Marina
Surzhevskaya

Beyond the Fog

From the author

M. Surzhevskaya

The Charmed Fjords
Book #1

Magic Dome Books
in collaboration with 1C-Publishing

The Charmed Fjords
A Romantic Fantasy Adventure
Book #1: Beyond the Fog
Copyright © Marina Surzhevskaya 2021
Cover Art © Olga Kandela 2021
Cover Designer: Olga Kandela 2021
English translation copyright © Elizabeth S. Yellen 2021
Published by Magic Dome Books in collaboration with 1C-Publishing, 2021
All Rights Reserved
ISBN: 978-80-7619-380-2

This book is entirely a work of fiction.
Any correlation with real people or events
is coincidental.

Table of Contents:

Prologue. Sverr..1
Chapter 1. Olivia... 4
Chapter 2. Olivia...10
Chapter 3. Olivia...20
Chapter 4. Olivia...38
Chapter 5. Olivia...50
Chapter 6. Olivia... 61
Chapter 7. Olivia...80
Chapter 8. Sverr... 95
Chapter 9. Sverr.. 123
Chapter 10. Olivia.. 139
Chapter 11. Sverr.. 150
Chapter 12. Sverr..162
Chapter 13. Olivia.. 174
Chapter 14. Sverr..187
Chapter 15. Sverr..209
Chapter 16. Olivia.. 229
Chapter 17. Olivia.. 242
Chapter 18. Olivia.. 256
Chapter 19. Confederation...................................... 274
Chapter 20. Sverr.. 287
Chapter 21. Olivia.. 302
Chapter 22. Olivia..322
Chapter 23. Olivia..344
Chapter 24. Sverr.. 363
Chapter 25. Confederation......................................382
Chapter 26. Olivia.. 403
Chapter 27. Olivia.. 414
Chapter 28. Sverr.. 433
Chapter 29. Olivia.. 450
Epilogue..460

Prologue. Sverr

THE SWEEPING PLATFORM of the tower glistened in the setting sun. With my fingernail I scratched a line in the tally marks, adding another notch to the black granite. I shook out my arms, stood up, and nodded at the guards who were standing motionlessly by the staircase. They nodded back in unison.

In the lower chambers, coals were smoldering in the fireplaces. I stretched out my hand and a flame sparked and danced toward my fingers. I had no time to play, though. I unstrapped my weapon and laid it on a nearby stand. It had been an endless, grueling day, and the fact that I barely slept all night didn't help. I massaged my neck, hoping that would wake me up. Two hours of sleep in three or four days is too little, even for the riar.

But apparently my day wasn't even over yet.

A tentative knock on the door and a familiar odor signaled that I had a visitor.

"Come in, Irvin," I said after a moment's hesitation.

The *a-tem* bowed on the threshold and displayed the palms of his hands, as was our custom. I wearily waved my arm at him.

"Go ahead, but keep it short. I'm exhausted."

"The Confederation, Lord Sverr," Irvin's blue eyes

The Charmed Fjords

sparkled with derision. "They've sent another message."

"By carrier pigeon?" I smirked. "Or have they already advanced to knotted strings?"

"This time they used ordinary paper," Irvin crowed. Acting like he owned the place, he strolled over to my small table, where a jug of excellent wine from Sheroalhjof sat. I watched him audaciously pour himself a cup, down it, and smack his lips in satisfaction. "It's the same old story: their intentions are friendly and they look forward to receiving a response from the lost lands, blah blah blah. They think they can lure us with all their scientific advances, which of course we desperately need."

Irvin poured himself another cup of wine, taking advantage of the fact that instead of looking at him I was gazing out the window, lost in my own thoughts.

"I think the message will come in handy for certain purposes, but of course the paper is kind of stiff..."

"We're going to answer them."

I continued to gaze out the window, at the majestic mountains, the gray-green forest, the rugged shore of the fjord and its dark waters — Irvin always said the fjord was bottomless.

"What?" Irvin finally stopped talking.

"We're going to answer." I turned away from the window and saw his bewildered expression. "And we're going to invite them here. I'll write the invitation personally. Yes, we'll be delighted to welcome our lost brothers, our long-awaited kin from the other side of the Great Fog. We've been waiting eons for this reunion. And of course we long to submit to the Confederation."

Irvin choked on his wine and began to cough. Feeling spiteful, I just stood there instead of slapping him on the back. That's what you get for guzzling my wine.

"Have you lost your mind, my *riar*?" Irvin finally

Book One: Beyond the Fog

croaked, his eyes widening like saucers. I shot him a haughty look and he shrank back.

"What for?" he repeated. "Wouldn't it be better to just say nothing, like the last time? And all the times before that?"

I shook my head, considering the options.

"Invite them here?" A look of disbelief crossed Irvin's normally impassive face. "But, Sverr. We can't let the people of the Confederation come here. That would be suicide."

"No," I said slyly, narrowing my eyes. A formidable plan was beginning to take shape in my mind. "This is what we have to do. We've been silent for too long, my *a-tem*, and that can instill fear — anxiety, even. Not to mention senseless thoughts. But we need a little more time. Knowledge, too. What we have now isn't enough. We'll welcome those people and ease their fears. We'll show them around, and let them try things out, and convince them they're superior and strong. Then finally, we'll get them to let down their guard. Oh, yes," I said, smiling as I envisioned the details of my plan. "We'll welcome our guests."

"But what will we show them?" Irvin couldn't contain himself.

"What's much more important is what we won't show them," I laughed, sitting down at my massive desk and taking out the items I needed to write the letter. "Say, does the tribe at the base of Gorlohum live there?"

"Yes, but you said that the Confederation thinks we're barbarians, Sverr. Beasts, even," Irvin added with a shudder.

I looked up.

"Isn't that true, my a-tem?" I said, grinning.

Chapter 1. Olivia

"DR. ORWAY, how long will the expedition to the land of the barbarians take? How many people are going? Aren't you afraid to get face to face with those primitive beasts? Is it true that they think it's acceptable to have sex with a woman whenever and wherever they want? Aren't you frightened of the barbarian customs? Does your husband approve of you going on this expedition, Dr. Orway?"

I smiled benignly, willing myself not to scream. The press conference had already been going on for more than two hours, and Sergey looked at me pleadingly, silently begging me to be patient for a little longer. I smiled again. For Sergey's sake I would sit here until morning.

"My husband can't object because I don't have one," I breezily answered the excited journalist. Everyone in the room burst out laughing. But I had already turned serious and leaned back into the microphone. "But if I did have a husband, I'm sure he would understand the importance of this mission that my colleagues and I have the honor of carrying out." The room grew quiet and attentive. I tried to ignore the camera flashes as I continued. "The world of the fjords, which is nearly a thousand years old, is cut off from us by an impenetrable wall. I won't go into all the historical details about what happened. I know you're all smart and

Book One: Beyond the Fog

informed" — more chuckles at this little bit of flattery. I pressed a button and an interactive world map appeared on the wall. I stood up and used my laser pointer to outline the territory between the rocky mountain range and the ocean. "As you all know, in around 873 the Lintoren volcano erupted, and a wall of ash and fog formed and separated an enormous swath of land from the rest of the continent. We came to call those lost lands the fjords, but we don't know for sure what they're made of. All we know is that the development trajectory in our world and in the world beyond the wall diverged. Our probes and spy planes have only gathered fragments of information, but we managed to piece them together into a single image. From that, we could draw some rudimentary conclusions. The data suggests that the world of the fjords has remained rather primitive, without the slightest trace of scientific or technological progress. And yes, you're correct. The peoples that populate it are mainly barbarians and half-beasts nowhere near as advanced as us. To us civilized people, their customs, predilections, and lifestyle seem not only primitive but also blatantly amoral. That's why this study mission to the fjords is so important. All of us — every citizen of our Confederation — is responsible for the planet: for its development, well-being, and prosperity. So it's imperative that we turn our attention to the massive fjords and put our research expertise to use. Crossing over into the world beyond the Fog is the greatest breakthrough in our history..."

I talked and talked, smiled, blinked from the camera flashes, and smiled some more. My jaw began to ache from talking so much, but when I looked over at Sergey and saw him beaming, I continued.

It was only after the press conference ended and the last reporter left that I allowed myself to exhale. I let my head drop onto my folded arms.

The Charmed Fjords

"You're brilliant," Sergey said, stroking my hair. "You're not just a talented scientist — you're also a phenomenal woman. Everything went perfectly, Liv."

I forced myself to straighten up. I smiled wearily.

"I don't get those people who like public speaking," I complained. "Those reporters were like a pack of wolves. It feels like they pumped all my energy out of me and sucked my brain out through a straw."

Sergey laughed and sat down on the edge of the table. He flashed a smile, the one that always made me melt. I caught myself just in time — if I spent more than a second thinking about that look on his face I'd be in trouble. I rubbed my eyes. It felt like there was broken glass under my eyelids.

"Well, by the time that pack of wolves left they were eating out of the palm of your hand," Sergey assured me. "Even the women."

I guffawed.

"I mean it, Liv. I saw how they looked," Sergey exulted. "That guy on the end was all set to propose to you, I swear. Even the old geezer in glasses got fired up and started smiling. He even showed off his missing front tooth. And everyone knows he's the harshest critic out there — did you know he's the reviewer for that magazine *Eye*? But you even managed to inspire him. You have an amazing gift for getting people to fall in love with you."

I wrapped my arms around myself and shivered, suddenly feeling cold. I felt totally depleted.

"How's Mia?" I asked, trying to change the subject.

"Everything's fantastic." As always, Sergey brightened when he talked about his wife. "You know she's been dying for you to come visit."

"I've been busy. You of all people should understand that," I said, disengaging my arms. "This expedition is taking up every waking moment."

Book One: Beyond the Fog

"Yes, I know." Sergey turned serious and looked at me searchingly. "Liv, I need to ask you something. Are you sure you have to go? I mean, of course everything you said about the mission and all that is true, but it's dangerous," he said in a malicious tone that caught me off guard. "It's really frigging dangerous! No one has ever been on the fjords. The beasts have never once said yes to us. And this invitation, doesn't it seem suspicious to you?"

"Why?" I asked in surprise. "What's strange about the fact that they want to make contact with us? We can contribute a lot to their lives, Sergey — education, medicine, technology. It's true that they developed differently from us, but I'm sure they're not really so primitive. After all, we know they're intelligent beings. They're different, but they're intelligent. Their message confirms it. We've been waiting for ages for a response from the other side, and we finally got one."

"But they're beasts! Savages!" He suddenly grabbed me by the arm. "Damn it, Liv. I understand how excited you are as a scientist, but good grief. Remember the ritual the probe recorded? It was a nightmare. I'm positive the savages practice human sacrifice."

I shuddered at the recollection. The fragmentary images the probe picked up would horrify any person living in the modern world: the naked men around the stone, the girl lying on it, all that blood. It was repulsive.

"That hasn't been proven, Sergey," I said quietly, gently extricating myself from his grip. "Don't worry about me. Everything will be fine. After all, I'm tough, have you forgotten?"

I winked playfully, but my old friend didn't share my optimism and he continued to stare daggers at me.

"I have a bad feeling about this, Liv."

"Feeling?" I said, bursting out laughing. "Since when

The Charmed Fjords

does a leading expert at the Academy of Progress believe in feelings?"

He laughed too and rumpled his hair.

"I guess that means you won't reconsider?" Sergey furrowed his brow.

I shook my head.

"Everything's already decided, Sergey. It's too late to turn back now."

"You've always been braver than me," he said, smiling. A strange look flickered in his eyes and I turned away. Yes, that was probably true. It's just that I rarely had a choice. Still, he was right — I'd volunteered for the expedition to the fjords. The committee had spent more time reviewing my application than the others. And yes, I was the only woman going on this trip beyond the Fog. Admittedly, the thought of that sometimes made my heart stop in fear. But I had to go.

"OK, I got it," Sergey sighed. "Want a ride home?"

"No, I want to finish my report."

"Yep, once a workaholic, always a workaholic." Sergey laughed with his familiar nonchalance. "Just don't stay too late, Liv."

"I won't."

I waited for Sergey to leave and went to stand by the conference room window, looking down at the road leading to the Academy. After I saw his bright red sports car speed through the gate, I put on my jacket and headed for the exit.

When I got outside I saw that it was about to rain. The pavement smelled of moisture and the approaching fall. I always thought fall tasted like dust, with a tinge of bitterness. It had always been my least favorite season. Something about fall always made it hard for me to keep from crying. It was a good thing that none of my colleagues had an inkling about what lurked beneath the perpetual stoicism of Olivia Orway, a leading anthropologist at the Academy. Of course, I would

Book One: Beyond the Fog

never let on, not even to Sergey — especially not to him.

I thrust out my chin and strode toward the underground parking garage.

Just as I expected, the rain started to gush as soon as I drove out through the gate.

Chapter 2. Olivia

EIGHT PEOPLE WERE CHOSEN to go on the expedition. They were all upstanding citizens of the Confederation and experts in their fields. Then there was me, the once-timid girl. Things were different now, though — I'd become a leading anthropologist at the Central Academy of Progress, a teacher, and a scholar. And I'd achieved all of this by the ripe old age of twenty-seven. I tried not to broadcast my age because I didn't want my male colleagues to be jealous or resentful. That was the last thing I needed. As it turned out, the men going on the expedition had known me for a long time, so I felt comfortable with them. I was delighted to learn that the scientist appointed to lead the expedition was my favorite professor and mentor, Maximilian Shach. Even after all these years, whenever I was around this white-haired, wise man, I trembled in deference to him just like I did the very first time I crossed the threshold of the Academy.

"Olivia, there you are!" Max gave me a big smile as I climbed onto the heliport.

On the day of our departure, the sun peeked out from behind the clouds for the first time in a week. I took that as a good omen. I squeezed Max's hand excitedly and nodded to the other team members. Our group consisted of four soldiers and four scientists. The invitation from the savages was explicit: we could bring eight people, tops.

Book One: Beyond the Fog

Scratch that — not the savages. They were *ilgs*, the children of the cliffs and the water, the people of the fjords. That's what they called themselves in their letter. My people, on the other hand, called them a "primitive and undeveloped life form." When I thought of what awaited me, my heart stood still and my stomach somersaulted. Would I really get to see firsthand what until then we'd only glimpsed in the occasional videos our probes sent back? Was I going to immerse myself in the world of the fjords, and have a chance to understand and experience the lost civilization? Was I really going to see their world? No doubt about it, it was no small feat.

The most important thing was to come back alive.

"Ready, Olivia?" Maximilian asked.

I nodded confidently.

"Of course. I'm ready."

We clutched our hats, watching the helicopter swoop down.

The Wall of Fog, which separated the two worlds, was on the northern border of the United Confederation. That's where the Academy's plane would take us. But first we had to take the helicopter to the aerodrome, where we'd board that plane and set off for the wall. Then we'd need to walk a few miles because all technology breaks down when you approach the Fog.

Someone would meet us next to the wall and open the passage that's usually closed to people.

I took a deep breath.

"I'm ready," I repeated to myself.

Sergey hadn't come to see me off. Then again, I had told him he didn't need to.

The Charmed Fjords

❊ ❊ ❊

The trip was shorter than I'd expected, but maybe that was because I was so tense. Once we got on the plane, the mood turned serious as everyone abruptly stopped laughing and joking. We didn't even look at one another; I think we were all privately wondering if we'd made the right choice in coming. We could still turn back — at least, in theory. But everyone believed in this mission, so no one actually yelled out, "Let me go!"

Surprisingly, I managed to sleep a little on the plane even though I'm not usually a great flier — the sleeping pill actually worked and I fell into a dreamless doze. By the time I woke up, the plane had already started its descent. I looked out the window and saw squares of earth, mountains, and the wall of Fog between the cliffs. It started off sharply and densely, separating people from the fjords. Like everyone on the planet I was familiar with the wall: we'd all seen it many times in paintings, photos, and videos. I'd even seen it in person once, on a school trip. I remember that I was completely in awe of it — no photo can truly capture the overwhelming power of a fog barrier. It's impossible to penetrate, and people have gotten lost in the white haze and died before finding their way out. When you're near it, all technology stops working. The Confederation only managed to get probes in a few times, hiding them in tree seeds and tossing them over. The few images that came back frightened and horrified humanity.

Nevertheless, we were acutely aware not only that the ilgs existed but that they were intelligent beings.

I pulled out my backpack and shuddered.

It was finally time to see the fjords up close and personal. There was no way I'd miss this. It was the purpose

Book One: Beyond the Fog

of all my years of hard work as a student and now as an anthropologist.

"Let's go," a stately soldier barked at us. "Yurgas Lith. Security," the metal tag on his uniform proclaimed. Yes, we were all wearing name tags even though we weren't sure the savages knew how to read. But they had answered our letter. To be sure, it was a short, dry response, but it was a response nonetheless. That meant they knew how to write and they shared a language with us.

I drew a deep breath. The fjords, which had been isolated from people for centuries, had inspired countless myths and tall tales. According to these stories, pretty much anything was possible on the fjords. Now it was time to dispel at least some of them, or maybe add new ones.

I shouldered my backpack and stepped out of the plane onto the ladder. The sun was hidden behind storm clouds, but it wasn't raining. We lined up on the ground and looked at the commander and Max.

"The plane will wait for us to return," Yurgas said, his eyes moving over each of us. "In keeping with the agreement, we'll spend seven days on the fjords and come back at noon next Thursday."

"Let's hope we all come back in one piece," joked Klin Ostrovsky, an expert on rare life forms. Yurgas glared at him.

"The jokes stop now. On the other side of our enemy's wall, we stick together and you follow instructions. Any questions?"

We hesitated, hiding our smiles. What are you supposed to make of soldiers? Our amusement faded when we all remembered why we were here. We sure hadn't come for a stroll in the park. We'd had to memorize enough rules to fill a doctoral dissertation.

Yurgas glowered at our wavering formation and nodded curtly. "Follow me," he said.

The Charmed Fjords

We goose-stepped for a while along a path that wound between green grass sprouting densely next to the wall. The vegetation was luscious and its colors were vivid. Even my friend Clys probably didn't have vegetation like this at her house in the suburbs, and she was a landscape designer who knew everything about grass. From what I could guess, the climate and the wall of Fog created a perpetual irrigation system that made the vegetation lush.

I let my mind wander, trying to avoid thinking about how we would soon be entering the fog — the deadly fog that no one had ever returned from.

A wave of fear suddenly overpowered me. My throat constricted and I reached into my pocket for my inhaler.

"Everything OK, Liv?" Maximilian leaned toward me, a look of concern on his face.

"Yes, professor," I said, pulling my hand out of my pocket and taking a breath. I smiled apologetically to Yurgas, who had turned around. The inhaler could probably wait. Max gave me an encouraging look and kept going.

Two hours later we had approached the wall.

The most disconcerting thing was that the closer we got to it, the less noticeable it became. It just looked a little different, like the colors had dimmed. If you don't realize you're stuck in the fog, you can easily get lost in it. When you turn around, you no longer see what you thought was there — all around you there's nothing but fog.

That's why markers — pillars, and stretched-out barbed wire — had been placed here long ago: to prevent wanderers from getting disoriented. There was a single passageway, and it was blocked by a gate guarded by a sleeping sentry. Someone had been keeping watch here out of a long-ingrained habit even though no one ever left the fjords. This basically meant that the guards monitored curious, reckless people who had stupidly decided to sneak

Book One: Beyond the Fog

into the Fog.

Yurgas exchanged a few words with the sentry, who raised the gate for us to pass through. We were at the final frontier. I snickered at my own joke. Come on, Dr. Olivia, you've always dreamed of discoveries. So then, onward.

Our group fell silent. Everyone was looking apprehensively at the white shroud ahead of us. Klin put his fingers together in a protective triangle and laid them on his forehead. I heard Maximilian whispering something. Was he actually praying to the One? I never would have pegged my professor as a religious man. I didn't pray or ask the eternal powers for protection. I just walked behind Yurgas, placing one foot ahead of the other and trying not to think about what would happen if the savages didn't come to meet us.

The fog thickened. We didn't turn around. We didn't even look at one another — we were too scared. Each of us had our eyes glued to the person directly in front of us. There was a reflective strip on the back of our uniform, crossing it in a yellow line like a ray of light. It was meant to help us orient ourselves. The sounds of our breathing and steps sank into the fog, while time stretched like molasses pouring out of a jar. It felt like we'd been walking in this haze for a ridiculously long time, like a year, or maybe even a century.

"Stop!" Yurgas's voice rang out unexpectedly loudly and Klin flinched ahead of me.

"What's going on?" Maximilian asked behind me. I wanted to shrug because like everyone else I had no idea, but I checked myself. The fog had suddenly begun to dissipate, as though it had been seized by a gust of wind, but the air was completely still. I could see a few yards of clear earth, forming a small open space where our group stood. And then —

"Holy cow," Klin said in a barely audible voice.

They started to appear out of the haze. The ilgs. There

The Charmed Fjords

were at least ten of them. Their tanned, naked, hairless torsos were so chiseled that even the men couldn't take their eyes off them. Their loins were covered in dark checked pieces of cloth that revealed their pelvic bones and ended at their knees. Below that were hides wound around their legs to function as shoes. Their shoulders were covered in furs, complete with animal snouts. There were wolves, foxes, jaguars. My eyes traveled upward to their faces. I shuddered at the sight of the cavities of the eye sockets, bloodstained foreheads, lips, and cheeks. What monsters! After a few moments I realized I was looking at masks smeared in blood — or more accurately, skulls of large animals placed over the barbarians' heads.

I quivered in horror.

Yurgas snapped out of it first — clearly he was no stranger to nightmares. I guess our commander had a shred of courage and had been in combat. He unclenched the hand that had been groping for his pistol and tentatively stepped forward.

"My name is Yurgas Lith. I'm commander of the experimental expedition to the fjords. Your leaders have approved our visit. I am requesting that you provide us with escorts and negotiators."

I snickered softly. It was safe to say that Yurgas wasn't the most diplomatic guy around. Could he possibly say something more pompous?

The ilg who was standing on the end turned toward me and I found myself staring into the empty eye sockets. The hide of a black wolf hung on his shoulders, and deep inside the bony dark holes I caught a glimpse of gold-colored irises. Or maybe I was imagining that. But I knew I wasn't imagining the barbarian examining me. His eyes bored into me attentively and keenly, and they didn't move from my face. I began to feel uneasy — creeped out, truth be told. What were

Book One: Beyond the Fog

these ilgs thinking? Their tanned bodies looked like lifeless figurines cast in bronze.

"Can you hear me?" Yurgas raised his voice. "Do you understand human language?"

I heard Maximilian hiss warningly next to me. The ilg with the wolf hide slowly turned his head and rested his gaze on Yurgas. He made a gesture with his palm that clearly signaled that we should follow him and the others. Moving in unison, the tanned savages silently separated and formed a ring around us. The black wolf took the lead and we obediently walked behind him. He walked on and on without once turning around or saying a word. In the white haze of the fog that had formed again, the pelt-clad silhouettes seemed like specters or the frightful monsters you see in nightmares. I kept the black fur in sight so I wouldn't get lost, but after a while my gaze wandered dreamily to the ilg's back, which was visible underneath the fur. I'd never seen anything like it. It was expansive and tanned, with muscles so prominent you could trace them. His broad shoulders and arms also sported protruding muscles and interlaced tendons. I was clearly looking at a spinal column that was accustomed to heavy burdens. There were clefts on each side of his waist. Strong glutes peeked out from under the sash he wore on his hips.

As a trained anthropologist I could say confidently that I was looking at a magnificent specimen of the male body. I would even go so far to say that it was the best one I'd ever had occasion to see. It was the kind of body that deserved to be sculpted and displayed in the national museum so people from everywhere could come and gaze on the exemplar of male physique.

My throat suddenly went dry and I gulped. The ilg turned around and I stumbled. The eye sockets in the skull flashed gold. The ilg's probing look made me freeze on the

The Charmed Fjords

spot.

I swallowed in fear and looked to my right, where Maximilian had been walking. But he wasn't there. There was no one next to me except the frightful ilg with the black wolf around his shoulders. He took a light step toward me, and his feet, clad in the high fur boots, glided silently along the ground. I shuddered and tried not to cry out in terror.

"Are we lost?" I asked stupidly, just to say something. The silence pressed down on my shoulders, like the fog and the motionless, menacing figure of the ilg. The bloodstained skull bent over me, and before I knew what was happening, the ilg lifted a hand to my chin and caressed it. I clenched my teeth, barely managing to suppress a scream. Never show the beasts you're afraid. Never cry out, turn your back, or run away. Never. Not even if you really want to. So I stood there, straightening my back until it hurt. I raised my head and stared unflinchingly at the skull that concealed the ilg's face. He stroked my cheek with a blazing-hot finger. The ilg leaned in closer and whispered, "Are you afraid?"

I was so surprised to hear normal human speech that my fear dissolved. But I nodded. "Yes."

"Of what?" the ilg asked quietly. I could now see his eyes — the gold irises, dilated pupils, and dark lashes.

"What?" I didn't understand.

The barbarian's finger was sliding along my skin. I bit my lip.

"What are you afraid of?" His quiet voice held a trace of mockery.

I was taken aback. What was I afraid of?

"Er... of dying?"

"You're lying," he said. He touched my lips again and I gingerly stepped back.

Then it hit me: the ilg was right. No, dying didn't scare me. I was a scientist and I understood full well that death is

Book One: Beyond the Fog

just an inevitable part of existence, so there's no point wasting your energy worrying about it.

The ilg sneered. He withdrew his hands, turned, and silently headed off into the fog. I followed him, too discombobulated to be able to think or analyze. What on earth had just happened? Who was he, anyway?

Only one thought consoled me: the barbarians of the fjords were completely intelligent and able to converse coherently and sensibly. Apparently they weren't as primitive as we thought. At the same time, I wasn't sure if I should feel happy or distressed about this.

Chapter 3. Olivia

THE FOG DISAPPEARED so abruptly I didn't even notice the change. The next thing I knew, we were standing next to a narrow passageway between the cliffs. The other members of the expedition were standing there waiting. Maximilian broke into a smile when he caught sight of me.

"Liv! Praise be to the One, you're here! There's something off about this fog. Did you notice? I couldn't identify its properties, though. I'd need to take samples, but I don't know what they'd show."

"They understand us," I whispered to Maximilian.

He shot me a look and nodded. "Have you spoken with them?"

I didn't have a chance to answer, and Max shut his mouth when the ilg wearing the red fox skin raised his hand to get our attention. He pointed to the narrow slit in the cliffs, which seemed to lead straight into a darkened hole.

"No way am I crawling in there," Klin muttered.

"Come on, it's late," Yurgas grunted, heading into the darkness. "Hurry up, everybody!"

We followed the ilgs through the granite tunnel. When we emerged on the other side, we stopped short at the edge of a clearing. A passing gust of wind was so strong I had to shut my eyes. After I opened them again, I blinked a few times to adjust to the light. I immediately cried out in amazement

Book One: Beyond the Fog

and awe.

"What the... am I seeing things?" a soldier whose name I'd forgotten whispered beside me.

I nodded, spellbound by the landscape before me. Mountains with emerald-green slopes and snow-covered summits rose majestically. Deep, inky water snaked between the craggy, broken shores. All around us were forests and lakes that seemed to belong to a fairytale world no humans had ever laid eyes on. Rainbows shimmered above waterfalls. Flocks of white birds sailed overhead. The most pristine blue sky imaginable was reflected in the water.

The sight was so breathtaking I had an urge to cry. I felt tears rolling down my cheeks and my heart was pounding so hard I thought it would burst through my rib cage.

Never had I seen such beauty or such intense colors. I'd never tasted salt carried by the wind, nor inhaled the millions of fragrances that were enveloping us on that cliff. It dawned on me that I was nothing more than a lab rat who had grown accustomed to the sterile environment of the Academy and the soggy asphalt odor of the city — I wasn't prepared for anything like this.

I convulsively grasped my inhaler. I stepped back behind the men and raised it to my mouth. I took a quick puff of the bitter medicine, which I hoped would ease my panic. Everyone else was too mesmerized to notice what I was doing, but the ilg in the black fur was scrutinizing me. I mustered up a friendly smile to let him know that my inhaler wasn't a threat. Who knew with these aborigines?

We only got to bask in the view for another couple of minutes before the fog descended, shrouding the fjords. Suddenly, out of nowhere came a clattering of hooves, and some peculiar, unfamiliar animals pulling a cart appeared before us.

"Holy crap!" Klin became animated. "Those are

The Charmed Fjords

mountain *ur-onoks*! Excuse my ignorance, but didn't those animals die off five hundred years ago?"

"They did die off," muttered Jean, our linguist. "On our side of the Fog. But here they pull carts, as you can see."

I silently examined the cobbled-together vehicle.

"I guess they've already invented the wheel," Max said under his breath. "And nails too. Well, what do you know. And what have we here? How fascinating."

Max's eyes gleamed with a scientist's excitement. I chuckled. But I had also put on my scientist's hat and was looking around curiously. The medicine had calmed me and my heart was beating regularly again. One of the ilgs gestured toward fur-covered wooden benches in the carts and we climbed in. Then the ilgs mounted the ur-onoks, which looked like horses that instead of manes had sharp spikes running down their long skulls and tensile necks. I noticed their fangs, which suggested that they were predators, not herbivores.

The hard bench was uncomfortable, and the low side of the cart seemed too rickety to lean on. "Fi-i-i-i-irrr," the ilg who was driving shouted, and we abruptly began to roll down the hill, right into the tall, emerald-green grass. I turned sideways and grabbed the ledge in the hopes that it would keep me from falling out in case we went over a bump. The ur-onoks plodded on without forging a path even though there was an imperceptible tread in the green carpet. But this track indicated that the path got some use.

My companions were excitedly turning their heads right and left, trying to see more, but there was nothing but the monumental trees of the forest around us. The grass was so high we could see only the shafts, leaves, and silver brush crowns down below, which showered us with a glimmering pollen when the cart flew through them. The distant snow-capped mountains peeked above the forest, but that was

Book One: Beyond the Fog

pretty much all we could see. That and the sky, which was dazzling. It was like a vivid sapphire pool spotted with feathery white clouds. I couldn't remember ever seeing a sky like that in the city. Or had it been too long since I'd actually looked up?

After two hours of jostling around in the cart, everyone looked somewhat deflated and we all stopped trying to glimpse anything new in the endless block of green. It felt like hours passed, but the scenery never changed. The ilgs galloped forward and back. We bounced along on the bumps and cursed through our teeth.

"Hey, are we almost there yet?" Yurgas could no longer restrain himself.

No one answered. Not then, not when he asked again an hour later, and not when he asked yet again two hours after that. Weary of the dancing foliage, I covered my eyes and started thinking about the first report I would record on my dictaphone. I had to make sure to describe every step in detail so that later on we could sort out and analyze the findings. I couldn't bring myself to start recording on the way, but I composed an outline in my head.

Another three hours went by, and then night fell on the fjords. It happened suddenly, from one second to the next. All the colors drained out of the grass, which then converged into a single solid wall. Immediately after that, the velvety sky began to blaze with huge, golden, sumptuous stars. They were so bright we craned our necks so we could take them in. There was so much artificial light in the city you could rarely see stars. These glowing stars were so captivating I wanted to jump out of the cart, lie down in the grass, and stare at them.

"Stunning," Maximilian stammered. But for some reason he frowned. "Interesting..."

"This bench has scrambled my intestines," Klin

The Charmed Fjords

grumbled. "Are we ever going to get there?"

"Look, we may be bouncing around, but at least we're alive," Jean pointed out philosophically. "Then again, they might roast us when we arrive."

"Always the optimist, aren't you," Klin chuckled.

I didn't say anything. Even though my body ached from sitting in such an uncomfortable position for so long, I wasn't about to complain. When the cart suddenly emerged into a clearing and stopped, I didn't realize immediately that we'd reached our destination.

The ilgs dismounted their animals and again surrounded us.

"Follow me," the one wearing the wolf hide ordered.

Grunting and stretching our stiff bodies, we climbed down off the cart and tried to take in our surroundings. In the light of the stars and a few torches planted in the ground, we could see tents made out of hides and crude canvas. There were around twenty of them, but it was too dark to get a good look. The shadowy ilgs, and especially their horrible animal skins, looked even more menacing in the half light. A tremor passed through me.

The ilg who seemed to be the leader came and stood in front of us.

"I'm sure you're tired from your trip. I'll answer your questions in the morning. For now follow me and I'll show you where you can rest."

Jean smiled in delight when he heard the ilg speaking a familiar language, and everyone else also brightened visibly. We set out behind the ilgs, but a couple of them blocked my way, cutting me off from my companions.

"What's going on?" Yurgas asked, frowning.

"The woman can't sleep in the same house as the men. She needs to be separate," the same ilg explained. The other ilgs were silent, as before.

Book One: Beyond the Fog

"What?" I asked in alarm. "Meaning?"

"The woman is separate," the wolf ilg replied sharply in a tone that made it clear he was the boss.

Yurgas scowled, clearly unsure what to do next. It was probably a bad idea to argue with the aborigines or break their taboos. In any case, I was so tired that I was willing to spend the night in the women's tent as long as there was a horizontal surface for me to stretch out on.

"Take it easy, Yurgas. I'll be fine," I said, trying to calm him. "Separating men and women is normal for a lot of peoples. We need to respect the customs of our welcoming hosts."

Yurgas frowned in displeasure but bowed his head.

As I spoke, the ilg in the black fur looked at me so intently I could feel his eyes searing a hole in my skin. I glanced at the eye sockets of his mask.

"I'm ready," I said as considerately as I could manage.

He nodded slowly and set out toward the dark tents. I glanced back at my colleagues, who looked anxious and worried. I smiled to show them I wasn't the least bit afraid, and followed the ilg.

Quiet surrounded us — a dense, sticky quiet, just like the night itself. I couldn't hear crickets or even any other insect at all. Maybe there just weren't any insects here. The ilg stopped next to the outermost tent, pulled aside the flap, and waited for me to enter. I gingerly stepped inside, expecting to see local women, but the tent was empty. There was a bed made of the hides that seemed commonplace here, a fireplace with hot stones and a kettle, and a corner occupied by a few earthen dishes and a round, dim stone that illuminated the furnishings. I looked around.

"So... I'll be in here all alone?" I turned to the ilg in surprise.

He nodded and pointed at the bed.

The Charmed Fjords

"Get some sleep. I'll be back in the morning."

The flap fell behind him, closing off the entrance. I stood there a little longer, blinking dumbly. Finally I just shrugged. I couldn't change the situation, so I might as well accept it. Feeling relieved that the trip was finally over, I shrugged off my heavy backpack and took off my shoes and jacket. I listened for sounds outside and then went to crouch down by the kettle, which was filled with sloshing warm water. I used it to wash up, and then dug wet wipes out of my backpack and rubbed them over me. Finally I felt more like myself.

I didn't hear so much as a rustle from the other side of the hide — it was as though the world around me had been deserted, or that it had frozen. I hesitated, pondering what to do. I had one more urgent need. I just hadn't expected to be alone, without any backup. And I hadn't remembered in time that I wasn't only a scientist — I was also a woman.

But my body needed relief, and I peered out from behind the hide. My eyes adjusted to the darkness and began to distinguish the outlines of the other tents and the trees beyond them. Close by there were dark bushes, which could definitely do the trick. Looking around and listening closely, I slunk toward them and unfastened my jumpsuit.

"Not here," a voice said in the darkness, startling me so much I nearly peed in my pants. I gasped at the sight of the ilg, who seemed to be woven out of the darkness.

"Damn it! Did you have to startle me like that? I almost... oh, never mind. I need to, er, take care of a natural bodily function, you understand? Could you just go over there and let me do it?"

The ilg leaned over me. "I could," he said. I detected a note of mockery in his voice. "But there are snakes here."

I jumped away from the bushes, pulling my jumpsuit over me in terror.

Book One: Beyond the Fog

"Follow me," the ilg said, nodding. His silhouette seemed even more imposing in the darkness. We went back into my tent. The ilg took a few steps and pointed to an earthen basin in the corner that I hadn't noticed before. "Here," he said.

"Er, in here?" I asked in confusion.

He guffawed distinctly and nodded again. He looked at me expectantly.

"Snakes," he repeated. "Don't leave the tent at night."

I looked askance at the basin. Well, what was I really expecting? Sewerage and indoor plumbing? Yeah, fat chance.

"OK, got it." I sighed in resignation. "Thank you."

The ilg stood there motionlessly and I felt like an idiot, shifting my feet and clasping my unfastened jumpsuit to me. The ilg looked at me again, shook his head, and walked out. I waited a moment, listening for noises, and then crouched down with relief over the basin. I covered it with a wide earthen lid that was sitting there, chuckling at myself. No doubt about it, I was spoiled by the benefits of civilization. The nighttime receptacle in the corner filled me with disgust, and I wanted to get rid of it right away. But if there really were snakes in the grass, it was best not to go out for a stroll.

I washed my hands and sat down on the hide in the opposite corner. I reached into my backpack and pulled out a superlight sleeping bag. I opened it, waited for it to inflate, and climbed in. The thin fabric made of aushlene fiber immediately enveloped me in warmth and all I wanted to do was shut my eyes and fall asleep. But I suddenly remembered why I was here and turned on my dictaphone.

"Report number one, Olivia Orway, anthropologist. We have arrived at the ilgs' settlement," I began softly. I stopped and digested that statement. We have arrived at the ilgs' settlement! On the lost fjords! Even I couldn't believe I was saying that.

The Charmed Fjords

I exhaled, holding back my emotions, and gave a concise account of everything I had seen on the way. I described the behavior and appearance of the ilgs. As I did with all my reports, I concluded with a summary: "Initial impression: the ilgs are intelligent beings. They have the ability to domesticate wild animals, they build dwellings and carts, sew clothing, and manually produce earthen dishware. While I saw only males, the fact that I was separated from the main group suggests that there are gender taboos among the local population. Most likely, this is an opportunity to observe a primitive communal system based on hunting and gathering. The expedition was received amicably enough, and so far I have not seen any signs of aggression. One ilg communicates with us. Judging by indirect signs, he seems to be the local leader. His speech displays a slight distortion of sounds, but he pronounces words correctly. We clearly have the same linguistic base. Further observation will offer a fuller picture of the life of the ilgs. End of report."

I clicked the button, returned the dictaphone to my backpack, heaved a sigh of relief, and closed my eyes. Fortunately, I'd gulped down some dry biscuits during the trip, so for the time being I wasn't hungry. In any case, I was too tired to think about food. Right now, sleeping was more important than eating.

❊ ❊ ❊

The next morning I was awoken by sounds coming from somewhere nearby. I opened my eyes and for a moment stared in confusion at the dark canvas roof above, unable to figure out what had happened to my white ceiling with its silver built-in lighting fixtures. But in an instant everything came rushing back to me. I stretched and unzipped my

Book One: Beyond the Fog

sleeping bag. The sight of a man in front of me startled me so much I nearly cried out. He was crouched down motionlessly, like a statue of a forgotten deity, and gazing at me. My fear quickly changed to admiration: never in my life had I seen such a magnificent specimen of the male species. The interloper had dark hair that was short in the front and hung to his shoulders in the back, and there were even lines shaved on his temples. These features, combined with his amber — almost gold — eyes gave him an otherworldly look. I sized up his face: it was masculine, with finely delineated, slender lips, a well-defined chin, and prominent cheekbones. He had a small bump on his nose and a couple of scars over his brows, but rather than spoiling the portrait, these blemishes made him look even more manly. A vertical black stripe bisected his left cheek, eyelid, and forehead. He was naked except for a leather sash hanging over his hips. A beautiful, unusual necklace strung with fangs and feathers hung down over his hairless chest. He had tanned skin, powerful arms, and sun-bleached hair on his arms and legs. A broad black ring that appeared to be made of an opaque stone encircled his neck like a collar. I wondered what it was. Did it indicate he had a subordinate status? Or was it just ornamentation?

    He appeared to be around thirty years old, but I could have been wrong. I was certain that this was the ilg who had been wearing the wolf's head the day before. His golden irises had been noticeable even under his mask.

    I mentally catalogued what I was looking at so I wouldn't forget to include a description of the ilg's physical features in my report. I sat down sideways on the bed. It took all my willpower to rein in my professional curiosity and impulse to touch this sculpted face — which of course I needed to do to examine the shape of the skull, feel the face bones, and inspect the muscles, sinews, and quality of the

The Charmed Fjords

skin. No doubt about it, this was an outstanding model. But it would probably be unwise to perform a full examination right now — better to wait a while, after building rapport with him.

"Good morning," I said, remembering my manners.

He cocked his head and continued to examine me.

"My name is Olivia Orway," I said, smiling and trying to sound friendly. "I'm an anthropologist. That means I'm a scientist who studies anthropomorphic biological species. Sorry, that was probably too technical." I bit my lip and thought for a moment. I pointed to myself. "I study people. People like me. Or like you. Do you understand? What's your name? Do you have a name?"

"Anthropomorphic species," the ilg repeated, looking at me unblinkingly. His tone was cryptic. What exactly was he thinking? Was he making fun of me? Did he not understand me? Or was he merely curious? I couldn't tell. I'd need to make a note about the distinctive voice intonations.

"Yes, that's right," I said cheerily, pulling the sleeping bag off my shoulders and smoothing my hair. "We're both anthropomorphic species. And if it's all right with you, I'd like to examine you more closely... if that's allowed."

The ilg cocked his head again. He nimbly straightened up and unfastened the sash, letting it fall to the ground. I blinked. I opened my mouth. I shut it. I gulped. I felt my face turn bright red. So much for being a professional anthropologist — I had gone back to being nothing more than a senseless first-year student.

In my defense, I was caught off guard. How else was I to react when I saw before me a smooth, large, and — how else to put it? — attractive male organ? It wasn't aroused, but even in this state it made a staggering impression.

"OK, I can confirm that the genital organs also correspond to human ones," I stammered hoarsely, trying to

Book One: Beyond the Fog

tear my eyes away from the ilg's groin.

"Do you want me to take off my *naches*?" I heard a voice say above me.

I blinked in confusion and forced myself to lift my head. "What?"

"My naches." The ilg pointed to his leg, which had hide wrapped around it.

"Oh, right, your shoes," I said weakly.

"Should I take them off?" He raised his dark brows. "You wanted to examine me."

Without waiting for me to answer, he leaned down, untied the leather laces, and loosened the fur. He stood up again, his eyes fixed on me. He was now totally naked. And tanned — his entire body, except for the many scars that dotted it, was tanned. I had no words. Without any prompting from me, the ilg turned, giving me a view from the back. Before me stood a bronze form pocked with white scars. There was sun-bleached hair in a few places where men are supposed to have hair, a chiseled back, strong glutes, and developed thighs. Damn!

I gulped and the ilg turned back to face me. He stood there, spread his legs slightly, bowed his head, and looked at me. He didn't move a muscle, not even to blink. I could have been looking at a statue, not a man. He didn't look embarrassed or uncomfortable, so I supposed that walking around naked was normal for an ilg. That seemed logical — I wouldn't exactly call the hip sash clothing. I pointed to the piece of leather, which was now lying on the ground.

"Do you always wear that? You don't have any other clothing?"

"I have a *shirs* for when it's cold. And a warm shirs if the mountains get angry."

"I see. A shirs and a warm shirs, well, well. It would be great if I could see them. It sounds like those are also hides,

The Charmed Fjords

but I'd love to see how they're sewn. Do you bind them or sew them together?" Finally I was able to call up my scholarly enthusiasm and dull my female embarrassment. It wasn't easy, though. I'm a scientist, but I spend most of my time staring at skeletons, not this sort of living, potent embodiment of male vigor.

I flung off of my sleeping bag and stood up, reminding myself why I was here.

"What's that?" I asked, reaching toward the dark ring around the ilg's neck. In a flash his fingers closed around my wrist. His golden eyes narrowed and the pupils stretched into slits. I stared at them in astonishment. He was so tall I had to tip my head back.

"Never touch that," he said quietly.

I hoarsely drew a breath, sensing an unveiled threat. I had no idea what I'd done wrong, but clearly I'd violated an important taboo among the aborigines.

"I'm sorry," I said, lowering my head to indicate obedience and humility. I tried to sound neutral and benevolent. I let my body go slack and didn't display any aggression. "I had no idea. I didn't mean to insult or offend you. It's just that where I come from we don't have necklaces like that. And you're allowed to touch other people's necks. I'm so sorry."

I froze, trying desperately to keep my breathing even and my body relaxed. I could physically feel terror rising up from my innermost depths and flooding my mind with blackness. Red spots swam in front of my eyes and my blood throbbed a warning signal in my temples. *Run away, run away, death, death...* I felt like I was already hearing those words.

I wasn't sure what would have happened next, but the ilg loosened his fingers and I immediately began to breathe easier.

Book One: Beyond the Fog

"I accept your apology, Olivia Orway," he said slowly.
I jerked my head up.
"Hey, you remembered!"
"Of course I did." He chuckled and, to my surprise, smiled. "It's not that hard. Your name isn't complicated. My name is Sverr Ragnar Helengvel Hrodgeir."

I took a breath. "It's very nice to meet you, Sverr Ragnar Helengvel Hrodgeir. That's what people say where I live."

For a moment I caught a glimmer of delight and surprise in his eyes, and I was thankful for my good memory, which was one of the traits that had helped me become so successful at such a young age. People called my ability to memorize things a gift, but I didn't think of it as anything special. It was just a part of me I was thankful for.

The ilg nodded slowly, and then said, "Now I want to examine you, Olivia Orway."

I balked. "What?!"

"I want to examine you more closely." The ilg repeated as though I were a backward aborigine.

"But — "

Did he want me to undress? Yes, he seemed to want me to do what he had done — take off all my clothes. But I couldn't do that.

"That's not done where I come from," I stammered, feeling like his golden eyes were casting a spell over me. Oh, damn it all. I'd sure put my foot in it. "See, if I were a man or if you were a woman... but... where I come from a woman doesn't undress in front of a man she doesn't know."

"Men don't undress here either," he interrupted me curtly. "But you wanted to examine me, Olivia Orway. I did what you wanted. I exhibited..." He knit his brows, choosing his words carefully. "Hospitality."

"But... I can't do that!" I exclaimed in despair. At the rate I was going I'd destroy the whole mission. And for what?

The Charmed Fjords

For my female hang-ups? That's an F, Dr. Orway. Please leave the classroom. You're not worth peanuts as an expert. You're just a hysterical chick, not an expert. But I really couldn't undress. I was panicking so much I started gasping for air. I glanced over at my backpack, which held my inhaler.

I know that when I'm dressed I look completely normal. I'm far from the prettiest girl in the Confederation, but I'm not the ugliest one either. I have dark wavy, shoulder-length hair, light-green eyes, and a slim figure with curves in all the right places. It's true that it would be nice if my hips were a little narrower and my chest a little bigger, but by now I was used to it.

But undress?

No way!

The most important thing was to not panic. I needed to think of the ilg as an animal — nothing more than a subhuman, uncivilized beast. I mean, I don't get embarrassed when I undress in front of my friend Clys's cat when I'm cat-sitting for it. This was almost the same thing.

I peered into the mischievous golden eyes and grew weak. No, this wasn't the same thing, not at all. It was safe to say that it would be easier for me to undress in front of an auditorium full of students at the Academy of Progress than in front of this ilg.

"I... can't," I sputtered hopelessly.

"Why not?" The ilg pierced me with his eyes. Once again, a single thought — that I undress and stand naked before him — made me blush. He breathed in sharply.

"It's just not something my people do. It's like..." I tried to come up with a comparison. My eyes rested on his neck. "It's like how here it's wrong to touch that ring. Do you see what I'm saying? It's taboo. It's forbidden. I'm a woman and we don't take our clothes off in front of men if... if we're not in a relationship."

Book One: Beyond the Fog

"Relationship?"

"Yes, exactly. A relationship. Marriage. Well, or love. Feelings. Where I come from, a woman undresses in front of a man she has feelings for. Do you understand?"

The ilg raised his eyebrows again. "So your women don't undress when they just want to copulate?"

I blushed again. This was ridiculous — I hadn't blushed once since I was a teenager. I'd been sure that I was no longer even capable of it, yet now here I was, doing it for the third time in fifteen minutes.

"Yes, that does happen," I stammered, "if they really want to."

"What do I have to do so you really want to?"

I shut my eyes for a moment, searching for the right words, and my reason.

"You don't have to do anything. I'm a scientist, you see? I..." I fell into thought, unsure how to explain. "I don't get into relationships with men!"

The ilg raised his eyebrows and circled me, looking closely.

"Why not?"

"Because my life is dedicated to science!" I shot back, starting to seethe at all these questions. "And to studying and research. There are no relationships! Do you get it?"

"No."

He stopped behind me and I could feel his breath scorching my temple, along with the heat of his body, which was too close for comfort. I tried to forget that he was still naked.

"Er... it's hard to explain..."

"Even for a scientist who studies anthropomorphic species?" There was that mockery again — it was obvious now.

I opened my mouth. Yep, your barbarian has outdone

The Charmed Fjords

you, Dr. Orway. Touché. Conclusion: ilgs are not the least bit stupid — at least, not this living, breathing, golden-eyed ilg beside me. He reacts quickly and intelligently, he remembers complex words the first time he hears them, and he responds multisyllabically.

Interesting.

I finally stopped blushing because the scientist had replaced the woman in me. I wouldn't say I pushed her away, but that I shoved her into a closet and locked it, opting to study this curious specimen. As everyone knows, where I come from a scientist is a sexless being.

"Why don't we say we've identified two taboos that our peoples have," I said, trying to smooth things over. I turned and found myself standing nose to nose with the ilg. He couldn't have been closer and I didn't much care for it. "Here touching someone's neck is off limits. Where I'm from, women don't undress in front of strange men. But I really appreciate your hospitality. And if you want to do a deeper examination, I'm sure any one of my friends would undress so you could look."

Sverr bowed his head slowly and his lips arched into a smile. But they didn't open. I made a mental note to try to examine his teeth and count them. The narrow pupils were making me uneasy. Did my people and the ilgs really have different genetic codes? Or was I just imagining it because I was groggy? Now I wasn't even sure if I'd really seen that brief, frightening miosis. If only I could do a blood test.

Feeling like a thirsty vampire, I fixated on the ilg's arms with their prominent veins. I'd just need a couple of drops. But for some reason I doubted that this aborigine would be pleased to have me stick a needle in him. Maybe I'd be able to get hold of some little hairs or pieces of skin?

The ilg scowled and took a step back. Apparently I'd gotten carried away with my inspection and plans. I supposed

Book One: Beyond the Fog

I'd turned the ilg against me when I made a fool of myself in refusing to strip. And I was going to have to write a report and describe everything in detail. Damn! I feared that the scientific council wouldn't look kindly on my bashfulness.

I stifled my aggravation, spread my arms, and smiled broadly to demonstrate goodwill.

Sverr snorted distinctly as he looked at me. "I get it, Olivia Orway." He started to head toward the opening in the tent. "I'll wait for you outside. The others are already there."

"Everyone's already awake?" I asked happily. "OK, I'll be right there."

The ilg pulled on his fur naches and leather sash, turned, and, just as he was before — that is to say, exposed — walked out of the tent. I collapsed onto the bed and exhaled. Only then did I realize how tense I'd been.

I chuckled nervously and quickly set about putting myself together. Something told me that the ilg would get tired of waiting and would just walk in without knocking. I didn't want him to find me on that basin.

Chapter 4. Olivia

AFTER HURRIEDLY WASHING UP and straightening my clothing, I threw aside the tent flap and stepped outside. Squinting in the morning sun, I could now see that there were around thirty dwellings. They stood in a circle around a stone hearth that was evidently used for cooking. There was no enclosure or any other protective structure around the settlement. All I saw were soaring, dark-wood pillars carved into whimsical shapes standing along the perimeter of the camp. Did the ilgs really not have any enemies? Were there no wild animals around? I made a mental note to investigate what wild animals lived here.

I could make out the sounds of the forest beyond the tents. The forest was nothing like anything I had seen in the Confederation. There was a forest outside Craos — the city where I lived — and Sergey had a small vacation house there that we would stay in on weekends when we were students.

Only now, as I looked at this forest on the fjords, did I realize that the forest I knew wasn't even really a proper forest. I guess you could call it a wood, but nothing more. But here, past the tents made of animal hides, those were real trees — trees so massive it looked like they were bobbing against the tops of the clouds. They had dark, rough trunks with thick moss growing on them. The branches were curved and covered with broad leaves. The grass surrounding them

Book One: Beyond the Fog

was succulent, thick, and high. In some places it was even taller than me. And all of this was substantial, monumental, indigenous, and ancient. From the looks of it, these trees were thousands of years old. This forest had probably witnessed the creation of the world. There was a slate-gray cliff on the right, with dozens of delicate waterfalls streaming from it, flowing into a lake at the bottom.

"That's the base of Gorlohum," a voice behind me said, making me jump. I spun around and found myself staring into a pair of mesmerizing golden eyes. "It's the mountain of the ancestors."

The first thing I did was brush against the ilg's hips, but luckily now they were covered by a piece of plain fabric. I looked up and let out a whistle. Beyond the imposing tree crowns, the outline of the rock face looked blue, and was dark at the top. A white cloud floated up above.

"Gorlohum is merciful today — his breath is snow-white," the ilg said.

"Oh, it's a volcano," I said. "You live at the base of a volcano."

The ilg shrugged. I looked warily at the clouds. I really hoped Gorlohum wouldn't choose today to get angry and spew lava everywhere.

"Has Gorlohum been merciful for a long time?"

"Gorlohum's black breath hasn't been seen for many, many years. Don't be afraid, Olivia Orway."

"Liv," I corrected him reflexively. Seeing his confused expression, I explained. "You can just call me Liv. Where I live it's common to have nicknames."

"They're so short," the ilg said mockingly. His eyes gleamed. "You can call me... Sverr. Liv."

"Thank you," I said with relief. I was actually worried I'd stumble on his unwieldy name.

"Olivia, is everything OK?" Maximilian was striding

The Charmed Fjords

toward me, followed by Yurgas and the rest of our group. Yurgas was looking at me disapprovingly but I had no idea why. I decided to ignore his expression; maybe I was just imagining it.

"Everything's great. I slept really well," I said brightly. "And how are you?"

"Impressed," Maximilian said, waving an arm toward the forest. "Did you notice? Those are obsolete evergreen *irshit*. They haven't grown on our land in ages. And those are extinct mosses and trees. I nearly lost my mind when I saw all of it." Maximilian removed his glasses and started wiping the spotless lenses. I instantly recognized his tic, which I'd been seeing for many years — he always started cleaning his glasses when something was troubling him. He put them back on and shook his head. "It's unheard of, Liv. It's just incredible."

Murmuring under his breath, he walked away to examine a bush. The other men also looked slightly dazed. Perhaps it was because they weren't used to breathing such clean air without a trace of smog or dust.

"Let me show you the settlement," Sverr said, breaking into my thoughts. "Then we'll eat. Follow me."

We nodded and set off behind him. The settlement had come to life. Ilgs were streaming from their tents, watching us with inscrutable expressions. But the aborigines weren't acting aggressive, and eventually even Yurgas stopped darting his eyes around distrustfully, and he took his hand off his stun gun. The tour was short because there wasn't anything in particular to see. There were the thirty or so tents where the ilgs lived, all with nearly identical interior decoration. Each tent contained sleeping pallets covered by pelts, rudimentary hearths in the center, holes in the roof for airflow, small, low wooden tables piled with earthen dishware, and a variety of utensils along the walls. The

Book One: Beyond the Fog

dwellings were clustered around the main building, which was smeared in clay and had a red roof.

"The *shiar*," Sverr said, pointing to it.

"Shiar? What does that mean?" Max asked with interest. He turned to me and said, "Liv, you've probably noticed that the ilgs have a lot of words we don't understand even though the foundation of the language is the same. Some words probably came into being here as crafts evolved or new objects, like the wheel or needle, appeared. But the ilgs gave them names different from ours. It's astonishing, isn't it? So what does shiar mean?"

"Shiar is shiar," Sverr answered flatly with a shrug. We didn't try to press him. There'd be plenty of time to find out about everything, including that mysterious building with the red roof. As we checked out the dwellings, implements, and carts with the beasts of burden, more and more ilgs began to gather around us. They trailed along after us, stared at us unblinkingly, and sniffed the air around us.

"The gene pool is extraordinary," Jean, the linguist, muttered beside me. "Simply extraordinary. Have you seen it, Liv?"

I sure had. It was impossible not to see how gorgeous the ilgs were. They looked like the bronze statues that stood in our anthropological museum. Their muscles had clearly developed from their way of life, not from working out in a gym, and they'd undoubtedly gotten their scars in battle, not in the studio of some trendy artisan. Clad only in the sashes they wore on their hips and their naches, the ilgs made a head-turning impression. Most of them had light hair, ranging in color from red to wheat, and their eyes were an intense blue or green. Isolated from the rest of the world, the barbarians had apparently preserved their original physical traits. They hadn't had an opportunity to mix their blood with other ethnic groups, so what I saw before me now were

The Charmed Fjords

perfect samples of a genotype that was virtually gone in the modern world. Dark coloring had long been dominant in the Confederation. My light green eyes were practically an atavism, and I was secretly proud of them. But here I saw dozens of men with eyes ranging in color from mint to almost lemon. It was amazing.

But the interesting thing was that only Sverr wore a dark ring around his neck — although most of the other men wore similar adornments, they were made of leather. Numerous strands of feathers and animal fangs, long, plaited hair, leather belts and bracelets, and strokes of red paint on their faces and bodies completed the portrait of the local population. I desperately wanted to examine everything more closely, but once again I forced myself to be patient. It was hard, though — I was already fantasizing about bringing just one barbarian back to my lab, if only for one day.

I only stopped daydreaming when I felt Jean elbowing me in the side.

"They're looking at you," he whispered.

I turned my head, trying to be discreet about it, and saw that he was right: the ilgs were looking at me. It was kind of intense, like they were checking me out. They were leaning their heads down, inhaling, and squinting, studying me from head to toe with a puzzled look on their faces.

"What's up with that?" I instinctively moved closer to my colleagues. "Why are they looking at me like that?"

"And why haven't we seen a single woman yet?" Yurgas added. His fingers clenched again, as though he wanted to draw his stun gun.

"Calm down, Captain Lith," Maximilian hissed at him, his eyeglass lenses glinting. "There's no need for weapons here."

One of the ilgs pulled away from the crowd and barked something. His words were throaty and staccato, and totally

Book One: Beyond the Fog

incomprehensible. He was looking straight at me. Sverr languidly turned to him and answered in the same incomprehensible language.

"So much for a common language," Jean snorted. "I can't even figure out what language group that is."

The blue-eyed ilg I hadn't noticed before opened his mouth again, and even without speaking the language, I could hear the wrath in his voice. Sverr responded gently and quietly. The crowd of ilgs retreated and the chattering died down.

Our little group, clad in black jumpsuits emblazoned with the logo of the Academy of Progress on the chest, also quieted down, looking around apprehensively.

"What's happening?" I couldn't contain myself.

"Nothing," Sverr said, turning to us. "I explained that you're our guests."

"Why do you speak different languages?" Yurgas wanted to know.

"I'm speaking the language of the northern fjord," Sverr explained. "I can communicate with both you and them. I'm the one who answered your letter."

"No way!" Jean threw his hands up. He was short and scrawny and looked up at the ilgs like they were gods. "So you're saying that there was even a linguistic division on the fjords? Would you mind asking them to say something else? I'd like to try to figure out the foundation of this dialect."

"Yes, later." Sverr gave another one of his close-lipped smiles. "I'm sure you're all hungry."

"You have no idea!" the long-limbed Klin, who was like quicksilver, exclaimed. "This tour of your landmarks is exhausting!"

The men burst out laughing. Sverr bowed his head and set off toward the center of the settlement, back to the immense hearth, from which the smells of food were wafting.

The Charmed Fjords

"He didn't answer the question about the women," Jean whispered to me. "Did you catch that? Maybe women don't exist here? There are only men all over the place. It's odd."

I had noticed. I'd also been thinking about how Sverr was the only person in the tribe who spoke our language. Was that how things were? Beside me, Maximilian was painstakingly cleaning his glasses.

❀ ❀ ❀

It turned out there was no reason to worry because as we approached the fire, we caught sight of the previously invisible specimens of the fair sex. Dozens of women of various ages were bustling about the fire, doing the things that all keepers of the flame have been doing since time immemorial. They were cooking something in a cauldron, chopping vegetables and thick stalks, tossing coals and muttering, burning their fingers on the boiling water. There were children running around them — grubby, buoyant children, just like all children the world over.

I heaved a big sigh of relief at the picture, because at one point I had truly been frightened. The other scientists also relaxed and livened up noticeably. Sverr beckoned to us and quickly said something to the women. They stared at us just as openly as the men had a little while before. One of the aborigine women, who had a mass of blond, filthy braids, pointed at Jean and chirped something in her unintelligible language. The other women laughed, and even with the language barrier it was clear that they were gossiping.

Jean scoffed. "You need to admit that the local beauties aren't nearly as attractive as their men," he grumbled.

I nodded in agreement. The women were stocky and short, and their gray tunics didn't conceal their stumpy legs

Book One: Beyond the Fog

and muscular arms. Their faces looked crude — almost masculine. Jean snorted triumphantly.

"Maybe we should give them a mirror so they don't decide to make fun of all of us?"

"In the animal kingdom, the females are often much less flashy than the males," Klin mused. "It's the law of nature, my friend. The men are the ones who need to prove they're entitled to mate."

Jean chuckled scornfully. "What barbarity."

"Jean, quiet down," Maximilian said, and turned to Sverr. "How far apart are the local settlements from each other?"

Sverr shrugged and directed us toward some hides around the bonfire. He sat down cross-legged, and after a moment's hesitation we followed suit.

"The Lon-ir clan is ten days from here, to the east. The Os-lor clan lives on the banks of the Black Lake, and that's even farther."

I quietly pulled out a small notepad and wrote: "The barbarian can count to ten."

"Is their way of life like the one in this settlement?"

"Somewhat."

My colleagues exchanged expectant glances.

"And how many people like you are there? Who would understand our language?"

Sverr shrugged again. I'd already noticed that Sverr made this gesture automatically whenever he didn't feel like answering a question.

"What's the meaning of the rings around your necks? Why are they made out of different materials?"

Another shrug.

We bombarded him with questions. Sometimes his answers confused us even more. Meanwhile, other men were drawing toward the fire, but a lot fewer than we'd seen a half

The Charmed Fjords

hour before.

"They're hunting," Sverr said nonchalantly. "They need to go get food."

"Right, of course," Yurgas muttered. "Could we see it? Your hunt?"

Sverr looked thoughtfully at the fire and nodded. "Soon."

My colleagues shifted excitedly in their seats but I frowned. Men are all alike. Just offer them a chance to kill a defenseless animal, and they all immediately turn into savages. I had no desire to watch an innocent creature get slaughtered, but as a researcher I had no choice but to go along.

Meanwhile, the women had already ladled some sort of stew into earthen bowls and covered them with broad leaves. The woman with the braids knelt down and held a bowl out to Sverr. He nodded and took it from her hands. The process was repeated for every man sitting next to the hearth.

"Looks like the men come first around here," Klin jeered. "I think I could get used to someone bowing down to me at every meal."

Jean poked him in the back and he coughed.

I stared at my plate. It looked like fish, but I couldn't figure out what was on the broad leaf. It seemed to be a piece of smoked black something. We'd packed enough dry food reserves and canned goods to get us through the trip, but we'd come here to learn about the ilgs, hadn't we? I inhaled, broke off a piece of whatever it was on my plate, and stuck in my mouth.

My splendid colleagues — those courageous men — watched me expectantly, waiting to see if the local food was poisonous. I briefly considered keeling over and going into spasms, just so I could see the looks on their faces. But then I remembered that I was no longer a student, but a scientist.

Book One: Beyond the Fog

I swallowed and smiled. "It tastes like cod," I said.

"The fish here has the same name," Sverr said.

"It's delicious," Jean said with surprise. The others nodded. Even our silent soldiers, who generally just frowned and darted their eyes from side to side, seemed to relax a bit. But I had noticed that before eating they'd all drunk a capsule of poison antidote. Of course, that morning we'd all already drunk it, but the soldiers had double doses, just in case.

While they were eating, my colleagues again tried to interrogate Sverr, but he just frowned at them and pointed at his plate. I noted on my writing pad: "The ilgs don't like to converse while they're eating, and they eat fast."

I smiled with contentment. On the whole, everything I was seeing matched the level of development we were expecting. Based on what we'd seen so far, I'd say the ilgs had remained at roughly the same development stage as the legendary savage berserkers, and perhaps had even slid backward a bit. Before the volcano erupted, the occupants of these lands lived in tribes, hunted and fished, and knew how to make utensils out of clay and torrefy knives. And that was exactly what we were seeing right now. True, they did use the wheel, needles, and other objects, but there was no way they had our developments, like stun guns or hovercrafts you could use to fly through the air. The gap between their development and our civilization was cosmic. The barbarians were barbarians through and through, while the fjords were a living museum of exhibits preserved in an unchanged state.

I put a small leaf in my mouth and chewed on it thoughtfully. Maximilian was too excited to eat. He couldn't stop looking everywhere, so eager was he to explore the lifestyle and tastes of the natives. His eyes danced with an infectious liveliness that filled me with wonder, too. I couldn't remember ever seeing him like this.

Then again, why hide it — I also couldn't wait to learn

The Charmed Fjords

everything about the local customs. It was a shame that the only person who spoke our language was Sverr. He seemed tired of our endless questions.

"You're free to do whatever you want until evening," Sverr announced, putting down his empty plate. "I recommend that you don't go far from the settlement. There are a lot of wild animals in the forest."

"What about you?" Yurgas asked, jumping up.

"I have to help the others get ready for tomorrow's hunt. You're welcome to join us if you want."

Not surprisingly, the men wanted to — even our perpetually glowering security agents, Luke and Reese. I chuckled in understanding and decided to walk around the settlement in the meantime. But Max shook his head.

He leaned over to me and said so softly I almost couldn't hear him, "Olivia, please don't wander too far away from us." I looked anxiously into his pale eyes.

"Why not?"

"I can't explain. Please just trust my instincts. I don't like the way they're looking at you."

I scowled and looked over at the ilgs. No one was looking at me. Just Sverr. But he only glanced at me and then turned to Jean.

"Stay with me, Liv," Max said, once again speaking in his normal tone. "This old guy will feel better."

I looked at him in surprise. Old? I'd never heard Mr. Shach say anything like that before. I nodded wordlessly. There was no need to say anything.

"You don't trust them?" I asked as quietly as I could.

The idyllic-looking picnic had even made Yurgas relax. He was almost smiling as he gazed at the children playing next to the tents. The women were busily cleaning up from breakfast, while the men had left almost in unison to do whatever it was the ilgs did. The forest looked majestic, but

Book One: Beyond the Fog

not threatening. What was Max worried about?

"I trust them. I just don't trust him." He spoke so softly that rather than hearing his words I read them on his lips.

I turned my head. Sverr was now looking at me point-blank. Once again, I got the impression that the pupils had narrowed in his golden eyes.

Chapter 5. Olivia

ALTHOUGH YURGAS KEPT hissing warnings and admonishing us to stay close together, we were all eager scientists at heart and we couldn't wait to scatter like cockroaches.

When we finished eating, we thanked Sverr and the women, who knelt before us one more time before heading off to take care of their own chores. Klin went to marvel at a shrub that was extinct in the Confederation, while Jean began interrogating a young ilg, trying to decipher the combinations of sounds coming out of the boy's mouth. The soldiers poked around the settlement, apparently looking for things like bombs and nuclear weapons, which of course didn't and couldn't possibly exist here. Max and I set out for the periphery — or more accurately, he set out and beckoned to me to join him.

Once we got past the tents, we could no longer hear any sounds from the encampment. A bird was singing somewhere out of sight, and the broad leaves of the trees were rustling in the wind.

"It's almost autumn back home," I murmured pensively. Max stopped next to a black pillar and craned his neck to examine it. I gazed at it too, jotting down mental notes out of habit: it was around three yards high, smooth, and black, and scored with irregular notches along the entire

Book One: Beyond the Fog

surface.

"What do you suppose this is?" I asked as I circled the pillar. "Do you think it has some meaning?"

I caught Max's eye and immediately felt embarrassed. "D for you, Dr. Orway. Go study for your makeup exam. Of course these pillars have meaning! In a system like the one here, all objects have a functional or religious purpose. It takes the tribes too long to create something like a knife or plate, so they don't make things for no reason. These black staffs aren't growing here naturally, so they must have been put here for a reason."

Trying to compensate for my naive blunder, I ran a finger along a hollow on one of the pillars.

"Wood, with a drawing that was presumably made with a knife. But the wood is odd. Is it burned?" I rubbed my fingers. "Maybe it's a species we don't have? What could these pillars be for?"

"I'd hazard a guess that they have something to do with the local religion," Max answered, "but if that's the case, it's surprising that they're standing here of all places. If they're important for the tribe and they're objects of worship, they should be in the center, closer to the fire, because as we know, fire symbolizes life and warmth. But they're here, on the periphery."

"So they're not religious pillars, but something else?" I always enjoyed listening to Maximilian's thought process. "By the way..." I glanced around to make sure we were alone. "What made you say that we shouldn't trust that ilg?"

Maximilian removed his glasses and began rubbing the lenses.

"I know it's an irrational feeling, Olivia. You know I'm a scientist, and I'm guided by facts. The facts on the ground are that Mr. Sverr has been very gracious in inviting us here, showing us the ilgs' way of life, and answering our questions.

The Charmed Fjords

And we're seeing exactly what we expected to see."

"Is that a bad thing? It means our hypotheses based on the images from the probes have been correct."

"It's not a bad thing," Maximilian said, frowning. "But... I'm saying it's an irrational feeling, Liv. As Gustav Rindor proved, you can use intuition to explain things that don't exist but are the sum of signals we've received but not processed. And they give us feelings — premonitions, you might say."

I nodded. Naturally, like every self-respecting scientist, I had studied Rindor.

"So, Olivia, my unprocessed signals are screaming to me that there's something fishy here."

I gazed anxiously at the landscape around us. Maximilian's words were unsettling. But before me there was nothing but a tranquil — even mundane — scene: the tents, the trees, a woman with a squealing little boy, Klin bending over some shrubs. Suddenly Yurgas appeared. He nodded to us, satisfied that we weren't in danger, and continued his rounds.

"But why do you think that?" I was confused.

Maximilian shrugged, reminding me of Sverr for a moment. "Maybe I'm just a senile old man," Maximilian said, sounding fatigued. I was taken aback. I'd never expected to hear him talk like that. Now I looked at him through new eyes. How old was Maximilian anyway? He looked to be at least seventy. But he was exactly the same — white haired and wise — as when I first arrived at the Academy. He hadn't changed a bit in the last few years. Or did it only seem that way to me?

"Let's get back to the pillars, Olivia," Maximilian said cheerfully, breaking into my thoughts. "I'm ready to hear your hypotheses."

For the next two hours, Maximilian and I made a close

Book One: Beyond the Fog

study of the settlement and took notes. I pulled out my dictaphone and started to record, afraid of omitting something important. We didn't speak any more about intuition.

SVERR

I turned the round can over in my hands, sniffed it, and tossed it back into the sack. Steps outside the tent and a pungent odor announced that I had a guest, so when Irvin stepped into the tent I just nodded at him.

"Looting, my riar?" the a-tem asked with interest, removing the bull's skull from his head. "That's cruel."

"Suck it up," I muttered, and went back to picking through the contents of the bag. "I'm not looting. I'm studying the enemy. Anyway, as far as I remember, looting is your job."

"Need me to create a diversion?" Irvin crouched down beside me. "What's this?"

I pulled out a metal rod and rolled it over in my hand. "It looks like that stun gun thing. Put out your hand."

"The stun gun that can even paralyze a horse? This thing?" Irvin asked suspiciously.

"Exactly. Come on, give me your hand."

"Sverr!"

"Irvin!" I mimicked him. "I've already tested it out on myself. Anyway, you're not a horse."

"You're just a bastard," Irvin grumbled, screwing up his eyes. But he obediently stuck out his left palm. I turned the rod, set it on Irvin's skin, and pressed the button. He leaped up as though he'd been singed. His pupils narrowed. "Damn it! That burns!"

"Does it hurt?"

"It's tolerable," Irvin grumbled in annoyance.

The Charmed Fjords

I grunted with satisfaction and reluctantly put the stun gun away. It was a fascinating object. I wanted to keep it for myself.

Irvin was studying me. He frowned. "Sverr, I don't like any of this."

"You never like my ideas or decisions. Your job is just to tell me why I'm wrong."

"At the moment you're especially wrong."

"My, what a stubborn a-tem I have."

"The tribe doesn't like outsiders. You yourself know that. How much longer do you plan to continue your fun? What are you accomplishing? I don't understand you."

"You'll understand, Irvin. Everything in good time. The tribe will be patient. We need knowledge, my a-tem — not the pieces of knowledge we already have, but much more."

"But for what?" Unable to restrain himself, Irvin jumped up and began to pace the tent, his forehead creased in anger. "We've gotten along just fine for ages without outsiders or the world beyond the Fog. Why now?"

"Because the Fog has begun to dissipate!" I yelled.

Irvin stopped short and stared at me in horror. "What?"

"Just what I said." I hurled the bag aside. "For now we're keeping it secret, but the Hundred is worried."

"Benevolent Gorlohum," the shaken Irvin whispered. "What will happen now?"

I turned away so he wouldn't see how agitated I was. "We'll straighten it out. Let's go. I hear people coming."

"Sverr..." Irvin stopped by the door and looked at me intently. "That outsider, the woman..."

"Olivia Orway," I said, drawing out the vowels and licking my lips. "I've prepared something special for her."

"You're playing with fire, Sverr."

"As usual," I interrupted him.

Irvin raised his eyebrows disapprovingly.

Book One: Beyond the Fog

"Speaking of which, it's time to go have some fun. I'm getting bored."

The a-tem winced.

OLIVIA

"What's going on?" Max and I reluctantly tore ourselves away from the pillars and looked curiously at the commotion in the center of the settlement. The women were placing small children in leather pouches and hoisting them to their shoulders, and the men were donning the animal skulls we had already seen.

"Where could they be going?" I shrugged because of course I had no idea.

Yurgas was beckoning to us from the tents.

"Well, let's go, Olivia," Maximilian said with a smile. "In any case, for now it's just a guessing game with these pillars. We need to learn more about the local customs and it looks like we're about to have a chance to do that."

I stuck baggies with samples of the black wood into the pocket of my jumpsuit and returned his smile. "All right then, let's go."

Our colleagues had already gathered by the fire, which by now was just smoldering. Jean was turning his head so his glasses shot out sun flashes, which a pudgy, grubby child was chasing as though they were rabbits. Sverr appeared from behind the trees and we headed toward him and began peppering him with questions.

"What's going on? Where's everyone going? What happened?"

"They're going to the basin," he said, as though that explained everything. "Tonight we're having a joyful event, the *shatiya*, so now everyone needs to bathe in the basin."

The Charmed Fjords

"Must be some ritual," Klin whispered to me. "I hope it's not the basin you cook stray scientists in."

I snickered and then immediately clapped my hand over my mouth. The ilgs all looked solemn and serious, so we mimicked their expression and took our place at the back of the procession. The men in their bone masks and hip sashes walked in front and on the sides, simultaneously guarding the women, children, and us. The path ran between two emerald hills, and I again fell under the spell of the scenery. The fjords were stunning. The ilgs trod softly, lightly, and silently, and we tried to imitate them. Everyone looked at me in irritation whenever a dry branch crunched under my shoe or a frightened bird took flight.

Sverr went to walk in front, so I couldn't ask him about the ritual that awaited us, if indeed it was a ritual. A tall, strapping ilg was walking beside me. I caught occasional glimpses of watchful blue eyes through the skull. I was surprised to see a stone ring around his neck. That meant there were at least two of them. Maybe this blue-eyed ilg also spoke my language?

"Where are we going?" I asked, trying to sound friendly and unconcerned.

The ilg turned away. I sighed. Well, all right then. I guess there wouldn't be any conversation. Too bad.

Around twenty minutes later, we emerged by the base of the cliff, where there were a few round, natural stone depressions. There was dark red clay inside the rocky basins.

The ilgs stopped and began undressing, exposing their muscular bodies. Around half of the women formed a semicircle in the shade of a sprawling tree, like they were watching a play, while the other half giggled and bustled around the men, holding narrow-necked earthen pitchers.

"What are they doing?" Jean asked, squinting as he watched an aborigine woman pour a viscous golden liquid

Book One: Beyond the Fog

from a small pitcher over one of the men. He narrowed his eyes like a cat and turned around so the woman could anoint his shoulders, back, and hips. There was a pungent, spicy fragrance in the air.

"It's the sap from the tree that grows in the valley." We all started when we heard Sverr, who had crept up behind us. He was holding the same type of pitcher, and we examined it curiously.

"It looks like oil," I said, smearing a golden drop between my fingers and sniffing it. "Only thicker. I don't recognize the smell." It tasted good, though, and I had an urge to lick my fingers. "Why are the women putting this sap on them?"

Sverr flashed one of his close-lipped smiles and shrugged. "So it's harder. Anyone who wants to can participate in the shatiya, but they need to prove they're worthy."

"What's a shatiya?"

"You'll find out tonight. Yes..." Sverr frowned, as though making a decision. "If any of you want to join us, you can. All guests are allowed to join us in the basin and the shatiya."

My colleagues exchanged glances. We were all totally confused. Say no more!

"Maybe next time."

Sverr nodded and went to join the other ilgs.

"Looks like he doesn't plan to join in their oil rub," Yurgas snorted.

I sank down on the grass, reveling in the luxuriant fragrances of the earth, water, flowers, and golden sap from the unfamiliar tree. It was still on my fingers, and it was like it had penetrated my blood — my entire being now smelled sweet and spicy. My head was starting to spin and my knees were shaking. It could have been from the blazing sun, but it

The Charmed Fjords

also could have been from the sight of the half-naked men gleaming from the drops of oil on their tanned skin. My colleagues were standing nearby, fanning themselves with wide leaves, so they must have been hot too. We shouldn't have been hot, though, because our jumpsuits were made of a special material that conserved the body temperature of the person wearing it. It was impossible to be hot in them. But I could see that the men's faces were flushed and covered in beads of perspiration. I for one was dying to pull off the damned black fabric with the reflective stripe and don a loose tunic like what the aborigines were wearing.

"It's so hot!" Klin couldn't contain himself. "Back home we're going to get snow pretty soon."

"It's like we're at a resort," Jean snickered. "Enjoy the sun while you have the chance."

I discreetly pulled down the zip slider on my jumpsuit. The breeze cooled my neck and chest and I began to breathe more easily. I took out my dictaphone and got ready to turn it on.

"Holy shit," Yurgas said in astonishment. "It looks like they're going to fight."

I looked over at the ilgs and my jaw dropped. They had already climbed into the wide rocky basin, right into that red clay. They broke into two rows and stopped, staring at the round opening in the cliff.

We moved closer.

A stream of water gushed from the cliff into the basin, creating a natural gong. The two rows of ilgs let out a roar and charged at one another. Each one tried to knock his opponent into the clay, which the water quickly turned into a red mash. The barbarians bellowed, shoved, and bared their teeth, their sap-smeared bodies ducked and glinted in the sun, and their fingers slid over each other. The women laughed and shouted, cheering them on. One of the

Book One: Beyond the Fog

barbarians who looked to be no older than seventeen fell down and tumbled over the side of the basin. Shrieking like animals, the women pelted him with lumps of red clay, and the boy walked off dejectedly.

The others continued the battle, if you could really call it that. There was little room and the ilgs' bodies were too slippery for them to truly hit each other, so they tried to knock one another over or shove one another out of the basin as the women barraged them with clay.

The spectacle was so enthralling that I only came to my senses after I noticed I was standing practically on the edge of the basin with a lump of red clay in my hand. The zipper of my jumpsuit had fallen down a bit more, and my body burned in the blazing sun and my cheeks glowed. When the next ilg fell out of the basin and onto the ground, I also had an urge to yell and fling clay at him.

But then a feeling of shame flowed through me and I skulked away, panting.

I felt someone's eyes on me and looked up.

Some of the ilgs were standing off to the side, just watching the merriment. Sverr was with them. He was sitting up against a rough tree trunk, and his golden eyes shone mockingly.

I let the lump of clay drop to the ground and wiped my palm on the grass, feeling embarrassed. I pulled the zipper of my jumpsuit all the way to the top and went to join my colleagues. They were also enthralled by the spectacle. Klin was shouting, Jean was shaking his fists, and our military guards seemed to be itching to join the fight. Only Maximilian was watching calmly — he even looked sort of displeased.

But I was in no mood to think about his warnings. I sat by the base of the cliff, on the silky, emerald-green grass under the azure sky, and watched the magnificent, oil-smeared men wrestle in the mud. When would I have another

The Charmed Fjords

opportunity to savor such a sight? I was pretty sure I never would. So I decided to turn off the scientist in me for a little while and just be a woman. There was no harm in looking, was there?

One of the ilgs let out a battle cry and I again fell under the spell of the action in the basin. There were now half as many men as before, and among them I noticed the fair-haired ilg with the blue eyes — my silent escort. He was clearly winning, easily knocking his opponents down. Smeared from head to toe in red clay, shining from the oil and sweat, the blond ilg was the epitome of primitive savagery.

I swallowed a thick lump in my throat and, summoning all my willpower, looked away. No doubt about it, such a sight could make a weak, civilized woman like me go crazy. Chuckling at my reaction, I decided it was time to go back to being a scientist. But as soon as I took out my dictaphone, another ilg flew out of the basin while the women leaped up and stamped their feet. The men stopped the fight and lifted their palms, smiling. There were six left — the strongest of them all. Or at least the hardiest ones.

I stood up and tucked my dictaphone back into my pocket. I could record my notes later; for now it looked like the fight was over.

I chuckled as I realized this whole business had unnerved me.

Chapter 6. Olivia

AFTER THE EPIC BATTLE in the basins, the tribe gathered and, with my group trailing behind them, walked a bit farther along the side of the hill. We stopped when we got to a volcanic pool filled with water. The aborigines immediately began pulling off their meager garments and jumping in. But the ilgs who had just triumphed in the fight didn't join them. Instead, they strutted around with their chests puffed out, as though the caked red clay on their bodies were a coveted prize.

My group lingered on the shore, gazing longingly at the babbling water. Sverr came over and looked at us mockingly.

"There are no predators here. You can go in. There's nothing to be afraid of," he said.

My colleagues exchanged glances, unsure of what to do. I for one was itching to get in the water and wash the dirt and sweat off my body. Disinfecting wipes are all well and good, but nothing can replace a real bath.

"We could take turns," Klin said. "Didn't we come here to learn about how the aborigines live?"

Everyone else nodded. Yurgas crouched down at the edge of the stone pool, took a sample of water, and dropped reagent into it. He grunted in satisfaction. "It's pure freshwater. You can wash up in it. First Maximilian and Jean. Then me and Klin, then my guys."

The Charmed Fjords

Sverr bowed his head and turned away, but not before I glimpsed a trace of ridicule in his golden eyes. That set me off. What did our hospitable host find so amusing?

"Do you think we're funny?" I stammered, unable to contain myself.

"I think you're..." he snapped his fingers, trying to find the right word. "Unusual."

"Right you are," I agreed. "We're different from you."

"Oh, yes." His golden eyes gleamed in the sun like coins.

"Sverr, I've been meaning to ask you something: your eyes are a remarkable color. I haven't seen anyone else in the tribe with gold eyes. It looks like everyone else's are blue or green. And you have dark hair, but everyone else is fair. Do your relatives look like you? With the same eyes and coloring? Does everyone where you come from look like you?"

The ilg bowed his head and peered at me.

"Not everyone. But a lot of them," he said curtly. He gestured toward my colleagues, who were peeling off their jumpsuits. "What about you, Olivia? Don't you want to cool off? It's hot out."

His eyes slid over my face, which I knew was breaking out in a sweat. I bit my lip and glanced at the enticing water, feeling envious of the aborigine women frolicking in it. Oh, well. The women had gone over behind a rocky ledge where they weren't visible, but to get to the ledge I'd need to walk a few yards in view of everyone.

Max shot me a sidelong look and curtly shook his head. Sverr looked pensively at Max's back.

"I'm not hot," I said hoarsely.

Sverr narrowed his eyes. "Is that so? It sounds like you're out of breath. Go in the water. You'll feel better."

No kidding. I ached to rip off this ridiculous get-up. I felt like I was wearing a spacesuit.

Book One: Beyond the Fog

"I feel fine," I muttered, trying to resist an urge to unzip my jumpsuit.

Sverr leaned toward me and then did something I wasn't expecting: he lowered his head and sniffed the air next to my temple, like he was a dog. I reeled backward.

"You should take a dip, Olivia Orway," he drawled, straightening up and staring into my eyes. I boiled with anger. He abruptly turned away and went back to the other men. I could swear he was whistling under his breath. Dumbstruck, I watched him go. I glanced around to make sure no one was looking at me and then smelled my armpit. I didn't smell bad. I scowled and looked around. I just smelled like myself, a stickler for cleanliness. You should take a dip? He had some nerve.

"Come on, what do you even know about soap here?" I muttered angrily, sniffing myself again. "I don't smell bad!"

My colleagues had already cooled off and were now chortling as they climbed back into their jumpsuits, which were also made to absorb extra moisture. I couldn't help noticing that Maximilian hadn't undressed, but just rinsed off and splashed water on his arms. But Klin, Jean, and even Yurgas had splashed around with abandon, not feeling the least bit bashful in front of me or the aborigines.

Everyone seemed to have forgotten about me, so I decided not to be a pest and go off on my own. I didn't feel like watching my colleagues get out of the water.

I started walking along a path flanked by bushes that had small leaves I didn't recognize. After a moment's thought I took out my dictaphone.

"Recording number five, Olivia Orway, anthropologist," I began. "We just witnessed a strange event. It was supposedly for entertainment, but it also might have been a ritual."

I gave a vivid description of the skirmish in the clay,

The Charmed Fjords

but I didn't include my personal reaction. I paused. I knew I should spend some time processing my emotions, but I could do that later. I concluded my report, turned off the recorder, and studied the scenery. I'd skirted the cliff and had strayed far enough away that the ilgs' voices sounded distant. On this side, the volcanic pool looked deeper: the water was dark blue and in the center it was practically black. The soil around it was dotted with short grass and low bushes, and I could see a few crevices beside them. Dang, it was the base of the volcano. I craned my neck to look for the majestic summit, which was somewhere in the clouds. Never in a million years did I imagine I would end up here.

    I glanced over my shoulder to make sure no one had followed me. The path was clear, so I crouched down and put my hands in the water. It was frigid. For some reason I was expecting it to be like steamed milk, but no. Now I understood why Yurgas had snorted like a walrus. This water was rather nippy. Maybe it was warmer in the shallow part. In any case, it was just the relief I needed, and I really wanted to plunge in. I quickly unzipped my jumpsuit and splashed water down the front. The smooth surface of the water rippled as though it were alive.

    I scrutinized my disheveled reflection and frowned. For a split second I could have sworn that something or someone was in the water.

    No, that was nonsense. I put my hand in again. Water spurted into the air and I jumped back.

    "What the — ?" I gasped. Then I noticed Sverr close by. He looked at me, turned to the water, and then shouted something. The blue-eyed ilg who had walked silently next to me all the way to the basin emerged from behind the bushes. He was now covered head to toe in dried clay. He dropped to his knees, thrust his hands into the water, and said something in a sharp, commanding tone. The water rippled

Book One: Beyond the Fog

again, seemingly on its own. I caught my breath and stared at it. I had the impression that the deep blueness was beckoning to me and calling my name. Just one minute more and I would see... what would I see, anyway?

The blue-eyed ilg sighed and stood up. He looked at me angrily and pointed.

"What was that? There was something in the water, wasn't there?" I stared at the two ilgs. They exchanged glances, the blond guy grunted something that sounded like an insult, and Sverr sniggered.

"I told you not to go far, Liv. There are snakes here."

"But you said it was safe in the water."

"Over there," he said, pointing to the left, where the ilgs were swimming. "It's safe over there."

I frowned and mulled this over. The other pool was just a few yards away. How could it be that it was dangerous here but not there? I suddenly noticed that Sverr and the other ilg were looking at the top of my chest, which was now exposed. The blue-eyed ilg's eyes had stopped flashing furiously and he was almost smiling.

I jerked at the zipper of my jumpsuit and retreated from them, trying to look composed. A look of animal hunger suddenly passed over Sverr's face. I hoped I wouldn't need to call for help. But he and the other ilg just grunted, swiveled around, and went back toward where the voices were coming from.

I sighed, double-checked that I was zipped up, and trudged off behind them, berating myself.

Luckily, no one had noticed my absence, and when Maximilian asked me what I was up to I told him I'd gone behind the cliff. I wasn't in the mood to explain, and in any case, I needed to process everything.

Who was that in the dark abyss?

I absently rubbed the bridge of my nose. How many

The Charmed Fjords

more riddles were the fjords concealing? How I longed to unravel them! I hoped I'd be able to solve even some of the mysteries here.

I wasn't convinced it was worth telling anyone about my little adventure by the water. I already felt like the weak link on this expedition, so the last thing I wanted to do was look even more stupid in front of the commission. Better to keep my mouth shut for the time being.

I felt better once I made that decision, but I was disappointed I hadn't had a chance to cool off properly.

❋ ❋ ❋

Night fell suddenly over the fjords, as though a bird had come along and spread its wings overhead. We returned to the tents and the aborigines dispersed, leaving us on our own. As we stood around debating what to do next, the ilgs sprang into action. We watched dumbly as the women dragged away the cauldrons and plates, laid down cords of wood by the fire, and hastily cleared an area in the center of the settlement.

"What are they doing?"

I shrugged. "Probably a ceremony or dance," I told Jean. "Or a typical tribal practice. They need to have fun, too. I wonder if they're planning to feed us?"

Now it was Jean's turn to shrug. Shrugging seemed to be contagious around here. I threw back my head and gazed at the stars twinkling in the velvety sky. The starry darkness was deep, infinite, and unfathomable. For now the sky was still dark blue, but I knew it would soon turn black, like an abyss. I hadn't seen a night like this in ages. Come to think of it, maybe I never had.

A muffled, strangled cry made me jump. Our group unthinkingly drew closer together.

Book One: Beyond the Fog

"Did you hear that?" Klin swiveled his head like a dog looking for a squirrel. "Did someone just scream?"

"It sounded like a woman," I said.

We fidgeted nervously by the tents, gazing at the fire burning in the center of the settlement. Suddenly, we all seemed to remember the fragmentary, dim images from the probe. We shuddered in unison. The dreamy carelessness I'd felt earlier in the day evaporated. I began to feel ill at ease and my blood ran cold. As soon as the sun set, a chilly fog enveloped the mountains.

"We need to find Sverr and demand that he give us an explanation," Yurgas said hoarsely, checking his stun gun.

As though he had heard us, Sverr's tall figure materialized beside us, startling us.

"There you are," he said, as though it were possible to miss us clinging together and standing stock-still. He was wearing his customary sash around his hips and his naches, and a wide fur pelt held together on one side by a leather buckle was slung over his shoulders. "Come on. The shatiya is starting soon."

Maximilian and I exchanged glances. Was this shatiya a ritual? But for what? What role were we expected to play in it? Questions flashed through my head, and judging by the look in Maximilian's eyes, I could tell he was thinking the same thing. The serenity of the day had dissipated and now I only felt frightened. How strange that we had all managed to forget that fear over a single day. We'd all even relaxed.

"Come on," Sverr repeated. He set off toward the tongues of the flame, which was casting long, orange reflections on the ground and tents.

"Stop shaking," Yurgas commanded quietly but sternly. "We all have stun guns. Remember? I could single-handedly knock out all these barbarians in their animal skins in five minutes."

The Charmed Fjords

"Glory to the Confederation," Klin snickered out of habit. But Yurgas's words had the intended effect. Really, why were we all so frightened? We'd all been trained in self-defense, and even the scrawny Jean was an excellent shot. It must have been the dark night, and all those hides, skulls, and fangs.

Sverr had settled down in the circle of light, and we took our places around him on mats woven from grass and tree branches. Everything looked completely different in the thickening darkness — it was like the idyllic daytime scene had never happened. The compact shadows danced with the tongues of light, and the burly ilgs approaching the fire looked like visitors from another world. Transfixed, I gaped at the shining tanned torsos, the brawny arms covered in red drawings, the animal skins, and the skulls over their faces.

"What are those headdresses called?" I asked Sverr, who was lounging on the ground to my left. The bonfire flame was flickering in his golden eyes, reflecting the twinkling sparks. I could feel myself falling under their spell.

"*Halesveng*," he said, looking at me. His gaze made me feel uneasy, and I had an urge to shift closer to Max, or even Yurgas. But I reminded myself that I was a scientist, not a fearful little girl.

"Why aren't you wearing yours now?"

A smile slowly crept across Sverr's face. "I'm not participating in the shatiya, just like they aren't," he said, nodding toward some men seated around the bonfire. Their heads were bare like his, and their faces seemed to be sculpted out of stone. "So there's no reason for us to hide our faces."

Hide their faces? From who? I was eager to find out what he meant but decided to ask him about other things.

"What is this shatiya, anyhow?" I continued.

"It's an ending and a beginning. You'll see."

Book One: Beyond the Fog

Meanwhile, the ilgs had begun to glide slowly around the fire. Even though their faces were covered with animal skulls, I could tell from the red markings on their bodies that these were the ilgs who had won the fights in the basins. The blond, blue-eyed ilg was among them — I recognized the ring around his neck. The ilgs ignored the spectators. They were focused on the fire and a wide tub next to it filled with jostling water. The barefooted men stepped softly on the packed earth like predatory animals, moving from the light into the shadows and from the shadows into the light. A long, drawn-out sound rose from somewhere off to the side, floating toward the dancing ilgs and wrapping them in a silver thread. I squinted into the darkness and caught sight of an old man sitting in the impenetrable shadows. He was also wearing a pelt and halesveng, and the skull and his brown body were smudged in red. On his knees he held an instrument that looked like two bronze plates, one on top of the other. He touched the plates with his long, gnarled fingers, making the openings in the metal ring out. The sound was so striking I felt like I could see it, and even touch it if I tried hard enough. It was the sort of sound that stirred up ancient, forgotten, and unsettling feelings. As his fingers ran over the plates, it was like he wasn't even playing an instrument, but rather the strings of my soul.

Di-in-shork-din-shork... The quivering sound soared higher and higher, and pulled and tugged at my soul. Silver and gold, ice and fire, the beginning and the end.

"This music is extraordinary," Klin croaked. "So much for the barbarians, folks."

A few women crawled over to us and held out steaming clay mugs brimming with a lapping liquid. Out of habit, my colleagues stuck capsules of neutralizer in their cheeks.

"It's an infusion of herbs and berries," Sverr explained when he noticed me studying the mug in my hands. "It'll

The Charmed Fjords

warm you up — it gets cold here at night."

As if on cue, I shivered. The fjords definitely cooled off after the sun set. The daytime heat seeped into the crevices between the cliffs, and was consumed by the nighttime fog and swallowed by the icy lake water. My jumpsuit was made of special smart fibers developed in the Academy's labs that were supposed to warm me, but they didn't seem to be working. I couldn't think of any other explanation for the chills running through me.

I wrapped my fingers around the earthen mug, basking in the warmth. The music began to speed up, and the ilgs started to move faster to keep time. The hides and grinning skulls converged, intertwined, and split apart. Their movements ran together, speeding up one moment and then a second later nearly stopping. During the lulls, a drawn-out, moaning sigh that seemed to be an incomprehensible word or prayer drifted over the fjords. I couldn't decipher it, but it didn't matter because I could see that the ilgs were interpreting it: their poses, movements, and intonation told me that the men were asking for something.

Their dance was bewitching.

"It's a prayer," Maximilian said, almost inaudibly. I nodded in agreement. Yes, the odd movement around the fire and the basin of water clearly indicated that this was a ritual.

"I wonder who they're praying to?" I whispered to him as softly as I could. "We need to try to find out about the divinities the ilgs worship. That will help us understand a lot of their life-cycle events."

"Yes, but we both know religion is too serious a subject to ask about. The ilgs might get angry and aggressive. We're lucky we're here to witness a ritual."

I nodded and raised the mug to my lips. The hot beverage warmed me and I began to breathe easier. My colleagues were also watching the primitive dance, nodding

Book One: Beyond the Fog

and occasionally whispering to each other. The other ilgs were watching silently, their faces impassive. But when they heard the sighing prayer, many of them raised their heads and repeated the indecipherable word. I covered my eyes, listening closely. The sound was like a splash of water, a chime, and a melody rolled into one. Then suddenly, it was a gong.

Jean was frowning and moving his lips, trying to reproduce the sound. Or maybe it was a word? Or a whole phrase? Who could tell? Jean leaned over and began running his fingers over the ground, apparently trying to note something or separate out letters he recognized. Sverr slowly turned his head and looked at Jean, who jerked his hand away as though he'd touched the fire. But he continued moving his lips.

The old man started to play the musical plates faster, and the thread of music stretched out like a bow string. I looked back anxiously, beyond the circle of light. The fog had rolled in and now concealed the outlines of the tents.

Maximilian was hunched over next to me. Always on his guard, Yurgas was pivoting his head and taking everything in.

We were jolted out of our reverie when the music stopped abruptly on a high, shaky note and a girl was pushed out of the shadows into the circle of light. She was naked.

"Cripes," hissed the genteel Klin, spilling his scalding drink on his knees.

I gulped. This girl hadn't been with the other women today. She was clearly young, but she had a mature, shapely body, with full breasts and wide hips. She was covered in dark, dried spots, starting from the hair below her belly and running all the way up her body, to her ribs, breasts, and neck. After a few moments, I realized with horror that the spots were blood — and it was smeared all over her body.

The Charmed Fjords

Was it hers or someone else's?

The girl stretched her hands toward the fire and water and quietly uttered a few words. I managed to pick out a few sounds I'd heard before: Lagerhjegg, Nerdhjegg.

Then she took a few steps and stopped in front of Sverr. Pressing her hands to her chest — but not enough to cover it completely — she said something in a foreign language. Sverr looked at her seriously but shook his head. The girl bit her lip, and I didn't need to speak her language to know she was insulted or aggravated. One of the savages smeared in clay gently pushed her back to the center of the circle, toward the fire.

She slowly turned her eyes on each of the men in turn. For a moment her face distorted. She shuffled forward unsteadily but the other ilgs pushed her away again. Another step as the music rang out again, and another shove. The shove was gentle, but it was forceful enough to keep her inside the circle. The ilgs' predatory movements, their fair, bloodstained hair, the grinning skulls, and the flying hides were stretching my nerves to the brink. I was paralyzed by a horrible premonition. I glanced beside me and saw Sverr's golden eyes boring into me. I realized he'd been watching me the whole time.

"What are they doing?" I wheezed idiotically. Anyone could see what they were doing. The predators were playing with their prey before... what?

Sverr looked calm, even relaxed. "This is the shatiya," he said. "It's..." He frowned, trying to choose the right word. "A union."

"What?"

My eyes were drawn back to the circle of light. The girl was darting about like a frightened deer, trying to break through the row of tanned bodies. She didn't have a chance. An ilg shoved her again and she dropped to the ground, into

Book One: Beyond the Fog

the orange light of the bonfire. I clapped a hand over my mouth to keep from screaming. The ilgs' hides concealed a lot, but they still left plenty visible. Now these men had flung off their hides and were wearing only those ghastly skulls on their heads.

"It's a union," Sverr repeated gently as he gazed at this frightful nightmare.

The girl arched her back and cried out when the first tanned ilg lay on her. The black ring around his neck shone dully. It was that blond, blue-eyed ilg.

Yurgas clenched his stun gun and dark red splotches appeared on his weather-beaten face.

"Are you afraid?" Sverr asked us, sounding surprised.

"This is horrible," Jean said, panting.

"Why?" Sverr seemed genuinely baffled. "This is a joyful event in every woman's life. All the girls here look forward to the shatiya. Don't you have this in the world beyond the Fog?"

"No," I squeaked. "We don't have anything like this."

The girl — the victim — was flopping around and arching her body. Now she was kneeling, her head hanging so low her dirty hair brushed the ground. One of the ilgs stepped on it so she couldn't get up.

I couldn't bear to look at the tanned, stone-faced men who were about to engage in this so-called union.

"Does this frighten you, Liv?" Sverr addressed me softly, forcing me to lift my eyes and look at him and, unfortunately, reveal my blazing cheeks. My head was still spinning. I felt like I'd downed a flute of champagne in one gulp. But that was impossible — even if there had been any questionable herbs in my drink, the neutralizer should have blocked their effect.

"Don't the women in your world go through the shatiya?" Sverr was uncomfortably close to me. He was staring into my eyes and our shoulders were almost touching.

The Charmed Fjords

"No," I said hoarsely. I trembled, trying to grapple with this hallucination. "What is all of this for? Why does it have to be like this?"

"Like what?"

"One after the other, with whoever she chose."

Sverr nodded in understanding. "That's how it was the first time. Glirda swallowed the special drink and experienced her first pain with her husband a few days ago. He'll become her protector. He'll provide her with meat and warmth. Now Glirda will share satisfaction and, er, children with the others."

"Children?" I was so horrified that all I could do was repeat what he said.

"Of course." Sverr's golden eyes were gleaming. "Children. A child is always a gift for everyone. For everyone who has danced in the circle of the shatiya."

I lifted my mug to my lips. Now this was starting to make sense. "Shared children. No one knows who the father is. Is that right?"

"Everyone's the father," Sverr said.

I shook my head, continuing to stare at the ground next to my feet. I couldn't stand to look at the spectacle of the moaning girl and the bestial carnality in full swing. To my disgust, my colleagues were fixated on the scene. Jean's mouth was agape.

The pieces were beginning to fall into place. If no one knew who a child's father was, all children had the same value. There was no rivalry — your son is stronger but mine is smarter — simply because no one knew whose son was whose.

"Does everyone take part in the shatiya?" I finally remembered that I had come here to do research.

"Anyone who volunteers and wins a wrestling match. It's the ones who are strong and healthy, and who hunt for

Book One: Beyond the Fog

food."

"Why aren't you doing this?" The words came out before I realized what I was saying, even though I genuinely wanted to know.

Sverr smiled. "I didn't want to."

"Is the girl allowed to refuse to go through the shatiya?"

"Why would she do that?" Sverr was confused. "She's perfectly fine. It's satisfying for the woman."

I glanced over at the circle of light. The bodies had shifted and now I could see the victim's face. It was true — she was perfectly fine. Her distorted face looked blissful: her eyes were half closed and her lips were parted. She was definitely enjoying herself.

"So when she was trying to run away it wasn't real?" I asked.

"No, of course it was real. Women are frightened of the shatiya. They're frightened and fascinated at the same time. They always try to run away, at least, in the beginning. Until the call."

I slowly lowered my mug to the ground. Jean was licking his parched lips while Klin was nervously quivering, stretching toward the light with his whole body. The music was winding around everyone, running through us like silver and gold strings, and tearing our souls out. The delicate fingers of the ilg sitting in the dark, the shimmering fire, the moaning...

I couldn't take it anymore.

"I have to go. I need to get some sleep. I'm wiped out." I was sure my nerves were betraying me. Yurgas turned his head and the look of lust in his eyes made me feel wretched.

No one paid any attention when I stood up, not even Max, even though he wasn't looking at the circle of light and had removed his glasses, which he couldn't see without.

I spun around and took off into the darkness, unable

The Charmed Fjords

to rid myself of the string vibrating inside me. Silver and gold, ice and fire... anguish surged through me.

I ran alongside the darkened tents. All I could think about was getting to mine, crawling into my sleeping bag, drinking a tablet of sedative, and falling asleep. I longed to bury the image of the warped, tortured bliss on that girl's face, the tanned, naked bodies, and the golden eyes.

I was almost at my tent when I felt someone grab me. Before I could scream a heavy hand clapped over my mouth.

"Keep quiet."

Sverr took his hand away. His face was dark under the light of the stars. He pulled me to him in a smooth, swift movement.

"You asked why I didn't want to participate in the shatiya," he whispered. His hot breath burned my temple. "I wasn't interested in the girl who entered the circle. I wanted you... I called you."

"What?" I couldn't think clearly anymore. What was he talking about? The only thing getting through to me right now was that string, which had snaked around my soul. It was shaking, and I felt like it was going to snap. It was pricking at my consciousness and scratching my mind.

I had a sensation of hands on me — burning, strong hands. Hands that wouldn't let me fall. Hands that were touching me and groping for the fastener of my jumpsuit. Hands that were pulling me into the dark tent, closer to the furs that were the bed.

"Take this off." Sverr's voice was rough and as scalding as his hands. But at the same time, it was caressing me. It was as though the tongues of the flame were heating me but not burning me — at least, for a moment. Sverr stroked my body greedily, tracing its contours. "Take this off. I want your skin, not this."

I deliriously jerked at the zipper, separating the fabric

Book One: Beyond the Fog

at my throat. I pulled it down. Sverr's burning fingers instantly began touching my exposed skin. He breathed plaintively.

"Very good. Now take it all off."

I pulled my jumpsuit off my shoulders and dimly tugged at the zipper. I was so nervous it got stuck.

Sverr muttered something and ripped off the fabric, tearing the material that, according to the specs, "can withstand four hundred pounds." But Sverr tore it apart as though it were flimsy cigarette paper. A moment later I was standing before him in my underwear, trembling and frightened. Or was I expectant? Was the music still playing, interspersing with my breathing, heartbeat, and moaning? Were those sounds really coming from me?

"Take the rest off," Sverr murmured. "Turn around."

I turned obediently and froze.

Damn it, what was I doing? What was happening?

"Obey, Liv. Now!" Sverr ordered. It was impossible to disobey him, and I didn't want to. But at the same time, I couldn't give him what he wanted.

"No." The word fell like a stone.

"What?" He didn't turn me to him, but instead walked around me and lifted my chin in his fingers. "Don't you dare disobey me."

"No."

My mind was a jumble of thoughts: about the expedition, the Academy of Progress, and a scientist named Olivia Orway. Who was she? I could barely remember. I was a woman, just a woman going out of her mind with desire.

"No," I whispered as though my life depended on it.

"You're rejecting me?" Sverr's voice dripped with fury, but also with astonishment. Now his voice felt like a fire that was no longer caressing me, just scalding me.

"Yes, I'm rejecting you. I'm not doing what you want.

The Charmed Fjords

Get out of here. Or I'll scream."

This was all stupid, strange, and painful. That drink had definitely been spiked — I was breathing like I'd just finished a marathon. I wanted this ilg. I wanted to feel his whole body against me, that body that he'd so guilelessly exposed to me just hours ago. I'd never wanted anyone so much, not even Sergey.

The memory of Sergey dulled my desire a bit, and I seized on the familiar, cherished image like a life preserver. Sergey, who was always disheveled and smiling. Or strict and serious. Or embarrassed. Or frightened. Or fierce. It didn't matter. I had to focus on him, not on the tanned body that was pressing into me, and not on the hands that were stroking my butt deliberately, like it belonged to him.

"You're not like anyone else," Sverr said. His voice was muffled and surprised. "You're resisting. Kneel down, Olivia Orway."

"Go to hell."

I clenched my fists and shook my head, trying to rid myself of the narcotic swirling through me. I needed to scream. I needed to call to Yurgas. At the very least, I needed to get to my stun gun, which was lying somewhere by my torn jumpsuit. I needed to destroy this ilg. I needed to find those damned men who had come with me from the Confederation. Maybe the barbarians had already devoured them? What good would our weapons do us if we were like rabbits in front of a boa constrictor?

"You're resisting." Sverr clenched my hair and studied me. In the dark tent his eyes shone like oozing lava. "Keep quiet. Do what I tell you."

"No!"

I somehow sensed that it was imperative to resist him. I couldn't succumb to him. I didn't know why, but intuition was guiding me, the same nonexistent intuition that my

Book One: Beyond the Fog

respected professor trusted. I knew it would be easy for the ilg to have his way with me, and to do everything he wanted to. I'd already seen how easily he'd torn the sturdy fibers. But this intangible intuition was screaming at me to stand my ground. The string inside me was quivering and bristling like needles — thousands or even millions of them. They were shredding my insides.

"Why are you acting like this?" he whispered, circling me. He was a shadow, darkness, a bronze reflection. He wasn't human. Damn it, what was going on here? What had we all gotten into? "Tell me. Do you really not feel anything? I'm calling you. Obey me!"

"No."

It was so hard to resist. I could feel how moist my skin was. I was seething with passion.

The ilg was also breathing laboriously. His body was tense and all his muscles were vibrating. I could feel it. Just a few more seconds, and we would both lose it. Or only I would. Because I couldn't resist anymore.

At that moment the ilg hissed like an angry cobra, an abyss opened inside me, and I fell in. For the first time in my life, I passed out.

Chapter 7. Olivia

I FELT A TICKLE in my nose and sneezed. Through the haze of sleep I realized I was cold, and I wrapped my arms around myself. I couldn't figure out how I'd managed to freeze in my high-tech sleeping bag.

My eyes flew open.

No wonder I was cold — I wasn't in my sleeping bag. Instead, someone had thrown a fur and a gray felt blanket over me. I squinted into the semidarkness. I jolted upright as everything suddenly came rushing back to me: the night, the flame, the girl in the circle... and me. And the ilg.

I surveyed the inside of the tent. I was all alone covered in these blankets. I gingerly lifted the fur, expecting the worst. I heaved a sigh of relief. I was still wearing my comfortable, utilitarian underwear, and my jumpsuit was beside me. My throat ran dry. Did that mean I hadn't dreamed the events of last night?

I carefully crawled out from under the hide and furtively examined my clothing. The zip slider was broken and the fabric was torn from the shoulder to the hip — not along the seam, but straight through the heavy-duty fibers. Fortunately, I'd brought along a special sticky tape that could hold the fabric together. Of course, the hermetic properties of the material were now destroyed and the jumpsuit wouldn't keep me warm like it did before, but at least I wouldn't have

Book One: Beyond the Fog

to walk around naked.

The worst part was I'd need to explain the tear to the men. I hopped up and splashed ice-cold water on my face. It did the job, but I yearned to take a shower. I would have given anything to linger under hot, streaming water, catching the drops in my lips as the water washed the dirt and fear from my body. But of course there wasn't a shower here. Here there was nothing that should have been in a civilized society, just like this society wasn't civilized. Here there were ilgs, who the night before had staged group sex, and one ilg who had nearly staged individual sex — with me.

When my thoughts turned to Sverr, my lower belly contracted painfully. Startled, I dropped my jumpsuit. What was happening to me? Why was I having this reaction? And yet, was it really so surprising? A woman needs a man, even if she's a workaholic scientist.

Scolding myself under my breath, I dug out my inhaler, took a puff, and calmed down. I realized that I hadn't had another attack last night, and thought that was odd. That surely would have repelled that savage who'd been hunting me, no doubt about it. I somehow managed to tape the rip in my jumpsuit together and gave the zipper a good pull. I took out my dictaphone and turned it around in my hands, pondering. What exactly was I supposed to report? That I'd nearly experienced a barbarian's "love"? I wondered how the Confederation's commission would react if they heard a recording like that.

But most important, how was I supposed to react now? Just like any other woman, I wanted to go find this ilg and give him a good slap — what had happened last night was not at all OK. Everything was still fresh in my mind: the boiling inside me, and the wild, unbearable desire. Even now it still reverberated inside me. That tea had to have been spiked, maybe with an aphrodisiac. No, I couldn't go around

The Charmed Fjords

acting like some sexed-up chick. Nothing like this had ever happened to me. Now I was angry and resentful, but as a scientist I understood that I wasn't entitled to emotions like that. After all, I was judging Sverr's behavior against the morals of my own, civilized society. Based on the shatiya alone, the codes and traditions were completely different here. I hadn't seen any disgust or distaste in the expressions of the ilgs watching that spectacle last night. The whole thing had horrified me, but clearly they didn't feel the same way. Perhaps Sverr had actually been showing me respect when he showed up at my tent for the sequel? Who knew with these ilgs? The girl in the shatiya had obviously asked him to step into the circle of dancing men. That meant she had wanted it.

I shook my head. O, omnipotent One! I had no idea how to behave now. Should I act like nothing had happened? Demand explanations? Take Sverr's behavior as a sign of hospitality?

I had to chuckle at that. For sure, I was shown respect here, but I didn't deserve it. I was a bad researcher. Where is your willingness to do anything in the name of science, Dr. Orway? Who else will have a chance to experience the savage, shall we say, for the record?

I burst out laughing and slapped my hand over my mouth. Yes, I did have an inappropriate sense of humor that occasionally conflicted with my image of a scientist. But I always figured it was better to laugh than to cry.

I hastily combed my hair and tied it into a ponytail. The morning light was already peeking through the slit in the entrance to the tent. I gave one last sidelong look at the hides in the corner. He'd even covered me up, the bastard. I checked my stun gun and attached it to my belt along with a packet of neutralizing capsules and other medicines, and thrust aside the canvas flap. When I stepped outside and

Book One: Beyond the Fog

looked around, I felt a twinge of surprise.

It was a quiet, calm, peaceful morning. There were no traces of the nocturnal orgy. For that matter, there was no one in sight — not the ilgs, not the other members of my group. Was everyone still asleep? That seemed strange. Considering the position of the sun, it was already almost noon.

I walked past the nearby tents, instinctively knocking on them as softly as I could. It was like the settlement had just died out. For a moment I felt uneasy, and I laid my hand on my stun gun.

"You overslept," a mocking voice said behind me, making me jump.

To my astonishment, it wasn't Sverr, but rather the blond, blue-eyed ilg who had been dancing in the circle at the shatiya the night before. He was leaning against a wide-branched tree. In addition to the hides I was now accustomed to seeing, he wore a heavy piece of dark fabric, which was thrown over his right shoulder and fastened under his left arm. He was holding an animal skull. The dark ring that matched Sverr's was shimmering around his neck.

"You understand me?" I managed to put two and two together. "How come you didn't answer me before?"

"Why should I have to talk to you?" he asked insolently, and I suddenly remembered that he'd been the first one with the girl, in the circle of the shatiya.

"Who are you, anyway?" I asked, not even trying to be polite.

"Irvin." His blue eyes flashed.

"What have I slept through?"

"The hunt. Everyone already left. But they didn't take you with them."

"And why not?"

The ilg shrugged in irritation. I understood anyway —

The Charmed Fjords

he didn't need to answer.

"Women don't hunt, is that it?"

"And they don't wear things like that." Irvin unceremoniously circled me, studying me up and down. Frowning, I turned around — this barbarian was looking too boldly at my butt under my black jumpsuit. Irvin clicked his tongue disapprovingly. How dare this savage, wearing hides and holding a skull, look at me with such disdain. That ticked me off. But really, why should it? Of course, women here didn't wear jumpsuits.

"Did all the members of the expedition go?" I asked hoarsely. "I mean, all the people from beyond the Great Fog?"

"One of them stayed behind. He's around somewhere," Irvin said, pointing toward the bonfire. "He's supposed to protect you."

He scowled contemptuously, showing me exactly what he thought of me, my guardian, and the entire expedition.

Luke was walking toward us, a glum expression on his face. I was surprised to see him. I was positive that Irvin had been talking about Maximilian. Had he really decided to be part of an animal slaughter? Strange.

The ilg leaned toward me and snapped, "Go back to your tent. Go! There's nothing for you to do here. Got it? If you don't, you'll regret it."

I shuddered despite myself, but the ilg had already walked away and disappeared behind the tents.

"Thank you for staying to look after me," I said to Luke with a smile. This soldier was so taciturn I couldn't even recall if I'd ever heard his voice. Now he just nodded in displeasure and waved his arm, as if to say, "I'll be close by."

I thanked him again and set off on a stroll. I tried offering to help the women cook lunch, but they only darted their eyes at me from under their brows. I didn't see the girl from the shatiya anywhere, but that didn't really surprise me.

Book One: Beyond the Fog

After something like that, I didn't think it was very likely that she would just bustle around cheerfully doing housework. A tremor passed through me as I thought of her. Nebulous memories swirled around in my head. All I could see were fire and checkered light and shade.

"They must have spiked our drinks," I muttered under my breath, grimacing. "They definitely did. It had to be a local narcotic." It just wasn't possible that a group of scientists would instantly turn into animals that look at a female with an expression of dull longing on their faces. But that's exactly how my colleagues had looked last night. The expression on their faces wasn't one of scientific interest. It was lust — brutish, dark, frightening lust. Next to them, Sverr was a paragon of calm and indifference. There had been no lust on his face. In fact, there had been no expression at all on his face, right up to the moment when he seized me by my tent. But in the darkness it was hard for me to see if there had been any expression in the eyes of this strange ilg.

I shook my head, trying to push the image of him away. Enough of this. I was a scientist and I knew what I had signed up for. I had known I might find the local customs shocking. But that wasn't what was gnawing at me right now — instead, I was tormented as I thought about my colleagues. It had to be because of a drug. There was no other possibility.

I looked around to make sure no one was watching me and then slipped a capsule of neutralizer into my mouth and chased it down with a gulp of water from my canteen. Then I set to work. In a few hours, using my miniature camera, I managed to photograph the settlement, the black pillars around it, the bushes and trees, and even the little boys running around the smoldering hearth. No one bothered me, and after taking the first few shots on the sly, I grew bolder and started photographing openly and often. I tried to document everything I could. I worked fast, without taking

The Charmed Fjords

time to think about what all the objects signified. I was stuck using an ancient film camera — it was a surprising choice, but the only option because as soon as we crossed through the Fog, all our modern technology glitched. Phones, sensors, supersophisticated prospectors connected to the satellite, and all the tracking and communication methods stopped working. Fortunately, our stun guns functioned, presumably because their system was simple: a trigger, nerve-paralyzing ray, and a chamber that held the machinery. That was probably why the film camera also worked. There was no way to use anything connected to the internet or a satellite.

When I eventually pressed the button and nothing happened, I rewound the film, pulled it out, and stuck it in my pocket. By the time the men returned I'd shot four rolls and was congratulating myself on my productivity.

But my mood plummeted when I saw the hunters emerge from the forest.

My mouth dropped open when I caught sight of my colleagues. Thank the One, they weren't wearing skulls or sashes around their hips, but Klin had a dark stripe on his face, just like the ilgs, and Yurgas was talking animatedly to Sverr. Sverr looked at me indifferently as he passed by.

Several men were holding sticks that a slaughtered wild boar was swinging from. The ilgs' black knives, hands, and even their tanned bodies were bloodied, as though they hadn't simply finished the beast off, but also given it a big hug before it died. I was most disgusted to see the blood spots darkening on my colleagues' clothing. Jean snorted when he saw me looking at him and Maximilian lowered his eyes.

I bit my lip. What had happened to these people? Clearly nothing good.

"Why didn't you wake me before you left?" I asked, mustering up a smile to conceal my annoyance.

"Someone sleeps like a rock," Jean said, snorting again.

Book One: Beyond the Fog

"But that's understandable."

He exchanged a look with Reese, the soldier, who smirked back. The ilgs lugged the carcass over to the bonfire, where the women were already fussing and happily greeting the haul.

I scowled.

"Let it go, Liv. You wouldn't have been able to come along anyway," Klin said, spreading his arms. "Hunting is just for boys, you know that. Look what they painted on me." He laughed and pointed at the black stripe. "I took the last shot, can you believe it? I killed that animal. They let me do it."

I couldn't hide my revulsion. "Klin, you're a scientist! Do you actually like killing?"

"I'm a man before anything," he said. His mood darkened immediately and he turned away. "You wouldn't understand."

I opened my mouth, staring at him. Fantastic. Right, I wouldn't understand. What was the good of my high IQ?

"OK, don't get mad at me." What with everyone looking at me funny, I didn't want to end up by myself. Klin and I had always had a strong connection — at least, that's what I thought. "What was the hunt like?"

"It was amazing, Liv!" Klin livened up. "It was unbelievable! You can't imagine the drive and what it felt like. I've never experienced anything like it. No stun guns, just you and the animal, one on one. Sverr taught us everything: how to wait in ambush, how to look for tracks, how to chase it into the trap. I prayed to the One. I thought I'd swallow my heart. Then I saw that boar's face. Did you see what it looked like? It's gigantic!"

That slaughtered little boar wasn't gigantic. It wasn't even medium sized. To me it didn't even look like an adult. But what did I know? I'm an expert in anthropomorphic

The Charmed Fjords

species, not wild boars, so maybe I was wrong.

"Cool," I said, trying to muster up some enthusiasm. I added innocently, "How'd everything turn out last night?"

Klin's cheerful ardor disappeared as if blown away by a wind, and I glimpsed an indecipherable expression in his dark eyes. Was it apprehension? Or maybe fear?

"I left right after you," he said with a shrug. "But unlike you, I left by myself."

"Meaning?" I asked in alarm.

"Oh, come on, Liv," Klin shot back. "Everyone knows."

He walked toward the bonfire, where the ilgs were laughing and chattering.

My mouth agape, I watched him retreat. I took a deep breath and set off after him, planning to find out exactly what it was that everyone knew. Before I could get very far, grabbed me by the elbow and pulled me aside with an unexpected agility. He didn't let go until we were next to the tents, where the fog was drifting in and dampening the hides.

"Come with me, Olivia."

"Did something happen?" I immediately switched gears.

"Yes," he muttered in exhaustion. "Our expedition happened. Blast it!"

We reached one of the black pillars and he sank hopelessly to the ground. I looked at him in surprise.

"Max, are you all right?" I leaned down anxiously.

"Liv, we need to get out of here," he said. He raised his head and looked straight at me. I could see my own reflection in his glasses. I was a small figure with unkempt hair.

"What —"

"There's something going on. There's something going on with everyone, you understand? Today I took a good look at our group. These are people — scientists — and I've worked with you. I know all of you, every little thing about you, every piece of dirty laundry, if you will. But now..." Max said

Book One: Beyond the Fog

angrily, making a chopping motion with his hand. "It's like they're all strangers! Last night at that horrible spectacle, today on the hunt. I don't recognize them anymore. I don't even recognize myself. There's something not quite right on these fjords. Everything's off."

I couldn't disagree with that. I sat down next to him and leaned back against the pillar. "Do you think they're poisoning us?"

"I tested last night's food and drink." Maximilian chuckled at the incredulous look on my face. "I have a bunch of reagents with me, Liv. I wasn't born yesterday. I was a hundred percent sure they were poisoning us or drugging us. I mean, my colleagues couldn't possibly voluntarily become..." Max trailed off. I didn't ask him to clarify. Obviously, something had happened after I left — something that was making Max tremble and repeatedly remove his glasses, forget why he'd removed them, put them back on his nose, and then pull them off again.

Damn it! I was pretty sure I didn't want to know what happened the night before.

"They couldn't... not them," Maximilian repeated plaintively. "But not a single test was positive. Do you understand? It was just ordinary grilled fish and ordinary herbal tea. Nothing! And yet they felt all of it. Even I did. Even you did."

"Me?"

"You know, you're better than us," Maximilian said suddenly. His statement caught me off guard — he had never once praised me during all my years as a student or scientist.

"I mean it. You're the best. You had the highest neuropsychic connection indicator, the best academic performance, unconventional thinking, ability to cope with stress — all despite your past. Don't look at me like that. I know everything. Remember, I recommended you for the job

The Charmed Fjords

at the Academy of Progress. And they don't accept people with —"

"With a red mark," I finished calmly. "I know. And I'm very grateful for your help."

Max cut me off with a wave of his arm. "I'm not talking about your 'dangerous' mark, Liv. I'm talking about the fact that you have an astounding mind. You're an extraordinary scientist. Even yesterday..." he suddenly looked embarrassed and started stammering. He turned his eyes away from me. "I'm not judging you. I... just want to say..."

"What are you not judging?" I was tired of all this beating around the bush. "Tell me, Maximilian."

"You and that ilg..."

"Me and that ilg?" I clenched my fists.

"Yes." And I understand if... well, you're a free woman and the local gene pool is, er, impressive."

"Is that so?" I was so angry I wanted to stamp my feet and kill someone. A certain specimen of that impressive gene pool would be a good start, the one with the golden eyes It would help thin out the population, you could say. ""Did he tell you that? Sverr?"

"No," Maximilian said reluctantly. It was obvious that this conversation was making him uncomfortable. He was blushing. "On the contrary. When Jean hinted at it, that ilg barked so loud everyone just shut up. How can I describe it? He looked savage. But as I'm sure you understand, the guys know how to draw conclusions. The ilg left with you and didn't come back."

"That's just great. So everyone saw that he went after me, but no one bothered to check whether I was OK? It never occurred to you that someone could rape me, kill me, or eat me alive? Seriously? So you're not judging me? Is that so? If you really must know, nothing happened between me and that ilg. *Nothing.* Is that clear? I came here to work!"

Book One: Beyond the Fog

"Olivia!" Max dragged himself to his feet. "Listen to me. I believe you. Let's stop fighting. That's not what I wanted to talk to you about. I wanted to talk about how something is off here. I can't explain it — it's just a feeling I have. And something is happening to us here. It's like our dark sides are emerging. Do you see? The dark sides of all of us."

I must have looked bewildered because Maximilian snickered.

"What, you weren't expecting to hear a scientist say something like that? We need to get out of here. And I mean right away. I have a bad premonition, but it's not scientific. I'm going to tell Yurgas today that the mission is aborting and we're going home."

"But what about the research, the fjords, the ilgs? This is a breakthrough, Professor! It's the insight we've been waiting for so long!"

"Insight?" Maximilian burst out laughing. It was angry, ugly, saliva-filled laughter. "As if we didn't all long for this insight."

"I don't understand."

"Unfortunately, I don't either, Olivia. But there's one thing I can definitely say." He reached for his glasses but then stopped himself and clenched his fist. "You're going to think I've lost my mind. But not everything can be explained by science. It's true. Come on, let's go. I'm aborting the expedition."

He set off toward where the fire was burning, metal was clinking, and meat was cooking over the coals. I trailed behind him, ruminating over this mysterious conversation.

Our colleagues were seated on mats laid out on the ground. Apparently even their strong legs needed a rest. I settled in at some distance away, ignoring the sidelong looks they gave me. Sverr was opposite us. Through the flame I could see his hard-edged face and squinting eyes. He was

The Charmed Fjords

looking at me, and a smile played on his lips. A faint anguish awakened in me like a fiery tornado and I gasped. I pressed a hand to my stomach, trying to figure out where the feeling had come from. What sort of demon was this? I looked at Sverr again. He was no longer smiling. There was a slight crease between his brows and his golden eyes were filled with fury. The blond ilg who had approached me that morning put a hand on Sverr's shoulder. Sverr said something to him sharply and shook off his hand. Irvin scowled and then also turned to me.

I didn't like the look they exchanged. Meanwhile, the fog was creeping down from the dark hills, sneaking ever closer, concealing the outlines of the trees, pillars, and tents. It looked like the fjords had come to a standstill in expectation of a tempest. Just a little more, and it would descend on us in flashes of lightning and pelting, thrashing rain. Darkness fell abruptly, but this time I didn't see any stars. And last night it was noticeably colder. The women crawled among the crowd handing out hides, which everyone wrapped themselves in gratefully.

Sverr stood up, walked around the fire, and sat down next to me. I turned away.

"How was your day, Liv?" When I heard the soft voice in my ear I instinctively clenched my fists.

"Get away from me," I hissed at him. "In my world, strangers don't sit so close together."

"Are we really strangers?" He moved even closer, until his hot shoulder was touching mine. I shifted away. But he lowered his head and kissed my cheek, right there in front of everyone.

My fingers instinctively reached for my stun gun and I pulled it out of the loop. Out of my peripheral vision I noticed Yurgas jump up, and I saw a worried look cross Maximilian's face.

Book One: Beyond the Fog

"Get away from me," I said sharply, looking straight into Sverr's gleaming eyes. He looked me in the face without blinking or moving. Fear washed over me — unbearable, dreadful fear. Just then it hit me that Maximilian was right and we needed to get off the fjords. Something was definitely off here. I was nothing more than a certified idiot — not a scientist — if I believed that this ilg was a primitive being. Oh, no. A sophisticated mind shone in those golden eyes of his. He wasn't the least bit primitive.

A lingering quiet hung over the bonfire. It was a dangerous quiet.

Then Sverr shook his head and burst out laughing.

"They already showed me those silver tubes today," he said. "They don't look like a weapon, but they sure sting. You don't need to take it out, Olivia Orway. I got the message."

The ilgs began to talk loudly and the women drew away. I looked at Sverr. The laughter had faded from his eyes, and so had the smile. It was a foretaste — a dark, grim one.

I gulped and turned my eyes away, despairing in the sudden knowledge that I'd just made a serious error exactly what an anthropologist shouldn't do when she's on aborigines' turf. And just what a person without a "dangerous" mark in a personal matter wouldn't do. I'd assumed I was superior to the locals, and especially the local who had indisputable authority here. I'd rebuffed him, when I should have grit my teeth and endured. Even though the ilgs didn't understand me, they surely got the gist of what I was saying. The intangible intuition that Maximilian had talked about screamed inside me that I wouldn't be forgiven.

Fear washed over me again.

Sverr sprang up an walked away. A few moments later he was casually eating meat and holding court with Klin and Jean, who were staring at him worshipfully. He didn't give me another look. I dug my cold fingers into the fur. The

The Charmed Fjords

aborigines' supper went on normally and everyone seemed to forget about the little show from earlier. Like everyone, I was given a plate with meat and a drink, and we were even offered more furs so we could warm up. After we ate, there was music again — that same soul-wrenching music. Unable to take it, I stood up and headed back to my tent. I made a quick recording recapping the day, made sure my stun gun was ready, placed it next to me, and crawled into my sleeping bag. But I couldn't sleep. The silver strings were trembling inside me and summoning me. The sound was insistent and painful. I had an urge to wail and bury my face in the fur, or leap up and race outside. But instead, I bit my lips and burrowed into my sleeping bag.

Chapter 8. Sverr

I SOUNDED my call.
When nothing happened I called again even though I knew it would be painful for both me and the tribe. But she isn't responding. How can that be? No one can resist the riar's call. My wrath is so powerful that it chars the pillars and the sky grows angry. The fury seethes inside me so violently that I am blinded by pain. The tribespeople are looking on fearfully. They are anticipating the black shadow and the inevitable agony and chaos it always brings.

No, I can't make them suffer like that.

I calm down and close my eyes. No one should suffer right now, not while they're sitting by a bonfire feasting on a slaughtered boar. We killed it so we could fill the outsiders with the blood and stir up their hidden essence — the essence everyone conceals under a black curtain and is visible only to me. People of the Confederation, scientists, progress: I know the meaning of these words and I detest it. I detest it all — the words, their meaning, and the very people who long to bring all of that to us. But I know what they need and what they're looking for in the land of the fjords. They want what belongs to us — our land, our fortresses, our women, and most of all, our strength. But they won't leave with any of that, and they'll lose more than they expect.

But as long they're useful to me, I'll let them live.

The Charmed Fjords

Whatever the call and the fjords expose will stay out in the open. These people have no idea what awaits them. What idiots. The fjords won't release them, no matter where they are.

But I know I make an impression, and so does Irvin. Between their stun guns, high-tech clothes, and fancy instruments, these people are dangerous. I suspected it immediately but now I'm sure of it. It's not their puny weapons that scare me — I just need to understand them better. I don't have enough knowledge yet. The spirits of the fjords are on our side, but I need to act fast.

Time is pulsating and stretching out like sticky tar.

No, I don't bear any ill will toward the people who are trying to study us. Those four scientists are just people who want knowledge. I actually respect them for that and understand that urge. But they're not the last people who will infiltrate the fjords. They'll be followed by people who want to possess — it's inevitable. And I understand enough about human nature to know that I can't let that happen.

The people beyond the Fog have been trying to reach the fjords for centuries. We owe our lives to the Fog, which has protected us all this time. Why has it started to dissolve now?

Even Irvin doesn't grasp the magnitude of the danger. My a-tem is smart, but he doesn't know everything. He hasn't spent countless hours studying the people from beyond the Fog, like I have. He assumed the fjords were protected and that's how it would always be. And that's why I'm the riar, not him. I can sense the danger even know, while those people sitting on the other side of the bonfire smile as they feast on the boar we killed. But I can see each person's true nature hidden under their eager expressions. Yesterday we only let them take what belongs to the tribe; we offered it to them as we would to any guests. And they took it willingly. In

Book One: Beyond the Fog

fact, they pounced on it greedily, and that told me a lot.

But tomorrow they'll want to take things we aren't offering them.

The dark instincts have stirred in all but two of them. I wasn't expecting that, and when I think about it I feel uneasy. The old man and the girl are different from the others. They have the strength to stand their ground and not submit to the call of the riar or to their own dark sides. Why?

I replay the events in my head. That old man is dangerous. His frailty, gray hair, and weakness belie the fact that he is the strongest of all the outsiders. His instincts are dead, and that frees the mind. He's observant and too intelligent. There's something about him that puts me on my guard. He's able to see things the others don't see, even when they're staring them in the face. I'd bow my head before that wise old man and make him my mentor if I could. But that is obviously impossible.

And that girl.

The call is awakening again. It's so powerful I can feel it breaking me. It sounds on its own, without my command or desire.

I called her last night. I felt her soul. It was intertwined with the call, and I touched it. I even heard the response. It was searing. I wanted more, but she resisted. Rage and confusion filled me. How did she resist?

She resisted so forcefully that her mind darkened. If I hadn't caught her, she would have hit her head on the dirt floor. Maybe I should have let her fall.

I smirked silently and gazed at her though the dancing bonfire, the outsider with the dark hair and green eyes. I know I look at her too much. I need to understand why I long to feel her body under mine. It's not as snowy white and stunning as the body of that maiden of Aurolhjoll, nor as servile or docile as the bodies awaiting me in Neroaldaf. I have

The Charmed Fjords

the impression it's not as adept as the bodies of the captives from the southern lands. She doesn't look like the women of the fjords. There's a fire burning in her eyes, but it's devoid of fury. She smiles even when she's afraid.

And she bubbles over with curiosity. Admittedly, we have that in common. In her light green eyes I detect a thirst for knowledge like the one that once made me study the world beyond the Fog.

But this is also the outsider who insulted me, and I'm not one to forgive insults.

Irvin laid a hand on my shoulder, silently reminding me of my duty. I managed to suppress a yell, but I pushed his hand away. A storm is brewing over our heads, and all the tribespeople look supplicant. The women offer me food, spices, meat, themselves — they'll give me whatever it takes to calm my wrath.

I nod, letting them know that I'm not slighting those who have provided shelter and food. I can hear Irvin sigh. That green-eyed outsider is looking at me through the flame, and my desire is triggered again. I watch her gasp. Her pink lips open slightly and I can practically feel her breath on my skin. I imagine that her breath is also spicy, like the summer herbs steeped in the boiling water. She turns away and the first bolt of lightning strikes the fjords.

OLIVIA

That night I barely slept. A storm broke out over the fjords, and the thunderclaps sounded like the yowls of a wild animal. It was so unsettling that I only managed to doze off for a few minutes, and I awoke sharply, gasping for air through my parched lips. I grabbed my inhaler but each puff only made me feel more glum. I was relieved when morning

Book One: Beyond the Fog

finally came, and I hoped the day would be better than the night had been.

The night before, our group had gotten into a nasty blowout. Maximilian announced his decision to leave, but everyone else was violently opposed. Things escalated into a shouting match, and since we were by the fire, the whole tribe witnessed the shameful scene. Confident that the ilgs didn't understand a word we were saying, my colleagues didn't hold back. But of course, there were at least two people in the tribe who could understand. That didn't stop the scientists, though. Unfortunately, although Maximilian is a stellar scientist, he isn't much of a leader. He's never managed to put his foot down when it counts, and in this case it didn't help that he couldn't justify himself coherently. Instead of bringing up his bad premonition, he tried to reason with facts, but that was pointless because there were practically no facts. No one was threatening the expedition — rather, everyone was as hospitable as could be.

When the topic of this hospitality came up, Klin turned beet red and the soldiers, Luke and Reese, smirked. I was repulsed. I wasn't about to ask what had happened when I left the shatiya, but the looks on everyone's faces told me more than I wanted to know. Maybe they'd entered the circle of the shatiya or, to put delicately, continued communing with someone in a tent? The last thing I wanted was to hear details. And what if I'd been the one to set it all off?

These horrifying thoughts nauseated me. Everyone had seen the ilg follow me when I left, and then they assumed that I'd given my consent. Everything must have been OK because I hadn't screamed or called for help, and they hadn't heard any shots from the stun gun I always had on me. All I needed to do was fire one shot from the stun gun and the ilg would be knocked out of commission for hours. So since I didn't fire it, they reasoned that I didn't feel like I was in danger and

The Charmed Fjords

that whatever had happened between the ilg and me was consensual. And once that sort of thing was permitted for me, a woman, what was required of them?

Klin had summed it up truthfully: they were all men before anything else. So the shatiya may not have seemed so appalling to them — instead, it was captivating, and even arousing. How vile. I gathered that during the night, everyone except Maximilian had conducted in-depth research on the local customs. Could that be? Even Klin, who had a family at home, and Jean, who was in love with an Academy worker?

I grew queasier by the minute, and I couldn't endure my colleagues' sidelong looks. They didn't even ask me any questions, but I wasn't about to justify myself for the sake of their speculations and assumptions. No one brought up the previous night, and they acted like nothing had happened. That only made me feel more tense.

After a drawn-out screaming match that didn't produce a compromise, we agreed to discuss everything again the next morning and we went our separate ways. I hoped that today Maximilian would present better arguments for our departure. At this point, I was ready to leave the fjords, and especially Sverr. The inexplicable way I reacted to him was disconcerting and I wanted to get away from it.

The sun was barely up when I emerged from my tent. As my eyes adjusted to the light, I looked around. The women were already puttering around by the bonfire in the middle of the settlement. There were no men in sight. I stood there for a while, pondering what to do, and then tentatively made my way over to the women. I'd failed to connect with the men around here, but maybe I'd be able to bond with the women so I could learn about life on the fjords.

"Good morning!" I called brightly as I approached the group. I made sure to keep my palms open and body relaxed, and I looked them straight in the eye. Studying anthropology

Book One: Beyond the Fog

taught me that body language is powerful and often says more than words. When they saw me, the women stopped what they were doing and stared at me, but they looked curious and didn't seem aggressive. I pointed at a cauldron that one of the girls was cleaning. "May I help?" I asked.

I gingerly went closer and crouched down beside her. I touched a sheaf of straw the women were using to clean dishes.

"May I help?" I asked again.

The women looked at each other and then began speaking quickly in a flood of words that sounded like gibberish to me. The next thing I knew, they were nodding and handing me the straw.

I took it happily, proud of myself for getting my point across. You don't always need to share a language to communicate. I set about scrubbing the cauldron, trying with all my might to show how eager I was to do this chore. The women were watching me closely. After a few moments they started clucking and then burst out laughing. The woman who had handed me the straw knelt down next to me and demonstrated the right way to clean the cauldron. Another woman sat down on the other side of me, stretched her fingers out to touch my hair, and then drew them back.

I smiled again.

"You like my curls?" I swung my head. "They're actually kind of a pain sometimes. I always feel like a mess."

Of course the woman had no clue what I was saying, but when she saw that I was smiling, she became bolder. She stroked the fabric of my jumpsuit and her eyes widened in surprise. She ran her finger along the spot where I'd taped up the tear, and exchanged a glance with her friends. I kept rubbing the cauldron and smiling, looking around the group of women.

"Where's that girl?" I asked. "You know, that girl? The

The Charmed Fjords

shatiya? Is she alive?"

The women laughed. One of them placed her hands under her head and closed her eyes. "She's sleeping," I guessed. When they heard me say "shatiya," the women didn't wince in revulsion. Instead, they actually looked coy.

What the hell?

"Did you have one too?" I stammered, looking at an older woman. "You know, a shatiya?"

She rolled her eyes and smiled, displaying perfect white teeth. Judging by her wrinkles, she couldn't have been young. But once again, at the mention of the shatiya, she looked happy and not the least bit frightened.

"Does the shatiya happen a lot?" I continued my interrogation.

The women spread their arms uncomprehendingly. Feeling a little silly, I mimed the shatiya and pointed at one of the women. She nodded and smiled again, then held up one finger and made a sad face. The other women chuckled.

I guess that meant she'd also had a shatiya, but just one.

"Child?" I rocked my arms in front of my chest in a gesture every woman recognizes. She started babbling and her face fell. She pointed at the children playing nearby.

I stopped rubbing the cauldron with the straw. If I understood her gestures right, she'd given birth to a baby. But why did she look sad? I must be missing something.

The aborigines glanced at each other and crept closer to me.

"*Shir haam Sverr hjegg?*" the sad one asked eagerly.

"What? Are you asking me about Sverr? I don't know anything."

The girl touched the seam on my torn jumpsuit and repeated insistently, "*Shir haam Sverr hjegg?*" *Shir haam?*"

"No, there was no *haam!*" I spat in annoyance. "And

Book One: Beyond the Fog

there won't be!"

"*Sverr hjegg! Haalensvod! Shinga, shinga!*" the women began to squeal in fear. I winced. All right then. The locals were scolding me because I'd thwarted the advances of their golden-eyed man.

"His plan failed," I added angrily, and the women screamed even more vociferously. Women always understand each other even when they don't speak the same language. I waved an arm to calm them down and beamed at them. "I've heard that word, hjegg. They were saying it at the shatiya. They were singing it. That's not quite it. What was it I heard? Nerdhjegg... Lagerhjegg."

The old woman twitched and slapped me across the mouth with unexpected strength. I bit my tongue to keep from crying out. Were those words taboo? Or was I the only one not allowed to say them? But what did they mean? I put my hands together like I was praying and bowed my head contritely. "I'm sorry. I didn't know. I'm just a stupid civilized woman and I have no idea what I'm saying."

My repentant expression did the trick, and the woman mumbled something and nodded. Then she pointed to the sky. "Lagerhjegg," she said breathily. The other women watched with fascination. "Nerdhjegg!" She pointed at the water in the cauldron and then to the mountains. "Ulhjegg!"

I contemplated this. Those must be the local deities. What else would the aborigines talk about with such terror and rapture?

A young girl with a mass of small braids came closer to me and whispered, "Hellehjegg..."

That earned her a slap on the mouth from the old woman that was so forceful her skin split. The girl prattled on fearfully.

I tried to memorize what she was saying. It sounded like they honored three gods but there was a fourth one

The Charmed Fjords

whose name they couldn't say. Could that be right? I cautiously pointed toward the cliffs. "Ulhjegg?"

The women nodded vigorously. The old woman studied me. I pointed at the water and repeated the second name. The women began to smile and looked at one another playfully. Again I was puzzled. Maybe the water god was very happy, and that made them joyful rather than afraid? Nothing made any sense to me.

"Ir-vin hjegg!" the girl with the braids sang out. I guess she wasn't afraid of getting slapped on the mouth. Hmm. Irvin was the name of the blond, blue-eyed ilg. But what did he have to do with this? Now the language barrier really was a problem. Nothing made any sense.

"Irvin?" I repeated. "Irvin... hjegg?"

"Irvin hjegg!" the women echoed gleefully. "Nerdhjegg!"

"What nonsense with these hjeggs of yours," I muttered in annoyance.

"*Hjegg sald! Hjegg shundir!*" The women started jabbering again.

I shook my head. I was totally lost. Apparently there was another deity that ruled the sky. I pointed to the fluffy clouds overhead. "Lagerhjegg?"

The girls crouched down, covering their heads in fear. The old woman raised her hand threateningly, but she just scowled instead of slapping me. She wagged her finger and said, "Lagerhjegg." The name sounded harsh and angry. She gave me a sidelong look and added in a whisper, "Sverr hjegg."

Sverr? Either I wasn't a scientist worth my salt or they kept repeating the name of the golden-eyed ilg, somehow connecting it to this mysterious hjegg. How did those things fit together? I was thinking so hard I forgot I was holding the cauldron and I dropped it. I itched to grab my note pad and dictaphone, record everything, scribble diagrams, write down

Book One: Beyond the Fog

everything I knew, and analyze it all.

The oldest woman couldn't take it anymore. She snatched the dish from me and growled something, probably that I was hopeless at washing dishes. The other women livened up. They seized me by the hand and began to pull me somewhere.

I stood up in confusion. "What's going on? Where are you taking me?"

They chattered away in their cryptic language. I had no choice but to follow them obediently. One of the women thrust another, slightly smaller cauldron into my hand, and the others also picked up cooking utensils. They set off at a run along the path I'd already been on, but instead of turning off toward the basin in the cliff, they went downward. We soon emerged onto the gently sloping bank of a calm lake. Water lapped against the bank, but closer to the center it was darker, indicating that it was quite deep.

"You wash your dishes here?" I guessed. When I saw the women undressing, I added, "I get it. You bathe at the same time."

The young woman who had led me there pulled on my sleeve and mimed something. "Hydra? Shatiya?"

"Shatiya?" I repeated. "Yes, of course I saw it."

"Shatiya?" The woman brightened and pointed at me. Then she shyly placed a hand on my stomach. "Shatiya?"

"Yes, I told you I saw it!" I nodded vigorously. "How could I ever forget it?"

The woman smiled again and indicated that I needed to undress. I looked toward the path, weighing my options. It was true that I desperately wanted to pull off my jumpsuit and dive into the water. I was in the habit of taking a shower every day, and several days without one were taking a toll. The prospect of splashing around in the water was enticing. But could I do it?

The Charmed Fjords

On the other hand, I'd already noticed that the women of the tribe bathed separately from the men, so that meant it was unlikely that any men would show up. The water really looked tempting, and it also dawned on me that if I got in the water with the women we could understand each other better.

That decided it for me. I carefully undid my cursed zipper and stripped down to my underwear. Not surprisingly, seven pairs of curious eyes immediately turned to stare at me. The women began to squeal, clicking their tongues and pointing at my stomach and chest, which was covered with a white cotton sports bra. I forced myself to stand there calmly and not shield myself, and not try to hide my scars. It wasn't the nudity that embarrassed me, and that wasn't why I didn't like to take my clothes off in front of other people. Rather, it was because of all the ugly, repellent scars that crisscrossed my body.

The old woman shook her head and lifted her hand, demonstrating a wallop. I nodded slowly.

The women came closer and examined me up and down. The old woman snorted and waved her arm in a universal movement that said to her friends, what are you staring at her for, her world is just like ours.

I couldn't help laughing at the eloquence of her facial expression and gesture. Women are women, no matter where you go. I took one last look at the path and then pulled off my underwear and stepped into the stone pool. The frigid water took my breath away and I cried out involuntarily. The other women were already splashing around, and the youngest one yelped from time to time like a puppy. I ducked down, submerging my entire body. The water enveloped me like a cold blanket. I resurfaced and laughed again through my chattering teeth. One woman held out a piece of crude fabric and rubbed herself, showing me what to do with it.

Book One: Beyond the Fog

"I get it!" I shouted in understanding. There's the local soap for you. The rag had a bittersweet smell to it, as though it had been soaked in a solution of ashes, which was commonly done in tribes like this one. I hastily rubbed my body, feeling my blood start to circulate again and goosebumps form on my skin. I plunged back into the water and did a few strong strokes. The water was rejuvenating and my head suddenly felt clearer, as though I had washed it too. My thoughts turned to what I'd heard the women say. Who were these hjeggs? I could grill Sverr, but I had no desire to talk to him. I didn't even want to get anywhere near him.

I surfaced.

Even the word "hjegg" was strange. At the same time, it seemed familiar even though I didn't know what it meant.

Hjegg...

I ducked into the water and then stopped moving, with my eyes open. Something was rustling in the dark depths. Something huge. Suddenly a wave surged and the whole lake rippled.

I opened my mouth to yell but instead swallowed a mouthful of water. I leaped ashore and shook my head, flinging my hair all over the place. The old woman bellowed threateningly and shot me a look. Everyone jumped up onto the bank as if they were obeying an order. I crawled farther up onto the trampled grass and wrapped my arms around myself.

"There was someone in the water!" I shouted. "Someone weird!"

I stopped talking because the aborigines were frowning and twittering again. I thrust a finger at the water. "Who was that? What sort of animal was it? Do you know? It was massive!"

The old woman waved her arm, and I thought I was in for another smack. That seemed to be the way these

The Charmed Fjords

aborigines kept people from talking too much. I managed to leap out of the way and she screwed up her face disapprovingly.

"Do you know who was in the water?" I asked.

"Hjegg!" the girl with the braids whispered. I turned to her.

"No, I was asking who was in the water. I wasn't asking you about your gods! I was asking you about the animal in the lake. Do you understand?"

She just shook her head and her braids flew.

"Hjegg, hjegg!" the women began shouting again.

A moment later an ilg I'd never seen before appeared on the path. I grabbed my jumpsuit, clasped it to my wet body, and backed away toward the rocky ledges to get dressed. Out of sight, I pulled my clothes on, half listening to the barbarians' disgruntled exclamations. They sounded indignant and a bit frightened. I fumbled with the zipper, which caught again, leaving too much of my neck exposed. I ground my teeth in frustration at the sight of my unintentional décolleté. Now everyone could get a good look at my cleavage. What a piece of crap this jumpsuit was.

As soon as I emerged from my hiding place, one of the women grabbed me by the elbow to drag me back toward the settlement. I didn't resist, and I wondered what would happen next.

We returned to the tents. Following their routine, the ilgs gathered around the fire, and the one who had led me back pointed at me accusingly. "*Raanval hjegg! Hudra!*" she shouted.

"You're a fool," I muttered under my breath. Dozens of judgmental eyes stared at me.

"I didn't do anything," I shouted indignantly. "I have no idea what's going on."

"They're accusing you of waking the hjegg."

Book One: Beyond the Fog

I was surprised to hear Sverr's voice. I swiveled around and looked into his golden eyes. I immediately felt the blood rushing to my cheeks. What nonsense. I flared up and scowled. "The hjegg? What on earth is a hjegg? And how could I have woken him up?"

My colleagues were running out of their tents. Klin was zipping his jumpsuit as he ran and Jean was yawning. Max was frowning again, and as he got closer he began cleaning his glasses. On the other hand, the soldiers looked vigorous and ready to take action.

"What's going on here?" Yurgas demanded when he joined us.

"They're saying I woke something up. But I don't understand."

"Hjegg! Hjegg! Hudra! Hjegg!"

"What are they talking about?"

I shrugged and gave Sverr a sidelong glance. He didn't say anything, and I took that as a bad sign. His forehead was creased.

"It looks serious," Yurgas said somberly, peering at the ilgs, who were shaking their fists and shouting. They didn't shout for long, though. The next thing I knew, stones were flying at me. I reflexively backed away, but I resisted the impulse to run from this wrathful mob of barbarians. The women who just a short time ago had been smiling at me were now either looking at me angrily or turning away.

"But I don't understand. I don't understand what I did!" I said.

"That's a major offense, Liv," Sverr said flatly. "People are punished for that here."

"But what kind of offense is it?"

"You went in the water. You called the hjegg. He came."

"What? The hjegg? Won't you just tell me already what a hjegg is?"

The Charmed Fjords

The old woman furiously lifted her arm, clearly wanting to slap my face again. I dodged her and looked over at Sverr.

Out of the corner of my eye I noticed a sullen-looking Irvin, who had emerged from behind the tents. He shouted a few words, apparently trying to calm the aborigines. But they only got angrier.

"Hjegg! Hudra! Shatiya!"

"Shatiya?" Finally I caught a word I knew. "What are they talking about?"

"You need to be given away in a shatiya with the hjegg," Sverr explained confusingly. "Because he came for you."

"Come on, that's nonsense!" I gasped. "What hjegg? How could I possibly summon him? I didn't do anything! I was only swimming. But the women brought me there!"

"Are you a virgin, Liv?" The gold in his eyes was flaring.

I blushed again. This blushing was an awful curse. Why did this happen to me? Was I going to have to tell everyone my shameful life story? Here, in front of my colleagues?

"What does that matter?" I asked.

"Only a virgin can wake the hjegg. Virgins aren't allowed to go into the water by the cliffs."

"But she was there!" I pointed hopelessly at the girl with the braids. "She's younger than me!"

"She already has a child," Sverr said dully.

I was too dumbstruck to talk.

"Apparently some sort of beast has shown up in the vicinity," Maximilian said. "And the barbarians are connecting it with you, Liv."

"I did see someone in the water. I mean, I didn't know what it was, but it seemed huge."

"If I'm understanding correctly," Jean said, pressing closer, "the shatiya with the hjegg is some sort of ceremony of peace offering for the beast."

We exchanged anxious looks. Even a fool would have

Book One: Beyond the Fog

been able to see that I wouldn't care for this ceremony, and none of my colleagues were fools.

"Hjegg! Shatiya hjegg! Hudra!"

The furious hollering made us huddle closer together. We looked at each other nervously.

"I suspect they want to feed you to a predator," Klin said morosely.

Yurgas's eyes flashed under his knitted brows. "What are we going to do?"

"Whatever you do, don't use weapons!" Max drew back and turned to Sverr, who was silent. "Tell them that Olivia is innocent. She didn't know about the predator in the lake, and she didn't know your traditions."

"That doesn't change anything," Sverr said.

"Ignorance of the law doesn't absolve you of responsibility," Klin muttered, and I shot him a dirty look.

"This is all madness!" Yurgas hissed.

"Madness?" Sverr raised his dark brows and his golden eyes seemed to be oozing melted lava. We stared at him in fascination. The color of his eyes was changing, and they were almost shining.

"Well, the thing is..." Jean sputtered, reeling.

"You're saying that a custom the tribe has been honoring for centuries is madness?" Sverr fixed his gaze on Yurgas, whose forehead had broken out in a sweat.

"I didn't mean to insult your traditions," Yurgas croaked. To his credit, he managed to apologize, even though he reached for his stun gun. I suppressed an urge to press closer to the men, and instead straightened up and thrust out my chin. No matter what, I couldn't show any fear.

Sverr narrowed his eyes and looked at me, but in the lava of his irises I caught a glimpse of approval. I averted my gaze.

"We'll apologize," Maximilian said quickly. "And we'll

The Charmed Fjords

atone for our guilt. Olivia will apologize..."

"The only thing that will help is blood," Sverr said matter-of-factly. "Either Liv's blood or..."

"Or?" I asked hopefully.

"Or the hjegg's blood. If someone dares to kill the hjegg, we can cancel the shatiya."

"That's great. That works for us!" Yurgas jumped in, but stopped himself when he saw Sverr's expression. "Well, it would be helpful to know who this hjegg is, but our stun guns should do the trick, right?"

I lifted my eyes and saw Irvin scowling. He was looking at Sverr, and he had a hard, despondent look on his face. But Sverr was lost in thought, ignoring him.

At that moment, the crowd of ilgs heaved and rushed toward me like a wave, and the next thing I knew, strong arms snatched me and lifted me. One of the barbarians threw me over his shoulder and dragged me away as his fellow tribespeople shrieked approvingly. I cried out, more in surprise than in fear. Strangely, I still wasn't afraid. It was probably because I hadn't yet registered that this was a serious situation — not a joke or a play, but real life. I hadn't come to grips with the fact that I had somehow incited the fury of the locals and now they wanted to hand me over to some mysterious predator and let it tear me to pieces. What a glorious way to end not just my research mission but also my life.

"Let go!" Trying to wrench myself free, I pounded the ilg's back, but he just adjusted me on his shoulder and kept walking. I flailed my legs and turned my head but couldn't see much.

"Yurgas, no weapons, please!" I heard Maximilian shout.

"I can shoot them all down."

"You've lost your mind! Put away your gun!"

Book One: Beyond the Fog

"Yurgas, don't!" I yelled, lifting my head. "I'm fine!"

Yurgas appeared for a moment and then fell back behind the sinewy ilgs. The ilg carrying me dragged me to the path leading to the lake and then flung me on the ground. I jumped up and looked around. Before I had a chance to get a good look, a few ilgs pressed me against one of the black pillars lined up along the lake while a few more began tying me up, with my back on the pillar and my face toward the lake.

My jaw dropped. "Professor, I think I finally understand what these ceremonial behemoths are for," I cried triumphantly. "They're sacrificial altars."

Maximilian didn't answer. I looked into the crowd but didn't see any of the members of the expedition. I only saw the ilgs who were binding my arms to the pillar. My shoulders immediately began to ache.

Someone grabbed my jumpsuit, trying to rip it off me. The adhesive tape gave way, cracking and exposing the tear. Well, this wasn't fun.

"*Im Sverr hjegg!*" I could hear a muffled, drawn-out screech behind me. Sverr... yes, it was him. The tribe instantly quieted down. Even the women stopped squealing. The golden-eyed ilg appeared before me and his eyes shot daggers at me. I felt utterly defenseless. But I bit my cheek to keep from showing my fear. Sverr screwed up his eyes as he looked at me reproachfully. After a moment he turned toward the ilgs.

"*Im Sverr hjegg,*" he repeated. Looking at me, he translated: "I will wash away the blood with the hjegg's blood."

The barbarians were bewildered. They didn't look pleased. Apparently they would have preferred to see the beast devour me.

Sverr lifted a clenched fist and slowly ran his eyes over

The Charmed Fjords

the tribe. "*Skjran.* Tonight."

The ilg who had carried me over his shoulder stepped forward. Now I could get a good look at him. He was tall and broad shouldered, with light, sun-bleached hair, piercing blue eyes, and wrinkles that revealed his age. He was still strong even though he clearly wasn't young.

He poked me accusingly. "*Hudra! Ihnemeneg hjegg!*"

Sverr cocked his head and replied briefly. He spoke calmly, almost mockingly. The ilg winced dourly and glanced at me. He spit on the ground and shouted to the expectant tribespeople, "*Aphajol!*"

That was that, I guess. No one seemed to be in a hurry to untie me. Everyone was looking at me now, as though they were waiting for something. I looked at Sverr uncertainly. What was I supposed to do? Act happy?

"I'll pay your debt, Liv," Sverr said, "if you consent."

"If I consent?" I wanted to say that of course I consented, but I held my tongue. "Is there some condition?"

"I'll pay your debt, and then you'll become my *lilgan.*"

The men in my group had fought their way to the front of the crowd. Now Yurgas hissed in protest and Maximilian placed a hand on his shoulder. I feverishly considered my predicament. Obviously, the man who steps up to protect the woman is entitled to a reward. But lilgan? What did that mean? Maybe it was a lover? I wasn't crazy about that, but it was definitely better than dying.

"I consent!" I shouted. The wind hit my face and my voice echoed back from the cliff.

"Olivia lilgan Sverr hjegg," Sverr decreed, his eyes gleaming like molten gold.

I repeated after him and choked from the gust of wind pressing on my chest.

Then the world went quiet.

"Very good, Olivia Orway," Sverr said derisively.

Book One: Beyond the Fog

"Tonight you will fulfill your oath."

"Tonight?" Yurgas piped up. "Is she going to stand here all day?"

"Yes," Sverr snapped and walked away. The other ilgs followed him in a line, looking askance at me.

"Nonsense! I'll untie you."

"Don't, Yurgas." I stopped him. "Keep quiet. It's not worth provoking the tribe even more. I broke a taboo even though I didn't know I was doing it. It's good that Sverr intervened."

"I'm not sure it's a good thing," Maximilian said grimly. "You should have clarified the terms of the deal before you agreed to them, Olivia."

"What difference would that have made?" I cried angrily. "There wasn't much of a choice."

We were silent for a moment.

"What happened at the lake?" Maximilian asked.

"I did see someone in the water. It was some creature. I don't know what it was, but it was enormous. At least, that's how it looked to me — the water was cloudy." I wiggled my bound hands. "Please go. I'm OK. You don't have much time to collect specimens and study the barbarians. Let's just say I got lucky. How many scientists can brag that they sacrificed themselves for the sake of science? I literally was almost sacrificed."

My colleagues smirked and dispersed. After they left, I grew despondent. It was easy to show bravado, but being tied to a pillar wasn't terribly pleasant. I closed my eyes and began to think things over. Since there was no escape, I'd just have to accept my fate. And while I was stuck on this pillar, I may as well try to use my time wisely. What better opportunity than to try to sort out everything I'd learned since I'd gotten to the fjords? It appeared that everything here was connected to these hjeggs — whatever they were. I figured a hjegg was

The Charmed Fjords

probably a local predator, maybe a wolf or inhabitant of the mountains, or the snow leopards. The people here clearly both feared and worshiped this beast, which was a typical phenomenon among such tribes. I frowned in confusion when I remembered how the aborigine woman had pointed to the water and then the sky. So maybe there were a few totem animals, while the concept of the hjegg was universal and signified an object of worship. For example, the snow leopard was in the mountains, the wolf was on the ground, and the large fish was in the water. But in that case, why did I hear the word hjegg attached to Sverr's name? What could it mean?

I tugged my arms and shifted from one foot to the other. It didn't really help, and my body quickly grew tired in that position. But I had no choice. OK, moving on.

Maybe Sverr was the sacred being? Maybe that's why the word hjegg was added to his name and he wore that black ring? That seemed like a reasonable theory. There was plenty of precedent for something like that in the history of humanity, between the priests, sacred beings, followers of a religion, and people who communicated with gods or brought them sacrifices. Maybe that's why Sverr was able to negotiate the exchange and save me — he was special. In fact, it was obvious that he was different from the other ilgs, and the tribe did treat him differently. Was it that they were more respectful toward him? Or fearful?

My nose tickled and I sneezed. Out of habit I jerked my body to scratch, but then I remembered I was tied up. No doubt about it, today I'd get invaluable experience. I'd be able to report on what it felt like to be sentenced to death as I stood in the blazing sun against a sacrificial pillar. I kind of wished I wouldn't have to give that kind of report — I'd always preferred theory to practice.

But back to Sverr, I'd seen that everyone looked at him

Book One: Beyond the Fog

with a mixture of fear and veneration. Yes, that's exactly what it was. I'd been studying body language and gestures long enough to recognize those signals. Did that mean he was an acolyte of the hjegg? It would be nice to see that animal. Or was there more than one? Most likely there was more than one of them. It struck me as odd that the barbarians didn't have any images. A common feature of totemism is drawings or stone or wooden statues that embody the objects of the religion. But I hadn't seen a single one. I suppose they could be hidden somewhere — such as in the building with the red roof that we hadn't been allowed to enter. After all, that's where the girl from the shatiya had come from. Obviously, that's where she experienced her first pain with a man, as Sverr put it. That was one more rite I now understood.

I licked my parched lips. The sun had climbed higher, and it was getting harder for me to keep standing there. Droplets of sweat were slowly dripping down my spine. It was a good thing my hair was still wet from the swim.

OK, totems, religion. What else?

If there were no images of animals, maybe the aborigines worshiped the elements rather than beasts. Earth, water, fire... isn't that what the woman was talking about by the bonfire? Maybe that was it. But then how did the hjegg fit in? And who was Sverr planning to kill tonight? Maybe I was just confusing different words that were pronounced similarly but had opposite meanings. I wasn't a linguist and my hearing wasn't very acute. I'd need to talk to Jean and get his take.

I pressed the back of my head to the pillar and snickered. My colleagues had left me here, and the noises of the tribe were soft and muffled from where I was. In any case, the pillar was pretty far away from the tents.

"I hope a hungry animal won't walk by and decide I'd make a good snack," I muttered. Looking skyward, I added:

The Charmed Fjords

"Well, I wouldn't get scorched in the sun. That would be a pity."

Sverr appeared from behind me so quietly and unexpectedly that I started. He lifted a cup to my lips. "Drink, lilgan."

For a second I worried about poison, drugs, and other bad things, but ultimately my thirst won out. I greedily swallowed the ice-cold water and spluttered.

"Quiet. I'm not going anywhere," Sverr said with a chuckle. He ran his hand along my lips after I drank all the water and lifted my head. "You missed some."

I tried not to erupt at him. I needed to remember that he was taking care of me and giving me something to drink, I suppose so that I could do who knows what for him. "Where are my friends?"

"They're wandering around somewhere," Sverr said, looking me up and down. His otherworldly eyes were shining. "They're tearing up our grass and collecting soil and water. They're even collecting air. They want to take everything back with them."

Well then, my colleagues were taking care of business. It was just that when this ilg said it, it sounded unsavory.

"Well, that is the purpose of our trip," I explained awkwardly.

"And what's your purpose, Liv?" Sverr was standing uncomfortably close to me. I wanted to move away from him, but that's kind of hard to do when you're tied to a pillar.

"I study humans. I study them, I get to know — "

Sverr burst out laughing.

"What's so funny?"

"You get to know humans?"

"Yes. That's my job. I'm a scientist — an anthropologist."

"Can someone who doesn't even know themselves really

Book One: Beyond the Fog

study others?" Sverr leaned in closer, staring into my eyes. His lips were curved into a smile but his eyes were mirthless. I tried to read his body language. Was he showing aggression? Enmity? Desire?

I gulped. Yes — all those things combined, along with something else I couldn't quite make out. A strange feeling of power and strength was emanating toward me and pressing on me like a granite slab. It was radiating from the ilg in waves, nailing me to the pillar as forcefully as the ropes.

My lower belly stirred inside again, and my legs grew weak. What was wrong with me?

The ilg pitched backward and his breathing became shallow. He slowly ran his hand from my cheek to the torn piece of fabric. He stroked my skin, gazing at the contours of my breasts.

"Get your hands off me," I hissed.

"It seems to me that the people from beyond the Fog are ungrateful," Sverr jeered. "We gave you food and shelter, and we're sharing with you like we'd share with close relatives. But what do we get in return? What do you say, lilgan?"

He leaned down and breathed next to my temple, so close my hair blew. His rock-hard body pressed against mine and I struggled to breathe.

"What's a lilgan?" I tried to detach myself from the scene and pretend that someone else, not me, was the sacrifice, and that this man wasn't languidly studying the curves of my body.

Sverr laughed quietly and said, "I was wondering why you didn't ask about that sooner. How fascinating."

"Because when you tied me up I was thinking of other things! I was afraid!" I snapped.

Sverr raised his eyebrows doubtfully. "You were afraid? I don't think so. You weren't afraid. That also surprised me. A maiden is supposed to scream and cry, and hide behind

The Charmed Fjords

men. You don't do that, though."

He traced the circle of my breast, looking scornfully into my eyes. He pulled apart the fabric in the spot where he'd torn it and again touched my skin.

"If I answer, Olivia Orway, what will I get? And what will I get for bathing in blood for your offense?" His barely perceptible touch burned me like red-hot coal. "You could thank me..."

I thrashed about, trying futilely to get away from him. Where could I go, anyway? Behind me there was a pillar and in front of me was an ilg, and my arms and legs were tied. Should I scream? Yurgas was probably close by. He'd help me.

No, I couldn't scream.

Sverr was peering at me, observing, judging, and studying me all at once. I squinted and stared into his golden eyes. "What does hjegg mean?" I spat.

The ilg smirked and tossed his head. "You're persistent, aren't you? That's a good quality, but only for a warrior. In girls we value obedience and tenderness."

I ignored his hint. "It's an animal, is that right?"

"Yes." Sverr bowed his head but didn't take his hands off me. Instead, he squeezed his fingers on my waist and stroked me. I bit my lip, trying not to panic. "The animal is strong. And fierce. And hungry."

"How was I able to summon it? What does being a virgin have to do with anything?"

He ran his burning fingers from my neck to my waist. "Virginal maidens have been given to the hjeggs for centuries. Our people would tie them to the pillars and dance around them to call the hjeggs, singing the words to summon them. We'd win them over. The hjeggs would seize the maiden for themselves and people would say they gave her away during the shatiya with the hjegg. That meant the maiden became

Book One: Beyond the Fog

betrothed. But not to a man — to the beast."

His slow movements were now ravenous even though his fingertips were barely grazing me as they traced the designs on my jumpsuit. I began to shake. His muscles tensed and his lips tightened into a narrow line.

I tossed my head awkwardly, trying to rid myself of the hallucination. The agonizing caresses, his golden eyes, and low voice were all bewitching me. I felt like a mouse being toyed with by a boa constrictor right before the boa gobbles it up. I needed to remind myself that I was a scientist from the Confederation and he was nothing but a savage, a barbarian. I couldn't quiver like this, losing my head from the feeling of his fingers and the primitive longing in his eyes. I was a scientist... a scientist... a scientist!

"I see. So somehow the animals have developed the ability to sniff out virgins. Damn, that's an amazing example of evolution," I muttered hoarsely. Sverr smiled mockingly, and stroked my lips with his thumb. He wasn't exactly caressing them — it was more like he wanted to feel their surface. His finger was rough. An overwhelming ardor coursed through me and my head began to spin.

"What does the hjegg look like?" I demanded.

"Aren't you a curious one," he said, touching my lips again. "And stubborn. Here we teach women like that to obey. Or we kill them..."

"Where I come from women like that become scientists or old maids. Well?"

"There are different hjeggs. There are some that live in the deep waters of the fjords. There are some that live in the cliffs. Or in the place where the snow never melts."

And then there are some whose name you aren't allowed to say, I remembered. I sensibly kept my mouth shut. Or did I keep my mouth shut because I was having a hard time breathing? Even though it was almost like he wasn't

The Charmed Fjords

touching me, my mind was a jumble. Sverr was frowning as he looked at me like a hungry beast.

I jerked away from him.

"OK, lilgan," he spat with surprising venom.

"Will you just tell me already what a lilgan is?" I whispered.

"Too many questions and too little payment. You'll find out when the time comes."

He turned and walked away. My breathing returned to normal, but not as fast as I would have liked.

Then the sky turned hazy and a chilly fog rolled over the grass. I sighed with relief at this break from the burning sun. Cold air descended from the mountains. I wondered what the fjords were like in the winter. They were probably just as beautiful, and for a second I felt a twinge of disappointment that I wouldn't get to see it.

Chapter 9. Sverr

"WHAT EXACTLY ARE YOU up to? Would you care to explain?"

"Remember your place, a-tem," I snapped at Irvin, and he winced as though I'd slapped him.

We looked toward the settlement, which from our vantage point on the cliff was shrouded in a whitish mist. The charred pillars were clearly visible, though. One of them was occupied. The girl's thin body, dark hair falling over her cheeks, and bright eyes stood out. She was helpless tied up like that.

I spun around and scrutinized the water cascading down the stone cliff.

"I can calm the wild hjegg," Irvin said, breaking into my thoughts. "You and I both know that, Sverr. There's no need to kill anyone."

"Yes there is," I said flatly, and he screwed up his eyes in thought.

"So that's how it's going to be," he sneered. His blue eyes darkened like the waters of the fjords right before a storm. "But what for? The girl will become a lilgan, but then what? After you pay the debt she'll be bound to you, but what will you get out of that, Sverr?"

I gazed out over the fjords. The cold season would soon be setting in. The water near the shore would be covered in a

The Charmed Fjords

shell of ice, while farther out it would be blue-gray and perfectly smooth. Snow would blanket the fortresses and buildings, and Gorlohum would sleep. Winter was the time of quiet and calm. But inside me lava was bubbling and my heart was pounding. I feared this winter would be different from all the others because the Fog was dissipating.

"I went to the Fog again last night," I said, avoiding Irvin's eyes. "It's thinning. The barrier could disappear completely with a new dawn. And then people will invade us — different people, Irvin. People who want to take our land and strength."

"We'll destroy them!"

"Perhaps," I said, looking at him. "But at what price? We need knowledge. That's what they say in the Confederation: whoever controls information controls the world."

"We can interrogate these outsiders. They'll tell us everything they know if we hold a knife to their throats." Irvin shot a sullen look at the tents and I sneered.

"They're small fry, don't you see? They don't make the decisions, and they know even less than you and I do. I need more."

"Do you think the outsiders are guilty?"

"I want to make sure."

"I don't understand how this connects to killing the hjegg."

"It's connected. Everything is connected. The girl needs to survive and become a lilgan. I need her. That means that we're going to keep the oath."

Irvin pursed his lips and his face hardened. "Maybe you just want her, my riar? You kept everyone awake last night with your call. And you ordered me to cover the girl with the mist from the sea so she wouldn't suffer in the heat. Are you protecting her? Really?"

Book One: Beyond the Fog

I snickered wryly. "That's not the only reason. The mist reduces visibility. As for the maiden, you bet I'm protecting her, Irvin. We can't let her suffer. It's not for nothing that I left Neroaldaf to come here and act friendly to these outsiders. Even if I'm showing my strength, I'm still acting friendly." I jerked my shoulder, throwing off the wolf hide. The drawn-out sound of the hang drums floated over the mountain slope. I looked at Irvin. "I'll be patient and smile. I won't fall apart. And you'll hold back your rage, and if you can't do that, get out of here." Finally I snapped, "But since you're still here, make sure all our guests are in their tents. We can't let them see too much."

"I got it. I'm not an idiot," Irvin muttered. "And anyway..."

I looked back at the water. "Everything will make sense soon."

OLIVIA

The day felt endless. But I was an expert at spending time with my thoughts, so I had a productive day, sorting and analyzing the information I'd collected. Of course, I would have preferred to do this while sitting at my comfortable desk with a cup of strong coffee in hand, rather than standing against a sacrificial pillar, but sometimes in life you have no choice.

My colleagues dropped by a couple of times to bring me water and energy bars to revive me. They also brought me special capsules that slow down the body's natural processes, like the ones athletes use so they don't need to pee in the middle of their event. But I refused all the food they offered and tried not to drink too much.

Yurgas didn't come near me, but I noticed him out of

The Charmed Fjords

the corner of my eye a few times. Apparently, even though he was clearly displeased, he was continuing to do his job and look after me.

When the sun set, the tribe lit the bonfire and beat a measured rhythm on their distinctive drums, which were made from tanned hide stretched over a frame. Rather than floating through the air, the muffled sound reverberated off the ground and cliffs in a powerful echo.

Any other time I would have taken an interest in the music, but by now I was so exhausted I didn't care what happened. I just wanted to be untied. Standing still all day turned out to be unimaginably hard. My whole body was throbbing and my arms were so numb I was afraid I'd never feel them again. My legs were shaking and felt like cotton, my head was spinning, and my stomach was growling from hunger.

So when night finally fell, I was relieved.

The drums began to sound more regularly. I could sense commotion in the settlement behind me, but the only thing I could see was the thickening darkness in front of me.

"How are you, Olivia?" Maximilian asked as he approached. "You've been here all day. What have you come up with?"

"What do you mean, what have I come up with?" I turned my head to hide my smile.

"I know how you operate. Well?"

I shrugged apologetically. "You've already figured it out, Professor. I only had a few minutes to make a decision and react. Obviously, the first thing was to figure out what a lilgan is. I knew that no matter what Sverr said, we like it. It could be a lover or slave, but in any case, it's definitely a woman. So I could have been outraged and refused Or I could have consented, already knowing the answer, and that's a completely different scenario, right? I was afraid that Yurgas

Book One: Beyond the Fog

and his soldiers would need to intervene — and he had to know that. Then a war with the tribe would have been a sure thing. So..."

"So we buy time for more research, and we get a chance to see a new ritual and the local totem animal," Max sighed. "You've always impressed me, Olivia."

I was too flattered to respond.

"I think a major trait of yours is that you tend to underestimate danger and often forget about yourself. I admire your courage, but I think you could use a sense of self-preservation."

"I'm afraid that if I wasn't like this I wouldn't have been sent here," I chuckled. "Come on, we all knew what we signed up for, Professor. Anyway, now we can say the expedition was a total success, right? I'm alive and healthy. Everything is OK. And now we know what these pillars are for. But let's not tell the others about my little scheme, what do you say?"

"You're right. Our brave soldiers probably wouldn't understand. They think too one-dimensionally. Yurgas grinds his teeth so much I'm actually worried about his jaw." Maximilian took a breath. "You know he has feelings for you, don't you, Olivia?"

"Yes, it's pretty obvious," I said. "It's all right. It will pass."

Maximilian and I smiled at each other in understanding, but while I felt calm, he looked somber.

"Be careful, Olivia."

"Don't worry about me, Professor. I remember the orders. Say, what's the tribe doing right now?"

"The ilgs are dancing," Maximilian said, shaking his head. "But not like at the shatiya. It looks more like a dance of sorrow. I tried recording a more detailed description. You can listen later."

"Is Sverr with them?"

The Charmed Fjords

"No. He went off somewhere. We asked if we could watch him hunt the hjegg but apparently that's also taboo. We should be grateful they didn't tie all of us to the pillars."

"Yeah, there are a lot of them, enough for each of us," I joked.

The banging drums broke off abruptly and all was quiet.

"All the ilgs are dispersing now," Maximilian said with some surprise. "They're also telling me I need to go. I don't want to leave you, Olivia."

"No, go," I said wearily. "Your being here won't change anything. We'll play this game by their rules until it's over. I just hope this wasn't all for nothing and I'll be able to see that hjegg. In any case, the totem animal gives us an idea about the tribe's entire belief system."

"Right as usual, Olivia. I can't wait to hear your report. Remember we'll be right here, no matter what happens."

"I know, Maximilian. Don't worry about me."

Maximilian shifted his feet uneasily and knitted his white eyebrows. He looked distractedly at the settlement and pulled off his glasses. He put them back on, then took them off again. "Liv, I've been wanting to say..." Avoiding my eyes, he began to speak quickly. "You're probably going to think I'm crazy. Even I'm starting to wonder if I am. But..."

A young ilg appeared in my field of vision and barked a few words. "He's chasing you away," I said.

"But I think..." Maximilian whispered desperately, "we're missing something. Something important. And here, on the fjords, everything is different. We're not assessing the danger right. And..."

"*Hjel shord!*" the ilg repeated angrily.

Maximilian hurriedly said a few more words and then trod off behind the ilg. I stared after him in disbelief. Was the wind playing tricks on me, or did he say what I thought he said? "That ilg... Sverr. He... I get the impression that... he's not human."

The fog swirled in the darkness and I didn't immediately notice the man standing before me. The golden eyes flashed briefly in the semidarkness, and then once again I was alone.

❀ ❀ ❀

The drumbeat rang out again, piercing the silence. Ba-a-am! It was drawn out and muffled. Ba-ba-a-am! It didn't sound anything like the music from the shatiya. The earsplitting sounds were as sharp as an ax blade. Bam! Bam! Bam!

I squirmed. The solidifying darkness, the fog, and the strained thumps were putting me on edge.

Don't panic, Liv, I told myself. You're just afraid of the unknown. That's totally normal. If I knew what to expect, I wouldn't be so anxious. Anyway, isn't this exactly what I wanted? I was getting priceless in-the-field experience. Just one more ceremony to get through, and I had a front-row seat.

In any case, Yurgas and the others were right there. Along with his stun gun, Yurgas had exploding capsules that released poisonous gas. Just one was enough to take out a herd of bulls, not to mention this mysterious hjegg.

I chuckled in an effort to cheer myself up. Now I hardly heard anything — it was as though the settlement behind me had disappeared into thin air. There was only a single hand monotonously and rhythmically beating on the hide drum.

Then I heard a hissing sound making its way to the lake along the path. I clenched up. Was that a snake? Just what I needed. I'd always been afraid of snakes. I shuddered just thinking about the prospect of coming face-to-face with a

The Charmed Fjords

hideous reptile.

More hissing. It was loud and protracted. I could feel goosebumps popping up all over me.

There was the drumbeat again — bam, bam, bam!

I strained my eyes as I peered into the darkness. There seemed to be something rolling around. What the hell was it? It was like a piece of the cliff had suddenly started moving and turned into a shadow figure. Scratch that — two shadow figures. That was about all I could see. The fog and darkness were obscuring the outlines. From time to time there were movements, but then they would die down. There was a splash of water, followed by the drumbeats, which now sounded furious and spiteful. One, two — it sounded like someone was hitting the drum with a huge rubber beam. Then a roar rang out. It was so loud the mountains shook and I broke out in a cold sweat.

What kind of wild beast made a sound like that?

For a second the fog dispersed and I caught sight of tracks on the path: thick grooves streaking the earth. They formed a long, winding line, as though someone had been dragging something heavy.

"What is that?" I squeaked, feeling like a sacrifice in the true sense of the word. Something in front of me was pounding, but I was paralyzed by horror and all I could do was look into the darkness.

More banging, then a sound of stones showering down, and another roar, followed by a low-pitched, sustained rumbling, and two long shadows rolling around in the darkness. And still, that hissing.

Then something quietly dropped to the ground. Even the drum went silent.

When a figure emerged from the darkness, I nearly shrieked, just like a primitive aborigine. But I was too terrified to make a sound.

Book One: Beyond the Fog

Sverr stopped a few steps away from me. He looked around through eyes narrowed into slits. He was now totally naked, and his body was smeared head to toe in blood. His golden eyes shone like fire in the darkness.

"Your debt has been paid, lilgan," he snapped, and stalked off. Then another ilg appeared. It was Irvin. When he turned to me, I spotted a look of pure hate in his face. I couldn't imagine what provoked it. He spit on the grass and followed Sverr.

"Terrific," I said in the darkness. "It looks like I've made enemies of everyone, but I have no clue what I did wrong. And I didn't even get to see that hjegg. What am I going to tell the others? That something was moving in the darkness but I couldn't tell what it was?"

I had an urge to cry out. Maybe they'd bring the beast back and burn it? That's what barbarians usually did, wasn't it? Then we could get a good look at the carcass.

Anyway, was someone going to untie me?

I wanted to call out to my colleagues, but I was distracted by the shouting, rustling, and running I could hear behind me. Apparently the tribespeople were coming out of their hiding places. Then the music started up again — it was now sad, with protracted tones. I was worried everyone had forgotten about me, but mercifully, an ilg finally came to cut the ropes binding me. When I landed on the ground, I swayed for a moment on my weakened legs, but I managed to find my footing. I rubbed my swollen wrists. My colleagues rushed to my side and Klin thrust out a syringe holding a special solution. I took a deep breath and pressed it to my shoulder. I could barely feel the microneedle enter my skin, but it instantly gave me relief and the medicine soon restored me.

But then I started coughing and gasping. What a great time for an asthma attack.

"Breathe, Olivia," Maximilian said, putting my inhaler

The Charmed Fjords

in my mouth. I gave him a sidelong look but didn't ask any questions about the last thing he said to me. It wasn't the right time — I'd be able to find out later what he meant when he was talking about Sverr.

I nodded gratefully. "Sorry, it must have been all that pent-up stress," I said. "I'm fine now. What's going on?"

"It looks like a funeral meal," Yurgas said glumly. "I assumed the ilgs would be celebrating."

"The hjegg is the local totem animal," I explained as I set off for the tents. "That means its death is a sad event for the tribe."

"Did you see it?"

"I couldn't get a good look at it," I said evasively. "But I'll tell you as much as I can."

We stopped at the edge of the settlement, but the tribe wouldn't let us join them around the fire. A hostile-looking ilg pointed to the tents in a way that showed he meant business. Apparently the barbarians were done being hospitable.

I staggered into my tent, groped for my backpack in the darkness, and pulled out my tiny flashlight. In the pinpoint of light I used the basin in the corner and then took out a protein bar, which I devoured in a few seconds. The medicine I'd injected had worked its magic and I'd gotten my second wind. When I was done eating, I went over to the tent flap and tried to look outside, but was immediately shoved back in.

"*Ir shik!*" a burly ilg bellowed at me.

"OK, I got it," I muttered. "I'll sit right here. I won't move." Fabulous.

I ate another protein bar and stretched out on the pelt. Was I really going home soon? I felt like I'd been on the fjords for a year, not a few days. It was hard to believe that pretty soon I'd walk into my apartment, take a bubble bath, make coffee, and do all those things I took for granted, without any hides, shatiyas, or blood in sight. No Sverr either, for that

Book One: Beyond the Fog

matter.

My heart pounded wildly against my ribs. What was wrong with me? Was I really getting upset about leaving the golden-eyed ilg?

A ghastly sound like a cross between a bellow and a growl rolled over the distant cliffs. I leaped up. What was that? Maybe that creature? Or another one? And what exactly had I seen in the mist?

The hair on the back of my neck stood on end, just like when I was tied to the sacrificial pillar. I grabbed my dictaphone and pressed the button to record. But then I stopped. I had no idea what to say. The thing I thought I'd seen was too mystifying, or maybe it was just too improbable. I covered my eyes, replaying the images in my head over and over again.

I turned off the dictaphone and laid it down. No matter how much I wanted to, I just couldn't talk about it.

❋ ❋ ❋

"Liv, wake up!" Someone was shaking my arm. I flinched and tried to blink the sleep out of my eyes. Klin tugged at me. "Get up! The professor — "

"Maximilian? What happened?"

I flung off the hides, thankful that I'd fallen asleep in my jumpsuit. The bizarre day had totally worn me out. I yawned and grabbed my backpack.

"He's unconscious, Liv! It looks really bad."

"What did they stick in him?" I feverishly tried to remember what medicines I had in my first-aid kit while Klin listed them. "Right... but he didn't wake up?"

"Liv, it looks like he's in a coma."

I clenched my fists and dashed out of the tent after Klin.

The Charmed Fjords

The morning was chilly and a cool dew covered the grass by the tent. The ilgs were already awake, bustling around with hides and utensils. They glowered at us.

I sprinted into the men's tent and crouched down next to Maximilian. I checked his pulse, breathing, and pupil reaction. I bit my cheek. Things did look bad. For starters, Maximilian was no longer young, so a trip like this was probably a challenge for him.

"We've already packed up to leave," Jean said from the doorway. "Right now it's urgent that we get the professor home."

"We will!" I gasped. "We'll make a stretcher and we'll carry him. Or we'll ask for a horse. He'll live."

My colleagues nodded, but I saw uncertainty in their eyes.

"Come on, guys, let's get to it!" Yurgas ordered. "Klin, go look for that ilg, what's his name? Sverr? Jean, check the specimens. Liv, keep an eye on Maximilian."

The men ran off and I stayed with Maximilian. I stroked his wrinkled hand. "Please hang on, Max!" I whispered. "You've got to hang on."

Without the calm, wise Maximilian I felt like an orphan — for the second time in my life.

Everyone rushed around in a whirlwind of activity. The men returned and carefully transferred Maximilian to a cart pulled by two horses. I climbed in, sat down, and supported Maximilian's head to make him more comfortable. I didn't snap out of my daze until we started moving.

Were we really leaving? I looked up. The settlement was behind us. No one had come to see us off and I found myself feeling a bit regretful. I wanted to tell the women not to hold a grudge, and to apologize for my mistakes, even if I could only mime all of this. A few minutes later the tents had disappeared behind the cliff. Sverr and Irvin were on horses

Book One: Beyond the Fog

ahead of us. There were two ilgs I'd never seen before next to us. The members of the expedition sat silently in the cart. I was certain we were all processing the trip.

We didn't speak at all on the way to the Fog. The only sounds were the clopping of the horses' hooves and the rustling of the grass.

When visibility plunged, indicating that we were in the Fog, the cart stopped and the ilgs dismounted their horses.

"We need to walk from here," Sverr said.

The men placed Maximilian on the stretcher and we set off. We were practically running so we could keep up with the two barbarians ahead of us.

After a few moments, visibility completely disappeared and we had to keep our eyes glued to the person in front of us in order not to get lost. I was so out of it that I had no idea how long it took us to cross over. Time stretched and then disappeared. I grew tired, and that was the only way I knew we walked for a long time.

When the Fog began to dissipate, I couldn't hold back a gasp of delight.

"Are we really back?" Klin whispered.

Yes! I could already see the red signal lights on the pillars, with the gate beyond them. Yes, we were back.

The ilgs stopped and we followed suit.

"We need to say goodbye." I stood up taller and looked around until I spotted Sverr. The silent barbarians also looked at him and uttered a few staccato words.

"*Hjegg... riar...*" I heard them say.

Without so much as a glance at us, the ilgs dissolved in the mist. Irvin followed them, and as he passed me he shot me a look that made me squirm. It was a look full of loathing.

Sverr stayed where he was, though.

Yurgas stepped forward. "Thank you for helping to make the Confederation's expedition possible," he said.

The Charmed Fjords

"You'll thank us even more later," Sverr said with a laugh. He looked behind Yurgas — right at me. "Don't waste your breath. I'm going with you."

"What?" we exclaimed in unison, so loudly the Fog quivered. "What do you mean?"

"Isn't that what he said?" Sverr pointed at Maximilian. "He invited me. He said he wanted to repay our hospitality. I accepted."

I could practically see the wheels turning in my colleagues' heads. Did our professor invite Sverr to the Confederation? Well, why not? For one thing, it was against the rules — we knew too little about the fjords and their inhabitants. Was it possible that Maximilian had violated orders and invited an ilg to visit us?

"He said I was living evidence of a lost civilization, and that I'd be given a dignified reception by your Confederation."

My colleagues and I exchanged glances. What were we supposed to do?

"We didn't plan for this," Yurgus stammered.

"On the other hand, we could treat Sverr like another specimen," Klin chuckled. "The rarest one."

"Exactly," Jean said brightly. "And I'll be able to keep working on the ilgs' language."

Yurgas said nothing and looked on disapprovingly. He clearly would have preferred to leave Sverr on the fjords. "I can't allow this," he said gravely. "Remember that we were given precise orders. The reconnaissance mission does not provide for an ilg's crossing over to our side."

"Are you afraid?" Sverr asked ingratiatingly.

Yurgas turned crimson. He clenched his teeth and shook his head. "Hold your tongue!" he snarled.

"We don't have time to argue!" I shouted. "Maximilian needs help!"

"The professor had the right to make such a decision,"

Book One: Beyond the Fog

Klin said thoughtfully. "He had the authority as the head anthropologist responsible for corresponding with the aborigines. And if Maximilian thought we could do it..."

"At the moment Max can't answer for his decisions," Yurgas snapped. "And I'm not taking on that responsibility. I don't have the authority."

"That's right, you don't. It's Olivia who does," Jean said gently. "If Maximilian is incapacitated, she's the one who can make such a decision — only her."

Yurgas ground his teeth loudly. I opened my mouth to utter a decisive "no." Every fiber of my being was revolting against the prospect of Sverr going with us. *Danger, danger!* a warning siren wailed inside me, filling my head with a flashing red alarm.

"I — " I began. Sverr's golden eyes were looking at me mockingly. I froze in the realization that I couldn't say the word "no." I literally couldn't do it — it was like my tongue had gotten stuck to the roof of my mouth.

"Olivia, you don't want him to come, do you?" Yurgas asked, almost tenderly, and his tone was so different from how he usually was that I looked at him in astonishment. "You do understand that it would be irrational, don't you? We can't just take an ilg along with us."

The men's eyes bored into me — sharp, probing, thoughtful, impatient. But I could see only one pair of eyes and only one face. Sverr was standing off to the side and watching us with cool indifference, but my whole body was concentrated on him.

"The debt of blood... lilgan..." I could hear a voice whispering inside me, and I gulped. "Sverr will go with us. I authorize his departure and will take responsibility before the Confederation's commission."

It sounded like the words were coming out of someone else's mouth.

The Charmed Fjords

"That's your prerogative," Yurgas muttered in disappointment. A look of childlike resentment flashed across his face, but then it disappeared and Yurgas regained his composure. "All right, then. Let's go!"

A half hour later, we were out of the Fog. We were home.

Chapter 10. Olivia

WE WALKED RIGHT INTO a maelstrom — escorts, cars, uniformed military men, stares, and the airplane. Sverr was silent and appeared oblivious to the fact that people were staring at his naches, the hide flung over his shoulders, and his hip sash. He narrowed his golden eyes, swiveled his head, and examined the people and objects around him. When we reached the plane, he paused and frowned.

"Don't be afraid, it's for flying," I said, rubbing my temples in exhaustion. "It's not scary."

Sverr's dark brows wrinkled together over his nose.

"Yeah, I know it sounds strange. Just take my word for it. This huge metal thing really does fly. And it will take us to the capital of the Confederation. Let's go."

I headed onto the plane. After a moment's hesitation, Sverr followed me. He also looked wiped out: his eyes were dull and his cheeks were sunken, as though he hadn't slept in a few days. But he walked with a spring in his step. Soldiers and doctors were waiting for us inside the massive airship. Maximilian was whisked off to a special bay and relief washed over me — I knew he'd be taken care of and everything would be fine. We were taken to the disinfecting chambers. Sverr entered one of them nonchalantly and I watched him get misted with the antiseptic solution.

The Charmed Fjords

A few hours later we landed at the closed airfield of the Academy of Progress. The ladder of the plane was lowered and we peered out the windows.

"Cool," Klin muttered in bafflement. "Looks like we're celebrities now."

A big group of reporters, council members, and scientists had gathered to greet us. They'd even painted a red pathway on the asphalt to make it look like a red carpet. It was kind of uncomfortable. After all, I was a scientist, not a movie star. Sverr was looking at everyone derisively — if he was afraid, he wasn't showing it. He was silent, but I didn't have time to calm him or explain anything. When I got to the door of the plane, I went up to him and carefully touched his arm. He gave me a piercing look. I pulled my hand away in embarrassment.

"Time to go," I said.

When the crowd caught sight of us they erupted in cheers. Floodlights were switched on to illuminate our path. Sverr stepped out onto the ladder and the cheering instantly subsided. The silence was so heavy you could feel it, and it was a rough, like an emery board. Everyone stared raptly, but then, as if there had been no interruption, the air was again filled with shouts, cameras clicking, and microphones thrust in our faces.

"No comment!" Yurgas snapped. "The expedition will answer all your questions later. No comments now."

A group of soldiers surrounded us and escorted us to the Academy building, where another entourage was on hand to greet us. I spotted Hans Stesh, the rector and a member of the commission, rushing toward us.

"Welcome back!" he exclaimed, pumping our hands. "We knew you could do it! It looks like things went even better than we expected. You brought back an aborigine!"

"He speaks the language perfectly, Dr. Stesh," I broke

Book One: Beyond the Fog

in before the rector could say anything else. "Sverr is our guide, and he's the one who read and answered our message. He found the canister with the letter. We've brought back amazing news, Dr. Stesh." I looked at the scientists, who were standing there silently. "And we were able to verify it: it's possible to penetrate the Fog, and the fjords are populated with intelligent tribes."

"What a breakthrough!" Stesh said in awe. "That's simply unheard of, and it opens up fantastic potential: now we can study the flora and fauna, and especially the ilgs themselves. How unbelievable!"

"We can discuss that in the morning," Yurgas interrupted. I looked at him gratefully. Maybe he wasn't such a bad guy after all.

"Yes, we're exhausted," Klin said. "We'll give you our reports tomorrow. Right now I'd really like to see my family."

For a moment I remembered how Klin had looked at the girl in the circle of the shatiya. I shuddered and kept my mouth shut. I was afraid there were some things none of the members of our research mission would talk about.

"Very well," Stesh said with a sigh of disappointment. "I think we should put the aborigine into the quarantine bay."

"Why not just stick him in a cage?" I erupted in anger. "I told you that Sverr is our guide and he understands every word you say. He's the honored guest of the Confederation, Dr. Stesh, so please show him some respect."

"Do you have a better idea, Dr. Orway?" Hans asked, visibly offended. "Of course an ilg from the fjords is a guest, but you need to agree that he's a very unusual guest. The commission will decide tomorrow where he'll stay, but what do you suggest doing right now?"

I bit my lip and looked at Sverr. Now what? I couldn't leave him alone — our scientists would want to shut the poor guy up in the lab. No matter what I thought of him, I couldn't

The Charmed Fjords

allow him to go through that. After all, he really had been good to us: he'd helped us, guided us, and even protected us. And hadn't I also dreamed about studying the barbarian? Now my dream had come true. Maybe I should be careful what I wished for.

"I'm responsible for the ilg," I said evenly. "And since I'm responsible for him, I'll take care of his accommodation. Without Maximilian here, I'm now running the anthropology department. Max invited Sverr, so that means I need to follow through, and I need to continue our observations. This is priceless experience. I'll be able to see how the ilg reacts and behaves in an unfamiliar environment, and assess his learning speed and aptitude. And of course, I'll write a detailed report."

"But where will he stay tonight?" Stesh interrupted me.

A single word resounded clearly inside me: "together." "He'll stay with me," I said.

My colleagues stared at me in shock, thinking this over.

"What?" Hans said. "Well, without Maximilian here you are the head, and you do have the authority to make such decisions. All right, everyone. I'll see you all tomorrow at the closed-door council meeting. We'll take you home now. Congratulations again!"

We nodded and went our separate ways. Klin fell in step beside me and gave me a perplexed look. "Are you sure about this, Liv? I think you're making a mistake."

"Shut up, he's not going to eat me," I snapped, and looked at over Sverr. He was examining the benches, platform, and high ceiling. I flinched at the sight of him. In the glaring fluorescent lights of the Academy auditorium, he truly looked like a savage with his hides, the dark ring around his neck, his body smeared with blood and some other black substance, and the animal fangs dangling over his chest. He looked like the very definition of a barbarian. At least he

Book One: Beyond the Fog

wasn't wearing the skull on his head. I'd wielded my authority for nothing — I should have left the ilg here. But my conscience wouldn't allow that. Sverr was a guest of the Confederation and I was duty bound to make sure he was comfortable, and that was impossible in the Academy building. Anyway, I yearned to get home, so that meant the ilg would go with me. I called myself a leading anthropologist, so it was about time I acted the part. But why did I have a feeling I was being sucked into a funnel of misfortune there was no way out of?

"He's just an ilg," I muttered to Klin, and strode over to Sverr, who was already surrounded by a throng of scientists looking at him like he was a fantasy creature. They were scrutinizing him, whispering, and pointing at him. They seemed to be afraid he'd let out a bellow at any moment. It never occurred to them that he understood every word they were saying. Sverr's eyes were indifferent, but I could tell that in their golden depths an unnatural feeling was gleaming, as if a fire were kindling.

I was so furious that I flew over like a madwoman and pushed the scientists apart. Now I was positive that I'd made the right decision to not leave Sverr with my colleagues.

"Come on," I said angrily. I wheeled around and stomped off, grinding my teeth. My mind flashed with an image of the funnel — the black, sinister funnel I'd fallen into, the one my nonexistent intuition had screamed about.

All I wanted right now was to lock myself in a dark room somewhere and be alone for a while to think everything over. I didn't get to do that on the plane — after going through the disinfecting chamber we all zonked out, which wasn't surprising. Even Sverr had shut his eyes and sat motionlessly until the plane landed. But instead of feeling rested after my nap, I felt more tired. Now I rushed to the door, ignoring the looks of my colleagues and trying not to think about the

The Charmed Fjords

mistake I was surely making. But I had no other options. Wherever the ilg went, I'd have to be beside him.

A tall figure blocked my path and I nearly knocked him down. In a flash, Sverr seized me by the elbow and pulled me to him, shielding me protectively. I heard someone cry out in astonishment.

"Liv?"

"Sergey!" I wrenched myself free of the barbarian's grip and threw myself at my friend.

"I'm so sorry I'm late!" He kissed me on the cheek and glanced at Sverr, who had a dark look on his face. I looked uneasily from one to the other: the intelligent, meticulously groomed man dressed in a neat suit who worked at the Academy, and the savage ilg who was drilling us with a look that made me want to drop into a hole. Knocked off guard, I found myself at a loss for words. Was I supposed to introduce them? Somehow that seemed ridiculous.

"Sverr, this is my friend, Sergey," I began.

"Are true friends late when something important is happening?" Sverr asked with ingratiating ferocity. "I don't think so."

"What the hell?" Sergey asked, looking at Sverr in hostile disbelief. "Olivia, what is this?"

I cringed to hear Sergey say "what," but in fact, Sverr was baring his teeth like a wild animal. I was sure that in a moment he'd punch Sergey, and I knew exactly which of them would win the brawl. Sergey had no idea how to fight.

But then Mia came over just in time and saved the day. She stared open-mouthed at Sverr before taking Sergey by the arm. "Liv, we heard that the expedition had returned. Is it true that you brought an aborigine back from the fjords?"

She stared at the ilg with such an indescribable expression of enchantment and puzzlement that I had to resist an impulse to laugh. Sergey gave Mia a hurt look and

Book One: Beyond the Fog

then cast his eyes down.

"Sverr is a guest of the Confederation and the Academy," I said, feeling the tension hanging between us. "I'll tell you all about it later. Please excuse us. We have to go now."

"But, Olivia, how... where are you going? What a... Liv!"

"Later! I'll call you!" I waved them off, afraid of being bombarded with questions I couldn't answer right now. "Later!"

I saw Yurgas detach himself from the pillars and fix us with a disgruntled look. I was struck by an impulse to press myself to Sverr's warm body — just to feel support and know that I wasn't alone. But of course, the ilg wasn't there to help me out with that. So I straightened my back until my spine cracked, thrust out my chin, and marched toward the door.

Let everyone see that I was sure of myself.

SVERR

"We'll take my car. I parked it here before the trip," the girl said. She looked away and I could see she was agitated even though she was trying to hide it. But her trembling fingers, tensed neck, and pursed lips gave her away. It wasn't until we arrived in the dark corridor, where there was no one around, that Liv relaxed slightly and narrowed her eyes for a moment, thinking I wouldn't notice.

But I did. I noticed every breath she took and every movement of her eyelashes. I understood how she felt — afraid, confused, angry. But I didn't try to calm her down. It's not acceptable to console an outsider, and demonstrating strength right now would only spoil everything.

So I kept my mouth shut, not dispelling her doubts. Meanwhile, I closely examined our surroundings. The room

The Charmed Fjords

that seemed to be an auditorium wasn't as big as Varisfold, the hall of the hundred hjeggs. The ornamentation was sparser and more rudimentary. The stained-glass windows, oak staircases, and doors three times as tall as a person made no impression on me — I'd seen bigger ones. There were some objects that looked interesting, but I didn't have a chance to get a close look because Liv was in a rush to get out. We exited through a low door, and as soon as we stepped outside, I recoiled in disgust.

"You're right, it doesn't smell very good here," the girl muttered. "Especially after you've been to the fjords. I didn't really notice it before, but now I do. It's called smog. I live next to a park, though. The air is cleaner there. Here's my car. You can think of it as a wagon, but it goes without horses. You can get in."

I stood still, examining the metal machine. I'd read about things like this, but in real life it was different, just like that plane we'd flown on. How about that — the riar flew on a plane. How ironic!

"Look, I'm exhausted," Liv said, crossly pursing her lips. "Can you just get in, please? Trust me, it won't bite."

"I believe you," I said with a chuckle and got in the car. It was cramped and uncomfortable. I would have liked some elbow room.

The girl pressed a button and the car roared to life and sped off. I suppressed a smile. If she were a hjegg I'd estimate her speed.

Liv chewed her lip and silently stared at the road as she drove. I didn't want to interrupt her thoughts. She truly was tired — after all, she was just a human. But I would have liked to see more of the Confederation city — I figured I didn't have a lot of time. I'd need to do it before it was too late, and commit it to memory and understand it as much as I could.

The trip was short, and Liv stopped the car outside a

Book One: Beyond the Fog

tall gray building.

"This way," she said, getting out of the car. I followed her inside the building. "This is an elevator. It's a booth that takes us higher, understand?" she said.

"I'm trying," I said, again suppressing a smile. I forced myself to look afraid or bewildered.

OLIVIA

Sverr looked puzzled, and I could empathize completely. I couldn't even imagine what was going through his mind. Between the cars, the airplane, the weapons, the electricity, and the elevators, this poor ilg probably thought Gorlohum was disgorging him. I supposed that's why he didn't say anything, and just stared at everything through the golden eyes gleaming in his tanned face.

But I was too tired to explain anything to him.

Fortunately, I was the only one living on my floor, so we didn't run into anyone between the elevator and my apartment.

"Here we are," I said, smiling. "This is my, er, tent."

Sverr stopped in the doorway and looked around. "I see," he said with a snicker. "It's a big... tent."

"I can't complain." Was it my imagination or was Sverr being sarcastic? I unlaced my hiking boots and heaved a sigh of relief as I removed them and sank my toes into the soft carpet. "The Academy of Progress owns this building. A lot of my colleagues live here. There's a panic button you can press if there's an emergency. There are actually a few buttons because I'm a maniac about safety in my house."

"You live alone?"

"Yes." It would have been smarter to lie, but the ilg wasn't a fool. And what would be the point, anyway? If

The Charmed Fjords

Maximilian were the one hosting the ilg, everything would be much simpler. But he was in the hospital and here I was on my own. The most important thing was to not forget that I was a scientist. "It's just me. So there's plenty of room for you. Say..." I spun around to look at him and stared at his masculine face. I finally asked the question that had been bothering me the whole way here. "Why did you decide to come with us? Tell me, Sverr."

"And why did you come to the fjords?" He smiled, flashing his white teeth. "Out of curiosity, Liv. I was curious. I answered your letter because I'd always wanted to know what was beyond the Great Fog."

I frowned. Curiosity? I supposed that was a valid reason. After all, humanity progresses because people are curious.

But was he telling the truth?

"You mentioned you grew up somewhere else." I decided that conversation was better than heavy silence. "Does that place have a name?"

"Neroaldaf," he said. His golden eyes shone softly. "That's my home. It's where I was born and grew up."

"Neroaldaf," I repeated. "Is your tribe big?"

Sverr smirked and shrugged.

"Bigger than the tribe we visited?"

"A little." A taunting expression danced in his eyes again and he shrugged slightly, brushing away my questions. He was standing motionlessly in the middle of my living room — huge, primitive, and completely out of place among the plastic shelves and plain furniture.

"So..." I waved my arm, feeling foolish. It finally hit me that I was alone with the ilg — the barbarian, the savage dancing at the shatiya. And no, I wasn't Max, who could get away with more than I could. But it was too late to turn back.

My spacious apartment suddenly seemed confining.

Book One: Beyond the Fog

The walls seemed to press in, pushing me closer to Sverr. He didn't move a muscle, but I almost felt his hands on me, and I felt his body heat. I wished morning would come faster. The next day the commission would decide what to do with him, he'd be taken off my hands, and I'd be able to breathe easy. I just needed to get through this one night.

A wave of panic washed over me like murky water, and everything around me suddenly looked gray. I raced to the dresser, pulled out my spare inhaler, thrust it into my mouth, and inhaled. The medicine coursed through me. I looked up to see Sverr still staring at me without moving. I mentally kicked myself and cowered in my anthropologist's corner. I turned around and straightened my shoulders.

"I understand that everything here is unusual for you. Ask me whatever you want. I'll try to explain. But first I want to take a shower and change. Feel free to look around, but please don't touch anything you're not familiar with."

"Go ahead," Sverr cut me off. He moved aside and his eyes slid over the furniture. He stopped by the bookcases. He glanced over his shoulder and added softly, "Don't be so scared. You're shaking."

I had no idea what to say. There's a barbarian for you! In one sentence he let me know that he was aware of all my fears and the feelings I was trying so hard to hide. And he managed to let me know that I wasn't the mistress of the situation in my own home.

The anthropologist in me again slunk to the corner my consciousness, letting the woman take over. I bolted into the bathroom. Before undressing, I triple-checked that I had latched the door.

Chapter 11. Sverr

I PULLED MY HIDE OFF my shoulders and tossed it on the floor. I sighed and covered my eyes, trying to calm my breathing. I was so close to carrying out my plan and achieving my goal. The most important thing was to stifle my fury and put up with the probing looks of these Confederation people, their snickers, curiosity, and unconcealed, rotten haughtiness. It's so obvious that they think they're better than me — the savage clad in hides — that it's actually kind of funny. But I'll laugh later, back home in Neroaldaf. Right now I'll bide my time and get a good look at the place, commit everything to memory, and absorb it all.

The odors of this world unnerved me — they're artificial and unnatural. Everything smells dead. The sweet scent of the girl in this ocean of stink is like a fresh breeze. It drives me wild, so much so that sometimes I can't help but get carried away and call her again. It's not powerful or even conscious. It's just the echo of the unfeigned call of the riar. But to my bewilderment, she continues to resist. Who resists the riar's call?

At the same time, I can see that she's afraid. I know that deep down, she's afraid not just of me, but also of herself. She doesn't understand what's happening to her, but she reeks of fear and I can see it deep in her eyes. It's only on the surface that her eyes look like the calm waters of the

Book One: Beyond the Fog

fjords when the golden rays of the sun caress the waves. They appear beautiful and peaceful. I want to see those eyes when I enter her. I'll look into her eyes the first time, even though that goes against everything the riar is supposed to do. Once the hjegg's blood was spilled, the outsider became nothing more than a lilgan. She is also stained with the hjegg's blood, and she is bound to the one who spilled it.

Irvin asked the right question — my a-tem is wise. Is the outsider worth the blood of the wild hjegg? I'll find out soon. Or maybe I'll find out now? What's the point of waiting? Once she's on her knees, the girl will submit, just like every girl who came before her. Will she continue to smile and play nice, unless it's not in my interest? After the moment of ecstasy women soften and turn subservient.

I winced in revulsion. It's not right for the riar to take advantage of a woman. But then again, it's not right to put up with insults. I've already put up with them once. I didn't do the killing, and I shed the hjegg's blood because of this girl.

I clenched my fists so hard the bones cracked. Again fury sparked inside me. I needed to curb that fury, accept it, and hide it as deep inside me as possible.

No, it wasn't for the outsider's sake that I was tolerating something that in the past I would have ripped a head off for. Everything I did was for Neroaldaf, for the fjords, for the green lakes, the blue cliffs, the white snows, the wind in the clouds, the wings and claws, and freedom and honor. For all of that.

My anger abated, as though washed away by the frigid water that lapped against the shores of Neroaldaf. I glanced at the papery wall that stood between me and the outsider. I couldn't see her, but I imagined the cool drops of water dripping along her bare skin. The call rises within me against my will. I can't contain it, and that surprises me too. I've silenced the fury, but the desire only burns stronger. Why?

The Charmed Fjords

I closed my eyes, breathing in heavily. My blood pounded in my ears and below my waist. I want her...

OLIVIA

I thought I'd find Sverr examining the furniture, but when I emerged from the bathroom, he was standing by the window with his hands clasped behind his back. A cold autumn breeze was blowing through the screen. It made me shiver.

"Sverr, it's late. I'm sure you want to rest. You can wash up in there. It's called a shower. I mean, if you want to. We don't have a lake or the ocean right here, like you do. We need to wash in the shower. There are no snakes — just a knob with warm water," I babbled. I was at a total loss as to how to behave. With a pang of surprise I realized that everything seemed simpler on the fjords. "I'll give you a towel. Here, look. You can use this to dry off."

I held a fluffy towel out to him. He bowed his head and studied it. Feeling awkward, I sidled into the bathroom, turned on the water, and watched it stream into the enamel basin. "See, you can come stand here. Do you understand?"

Sverr shifted his eyes from the faucet to me. He raised his eyebrows. "And there are no wild snakes? Really? I'm surprised."

"It's true," I said. "You can think of it as a home waterfall. Do you like it?"

The ilg snorted, dexterously slid off his naches, and approached the water. "Unbelievable," he muttered. "It's a miracle."

"Exactly," I said. I had the distinct impression that the ilg was mocking me, and I suddenly felt embarrassed. But if he was sneering I didn't see it because he'd started to pull off his only piece of clothing. I pivoted and lowered my eyes.

Book One: Beyond the Fog

"It's kind of tight in here," he said. "There's more space at the waterfalls. But the water is colder there."

"Uh-huh," I muttered, trying not to look in the mirror on the wall, which provided a perfect view of that damned ilg scrubbing the dirt off himself. But as though the mirror were a magnet, I couldn't keep my eyes off the vision of the tanned, muscular back with the water sliding over it. Truth be told, I also peeked at the part of his body below his back.

"I'll be, er, right outside this door," I stammered, deciding he was smart enough to find the soap without my telling him where it was.

I bolted into the living room and pressed my back against the wall. Why did everything need to be so hard? "Just one night, Liv!" I whispered as though I were reciting a spell.

The ilg emerged around ten minutes later. His hair was dripping — it looked like he'd forgotten about the towel. The black stripe crossing his face was gone, as were the spots of blood and red clay. This made his cheekbones, prominent chin, and shining eyes even more noticeable than usual. But he'd put his hip sash back on, and I silently thanked all the gods that exist for that. I gingerly shifted a little farther away from him and went into the kitchen, where I stuck a mug into the bottom of the coffee machine and pressed the button. I couldn't wait to drink the coffee I'd been dreaming of when I was tied to that pillar. Sverr followed me and surveyed the kitchen from the doorway.

"We'll go to the Academy in the morning. We'll need to answer a bunch of questions about you, your customs, and the ilgs. They're going to ask you all about your life, Sverr. Do you understand?" I looked over at him.

"Yes, I understand."

"Will you answer the questions?"

"Maybe," Sverr said. His gaze traveled over my bare feet,

The Charmed Fjords

my ponytail, and the white T-shirt and jeans I had changed into. My mouth ran dry and I froze when he started toward me. He was walking slowly, with a calm confidence in his eyes. My knees turned to jelly and a sweet contentment spread under my belly.

Sverr came to a standstill so close to me that I could almost hear his heart beating. He lowered his head and laid a hand on the back of my neck. It felt heavy, but not in a bad way. My heart dropped and lava began to simmer inside me. I looked into the barbarian's face and forgot where I was. He began to run his coarse fingers through my hair. He wasn't caressing me, though — it was more like he was examining me with his hands. Did the barbarian even know how to caress a girl? Or would he take me roughly, like an animal? Yeah, that was probably what he'd do.

Oh my God, what was I even thinking?

"I don't like your world, Liv. I don't like the smells, the buildings, your clothes, or your machines. But I am interested in what you and your people are like. Just like you're all interested in what I'm like. Isn't that right? You were drawn to the fjords by a desire to learn about me." He slowly pulled me by the hair. "I know you want this. Don't be afraid. Fear and desire are holding you captive and you can't tell which one is stronger. You said you study people, but you're afraid to look into your own soul, Olivia Orway."

"You don't know anything about me," I retorted.

"I might know you better than you know yourself," he answered quietly. "When you conquer your fear you'll be able to see what it was hiding with its darkness. But not before that."

"I don't understand."

"You're brave, Liv." The rough fingers stroked the back of my neck for a few moments. His proximity was making me uneasy. "But your courage wasn't born out of bravery. You

Book One: Beyond the Fog

just aren't afraid of death. You're indifferent to it. I already asked you what you're afraid of. Did you find the answer?"

"Why are you saying all of this?"

"I want the desire to remain, lilgan. Just desire."

The ilg gazed into my eyes. I wheezed. As hard as I tried, I couldn't suppress the spark that had ignited inside me. A fire burned in my body like lava racing through my veins. It was painful and hungry, sweet and bitter... Sverr smiled at the sight of my feelings reflected on my face. He squeezed my hair tighter and placed his other hand on my waist. I was suddenly aware how much smaller than him I was.

"If the women of the fjords walked around in clothes like these, they'd be taken right there on the ground, Olivia Orway," the ilg said hoarsely. "Right there, where they're caught. All of them, even the honorable wives, freeborn maidens, and captives."

"If the people on the fjords walked around in clothes like these, I think you'd stop noticing the women," I said, twisting out of his grip. "Don't touch me, Sverr."

I stepped away, looking warily at his tanned body and brutish sneer. What was I thinking when I decided to bring him home with me? It wasn't like he was an acquaintance from a nearby city who just needed to crash in the guest room — he was a barbarian, and on top that, a barbarian with his own notions of honor.

"Are you running away again?" he scoffed. "Go ahead, lilgan. Try to run away. The night is long. We'll have time for everything."

"We won't have time for anything!" I snapped. "Sverr, we need to talk."

"You want to talk? I've heard that after intercourse women want to talk, but do you need to talk before it here, too? I hope you don't mean you want to talk instead."

"Stay away from me!" I whirled my head around, trying

The Charmed Fjords

to remember where my pepper spray was. I wondered what the commission would do to me if I knocked out a valuable scientific specimen. I inched backward, not taking my eyes off the ilg.

"I'll be standing right here, Liv. You'll come to me on your own. Everyone voluntarily travels the path of their own fear." The amusement had left Sverr's face and he was now looking greedily at me. "But I'll catch you if you trip."

He stopped talking and I drew a breath. I craved him.

"You see, Liv..." Even his heavy, hoarse voice intensified my desire. If I felt like this right now, I couldn't even begin to imagine what would happen when he touched me for real.

I didn't even notice that I had taken one step toward him, and then another.

His golden eyes were blazing so vividly I thought I could see actual lava bubbling in them.

Just another couple of steps and I would feel his hands, lips, and body on mine...

One step.

A convulsive breath. A twitch... but not toward the ilg, who was gazing at me expectantly, but to the side, toward the shelves. My fingers closed around the spray can, I lifted my arm, and I sent a stream of pepper spray into the barbarian's face.

But instead of watching him recoil, I was overtaken by a panic attack and I struggled for breath. Tears ran down my face. I couldn't see anything, and it took all my concentration to breathe.

"Stupid lilgan," that goddamn ilg said. The same hands that I had just been daydreaming about seized me under my armpits and hoisted me up effortlessly. The next thing I knew, the raw city wind was scattering my damp hair. Sverr had simply thrust my head out the window.

Super. Now I'd probably catch pneumonia. But then

Book One: Beyond the Fog

the veil of fog lifted from my eyes and a vigorous burst of oxygen flowed into my lungs.

"Breathe, Liv."

I wanted to kill him for the sneer in his thick voice. I coughed and took another breath, as Sverr dangled me from the fifth floor and tears streamed from my eyes. But I was thinking clearly enough to wonder why the pepper spray hadn't worked on the ilg. It had certainly worked on me, even though I was certain I'd pointed the can at Sverr's face. It had only caught me in the corner of my eye, yet I was the one hanging by my feet and coughing uncontrollably.

The ilg pulled me back inside, carried me into the living room, and dropped me on the couch. "You're a stubborn one, aren't you?" he mused, looking down at me. He was like a mountain of muscles. "Where I come from, an attempt to poison the riar is punished by death. A painful death."

"Well, where I come from you go to jail for a few years if you try to accost a woman," I snapped after I managed to stop coughing and catch my breath.

Sverr squatted down. "Your practices make no sense, Liv."

I rolled my eyes wordlessly. What was I supposed to say? In his world things were a certain way, and he'd never understand my world. I wiped my damp eyes. Sverr was too close again. The pepper-spray shower had only temporarily weakened the attraction I felt for him.

"Get away from me," I croaked.

"You're giving me orders again?" Amusement flickered in his golden eyes.

"When we got to your land we respected your laws!" I shot at him. "We ate your food, respected your rituals, accepted the taboos..."

"You broke one of them."

"I didn't know about it! You can't blame me for not

The Charmed Fjords

living like you, Sverr. I respect you and your world. But you're breaking the rules of hospitality."

"Respect?" He placed a hand on the edge of the couch and leaned forward. I realized I'd fallen into a trap. "You're talking about honor, lilgan? I don't need to prove it to you, and not to any of the outsiders. My honor and strength are washed in blood. It's not up to you to judge them, or to talk about them. I follow the rules of hospitality, but I want what you yourself are offering."

"What am I offering?" I asked in surprise. "What gave you that idea?"

The ilg moved his hand and came closer, hovering over me.

"Do all the women beyond the Fog talk a lot?" he smirked. "Or just you, Olivia Orway? And do they deny their nature so forcefully?" He drew a breath. "You reek of desire, lilgan. You're responding to my call. I'm stronger than you — I'm the riar. So why are you resisting?"

"I'm responding to your call?" I asked with interest, trying to detach myself from the lava inside me. He'd already said something about this call, but I couldn't remember what. "What do mean by 'call'?"

Sverr sneered and bared his teeth, and then, to my surprise, placed his hand on my stomach. His heavy touch made me shudder. "You feel it," he said.

Fiery spirals began twisting from his hand along my skin. No, not along my skin — somewhere within it, inside me. It was a sweet feeling. And his face was so close to mine. Suddenly my fear receded, leaving only an understanding that no one had ever flustered me like this ilg. It was as though he were a living statue of an ancient god, a savage and unrestrained barbarian. How much bliss could he give me? Sverr was right — I was fighting my attraction to him with all my strength, and my female nature. After all, my body

Book One: Beyond the Fog

was already aching from unsated desire, and lava was searing my inner being. He was panting and looking at me ravenously, more like a hungry beast than a human. The most shameful thing was that it was he who was making me daydream like this. But wasn't that what my subconscious wanted when I invited Sverr into my world? All I had to do was overcome my fear.

In that moment, when the burning carnality conquered the cold voice of reason, I leaned forward and pressed my lips to the ilg's. They were rough and dry, just as I'd expected. He kept them closed. I carefully ran my tongue over them and thrust it inside a little more forcefully. His lips were slightly salty. Finally they parted and I touched his tongue with mine.

He abruptly pulled away and frowned at me. "What are you doing?" he barked.

I stared back at him in bewilderment. Chalk up another failure for Dr. Orway. Apparently the ilgs didn't like kissing. I guess I shouldn't expect any affection with this barbarian. My fear returned with a new potency and I jumped up.

"It's fine!" I muttered petulantly, angry at my momentary weakness. It seemed like tonight the woman in me was overpowering the scientist. I sighed. "It's just what people do. They kiss other people when, er, they want to feel good. You know, to find satisfaction. That's it. Let's just drop it."

Sverr was still crouched down next to the couch, eyeing me warily. "That's dangerous," he grumbled.

"What's dangerous? Kissing?"

"Yes. It's dangerous to push your tongue into a woman's mouth. If she bites it off, not even the riar will grow a new one." Sverr shook his head, deep in thought. "Same for the other body parts."

I choked in astonishment. Finally, unable to contain myself, I started laughing so hard I doubled over. How

The Charmed Fjords

incredible — the savage barbarian was afraid of kissing. Who would have guessed that? This was excellent news. I was definitely putting it in my report.

Sverr lowered his head and looked at me reproachfully. "It's best to take the woman from behind. You put one hand on her neck and the other on her hip. That way she can't escape and she won't hurt you," he said.

"And she won't bite off anything really important," I finished in my head. What savage customs. "Do you really only take the woman that way?" Thank goodness my researcher's instincts had kicked in again. "Don't you ever do it out of love?"

Sverr frowned. "No. Love is a bad feeling for me, lilgan. It's inappropriate. It can weaken the riar and cause a lot of distress for the woman. My life revolves around fighting and combat, so I can't get too attached to someone. I can't hold on too tight. Otherwise, I could lose myself, too. It's a bad feeling, lilgan."

"Are you saying it's always like that in your life?" I asked. "It's just like at the shatiya all the time? Without kissing?"

He nodded. His expression was both cutting and perplexed, as though he were trying to understand what I was talking about and why people needed to kiss.

"My tongue is still useful," he said. He shook his head, smiled again sarcastically, and stood up. He took a slow step and said calmly, "But it will also be good for you without this sort of touching."

I snorted, not sure if I should laugh or cry. So much for overcoming my fear. It would probably be best to go back to being a researcher and forget that I was a woman. I looked seriously at Sverr. "Let me explain. You're a guest in my home and in my world. As a guest I'll respect you completely. But please do me a favor and respect me, too. No touching,

Book One: Beyond the Fog

understand? If you get the impression that I'm responding to your desire, I'm sorry. We're misunderstanding each other."

Sverr cocked his head, looking at me intently.

I turned and, furious at myself, went into the bedroom for a time out. I hoped the ilg wouldn't trash my apartment while I was out of the room. Without undressing, I lay down on the bedspread and stared gloomily at the ceiling. The worst part was that my desire hadn't abated. All I could think of was the ilg's tanned body.

With a sigh of exasperation I flopped over and covered my head with a pillow. There was no denying it, the arrival of this barbarian in my life was making it harder and harder for me to remain a cold, impartial scientist.

Chapter 12. Sverr

THE BACK OF THE CHAIR cracked and I tossed it aside in irritation. I shut my eyes and inhaled the dry air that was so different from the air on the fjords. Everything here was strange and unfamiliar.

Even she was unfamiliar. I needed to remind myself of that and not move from in front of this window, even though I could only think about one thing: breaking through the papery door and taking that thin, delicate body.

I shook my head and tried to bury my desire — I knew it would lead to no good. I had to be more careful. I needed to stay focused on the task at hand and not succumb to pleasure.

I straightened up and tried to calm down. Focusing hard, I managed to quell the fury, the fire, and my call. I then set about examining the living room, and my first impulse was to chuckle. I recognized a lot of the objects, and it was easy to guess what the other ones were used for. I paced around the room, looking at everything. Wondering what the wall felt like, I laid a hand on it and tuned into the sensations. I felt only a faint prick. Clearly the people of the Confederation killed everything, even stone. I took a small glass ornament off a shelf and grunted. I don't like glass. It's used to give the children of Ulhjegg something pretty to look at to quiet them down, and the riars of Aurolhjoll have long honored it. The

Book One: Beyond the Fog

girl would probably like the shining towers of Aurolhjoll. At this thought, a spark of malice ignited in me. I cursed and put the ornament down. No matter what, I needed to keep my mind off what Liv might like.

Everything in this home was delicate and small, just like the lilgan herself. I was sure that if I just laid a finger on any object, it would immediately turn to dust. Nothing here was like the furniture in Neroaldaf, where every object was solid and built to last centuries.

I examined the three burners of the lamp with its evenly burning transparent vessels. I stuck my hand in and squeezed one of them. As I'd expected, the glass shattered and the electricity stung me. The pain wasn't excruciating, but it was unpleasant. I contentedly shook the fragments of glass off my fingers.

I spotted a wooden jewelry box filled with gleaming gold baubles. I picked up a thin chain holding a small pendant and dangled it scornfully. What a disgraceful trifle. It would be shameful to offer a freeborn maiden something like this. What kind of man would think that was acceptable?

I flung the chain back in the box and opened the doors of a cupboard standing by the shelves. It was filled with drab gray and brown pieces of fabric. There was almost nothing bright, gold, red, or embroidered. I was perplexed — Olivia was young. On the fjords, only hunched-over widows wore such dull colors. Then another thought flashed in my head: I wanted to see the girl in crimson. It would suit her. I pulled a black patch of lace off the top shelf and turned it over in my hands. My mind began to wander as I imagined what this lace would look like on Liv's curvaceous body. I snorted so vehemently I could see the steam surging from my nostrils. I hurled the rag away.

The living room was small — it only took a few steps to get back to the couch. It was a cramped, modest home. Was

The Charmed Fjords

my lilgan poor? By all appearances, she was. Why didn't she have a man who would protect her and shower her with precious gifts? Yet I knew that in this world things didn't work that way, and it wasn't unusual for women to live alone.

That made no sense to me. Why did they live like that?

I contemplated the question for a moment. I didn't think too hard, though, because I was tired and wouldn't have minded getting some sleep. I'd had to expend a lot of the hjegg's energy to take the people out of the Fog. It was a process that drained a lot of strength from me and I was now physically exhausted. But I was too stimulated by the new smells, sensations, and sounds. What would really wake me up was a good fight, but I was pretty sure I couldn't count on that.

I glanced at the door that Liv was hiding behind but then forced myself to turn away. I did another lap around the room. I picked up what looked like multicolored shining ink holders that were rolling around loose on the table. I knew they were pens used to write letters. I also had some, but the ink in them had dried out long ago. I ran the metal end across a piece of paper and admired the even blue trace it left. I wanted to take it, just like I was used to taking anything that caught my fancy, but I remembered that the customs were different here. I put it down regretfully. There were books and piles of paper next to the pens. Everything was thin and snow white. It was pleasant to write on paper like that. A desire to pilfer some paper began to nag at me. No! I was in the Confederation and I couldn't just take whatever I wanted. The Confederation wasn't the fjords.

Feeling annoyed, I went over to an opening that led to another room. This room was dominated by cabinets filled with kitchen utensils. I spotted some tall, delicate goblets sparkling on a shelf. More glass? Did the lilgan really like glass so much? Personally, I preferred gold or iron. I pulled

Book One: Beyond the Fog

out one of the vessels but I didn't know my own strength and it shattered in my hand. I cursed softly and looked for a place to put the pieces. I emptied the cupboard onto the table. I pulled out a second goblet more carefully, but it also splintered into two pieces between a ladle and a thin knife. This set me off. When I tried picking up the shards of glass they kept slipping through my fingers, so I just brushed them onto the floor. How I detested glass.

The fragments dispersed under my feet and I looked at them in disappointment. Glancing at the door to the room where the girl had fled to, I carefully moved the trash toward the wall.

Then the white cupboard in the corner began to rumble. Startled, I wheeled around sharply, pulling down the side shelf with my shoulder. I stared at the detritus in puzzlement. All these people's possessions were too fragile — as soon as you touched something it broke. For some reason that really got under my skin, and I realized it was a good thing I didn't have my sword or battleax with me. I tend to take my weapons out too fast. If I had them with me, I probably would have decimated this rumbling cupboard already. But it was too risky to go beyond the Fog with weapons — steel always awakened the dark, primordial side of people, especially the steel from Neroaldaf. I definitely didn't want to awaken anything. No, I wanted to calm their fears and make them less vigilant.

I took another turn around the girl's dwelling, giving special attention to things that caught my eye. Color portraits in dainty frames hung on the wall. One of them showed a young Olivia hugging the same little son of a bitch we'd run into at the Academy — that scrawny, feeble, spineless, yet arrogant guy. His eyes revealed an artificial, stupid sense of superiority, but there was also some fear mixed in. I couldn't help but notice how weak Liv became when that guy was next

The Charmed Fjords

to her. What was their connection? It looked like their connection was the past.

I pounded a fist on the wall and winced when I saw the indentation it made. Why was everything here so insubstantial? You could blow on something and it would fall apart. I didn't understand how anyone could live in a home like this.

Trying not to break anything else, I walked around the rickety little table, compact armchair, narrow couch, and scraggly plant standing on the shelf.

What a dreadful place.

I stopped in front of the rumbling white cupboard. When I opened it, cold air came rushing out and I saw shelves of food. Ah — this was a frosty refrigerator. In my home, Neroaldaf, we keep provisions in an underground vault where you can get lost. The vault is so big that when you light the lantern by the door, you can't see it from the farthest shelves, no matter how big the flame is. But it looks here people keep their food in a cupboard the side of a small trunk.

I stuck my head in and sniffed. I immediately ruled out a couple of boxes, but there was one that tempted me. I took it out, tore the stiff paper that was compressed as if all the air had been pushed out of it, and sniffed the meat again. Of course, it wasn't a freshly killed animal seared over an open flame, but it would have to do. That thing they'd tried to feed me on the plane — I think they called it an energy bar — was still stuck in my stomach like a rock.

I snorted, and this time the smoke coming out of my nostrils was impossible to miss. I was starving, and my beast was close by. I needed to eat and quiet the thoughts and desires I shouldn't be having.

I chuckled at myself. I forgot there was no maiden nearby yearning to hear the call of the hjegg, or to be with me even without the call. During the years of war, and on

Book One: Beyond the Fog

campaigns, there were always maidens, either captives or those who wanted to curry favor with the mighty riar. On the fjords every woman knew it was better to stand behind a man, and if that man was a hjegg, even more so. But this Liv, the girl from the foreign land, didn't know that. She was resisting.

I sniffed the meat again, pondering it. Suddenly I heard noises coming from the corridor. I jumped up and strained to hear them. I recognized the sound of the elevator. Then I heard someone walking. The footfall sounded light, like women's steps. Good, it didn't sound like anyone dangerous. I relaxed my shoulders and waited, smiling inwardly.

It looked like my lilgan had some guests, and they were women. Did the firstborn hear that I needed a maiden? This was going to be interesting. I needed to subdue the fury, and women and laughter were a sure way of doing that.

OLIVIA

Before I had a chance to fall asleep, the insistent warble of the doorbell rang out, then a key scraped in the lock and I heard a cheerful voice sing out, "Liv, are you back? Where are you?"

Damn, it was Clysindra. I moaned silently. She had my spare keys and I could always count on her to be extracurious. She couldn't have come at a worse time, when I had this ilg in my house.

I jolted upright, slid out of bed, and dashed into the living room.

To make matters worse, Clys wasn't alone — our mutual friend Rani was with her. They were standing in the living room gaping at Sverr and panting like dogs. He was gazing back at them in idle interest, with a mocking look in his golden eyes. Of course, all he was wearing was that piece

The Charmed Fjords

of fabric that covered his groin. Fixing my friends with a pensive stare, he lifted the raw meat he was holding and tore off a piece. He bit into it with his snow-white teeth, narrowed his eyes like an animal, and swallowed, not taking his eyes off Clys and Rani. Blood dropped onto his chest and slowly dribbled down all the way to the edge of his leather skirt. My friends, who were normally so levelheaded, gawked at this spectacle so raptly I felt embarrassed for them.

"Oh my God," Rani squeaked.

"What are you guys doing here?" I asked in annoyance.

"We heard on the news that the expedition was back," Clys said weakly, continuing to ogle the barbarian in my apartment. A telltale flush I'd never seen on her crept over her face. What was up with that?

"So you decided you needed to drop in on me?" I said.

"We were worried about you," Rani purred without taking her eyes off Sverr. I had the impression she'd never take her eyes of him if she were left to her own devices. I watched her look him up and down: from his preposterous sash around his hips up to his face and back down again. I thought she was either going to pass out or fling herself at the barbarian.

I shook my head. "Everything's great. I'm just exhausted. I'm meeting with the commission tomorrow and I'd really like to get some sleep."

"Is he a real barbarian? Does he talk?" Clys asked in a strangled voice as though she hadn't heard a word I'd said.

Sverr ravenously bared his teeth, cocked his head, and then, to my surprise, let out a wolflike growl. The low, guttural noise reverberated around the apartment and bounced off the walls. Clys, Rani, and I flinched as that damned ilg threw back his head and burst out laughing, looking pleased to have a good time at our expense.

"Holy cow!" Clys and Rani sputtered. Their eyes blazed

Book One: Beyond the Fog

like they were newborn kittens, and I wanted to fall through the floor.

Rani stepped toward the ilg in fascination. He cocked his head and narrowed his eyes. He looked like a cat lying in wait for a hapless mouse. I didn't like that look one bit. I started boiling with anger. What was he up to? If Rani had her way, she'd start groping him on the spot. Admittedly, I also wanted to touch the ilg when I first laid eyes on him, but it was purely for research purposes. But my friends weren't scientists, and they just had a primitive female interest in him.

That infuriated me.

I supposed I should have been glad to have a chance to see how Sverr behaved with new people. But I felt no satisfaction, only confusion. I had an urge to kick the barbarian and smack my friends in the neck.

My sudden bloodlust horrified me. I turned to Clys and Rani. "Guys, this is really a bad time," I snapped. I took them each by the hand and started to pull them into the hallway. The last thing I needed right now was their questions and curiosity. I had a hard time getting them to move. All I could do was yell at them. "I'll call you tomorrow! Right now I need to get some sleep and — "

"With him?" Rani spluttered, turning back to look at Sverr.

I exploded. "No, alone!" I shouted so loudly I was sure the whole building could hear me. How embarrassing. "Please! We'll talk later. I'm begging you!"

Clys and Rani exchanged glances. I could see they were offended. "OK, but you owe us a bottle of champagne and you have to promise to tell us everything," Clys said. I nodded. I was willing to do anything they wanted as long as they left. When they finally got into the elevator and the doors slid shut on them, I heaved a sigh of relief.

The Charmed Fjords

Back in the apartment, I found Sverr standing in the same place, taking his time eating the meat.

"No," he said, licking his fingers. "A woman on the fjords wouldn't even make it outside in clothes like those. She'd be taken on the spot, right where she'd put those clothes on."

I recalled Rani's lacy minidress and looked at Sverr. He was close to me, and the attraction was still bubbling in my blood.

I noticed the remains of the chair and broken dishes but kept my mouth shut. They were only glasses and I could easily replace them — it was no comparison to how I'd awakened the sacred beast on the fjords.

"I see you managed to find some food and you've had dinner. That's lucky for you because I'm a bad cook," I muttered distractedly.

I had a feeling I wouldn't be getting any sleep tonight, so I figured I may as well try to get some work done. I headed into the small spare room, where I had my desk and laptop. As the computer powered on, I tried to decide what to write in the report for the commission. For the first time in my life, I had doubts about whether I should share all my observations with the council. The doubt gnawed at me as insistently as a wild animal.

I placed my hands on the keyboard, reluctantly listening for noises in the living room. But it was quiet.

SVERR

I pushed on the door and stopped when I saw the sleeping Iilgan. Her head was on the desk, next to the glowing computer screen, another invention of this so-called progress. Her left arm was hanging down and her right arm

Book One: Beyond the Fog

was cushioning her cheek. I stepped closer, gingerly picked up a piece of paper, and carefully read the even lines. The letters were jumping around; they didn't want to come together to make words. On the fjords we used different symbols for writing, so it took a lot of concentration for me to decipher what she'd written. It was the report for her commission. Instead of giving in to an urge to spit on it, I read it. It almost made me laugh. "The barbarian can count to ten... Knows the letters... Knows the geographic location of other tribes... Understands and adopts understandings of hospitality, virtue, honor... The Gorlohum volcano is personified and is considered to be alive... Possible offering of sacrifices... The religion of the hjeggs has not been studied... The totem animal has not been studied... Probable worship of the elements... The topic must be studied more fully..."

I smiled, put the piece of paper down, and began to walk back into the other room.

The report didn't contain anything really dangerous, just like the others wouldn't. If there was anyone who had begun to figure things out, it was the old man — the old, wise man. He had seen a lot — I glimpsed the burden of a long life in his faded eyes. He commanded respect, and in another lifetime I would have knelt before him as before someone who was worthy of such an honor. Maybe that was why he was still alive. But whether he would come around was now beyond my control. The riar's fury is more frightening than his call.

The old man had not only begun to figure things out, he had also had a chance to tell the girl. I heard what he said when the girl was tied to the sacrificial pillar. But Liv either didn't believe him, hear him, or place any significance in what he said. That woman... My call and the blood of the murdered animal had dimmed her reason and now she was devoting all her strength to resisting.

The Charmed Fjords

That was a good thing. It meant everything would work out.

I looked back at her from the doorway. She was still sleeping. Her dark hair had fallen over her cheek, and her lips were slightly ajar. I ran the back of my hand over her mouth, as if I could still feel the touch of her lips. The heavy feeling sank into my groin again. I frowned in annoyance.

I remembered how Irvin and I had examined the book belonging to the people of the Confederation. It had drawings and descriptions — the kind that made your cheeks burn. We were around eight years old. Of course the adults took the book away from us and boxed us on the ears, but I never forgot the images I'd seen. I just never thought I'd want to mimic them. None of the women on the fjords aroused such desire in me. I usually never even asked their names. But now, looking at the quietly sleeping outsider, I wanted everything I'd seen that time in the book but was too young to understand.

Just touching her lips made me burn with a craving for her.

I seized her light body. She was delicate and thin, just like the little gold bauble. I wanted to snatch her away, hide her in the cave among the treasures, and not show her to anyone. Sometimes it was hard to subdue the longings I had in my blood. For some reason I had an especially strong desire to help myself to Liv.

I picked her up, carried her into the room that held her bed, and laid her on the blanket. She muttered something but didn't wake up.

She was weak, but at the same time, she was strong. In fact, her strength was astounding. The whole time she was tied to the pillar, she was silent. She never complained, cried, or begged for mercy. I had watched her from the shadows, waiting for her to begin begging. But she never did. She didn't

Book One: Beyond the Fog

call out or complain to the men who had come with her. No, she did the opposite: she got to work. She was silent and didn't show any fear. She was a worthy, proud maiden. If she were a daughter of the fjords, the men would bring her gifts to win her favor, but I would steal her away and lock her in my bedroom.

But Liv was an outsider. Her soul was dirtied with the blood of the hjegg I had killed. She was a daughter of the people beyond the Fog, who were bringing progress and disruption.

I brushed her dark hair off her face.

There were scars on her body. I had studied them when I lifted her and carried her to the hides when we were with the tribe by the White Lake. I shook my head. This time, I only looked briefly. The scars ran down her body in incisions, marring her soft skin. I wondered where they came from, but I knew she wouldn't tell me if I asked.

Apparently she had never been with a man.

A feeling of contentment spread through my body, giving me a sweet foretaste of what lay in store for me. She was so tender, pliable, and soft right now. How I wanted her...

I needed the deep waters of the fjords, where the frigid moisture meets you with a frozen embrace. Only the cold could suppress my desire for this girl. But the land of the water and cliffs was far away.

Deep in thought, I touched her lips. Inside I burst into flames, which blinded me to everything except this soft feminine body.

I clenched my jaw so hard it cracked. I needed to think about what was going to happen tomorrow, at that damned commission meeting. I needed to think everything over again and prepare. But my thoughts returned again to the girl lying next to me.

Chapter 13. Olivia

I FELT SOMETHING HEAVY pressing me into the bed. I shifted, trying to find a more comfortable position. From my half-asleep state, I vaguely registered different sensations. A burning body, burning breath.

Good morning, Liv!

My eyes flew open and I found myself face-to-face with Sverr's penetrating gaze. He began to slowly run his hand along my side. My body responded automatically with a shudder of pleasure. Sverr grinned and began to stroke me more assertively.

"You're so vulnerable when you're sleeping," he said quietly. "I like you that way."

He pulled me closer as though I belonged to him.

I blinked sleepily and tried to break away, but he turned me onto my stomach and pushed me harder into the blanket.

"Enough with the running away, lilgan," he breathed into my ear. "Enough! I know you want to obey me as much as I want to take you."

His hand reached under my hips and he jerked the top of my jeans. The thick fabric tore as easily as the fiber of my protective jumpsuit. Sverr pulled my pants down, baring my butt. I began to struggle harder as I felt my jeans fall somewhere around my knees.

Book One: Beyond the Fog

"Calm down!" He slapped me lightly and I cried out indignantly. What the hell? No one gets away with slapping the head anthropologist of the Academy of Progress. Did this powerful barbarian think he could just order me to obey him and give him satisfaction?

I twisted like a snake, trying to throw this colossus off me. Sverr clamped his teeth down around my neck. He wasn't playing this time. I cried out in pain. He released me, but he accomplished his goal: I stopped wriggling, but only because I was stunned by his savagery.

"I want to see your eyes the first time we do this," the ilg said, flipping me over. He stopped when he caught sight of my eyes and scowled.

He shook his head furiously, yanked my arms over my head, and pinned them to the pillows.

"Why are you fighting me?" he barked. There was a note of genuine surprise in his voice. "I know you want me! You answer me and then you get angry. May Hellehjegg take you!"

"You won't catch me!" I hissed. "Things aren't that simple in my world, Sverr."

"Desire between a man and a woman is the same everywhere!" he snapped. "Isn't this what your friends wanted when they were checking me out? To hell with your arguments." Sverr shook me lightly.

"I'm not them! I don't want — "

"Yes you do. I know you do." The ilg's voice sounded so convincing I ground my teeth. He was right — I did want him. But shouldn't I explain how things worked in this civilized world of ours — or rather, my civilized world? There was no point. He wouldn't understand.

The ilg was lustfully studying me. "Your resistance is only breaking both of us, lilgan, and it's breaking me more. This is too much for me. I can't bear to feel you respond and then hear you say no. I've been lying here for hours and I

The Charmed Fjords

couldn't even fall asleep because I felt you," he said, baring his teeth. His tense, feverish body was practically vibrating and the veins were popping out on his neck. I noticed with horror that the pupils of his golden eyes were dilated vertically again. What was that all about? So it wasn't my imagination after all? I didn't mention it in my report because I was sure I was imagining things — it was the only logical possibility. But now, in the morning light, I could see it clearly.

"Your eyes..." I whispered. "They're... inhuman..."

The ilg blinked and the pupils went back to normal. Then he let out a yell and rolled off the bed. "What are you talking about, lilgan?" he asked mockingly.

I propped myself up on my elbow, watching him walk away. Was I imagining things again? Was I still half asleep? I shook my head. Enough of this nonsense! This time I was positive — his eyes did change. My heart pounded against my ribs. What was it? Was it a lost atavism? A different eye structure? Or something else entirely? The thoughts were racing through my head so fast I even forgot about my momentary arousal.

What did Maximilian mean when he called Sverr inhuman? I wished he hadn't fallen into a coma before he had a chance to explain his theory. It occurred to me that his coma wasn't a coincidence, and a profound fear seized me. That ilg was incredibly strong. He'd torn the ultraresistant fabric without so much as a blink. He had some sort of mental power, and I could no longer explain my hallucination merely as desire. His pupils narrowed, and the tribe added the divine hjegg designation to his name.

Who was he?

Was he simply sacred or the keeper of the religion?

Or was he the being the others worshiped?

I tumbled clumsily out of bed and got tangled in my

Book One: Beyond the Fog

jeans, which were now around my ankles. I pulled them up carelessly and began rushing around the room. Why had I shut my eyes to all these signs? Why didn't I mention these crucial facts in my report? It was as though something inside me had made me either forget or not think about certain details, but why?

It had to be because my mind was occupied with the ilg's aggressive sexuality and the desire he kindled in me. Whenever I was near the ilg I lost the ability to think clearly. What an idiot I was. I hadn't written about my torn jumpsuit, or about how the ilg had come to me after the shatiya. I was afraid my colleagues would scorn me and ask prying questions. Among them I was the odd one out, while here I was a potential target of mockery.

I stopped short in the middle of the room, with one foot up and my mind surging a mile a minute. If I pushed out all the emotions and looked at the situation objectively, what would I see?

For starters, there was the expedition, in which each of us, with no exception, kept something secret. I concealed the information about Sverr's visit to me in my tent, my embarrassing suspicions, and the discrepancies. My guess was that my colleagues hadn't written about how the shatiya ended. All of us had something here, in the civilized world, that compelled us to lie — wives, families, friends, a reputation, a moral identity.

In other words, we hid important information because it compromised us. Everyone, except Max, had revealed unflattering sides of themselves that day. Of course, I had fended off Sverr's advances, but no one actually believed that because they themselves had succumbed to their baseness. The hides, the ancient rituals, the blood, the music: the fjords awakened people's ancient instincts, those that civilization had long hidden.

The Charmed Fjords

Or had those instincts been awakened by whoever had orchestrated this entire game — the shrewd manipulator who had imperceptibly nudged us into the abyss, allowed us to become a part of the tribe, and allowed the men to take the women of the tribe, knowing that the men would hide this incident, and with it their suspicions if they actually had any. I was willing to fight for my status as a scientist, but today the commission would hear only dry facts and an embarrassing statement: we had too little information to draw a conclusion. That's what I had written, and I knew it was also what the others would write.

Only Maximilian was willing to tell the truth. After all, he was the only one who had kept his head. On top of that, Max had such a solid reputation in the field that he wasn't afraid of anything. But he was on life support right now. The medicine we injected in him helped us get him back to civilization, but barely.

And almost the last thing Max said to me was that Sverr wasn't human.

I bit my cheek, trying to calm myself. Not human? Was that even possible? What had Maximilian seen or sensed that made him say that?

Sverr's strength and miosis weren't evidence. The ilg was used to physical burdens, and he did in fact have much more stamina than the average person from the Confederation. Yet I could take out my defective jumpsuit, and I imagined I saw a change in his golden eyes. At the same time, the shining irises weren't really that unusual — in history there were plenty such cases. One of my colleagues had even written a whole dissertation explaining the phenomenon. There were incidents of people being killed when their blazing irises got them mistaken for snakes.

Everything we had seen could be explained and understood, even that damned call he kept talking about.

Book One: Beyond the Fog

Why blame things on a mental stimulus? All you had to do was look at the ilg. He was uncommonly attractive and masculine, and he had an aura of savagery and strength about him — that was the whole mystique. He oozed sexuality and he was comfortable in his own skin. He was unusual. He was like an animal in a human body, arousing fantasy and forbidden desires, while I was a twenty-seven-year-old woman with raging hormones. There were no mysteries, just primitive instinct.

Or maybe not?

Damn it! I was no longer sure about anything.

No, scratch that. I was sure. And my intuition had been telling me for a while that there was something off about all of this.

On top of that, I did see the hjegg. Admittedly, I only glimpsed it vaguely and I saw too little, but I did see it, in the split second when the mist dissipated. I didn't believe my own eyes, and even now, I couldn't believe I saw it.

But if I publicly shared the hypothesis that Sverr wasn't human, I'd be a laughingstock. Maximilian was the one who could come up with bold theories and wild ideas — he had years of experience and he'd already achieved plenty, so he was allowed to make mistakes. But I wasn't. And before coming out and saying something, I needed to know for sure.

For that all I needed was one test. I would have liked to do a thorough genome sequencing, but I didn't have time for that. But I could recognize human proteins in the blood, and that was a quick process. All I needed was a drop of Sverr's blood.

I held up my torn jeans. How could I possibly get a sample? I doubted he'd just let me stick a needle in his arm so I could do some research. But I needed to confirm my theory before the meeting with the commission, and the clock was ticking.

The Charmed Fjords

What was I going to do?

I darted into the bathroom, which adjoined the bedroom. It was just big enough to hold a shower stall, toilet, and sink. I turned on the faucet and splashed cold water on my face, not caring that I was getting my jeans wet.

Then inspiration struck. Obviously I couldn't plunge a needle into Sverr without him noticing, but I could arrange things so that when I drew his blood he was focused on something else — a woman's body, for instance. My knowledge was only theoretical, but I suspected that during sex men didn't think with their heads.

I splashed more water on myself. I decisively, almost with a malicious excitement, tore off my jeans, and then pulled off my T-shirt and underwear. I pulled a smooth capsule with a needle from the medicine cabinet, took a breath, and looked in the mirror.

At one point in my life I had decided that science was the only future for me. Before that, I'd dreamed about something bigger. I loved to have fun, play sports, hang out with my dog. And I loved Sergey, and he also said he loved me. I believed him. Even after the dreadful incident that changed my life, I believed him. But I stopped believing him when I undressed in front of him and saw his look of horror and revulsion. To be fair, he quickly tried to wipe the expression from his face and he rushed to embrace me, but in that moment something inside me broke. I realized that beauty and scars are incompatible. They're like reagents that never mix.

Since then, my life was full of work, science, my department, a new job... and Sergey's wedding — the wedding of my best friend, who after all this time still felt guilty.

But there was no man in my life.

I forced myself to run my hand over my scars. They

Book One: Beyond the Fog

were repugnant — no woman should look like this.

In the years since the experience with Sergey I'd only undressed once in front of a man — he was a random stranger. It was like with Sergey all over again: the repulsed look, my inability to breathe, shame, suffocating panic, and the ever-present inhaler. From that moment I swore off men.

And now I'd decided to play the seductress? It was almost funny. But then a burning, sweet feeling began to flow through me and I narrowed my eyes. No, it wasn't funny, not at all.

I crept back into the bedroom. I looked askance at the rumpled bed. Was I a fool trying to carry out this plan?

I hid the capsule in the headboard and said — or rather, gasped, "Sverr..."

I spoke quietly, like a rustle, not a sound. A normal human being wouldn't even hear it. If the ilg didn't hear me, I'd know my suspicions were worthless.

But he did hear me. He came to the doorway and leaned his shoulder on the door jamb. His brow was furrowed and his lips were pursed disapprovingly. He hadn't bothered to cover himself, so I tried not to let myself look at his bottom half. He slowly sized me up, taking in my reddening cheeks, the neckline of my short dressing gown, my hands nervously pulling at the string, my bare legs. He looked again at my face and raised his eyebrows inquisitively.

I let out a tortured gasp. Damn it! Things were always much simpler in theory. In reality I just blushed and fidgeted nervously.

"You're right," I said, trying to steady my voice. "I... I want... it... I want you. I want to be close to you. It's just that it's complicated for me."

"Tell me more."

"What?"

"Tell me more, Olivia. Tell me what you want."

The Charmed Fjords

I jerked my head up and stopped playing with the string of the dressing gown. Really? So it wasn't just going to happen? He expected me to say something? I clenched my fists for a moment, like before my speech at the Academy, and braced myself. I said sharply, "I want to have sex with you. I want to feel your strength, your weight, your body. I want you to press me to this bed, lie on top of me, open my legs, and..."

I fizzled out, but I'd said enough for Sverr, who had been listening intently. He straightened up and in a split second was next to me. He gently pushed me toward the bed and bowed his head, studying me. I didn't resist him, and as I flopped onto the bed my dressing gown fell open. Sverr placed a knee on the edge of the bed and looked at me. For a moment I felt scared. But when I spotted the desire fluttering in his eyes, I realized with despair that this was going to go beyond touching. If only it weren't with him.

The ilg pulled on the string and flung the dressing gown off me. My body clenched up. A normal woman would hide her chest or lower belly from a man's gaze, but I was hiding my scars. Sverr separated my arms and then ran a finger along the scar under my breast.

"Was it a good fight, Liv?" he asked, continuing to stroke me.

I gasped inadvertently. It hadn't occurred to me that I'd enjoy this sort of touching.

"No, it was bad. Very bad," I replied hoarsely. "But I won."

He lifted his head and smiled approvingly and admiringly. I bit my lip, feeling pleased despite myself. Sverr didn't pity me like everyone around me did, and there wasn't a hint of revulsion in his eyes. I saw only unbridled desire — as if for him there was nothing surprising in such blemishes, and the only important thing was how I'd gotten them.

Book One: Beyond the Fog

The barbarian took his hand away and began running his tongue along the scar on my stomach. I flinched, trying to pull away, but he wouldn't let me. He just lifted his head for a moment, opened his golden eyes slightly, and went back to licking me. He went a little lower. He wasn't kissing me, but rather running his tongue over me, taking in my taste.

The unfamiliar wet movements began to arouse something savage in me.

I could feel his primitive hunger and beastly, burning desire. Then it hit me that I wasn't afraid. I didn't feel an ounce of fear, not even when he shifted and covered himself. The ilg was silent — he didn't compliment me, but I could see how tense his strong body was and how heavily he was breathing. He wanted me so openly that no words were necessary.

He dropped his hand and ran it along my stomach, making his way down.

"You're soft here," Sverr said in surprise. "You don't have hair?"

"I... we... women... we remove it," I stammered, trying to control my breathing. It came out as if it were no big deal. "All the hair from our bodies. Forever."

"Really?" He touched me again and his face looked predatory. "Hmmm... interesting..."

I couldn't restrain myself and pressed his hand, instinctively wanting to feel his touch. His rough finger touched my skin and I shuddered. Sverr's eyes blazed with interest and he began to caress me on his own more insistently. I shifted and arched my back.

The ilg gave out a strangled growl, greedily picking up on the obvious signs of my arousal.

"More, more," I whispered feverishly, yielding to him.

I grabbed his shoulders, and reveled in the bulk of his masculine body. I caressed his broad back, from his shoulder

The Charmed Fjords

blades down to the clefts of his lower back, and I touched his strong glutes. I was in such bliss that I never wanted to stop touching him. The ilg was also studying me: he was touching me, pressing me to him, caressing me. I couldn't restrain myself. I slid forward on my arm and ran my hand over him.

Sverr tugged my arm and pinned it to the blanket. He interlaced his fingers with mine, and with his knee separated my legs. A pinpoint of fear pricked me through the intoxicating fog of ecstasy.

The ilg seemed to sense it. He threw his head back and looked me in the eyes, and I felt the familiar lava begin to gather in me. It spread like a molten lake below my belly and started to boil. Pure desire replaced the blood running through my veins. Sverr inhaled heavily and swayed, peering ferociously at my blazing face. We both gasped for air, but my fear had dissipated. All that remained was uncontrollable desire. He swayed again and I submitted to him, gripping his shoulders. Oh, yes, he was rock solid, and the touch of his fingers drove me out of my mind and made me want to give all of myself to him.

The lava in me bubbled like champagne. I was no longer thinking, just feeling. I was feeling more vividly than I'd ever felt in my life. The pain came and then went away, burning up in the flame. I took refuge in his strong arms and cried out in ecstasy. It felt like all my nerve endings had burst, my receptors had gone haywire, and I turned into a lump of bare erogenous points. The golden eyes held and commanded me, while the tanned body moved on top of me. It wasn't until Sverr moved his head and gave out a choking growl that I suddenly remembered why I'd masterminded this whole thing. The syringe was in my hand, and I laid it on the ilg's leg at the moment when I felt a pulsation inside me. The needle easily penetrated his skin and was concealed again, and the syringe slid out of my hand onto the rug.

Book One: Beyond the Fog

Sverr stopped moving on top of me and gasped for breath. I was sure he'd felt the needle and guessed what I was up to, and that he'd immediately strangle me. And he could definitely do that — all my nonexistent intuition told me that. I hoped I was wrong, though. When Sverr lifted his hand, I burrowed into the twisted sheets. But all he did was tenderly run it along my cheek — he actually stroked me. He abruptly rolled off me and stood up. He looked down at me mockingly and said, "I'm going to go look for some food. You're not so good with that, lilgan."

With that, he walked out of the room.

I blinked vacantly, watching him, and sighed. I had just had mind-blowing sex with the most unromantic man in the world — simply put, with a barbarian. There wasn't a single kiss or tender word, but I'd felt such ecstasy that my scientific brain was broken. But I couldn't think about that now. I had to get to work. I leaped up and pulled off the sheets that still held the evidence of our tryst. I looked around furtively, picked up the syringe containing the ilg's drop of blood, and headed to the bathroom. I threw my dirty laundry on the floor and went into the shower. I hurriedly put myself together and stepped out, leaving the water on. In the corner there was a box with medicines and a few reagents. I put a neutralizer tablet in my cheek, getting rid of the undesired consequences of the intercourse. I only needed to do one test to find out whether the blood in the syringe was human. I settled on the toilet seat and took out a solution used mostly by criminologists but also sometimes by anthropologists and researchers. The capsule contained potassium and magnesium, and I knew that human and animal hemoglobin react differently with an alkaline solution. It would just take a few minutes, and the indicator would show a stripe: a green one if it was human blood and a red one if it wasn't. That was all I'd be able to tell for now. I needed a lab to learn more, but

The Charmed Fjords

at least I'd get an answer to the most important question.

I opened the cover, dribbled in the blood from the syringe, and closed it. As I waited, I could barely breathe. My thoughts immediately returned to what had happened five minutes before in the bedroom, the moist movements, heavy breathing, moans, and that unforgettable bliss. I needed to lean back onto the wall to regain my senses. I told myself it was all for the sake of research, for science. If I kept telling myself that, maybe I'd actually believe it. Suddenly I heard a knocking sound in the bedroom. I jumped up and almost dropped my equipment.

"Lilgan?" Sverr called to me quietly from behind the door.

"I'll be out in a minute!" I yelled back, not taking my eyes off the container. I willed it to hurry up, holding it to the light. Then my heart stopped.

Chapter 14. Sverr

I WANT TO DO IT AGAIN.
The lilgan went to hide behind the door and now I can hear her splashing around in the water. Is she upset? I crept over to the door to listen. Why should I care whether or not she's upset? I know she enjoyed it. I didn't have to wait long for her to experience her ecstasy. Her responsive body flared up in my arms like a torch and blazed so brightly and warmly that I lost my head. It was just as sensational as I imagined it would be the second I caught sight of her in the Fog. I knew immediately that I wanted her. Yet there was something about our union that troubled me. I knew her body was satisfied — I saw her energy and yearning — but it was a different story with her mind and soul.

I couldn't quite put my finger on it, though.

Maybe it was just that everything had happened in a way I wasn't used to. The raspy moans, dewy breath, her hands gripping my shoulders, and the foggy, ardent look in her eyes... Damn! Even thinking about it set my insides aflame all over again. I had an urge to drag her out of the shower and back to the bed. I'd lost control on that narrow bed in the small bedroom. I'd forgotten who and where I was. All I felt was the girl, who had so passionately responded to my call. I wanted to prolong our intimacy for as long as I could, as if it were something more consequential than a

The Charmed Fjords

mere union between a man and a woman. In Neroaldaf nocturnal satisfaction was never a secret — we didn't hide our desires behind deception or duplicity, and they were as natural as our other desires, like hunger or thirst. When I was done with whatever girl happened to be in my bed, she left and I had no interest in keeping her there or finding out what she was feeling.

But with this girl, I did.

I shook my head. I shouldn't have looked Liv in the eyes. I should have done everything like I always did, and not explored her body with my fingers and tongue.

A craving to break something flared up inside me again. The fjords were calling me. I felt suffocated in the world of the Confederation. Everything was new and unfamiliar here, and it really set me off. Even Olivia had that effect on me. She awakened new feelings in me, and I didn't like that. Yet I don't want to understand her. But I already know too much, and still I want more.

I stopped myself as I reflected that I wouldn't mind continuing that exploration right now. One short encounter was too little for me. But she was so silky, tender, and fervent that it couldn't last long.

I grunted and turned my attention back to the sounds behind the door. Where was Liv? The water had been running too long. She should have been done by now. For some reason, I felt on edge and could sense my temper start to build. I frowned and went into the bedroom, planning to break down the flimsy door if she didn't open it. I got a bad premonition. But then Liv appeared in the doorway, her hair dripping and her face flushed and steaming. She shifted her eyes.

"We need to get ready to leave, Sverr. The commission meeting at the Academy starts in an hour. Why are you looking at me like that?"

Book One: Beyond the Fog

I lifted her chin and gazed into her eyes. They were greenish-gray, like the waters of the fjords. "Are you in pain?"

I was certain that she had gotten pleasure out of our intimacy. But what now? I'd heard that afterward women were sometimes uncomfortable, but I'd never cared about the details. Whenever I wanted a woman, a maiden came to me, and afterward she left with gratitude and a gift. But apparently things were different with the people of the Confederation. I didn't know much about that part of human life. The books about relationships I'd happened to read just made me and my a-tem chuckle, and I never looked at them again. I was interested in weapons, ships, planes, and equipment — the frightening handiwork of progress.

She shook her head and her wet hair spurted droplets on my hand.

"No?" I lowered my hand and touched her stomach.

The lilgan rolled her eyes and squeaked, "What are you doing?"

I continued to stroke her. She was silky, without a single hair, and to my surprise, that drove me wild. I desired this outsider so intensely I lost myself, but at the same time I could feel irritation build in me.

These feelings confused me.

"Stop it!"

Liv was blushing again. Surprising even myself, I brought my finger to her lips. She opened her mouth and her tongue touched my skin. A sweet, dense longing unraveled inside me so powerfully I pushed the girl against the wall. I had a sudden urge to thrust my tongue into her mouth. I wondered how that would feel. Were her lips as silky and soft as the rest of her? I pulled at the rag she'd put back on. Liv began to pound on me, trying to push me away with her weak hands. I smiled. The ardor of the hunt ignited in my blood, as my prey began resisting me again. This time I wouldn't

The Charmed Fjords

throw her onto her back — I'd already had a chance to look into her eyes.

"Sverr, no!" she snapped so forcefully I was caught off guard. How could so much power come out of that slight body?

"No!" She slammed her little hands into my chest, panting. Panic gleamed in her green eyes. "Enough! We have to go. The council is waiting for us."

I would have been happy to throw that damned council into Gorlohum's boiling magma, but of course I didn't. I had to remember that I didn't come here for fun, but my pleasure with the girl was making me forget my purpose. Her presence made me go weak and lose control.

I pulled back sharply, feeling angry at myself.

"All right, lead the way, lilgan," I said, trying to slow my breathing and subdue my desire.

OLIVIA

I gulped down some coffee and opened the refrigerator. I stared at the shelves, trying to figure out what to make for breakfast. I pulled out a carton of eggs and looked at it, feeling at a loss. I didn't know how to cook — I always just made do with dry snacks or ate at the café near the Academy. But did I need to feed the ilg? I felt like I'd earned the title "worst host to the representative of the fjords."

And yet...

I felt myself turning red, and with irritation I pushed the memories away.

"What are you doing?" Sverr had come up behind me so silently and unexpectedly that the carton of eggs slid out of my hands and I found myself standing in egg yolks.

"Shit!" I said, crouching down. "There goes your

Book One: Beyond the Fog

breakfast."

"I'll live."

"But omelets are the only thing I know how to cook."

"You're afraid again, Olivia."

I shuddered and looked up at the ilg. His attentive eyes seemed to be trying to penetrate my soul. Or had he already done that?

"So you're a psychologist now, is that it?"

"The smell gives you away," Sverr said coolly. "Fear always gives off an odor. You smelled differently during the night — there was no fear. But now it's filling you up."

I straightened up slowly and looked Sverr in the eyes. Why didn't my years studying science prepare me for waking up with a man, for how I'd feel, or for what I'd have to say? And for how everything would be so acute? Was this just a scientific experiment? Did I do everything for the sake of science? Try telling that to my feelings, that they'd blow like a lethal tornado and completely carry away my brains as if they were as tenuous as a straw roof.

Not a single diploma could help me deal with this.

Sverr swayed toward me and placed his hands on the counter behind me, encircling me in his arms.

"Why does the whole world disappear when I look at you, lilgan?" he asked softly. My heart simultaneously stopped and seemed to crack like a fragile eggshell.

"We're going to be late..."

He smirked, as if he could see right through all my stupid, meaningless arguments. They just went into the inferno of Gorlohum, so to speak. For a split second I wanted to blow off the council and the Academy, barricade the door, lock myself in the bedroom with the ilg, and stay there forever.

I shook my head, grasping the absurdity of my longings. Sverr let go of the counter and walked away,

The Charmed Fjords

resigning himself to the fact that we needed to leave.

When we left the apartment I wasn't as lucky as the night before: in the elevator we ran into an elderly couple, Anne and John Bork. I girded myself for curious looks and even questions, but to my surprise, the Borks didn't pay any attention to me or my odd companion wearing hides. They were holding hands, smiling, and kissing furtively like teenagers experiencing first love. They were so absorbed in each other it was like nothing else in the world existed.

"What a beautiful morning!" the balding, chubby Mr. Bork exclaimed gleefully as he stepped outside.

"Just wonderful!" Anne answered with just as much delight.

I stared at the couple in disbelief and then looked up at the somber, leaden sky and the leaves falling onto the sidewalk. I shook my head — another dreary autumn day.

In the car Sverr looked out the window serenely as I drove. You'd never guess from his expression that sitting in a car wasn't something he did every day. In fact, if you looked at his golden eyes, you might assume the exact opposite: that Sverr was a figure no less important than the king of the world. He was decked out in his usual ensemble: the cloth on his hips, the hide wrap around his shoulders, the fur naches, and of course the fangs, the ring, and the other accessories he never removed.

I suddenly remembered how the black fang on the leather string swung over my face when Sverr entered me.

I gripped the steering wheel and clenched my teeth.

Better not to think about that, and in any case, it wasn't going to happen again.

When the arch of the bridge loomed in front of us, Sverr turned to look at me and said, "Stop."

He said it softly and it occurred to me that he always talked like that. He never sounded like he was giving an order

Book One: Beyond the Fog

— there was no haughtiness, just the cool confidence that whoever he was speaking to would obey. Clearly this ilg was used to submission in every aspect of his life.

I pushed on the brake pedal, turning off the road toward the sidewalk. Sverr got out and walked over to the cast iron enclosure by the river. I also got out of the car and leaned on the door. From this vantage point there was a breathtaking view of the city, and I felt like I was looking at it with new eyes, seeing it for the first time. I saw the fancy arches of the iron bridges, the thin steel and glass buildings, the rotating advertising banners and panels displaying smiling women with sparkling teeth, the low sky scraping its stomach on the spires, the falling leaves beating down like flocks of birds on the curbs.

Sverr rested his arms on the enclosure. The wind whipped the animal hide around his shoulders, and his nearly naked body looked savage against the backdrop of the city skyscrapers. I would have given anything to know what he was thinking as he gazed at my city.

I went to stand beside him.

"It's cold today. It'll be winter soon," I said, immediately feeling embarrassed. I was unable to look at the ilg. "You'll freeze."

He snickered. He stroked the cast iron enclosure, as though he were listening to it. I looked at his hands and gulped. Memories of our intimacy flashed through my head again. I clenched my teeth, trying to force myself not to think about what had happened between us. But even based on what was only theoretical experience, I was aware that I'd never meet anyone like Sverr. I was sure there was no other man like him.

I turned away sharply and stared at the river. The car was still running, and occasional passersby stopped and gaped at Sverr. Some young women stared at him with such

The Charmed Fjords

delight in their eyes that I felt irritated.

"We need to get going. There's that council..." I said. The ilg didn't notice the slowly gathering crowd; he was too busy eyeing the city buildings while he ran his hands along the cast iron enclosure. For a moment I had the impression that the bridge was chiming under his hand, like the instrument I'd seen on the fjords. *Di-in-shork...*

"Do you like it here?" Sverr asked suddenly.

I frowned. Did I like it here? I'd never thought about that before.

"Of course. It's my home." I pointed at the square on the other side of the river. "My parents used to take me for walks over there when I was little. My school is behind that building. Next to it there's the pastry store, which has the best cookies. On that side over there is the Academy. The first time I walked in, I was so happy I thought I'd faint. I still can't believe I work there. Yes, Sverr, I do like my world."

He gave me a probing look. "Everyone has to love their own home. I understand, Olivia. Let's go."

He turned on his heel and headed back to the car. As we drove away and I looked in the rearview mirror, I could see curious, disappointed-looking people staring at us.

We had to go upstairs from the underground parking garage of the Academy to the lobby, where my colleagues made a beeline for me.

"Liv! You look great! Want some coffee?" Klin gave me a friendly welcome and thrust a paper cup into my hand. After a moment's thought, he held out another cup to Sverr, but Sverr shook his head. I glanced in the reflective doors of the closed elevator. I was wearing a dark red skirt that fell below my knees, a light silk blouse, and heels. I hadn't had the time to put on makeup, but it was true that today I looked unusually good. Klin smiled joyfully at the ilg, who responded with a sober nod. "Everyone's waiting for you. I can't even

Book One: Beyond the Fog

describe the excitement. Everyone's come, even Anders Eriksen. They all want to see our samples and hear everything we have to say. And of course they want to meet a living representative of the fjords."

I gulped.

"Yeah, if the famous Eriksen has graced us with his presence, things will be heated. Not that they wouldn't be anyway. A hot night, a hot day," Klin continued.

"What are you talking about?" I asked in confusion.

"Rumor has it that last night there were explosions on the sun, or a comet passed, or something else happened that affected the activity of the people in the city. Didn't you hear? It was on the news."

"I didn't turn the TV on today," I stammered. "But tell me, how's Maximilian? Have you heard anything?"

"He's on life support," Klin said, suddenly growing serious. "In any case, he's not young — you know that. He's in a coma, so now everything depends on him."

I glanced at Sverr. He had his usual look of indifference, almost like he was detached.

I averted my gaze.

"OK, I'm ready," I said, trying to sound confident and clutching the folder containing my report. "Let's go."

A hum of voices greeted us when we walked into the conference room. Thankfully, there were no reporters — the first meeting was just for scientists. I headed over to my assigned seat, my high heels clacking on the floor. Sverr walked beside me, and I could see an expression of idle mockery sparkling in his golden eyes. My colleagues craned their necks and jumped up, trying to get a good look at the ilg.

When we sat down, the chairman of the council struck the table with his mallet to bring the meeting to order. "The extraordinary meeting of the high commission of the

The Charmed Fjords

Academy of Progress is now open."

A roomful of curious eyes turned to stare at the ilg, but he was unfazed. For Sverr, the most interesting thing was the collection of shining, gold-capped pens. He rolled one of them in his fingers, and then he shamelessly tucked it into his hide. He thought for a moment and then picked up all the rest of the pens lying on the table. The scientists looking on grinned quizzically. Anger begin to seethe inside me.

What a savage, stealing pens. What was so funny about that?

I fixed my gaze on the green glass bottle in front of me to avoid looking at the ilg or my colleagues.

The historians and land surveyors spoke first, delivering a detailed report on the separation of the fjords. Of course, the most important presenter was Anders Eriksen, a researcher who had devoted his life to studying the Fog. We had all read his work and now we listened to him raptly.

"According to our data, the Fog first appeared around the beginning of the N era," Anders began slowly. In my peripheral vision I could see Sverr's eyes shining. He wasn't moving. "We know very little about the event that created this barrier. At the time, our civilization was only at the beginning of its path: people knew how to read and write, they were building the first boats and stone houses, and they sewed clothing. But records were only kept haphazardly, and a lot of events were embellished. So now the theories we come up with are only based on sparse data. Anyway, at the beginning of the N era, the Earth's crust shifted. As a result, the volcano erupted. According to historians, so much fire and ash were disgorged that they buried entire settlements and the ocean started boiling. Every culture had its own explanation for the deadly eruption. Some thought the gods were angry at the people for committing sins, and others thought it was the Earth's own punishment. My people explained the eruption

Book One: Beyond the Fog

as the fury of the great Hellehjegg."

"Wait, who?" I cried out suddenly. The chairman looked at me reproachfully but Eriksen only smiled.

"That's what the ancestors of my people called the winged fire-breathing snake, Dr. Orway. They thought the eruption of the lava was a sign of his fury descending on the world. The snake is no longer worshiped, but to this day you can find temples to Hellehjegg in the mountains of my country. They say a fire burns perpetually in them even though no one lights it." Anders trailed off and went back to talking about the Fog. "As we all know, religions often have a factual foundation. Over time that foundation changes, and becomes cluttered with myths and legends and takes on a form that's convenient and easy for people to understand. But we're not going to talk about theology right now. Let's get back to the eruption. After the lava froze and the ash fell, people saw that huge swaths of our planet were hidden by the Fog. That's what we called the poisonous, impenetrable substance. People would completely lose their sense of direction inside it. Scientific and technological progress was no help. Technology got stuck in the Fog, just like people. But!" Anders paused dramatically and looked at his enthralled audience. "A few years ago, we discovered that the thickness of the Fog was patchy in different sections, and that it was dispersing. We hypothesized that we'd soon be able to pass through it. We did a spectral analysis along the entire perimeter of the Fog and this is what we found" — he pointed at markings on a map — "there are three places where the thickness of the Fog has shrunk to almost one-twentieth of what it used to be. That inspired us to start looking again for a way to get to the other side, and you can imagine how surprised the researchers were when they got an answer from the fjords." Eriksen smiled faintly at Sverr, and a photo of a piece of parchment appeared on the screen.

The Charmed Fjords

"As you know, we launched another message into the ocean and we hoped the Anfin current would carry the canister under the Fog. That's exactly what happened. The ilgs received our message, and our guest — Sverr, who you see over there — not only responded, but also told us the exact location where he'd be able to meet the group from the Confederation. We also found the canister with the response in the ocean and immediately began to prepare for the mission — the successful mission, I might add. And all of this was possible because the Fog thinned out."

"But why did the Fog start to dissipate?" an impatient listener asked.

Anders was silent for a moment.

"We haven't figured that out yet," he said with visible regret. "Just like no one has been able to explain why it appeared in the first place. Maybe it's a natural process. In any case, we're far from knowing everything about our planet, and to this day some phenomena are mysteries. The Fog is one of them."

He gave a little bow and sat down. Sverr wasn't moving; he'd lost interest in the pens.

Yurgas was next to give his report. It was short and dry. He described the geographic location of the tribe, the number of aborigines, the gender ratio, and the types of weapons. As I half listened to his droning speech, my eyes wandered around the table, taking in the three dozen people sitting around it. They were all distinguished scholars and politicians who held the fate of the entire Confederation in their hands. I was seeing some of them in person for the first time. It occurred to me suddenly that I'd become somebody, but the realization didn't give me any pleasure.

Sergey wasn't at this council meeting because he studied other things. With a twinge of surprise, I remembered that I hadn't called him to explain things to him. I actually

Book One: Beyond the Fog

felt relieved, and anyway, it was a good thing I hadn't called him. Sergey had long been living his life, and now it was time for me to focus on mine, whatever it was.

I glanced over at Sverr and caught him boring a smoldering look into me. It was so intense I was sure that in a few seconds my colleagues would start to whisper and snicker about me. I frowned and looked away. But still, my breath caught and I felt weak in the knees. Then a sweet wave washed over me — the memory of his hands pressing me to the bed, his tongue licking my skin.

I clenched my fists under the table, digging my nails into my palms. By now, Klin was concluding his report and then it was Jean's turn. He pontificated on the specificities of the ilgs' linguistic culture, the composition of syllables, linguistic modulations, and on and on. The linguists exclaimed excitedly and wrote everything down. Their pens flashed in the sun and sheets of paper rustled. No questions were allowed until all the reports were done. The audience was a little miffed about that, but they managed to stay quiet.

"Now we'll hear the report by the anthropologists, Maximilian Shach and Olivia Orway," the chairman announced. My heart sank. "As you know, our esteemed professor is on life support right now." There was murmuring around the table. "The professor fell into a coma when he was on the fjords. Fortunately, we managed to get him to the hospital and the doctors are doing everything they can. We all hope that Dr. Shach will regain consciousness, and then we'll look forward to hearing his report. In the meantime, his deputy, Dr. Orway, will speak."

I gasped and choked. I started coughing and saw my colleagues looking at me condescendingly. Then I felt Sverr put his hand over my clenched fist under the table. His face was just as detached as before — no one would have guessed he was touching me.

The Charmed Fjords

I took my hand away, grabbed a glass of water, and guzzled it. I pulled myself together and stood up.

"Good morning, everyone. Chairman, colleagues..." I rushed through the formulaic niceties. "As you understand, the main goal of our expedition was to look for and observe the people who live on the fjords. We were fortunate. This ilg found the canister with the message." I didn't meet Sverr's eyes, but I could feel his gaze on me in my entire body, as though it were searing my skin. "He was able to write a message in response and activate the mechanism to return the canister. As you probably all know, this is a relatively primitive device that's activated automatically after a certain amount of time. But that's just the background." Noticing that my colleagues were starting to look agitated, I stopped abruptly. "We didn't know anything about the population of the fjords. You could even say we knew less than nothing because all our probes only transmitted murky landscapes or a mess of silhouettes and shadows that led us to come up with frightful theories. But the people of the fjords received us hospitably." I found myself getting caught up in my narrative and stopped noticing everyone looking at me. In any case, now they were looking at me benignly and listening attentively. I gave a vivid description of our stay on the fjords, the encounter with the tribe, daily life, and their customs. I gave a brief and clinical description of the shatiya. My colleagues exclaimed and exchanged glances. "Such rituals aren't unusual to anthropologists," I continued, neglecting to mention how much it had shocked me. "Such things exist in different cultures and at different stages of development. The United Confederation has always been proud of its tolerance for other lifestyles." I paused, trying to gather my scattered thoughts and calm my racing heart. "On the whole, all of this is interesting, but it isn't important because there's a much more important discovery we need to talk about."

Book One: Beyond the Fog

The room fell silent as dozens of eyes stared at me. Some of them looked interested while others looked skeptical. I took a deep breath. For a moment a fire burned in me again, but I didn't look at Sverr. I couldn't. If I did, I knew I wouldn't be able to say what I needed to.

"What is much more important and valuable is that we discovered a new life form on the fjords, one that was previously unknown."

My colleagues could barely hide their excitement. A few of them jumped up and the chairman pounded his mallet. "What do you mean exactly, Dr. Orway? What life form are you talking about? A new plant or animal species?"

"A new species..." I faltered. I turned my head slowly. Yes, he was looking at me. Sverr, whose blood wasn't human, who two hours ago had been caressing me so lustfully... "A new race. And maybe also a new species. The ilg we have here in front of us is not a human."

Now everyone leaped up.

"Do you understand how serious that is?" the chairman shouted over the growing din.

"Yes," I whispered. "I do."

Sverr stood up slowly, his eyes glued to me. It was like I was the only person in that huge conference room.

"What a smart lilgan," he said with a smirk. Only I heard him. And I was frightened. I took a step back.

"Well then, Dr. Orway, who do you think this barbarian is?" the chairman shouted.

"Yes, who am I, lilgan?" Sverr asked, a smile playing on his lips. He looked at me with interest, as though he were actually waiting for my answer.

I took another step away from him. As a certain respected scientist demonstrated, there was no such thing as intuition — just an accumulation of unprocessed signals received by our brain. Now it was like puzzle pieces were

The Charmed Fjords

coming together in my brain: Max's words, the two silhouettes of the hjeggs in the haze, the golden, snakelike eyes in the split second when the fog dispersed, the way the other tribespeople worshiped Sverr, his strength and narrowing pupils, the guesses and hypotheses, the red stripe on the analyzer. The nonexistent intuition pasted all those images together into a single picture.

"Who, Liv?" Sverr repeated.

"A dragon," I whispered, hardly believing that I was saying the word aloud.

"We actually say hjegg," the ilg answered softly. I began to tremble.

"A dragon?" "Did she say dragon?" "Did I hear that right?" "Is this a joke?" People were speaking all around me, but I could only see Sverr.

"Dr. Orway, are you joking?"

"No... I..."

"What evidence do you have? Are you seriously saying that this savage is the snake from the ancient religion of the northern peoples? The great fire-breathing snake? Are you in your right mind, Dr. Orway? What proof do you have besides your raging fantasies?"

"His blood has a different composition. I hope our guest will allow us to do some tests so we can map his genome," I said, barely audibly.

As soon as I said it, I knew Sverr wouldn't allow it.

He shook his head and I was struck by a terrible, chilling sense of foreboding. Yurgas appeared behind Sverr and grasped him by the elbow.

"I knew we'd have problems with this barbarian!" he said. "OK, buddy. No sudden movements, let's go. We'll let the scientists figure out what's going on with your blood — "

Before he got all the words out, Yurgas was flying through the air toward the opposite wall. Sverr turned his

Book One: Beyond the Fog

head and looked around, scowling. Yurgas was a burly man who was at least six feet tall, yet Sverr had just flung him thirty yards across the room like a stuffed animal.

A deafening silence fell over the room.

"Sverr, please don't," I squawked.

The scientists were frozen in place with their mouths ajar. The chairman imperceptibly pressed a panic button and armed men burst into the room. After that, everything became a blur: shouts, mayhem, orders. Someone shoved me, and a soldier in a black uniform and helmet bolted toward me.

"Don't worry, everyone. Everything's under control."

"What's under control? What are you doing? Stop!"

No one was listening to me anymore. I yelled and looked around. The guards had thrown an electrified net over Sverr and he was trying to wrench it off. He tore the metal net with his hands, and his upper lip broke into a grin. Blue sparks of electricity were flickering all around, threatening to start a fire. It was hard for me to see the ilg among all the men in black, but I caught occasional glimpses of him as he threw off his attackers. The men were pounding him with rubber clubs and poking at him with their stun guns.

"Be careful!" the chairman bellowed. "That's valuable genetic material there, and our only specimen! Careful! Take him to the lab right now."

I went cold. The noise, the shouts, and the growling were suddenly gone. There was nothing but a sepulchral cold and me, the anthropologist Olivia Orway, who had just done something horrid.

"Don't touch him! Let him go! Don't treat him like that!" I looked around in dismay and caught Anders Eriksen's eye. He looked at me reproachfully.

Or was I projecting my feelings about myself onto him? But I truly had good intentions and I only wanted what was

The Charmed Fjords

best: a breakthrough, a scientific phenomenon, a new milestone, a new race. It was unbelievable and we all knew it, so I thought everyone would share my awe. At the same time, I was expecting them to treat the ilg respectfully. After all, we lived in a progressive, developed civilization that was proud of its humanity. So how could these people act like this? What did they really care about?

Nothing but experiments, endless experiments. A cage. A lab. And then another expedition to the fjords to collect more rabbits? What would come after that?

I was filled with horror. What had I done?

"Let him go!" This time I yelled so loudly the scientists shuddered and the soldiers momentarily stopped their assault. Someone grabbed my elbow.

"Don't worry. The barbarian is no longer dangerous. Everything's under control."

"Don't touch me!" I shook off the hands grasping me and darted over to Sverr, who was growling. Incredibly, even after being shot with the stun guns, walloped with the clubs, and shocked by the net, he was still conscious and fighting. He was bellowing, hurling away his attackers, and diving under the arms holding weapons. His fur cape was flying, his eyes were shining, and his body was moving in a way that made it clear that killing was nothing new to him. A turn, a punch, a skull cracked under a helmet, and shrieking all around.

Then a shot rang out. Yurgas was kneeling next to the wall, squeezing his pistol.

Sverr fell over, and so did I. Blood spurted everywhere. My heart gurgled and nearly stopped.

"You idiots! Did you kill him? Have you lost your minds?" the chairman yelled.

"Get the woman away!"

"Liv, please..." someone, I think Klin, said to me.

Book One: Beyond the Fog

"He's breathing."

He was breathing?

I lifted my head and looked Sverr in the face. The black eyelashes with the sun-bleached tips were quivering. It was barely noticeable, but I could see it.

"Don't die... Please don't die!" I'd do anything to fix my mistake.

"Take him to the lab. Hurry up!" the chairman of the council finally said. "If we lose this ilg because of your guys, I'll write a complaint to the department."

Someone tried to pull me away again. This time it was Jean.

"Olivia, look at me!" Jean tugged at me and blocked my view of the soldiers lifting Sverr. His wolfskin still lay on the floor. "Liv! Get a hold of yourself! Everyone's looking at you! I understand that this spectacle would be hard for anyone, but I didn't think you of all people would... I can't believe what I saw."

"Dr. Orway, when will you be able to provide a more detailed report on your conclusions? How did you reach them? What connects you to this ilg?"

I threw Jean off me. My mind was moving frantically, like a bird trying to escape from a trap. Bitterness and a murderous fury were dancing in me. I was furious at myself, the council, and all these people.

A man with a look of icy politeness in his eyes loomed in front of me.

"Dr. Orway?" His voice was cold and hateful. His parka bore a small patch from the special unit of the Confederation. "Please come with me. We need to ask you some questions."

"I'm not going anywhere."

"Please don't put up a fight. It's in your best interest to come with us."

"I'm not going anywhere," I said emphatically, craning

The Charmed Fjords

my neck to catch a glimpse of Sverr.

The man scowled and took my arm.

"Don't touch me!"

"Dr. Orway, you're not yourself. We'll get you help."

"You and your help can go to hell!" I sneered. I no longer cared about being polite. I tried to evade this disagreeable man, but he grasped my shoulder, holding me back.

"Get your hands off me!"

"You're coming with us." Apparently he was tired of standing on ceremony with me, and he nodded to two men I hadn't noticed before. Moving in lock-step, they took up positions on each side of me and grasped my arms. "Please don't resist."

"Let me go!" I jerked my arms, trying to break free, but they were holding me too tightly. Panic tore through me, and I struggled to breathe. "Let go!"

"The barbarian opened his eyes." A surprised voice stopped everyone in their tracks. The soldiers in black were blocking the stretcher holding Sverr, so I couldn't see anything until they began to run every which way. Their faces all wore the same terrified expression.

"What the hell?"

"Who is this guy?"

"Holy shit! Emergency evacuation!"

In the ensuing chaos someone pushed me and I dropped to my knees. When I lifted my head, the first thing I saw was the familiar golden eyes. Then before I knew it, I saw his quickly changing body. The ilg turned dark, as though an enormous shadow were over him — a winged, spiked shadow. Then Sverr began to metamorphose. The next thing I knew, the human being disappeared completely. Right there in the middle of the conference room of the Academy of Progress, a monster stood. The hjegg. The winged snake — the dragon. A creature unknown to science. It was a huge, dull-black

Book One: Beyond the Fog

creature, with thick layers of scales on his body, a crest stretching from his forehead to the end of his tail, powerful wings, and the snakelike golden eyes with vertical pupils. The frightful eyes seemed to be looking for someone in the crowd of screeching, screaming, collapsing people.

The dragon idly lifted a clawed foot, brushing aside the nearest row of people. The soldiers rolled away like bowling pins. The magnificent auditorium of the Academy, which could hold up to a thousand people, was too small for this creature. The dragon's tail slapped against the arched windows, knocking out the glass along with chunks of the wall. The narrow head swung and the eyes stared unblinkingly at the crowd.

The security guards finally snapped into action and let loose a flurry of bullets, which bounced off the gleaming membranes of the dragon's scales with a clang. Crouching down, I tried to creep backward without anyone noticing. I had a feeling I knew who this creature who used to be Sverr was looking for. Or was this still Sverr? How was that even possible? Apparently even I didn't totally believe it was possible. I mean, it defied the laws of physics. All my common sense and scientific training told me it was impossible, but the scene in front of me told a different story: a dragon was smashing up the majestic auditorium of my beloved Academy.

"Maybe I'm on the fjords and this is just a dream?" I whispered under my breath, continuing to crawl away. "Maybe they put something in my drink and I'm having a nightmare?"

There was no way anyone could hear me in the din.

But the narrow head with the black crest jerked up and turned toward me. The large nostrils sniffed and let out two plumes of black smoke.

"Get away! Get away! Get the injured ones out of here!

The Charmed Fjords

Right now! Evacuate! We need reinforcement. This is an emergency."

Emergency was an understatement. There was a dragon in the room.

My back bumped into a step. I looked up. Right at that moment, the dragon took off. The huge wings spread and before I could even take a breath the monster overcame the distance between us. The powerful gust of wind the dragon's wings created knocked everyone off their feet. Then a massive foot grabbed me, squeezed me, and flipped me upside down. I began to scream, but then was struck by a coughing fit. Tears streamed down my face and my ears clogged. I was flummoxed and no longer knew where I was. The dragon made another circle, and at full speed smashed through the window and broke off half the wall. Shards of glass and splinters of wood rained down on me and I covered my head with the one arm that wasn't pinned to my body. Through my shock I realized that shots were still being fired at us and no one seemed to care that I was dangling from the hjegg's foot.

Chapter 15. Sverr

THE PAIN SCORCHED my chest. The lead had entered me through the right side of my body, under my ribs, and then stayed there. It wasn't lethal. I could handle it. And that was just what I planned to do — this wasn't the pain that would make me call my beast. I'd wait until they imprisoned me and then just walk out. Neither stone nor iron can stop the riar of Neroaldaf. But the humans got angry. They stung, bit, and pummeled me. Still, it was no big deal. But then Liv started to scream. That triggered the fury in me, and the fury of the beast was awakened.

The world changed again. It was different now. The humans were small and insignificant, the walls were flimsy, and I had wings. Fury and fire, claws and fangs.

This wasn't right. It wasn't supposed to happen this way. Damn it! Things weren't going according to plan. I should have just left inconspicuously. Never mind, I can feel my regret later, once I'm back in Neroaldaf. It's too late now. The hjegg was wailing as he flung off the people of the Confederation and nearly gave in to the urge to burn that auditorium to the ground. I scooped the girl up with my leg and soared into the sky. I remembered just in time that I'd need to fly low or else the lilgan would die. Humans are weak and always die if you carry them into the clouds. When they're up that high they either suffocate or freeze. My armor

The Charmed Fjords

and fire protected me from everything, while my fury goaded me to soar skyward, to the place where there were no worms with weapons. The iron in their hands spewed fire. What an insult! I was tempted to unleash all my power. Take that, humans!

But I contented myself with swinging my tail and smashing the wall.

The girl shouted something and I looked down in irritation. That traitor. What had made me decide to take her with me? I should have just left her there, but I couldn't bring myself to do that. No, I needed to take her with me. I needed to punish her and exact my revenge. The fire in me was boiling like lava and clouding my judgment. That's how it always is. It's hard to get hold of the beast and even harder to control him, and then to remain yourself after the merging and not dissolve into the hjegg's power.

"Fighter planes!" What on earth was she shouting? "They'll send the fighter planes after you!"

I exhaled smoke, holding back my fire for the time being. The lilgan was shouting about human planes. I knew all about those. I shook my head, releasing a smoke of crimson malice that blurs the vision and the brain. When I become the hjegg, it's easy to lose my wits, but right now I needed them more than ever. Did she say airplanes? I flew in one, and I could sense its might. But it was nothing but a heap of dead metal, a weapon. I'm stronger and faster. All I need to do is ascend higher and higher and they'll never catch me.

But I have the girl with me. I can't do that. If I fly higher she'll die. With her in my clutches I need to fly so low my belly nearly brushes against the roofs of the buildings. If I don't do that, by the time I get to the fjords I'll just have a corpse on my hands.

Then again, what do I care if she lives?

Book One: Beyond the Fog

I already got everything I needed. I found out what the humans know about the Fog — no more than us, it turns out. I didn't even find out what's making the Fog dissipate. What a useless trip.

I looked around. I needed to reach the cliffs, but the girl was right. There were planes coming after us, and soon they'd be too close for comfort.

I hissed angrily. The fire was boiling in me. I am strength. I am fury. I will annihilate them!

But I am also reason. I must keep remembering that. But I exhaled a stream of fire anyway so they could see who's boss. Just a small one, enough to set a roof aflame. I flew off above the buildings, not toward the forest. Down on the ground I could see minuscule people shouting and pointing. I longed to burn them, too. The People of the Lakes and Cliffs know what to do when the black hjegg flies overhead: hide and pray to the ancient firstborns. But here the people are stupid. I must punish them, and the only way to do that is to burn their homes. Then I must plunder their gold, abscond with their women, and help myself to whatever I want. Yes, burn it all.

I roared querulously but held back my destructive wrath. I'd made too many mistakes. These humans weren't supposed to know about me. But what was the point in regretting that now?

I held my fire back and summoned the thick haze. Clouds gathered below my wings. Under my power they darkened instantly, and lightning flashed inside them. A dense cloud enveloped me, concealing me from the humans and their planes. They'll never spot me. The hjegg growled but the storm calmed him and tickled his skin with bolts of lightning. My urge to decimate whatever lay in my path melted away.

"Sverr! Where are you taking me? It is still you, isn't it?

The Charmed Fjords

Sverr!"

That lilgan was trying to talk to me again. She was an idiot too, just like the rest of them. Who tries to talk when the hjegg is carrying them to his lair? She should have been sobbing, praying, and pledging her virginity, body, and whatever other gifts she had to offer.

Well, she did already give me her virginity. I remembered how tender, moist, and silky the lilgan had been, and how much I'd liked that. The dragon flame singed my throat again. Malice and irritation were throbbing and converging inside me. It's not supposed to be like this.

No, I'll make sure the girl survives, but I did toss her from leg to leg to shut her up. It worked. Apparently she had no feelings.

All the buildings were now behind me. I sped up, rushing toward the Fog. I was weaker now, but I had enough strength left to pass through, and to carry Liv with me. With my strength, I could do it. The humans had not yet penetrated the shroud of Fog — that was the only thing saving the fjords. But how long would that continue?

I felt my anger rise again and I beat my wings. I had to get back. Faster.

My home was beckoning me.

Left to my own devices, I would land on the spot on top of the riar's tower, but I can't do that now. The surface is granite and the girl would get smashed to bits, so I'll need to land on the grass near the fortress.

OLIVIA

At some point I must have blacked out. Maybe it was from shock when I glimpsed the elongated silhouette of the dragon in the reflective windows of the skyscraper and the beast

Book One: Beyond the Fog

throwing me in the air, or from the storm and the lightning sizzling alongside us, brushing against the beast's scales, or maybe it was just from lack of oxygen so high in the sky. When I regained consciousness, I saw water below, and in the distance I saw the green cliffs of the fjords. Had we actually crossed back through the Great Fog to the other side?

I tried to yell, but all I could manage was a faint squeak. My shoes had fallen off somewhere and my feet were numb. My blouse was torn. Admittedly, that was the least of my worries right now. But that's how our brains work — we fixate on minor details to protect ourselves from shock. In this case, there was no way I could make sense of what had happened. I felt like I was either in a dream or I was delirious. My brain couldn't find any logical explanations or accept what had happened, both at the Academy and right now. A single word kept repeating in my head like a broken record: impossible. It was still impossible when the monster nosedived and unclenched his leg right above the ground. I rolled through the tall grass, all the way to the edge of the sea.

The dragon breathed out a flame onto the closest tree, turning it into a lantern, and lay down and flattened his wings. His silhouette began to flail and then it turned into a shadow. In a split second, Sverr stood up. It was the same Sverr who had been with me in the conference room, except now he wasn't wearing his hide.

He was also missing the bullet hole in his chest — the only sign of the skirmish at the Academy was a red scar and drops of dried blood on his skin.

"Get up," he barked and began untying a narrow boat from a nearby pillar.

"This is impossible," I said, speaking my thoughts. "It's physically impossible. Body mass and conservation of energy don't just go away. This makes no sense."

The Charmed Fjords

Sverr looked at me sideways and let out a bellow. I shuddered at the memory of the winged beast that had carried me across the sky.

"Get in the boat, lilgan!"

I leaped up, climbed into the rickety vessel, and settled down. Sverr gave it a shove, stepped into the water, and jumped in beside me. There was only one oar. With confident, even strokes, Sverr began paddling to the opposite shore.

"It's just not possible," I whispered.

Sverr didn't respond. He was frowning and it looked to me like he was getting angry. His forehead was creased and his pupils narrowed, and now I could see clearly that they weren't human.

"It doesn't add up."

"Enough! the ilg barked. "I'm sick of listening to this."

"So will you explain everything to me?" I asked, perking up. "How is it possible?"

"I'm not explaining anything to you, Liv." Sverr cut me off. He stood up and looked behind me. I could hear shouting from somewhere. With a jolt, I turned to follow his gaze. There were people running along the pier, which jutted into the water like a big tongue. The men were wearing cloth trousers and shirts with wide belts on top. Some of them wore sleeveless shirts that revealed their strong arms adorned in iron bracelets. A couple of them were wearing trench coats. All of them had some sort of weapon dangling by their sides: I saw knives, swords, spears, and even axes. Leather breastplates and boots completed their outfits. I could make out their weather-beaten, stern faces and dark hair, but they were too far away for me to be sure of what color their eyes were. I had the impression they were rather dark, though — either amber or light brown.

Sverr steered the boat toward the shore, passing a dock meant for tall ships, and a few minutes later the bottom

Book One: Beyond the Fog

scratched along the sand and he straightened up. When the boat approached, all the men bowed their heads in unison. A few of them ran into the water to pull the boat ashore.

Sverr stepped onto the sand.

"Greetings, riar," a towering man with streaks of gray hair said. He spoke with a noticeable accent, but I could still understand him. He used words I knew, but his pronunciation of some of the sounds was different enough to make it seem like he was actually speaking a different language. "It's been a while."

"All the best to you, Laif," Sverr said. Sverr glanced at me quickly. "Lock this lilgan in a room and guard the door. Don't let her go anywhere." He took a step and then stopped. He scowled at me, as though he were mad at himself for bringing me here. "Don't harm her. Feed her and give her clothes," he muttered.

Without looking at me again, he strode off. A burly guy pulled me out of the boat, threw me over his shoulder, and waded through the water to the beach. The men looked at me with a mixture of surprise and irateness. Some of them screwed up their faces in confusion. One of them peeled off his heavy linen trench coat and threw it over me. It covered me from head to toe.

"Looks like the riar has brought another outsider back. Where'd you get to be so shameless? Take this and at least cover up your private parts."

I looked down at my clothes. I was wearing a designer knee-length skirt, which revealed the edge of my stockings that had slipped down, and a silk blouse with a torn-off sleeve. I laughed hysterically. Indeed, all my private parts!

Someone gave me a gentle push.

"Move it."

I started to walk, but then stopped and exclaimed in surprise.

The Charmed Fjords

Up ahead, a city loomed on top of the cliffs. It was surrounded by a wall, and the central entrance, which was at least thirty yards high, was shaped like a dragon's grinning mouth. Instead of fangs, there were iron blades, and I shuddered at the thought of them closing down on me and pulverizing all my bones. Behind the dragon's head, there were buildings perched on the cliffs: some had red roofs, while others were topped with overgrown dark green grass that flowed downward like a living curtain. There were stone bridges whose arches hung over the waterfalls. The sharp peaks of the black cliffs formed a perimeter around the city like extended fingers and protruded into the sea. White seagulls circled and surged through the sky. A tall staircase led to the upper city, where buildings with delicate terraces towered. The city stood on many tiers carved into the cliffs, and was joined in a latticework of arches, cornices, enclosures, and roofs. Deep in the city, a tower as tall as a skyscraper ascended so high it seemed to be holding up the clouds. A spiral staircase without railings wound upward on its outer facade. Who in their right mind would walk down those hundreds of slippery steps? Someone who wasn't afraid to fall, I supposed.

"Do you like it?" Laif smirked into his beard. "That's Neroaldaf, girl. The best place on Earth. You should be proud you ended up here. Look over there, you see?" He pointed to some pillars standing along the sides of the city: six on the left and six on the right. A hjegg with outstretched wings sat on top of each one. From my vantage point on the shore they looked terrifyingly real. I felt a tremor pass through me, but then I realized they were only made of stone. "Those are the twelve founders of Neroaldaf, our riar's ancestors. They're all Lagerhjegg's children."

He sounded especially proud when he said "Lagerhjegg."

Book One: Beyond the Fog

"But how..." I mumbled in amazement, unable to finish my thought. I desperately wanted to know how they could build such a huge city on the cliffs without modern machines, cranes, or equipment. How could they erect those gigantic bridges and statues, and the tower that grazed the clouds? Who beveled the stone to create those extraordinary sculptures of the hjeggs? Slaves? Captives like me?

I looked at the sea. Long, narrow, wooden ships with high bows shaped into terrifying, leering creatures were bobbing on the water off the pier. I stopped walking to examine an intricate carving on a tree. It also depicted dragons, but they didn't look like Sverr. The wings were narrow, more like fins. Was it a sea dragon, maybe that mythical Nerdhjegg?

The men kept dragging me along, so I didn't have a chance to look closely.

"Enough staring. You can admire everything later. That is, if the riar allows it," one of the men said.

I approached the dragon's mouth with some trepidation, but walked through it into the city without losing any body parts. Now I could see all the details of the city up close: the ironwork on the windows and doors of the buildings, the stone-fortified embankment, and the black-and-gold banners fluttering over the tower.

"Neroaldaf is the only city that has the right to go into battle with Lagerhjegg on its flags," my guide told me proudly.

"Why is that?"

"Because when it came time to choose a seal, every child of the black hjegg wanted to take the image of Lagerhjegg for themselves," the peasant snickered with a sidelong look at me. "But the first riar of Neroaldaf was faster and stronger. He killed all of them."

The men laughed — they clearly told this story often. I just shook my head, continuing to take everything in.

The Charmed Fjords

The chimneys were smoking and the air smelled of cooked meat, fresh bread, spices, the grass that hung down from the roofs, and the ever-present salty sea. I also detected a faint smell of ashes. I inhaled deeply, feeling all the fragrances with my whole body. Here on the fjords they seemed to be both sweeter and more vivid. We continued along the embankment, which was paved in smooth cobblestones that cut into my bare feet. As much as I was enjoying the sights, I couldn't forget how numb my legs were from the cold. I stumbled along awkwardly. The young guy who had taken me out of the boat hissed in annoyance and threw me over his shoulders, so again I was hanging upside down. I tried to resist, but he kept carrying me to the tower. On the way I tried to register the details of this world. Snapshots of a life totally unlike mine flashed before me: the open door of a bakery, where a flame was sizzling and cooks were scurrying about; a woman beating a blanket made of bright scraps of cloth; a little girl running somewhere, clutching the skirt of her dark blue dress, her hair ribbons whipping in the breeze; two guys with enormous dogs on leashes who stopped to stare at us, as the dogs silently turned their yellow eyes toward me. I realized they weren't dogs, but wolves — actual wolves, not stone ones. We reached an iron door on which two black, unsheathed swords were crossed, stuck in the fold of the door for all eternity. Instead of entering, we turned into a narrow lane behind the tower. We followed it until it dead-ended. The guy who was carrying me tossed me to the ground like a sack of potatoes and pushed me through a low door.

"You stay here for a while," he ordered, gently but firmly, shoving me inside the room. "Then I'll decide where to put you. Or the riar will decide. I don't have any empty rooms in my house. For a girl like you this is good enough."

"Like what?" I asked in dismay, looking around

Book One: Beyond the Fog

nervously.

"You know. An outsider, and a shameless one too. Stay here."

With that, he left and the heavy door slammed behind him. I heaved a sigh and sank down on a crude bench against the wall.

"This is great," I said gloomily, looking around the room. "Well, it's not a tent. That's something to be happy about."

It may not have been a tent, but the room was tiny, like a storage closet. That might have been exactly what it was — wooden trunks with iron rims were pushed up against the walls. Naturally there was no bed, table, or shower. As I was thinking about my natural needs, the door opened and a gray-haired woman wearing a long dress and kerchief came in and plunked a tray holding food on one of the trunks. She also slammed down a round vessel.

"Here's a latrine for you if you can't wait," she snorted. She scurried out and the door closed again.

"Thank you," I said, too late for her to hear me.

A fresh sea breeze and the sound of people wafted in through a small window. Someone laughed heartily, metal jangled somewhere nearby, and a woman's voice called out. Some dogs began to bark. It was just like back home, where humans lived. Except that these weren't humans, were they? Or were they all humans?

I shook my head, trying to clear the fog in my brain. As a scientist, I knew that everything has a rational explanation. You just need to find it. I knew I would find it — if I managed to survive, that is.

But I'd have to start looking later. Right now I needed to tend to more mundane matters, like my weakened body. I pulled the tray toward me. It held a dish of thick broth and a mug filled with a fragrant liquid. I studied the spoon. I noticed

The Charmed Fjords

that all the dishware was iron or wooden. I was interested to see that the level of progress was clearly higher than in the tribe I'd already visited, but it wasn't like what I was accustomed to. It reminded me of the dark ages, what with the swords, handwoven clothing, trunks, and fortified wall. But they had plumbing and a sewage system? The city was clean, which wasn't the case in the history of the Confederation. I hadn't seen any ditches with feces, and my bare feet hadn't gotten too dirty — it was like the paving stones had been washed. And the people looked well groomed: the men were clean shaven or bearded, and their clothing was neat. Whatever. These riddles could also wait until later. I took a spoonful of the steaming, tasty broth and closed my eyes in satisfaction. It was hearty and scalding, with chunks of potatoes, carrots, and meat. I crunched the piece of pancake that was like a red crust and savored the melted, creamy butter. It was so delicious I nearly swallowed my tongue. The mug held a steaming drink made of lingonberry laced with honey. Did all the tribes here feed guests so well or had I just gotten lucky? My frozen body began to warm up, but I still enveloped myself in the wrap the guy had thrown over me. I was glad no one had taken it away.

Maybe he felt sorry for me? Or did he have designs on me?

I stopped to think with a spoonful of soup halfway to my mouth. All right, I'd deal with the riddles of the dragon and the city later, too. I didn't have enough information yet to come up with any theories. But why on earth had Sverr brought me here?

I forced myself to swallow. There was only one possible answer: he wanted to get revenge.

The ilg wasn't counting on me figuring out his secret. That's why he behaved calmly, and mocked, and even

Book One: Beyond the Fog

seduced, in his barbarian manner. After all, I had no facts. I only had suppositions, and the blood I'd drawn while we were having sex.

The soup suddenly tasted bitter. Based on my imprisonment in this little room and the things the men had said, I supposed I shouldn't expect anyone to roll out the red carpet for me.

But then what should I expect?

Dozens of possibilities started running through my scientist's brain, each one more frightening than the last. I gnashed my teeth. I managed to thoroughly scare myself before the door even opened. It would be better to eat and take advantage of the bedpan no matter how disgusting it was, and try to plot my next move. For starters, I could look to see what was in these trunks. Maybe I'd find what I needed.

My plan was thwarted, though, because all the trunks were shut with heavy padlocks. I also tried pushing on the door, but it was locked too. The window was so small not even a child could fit through it. I climbed up on one of the trunks and tried to get a glimpse of the street. I couldn't see much — just the stone wall of the tower in the distance, the edge of a cart, and the back of a horse. I seemed to be in some sort of household buildings — I wasn't even worthy of a room for a person. I wondered who Sverr represented for the locals. It was clear that he wasn't the lowest of the low. Then again, he wasn't even a human.

My brain stumbled again.

Better not to think.

But then I caught sight of some blond hair, blue eyes, and a large nose.

"Irvin!"

The ilg turned in surprise, trying to figure out where my voice was coming from.

"Is that you?" he frowned. "It's you! So Sverr's back?"

The Charmed Fjords

"Yes," was all I managed to say.

"And they've locked you up?" Irvin chuckled insolently. "In the storeroom?"

"I see you've lost your animal skull," I retorted. "And you changed your clothes. What happened? You got tired of running around the forest in the buff, Irvin?"

"Watch it, outsider," Irvin said, coming closer to me. He was now dressed almost like the other people in the city. He was enveloped in a trench coat with white fur and cuffs sewn with blue and silver thread. A dragon bared its teeth on his heavy iron belt buckle. "You can lose your head if you say things like that. We've tolerated a lot from the people from beyond the Fog — insulting our traditions, greedy curiosity, defiance of our customs. I don't know how Sverr put up with it all. I would have beheaded all of you and been done with it."

I anxiously clutched the window. "So are you saying that everything we saw was a lie? A show?"

"Putting together a show like that was too good for you," Irvin snorted. "You just saw the southern tribe. They speak a different language and have a different way of life, but we obey the basic laws of the fjords in the same way. By the way, don't tell anyone what tribe I was born to." He calmed down and started laughing insolently again. "Why are you in this shed? And where are your friends?"

"I'm the only one here." My voice shook and I coughed. Apparently I was frozen after all. The coughing fit was so overpowering that I doubled over, and when I finally straightened up Irvin was already in the room. He looked at my bare feet, mussed dirty hair, and torn clothing.

"Come with me. Fast!" he commanded.

"But Irvin-hjegg, the riar ordered — " the guy guarding the door started stamping his feet but stopped when he saw the look on Irvin's face. I bolted out of my cage and decided

Book One: Beyond the Fog

that it was better to be with Irvin than inside.

Irvin walked on, keeping his eyes straight ahead. I followed him, hopscotching along the pebbles and feeling lifted by the breeze. It was colder here in Neroaldaf than on the lands of the tribe at the base of Gorlohum. I wondered how far we were from the Fog.

We walked along the stone wall, which in places was wound with ivy. We turned into an opening and crossed a sprawling courtyard. The people we passed looked at me with interest, and I stared back at them. They looked just like people you'd meet anywhere. There were peasant men, and women in dresses, all of them busy with ordinary tasks: some were cleaning their battleaxes, some were feeding livestock, some were piecing a wheel onto a cart. There were no flames, claws, or fangs in sight. Not only that, I didn't see any acrimony at all. Everyone looked at me with the most run-of-the-mill curiosity and even good-natured amusement.

Just like any human beings.

I'd just had this thought when I caught sight of a wall charred to blackness. But it was a stone wall. It was as though a flamethrower had passed along it — even the stone had sintered, and the edge of the wall jutted out under the effects of incredible heat and hardened like a knobby growth.

I wanted to ask Irvin about it, but it was hard to talk while I was running, and I was too hoarse from coughing.

We reached a door. Irvin bent down to pass through and I followed him. When I got inside I couldn't contain my excitement. "Wow!"

In front of me was a cave — by the look of it, a natural one. The best part was that there was a hot spring under the water. I could tell because drops of water streamed down the low arches, and in the center of the cave the water was dark and shrouded in steam.

"Get in," Irvin said.

The Charmed Fjords

I wondered how deep the water was. I remembered another time I went into the water and ended up tied to a sacrificial pillar. But this time I wasn't given a chance to think about it.

"Now!" Irvin ordered. "If you don't hurry up I'll throw you in."

I cursed him silently and decided that with a little imagination, my underwear could work as a bathing suit.

I chuckled as I remembered how the ilgs had called my clothing by a city designer my private parts. What would the ilgs say if they saw my lacy underpants?

I hastily pulled off my clothes, sat down on the edge of a rock, and put my feet in the water. I moaned in glee when the wet heat enveloped my body.

"I hope the hjegg doesn't hang around here," I muttered, sliding into the water. When I emerged, I saw that Irvin was laughing, but I didn't understand why.

I grasped the edge and dangled in the scalding water. It occurred to me that I could combine business with pleasure and try to ask Irvin some questions. Since he was smiling, maybe he'd be cooperative.

"Say, Irvin, what's a lilgan? Is it a slave?" I shook out my wet curls and looked up at him. The water was black and opaque, and the steam was wrapping me like a cloak.

"She's a debtor," Irvin smirked. He shrugged off his trench coat and crouched down on his haunches. "She's the one for whose sake a man spills someone else's blood in order to protect her or get revenge. The lilgan can't hurt her protector, and he'll do whatever he wants when the time comes. The riar paid your debt and the price was very high: the hjegg's blood."

I nodded. It was more or less clear: I'd violated a tribal taboo and by killing the hjegg Sverr had paid my debt. So that meant I'd become his debtor. Then I'd brought him to my

Book One: Beyond the Fog

world, my home, and the Confederation council. Apparently that was why a beast had been killed in that lake. But I hadn't wanted to allow Sverr to leave the fjords. I felt the danger, but I'd still allowed him. I'd allowed everything.

I frowned. The mechanism of this strange connection between the lilgan and protector was yet another thing I'd need to try to figure out later.

"I understand. Why is it cold here? It was much warmer where the tribe is."

"We're much farther away from Gorlohum."

"How much farther, exactly?"

"Farther."

I could see that Irvin wouldn't tell me anything he didn't want to, so I didn't push it. He smiled as he looked down at me.

"There are fifty caves like this in Neroaldaf. Some of them belong to noble city residents, and some of them are public. Do you like it?"

"Who does this one belong to?" I asked, suddenly a bit scared. Irvin smiled again.

"This one is mine," he said. "You know, you're unusual. Although you are an outsider. Your skin is so light. It looks like snow in the water."

He drew himself up and began to undress. I watched in bewilderment as the clothes fell off his body and he plunged into the black water. He surfaced, blew out, and broke into a huge smile.

I wondered if I should be frightened, and if there was some sort of sexual undercurrent to this behavior. It certainly seemed like it to me. But the ilgs were different — I'd already seen that firsthand. Maybe Irvin also just wanted to warm up, and that was all there was to it.

But then he did a broad stroke that brought him right in front of me. He reached out and pinned me to the stone

The Charmed Fjords

wall.

"Tell me, outsider, why are you still alive? Why did Sverr bring you to his home? I really don't like that, outsider. He'll be angry by nightfall. I think you should tell me everything right now," he drawled, and I noticed with horror that his pupils were changing.

"Don't touch me, or else..." I jerked away, forgetting my trust. There sure was an implication in Irvin's actions, and what an implication it was.

"Or else what?" he sneered. "You still haven't figured it out, outsider? You don't have your guards or your stun guns here. You no longer exist. You're a captive in Neroaldaf, and that means you have no rights. You're not even very valuable — you were locked in the storage room." Irvin licked the water off my cheek and his voice became muffled. "If I decide I like you, I'll take you, outsider. So just try. Will you surprise me?"

"My name is Olivia Orway! Don't you dare touch me!" Overcome with rage, I slapped the ilg across the face with all my might. My hand left a white mark on his swarthy skin. The impact threw me off balance and I slid off the wall. I dropped down into the water and immediately felt something scaly and alive wind around my legs.

The terror took all the oxygen I had left out of my lungs. Was it some kind of aquatic snake?

A hjegg?

Irvin.

A flame burst above, briefly illuminating the dark depths. I saw there was no longer a man standing there. Deep in the water, specks of light glided along the scales of an enormous water snake, which wrapped its tail around me and pulled me down.

I flailed my arms, trying to break free and catch my breath. Up above me I saw another flash, and then through the shroud of water I caught sight of Sverr's face.

Book One: Beyond the Fog

Suddenly the mortal embrace loosened and I surfaced, gasping for air.

Irvin emerged beside me, shot me a mocking look, and spread his arms on the opposite side of the basin.

"It's nice to see you, Sverr," he said without a trace of shame.

Sverr looked down at us and said nothing, and then shook his head and looked at the man who was shifting his feet next to him.

"If I ever hear again that you've disobeyed my orders, you'll be fed to the wolves," Sverr said quietly. His golden eyes flashed even though his face remained expressionless.

"But Irvin-hjegg ordered — " the man began, but stopped when he saw Sverr's withering look. He hunched his head into his shoulders.

"Irvin, meet me in my chambers," Sverr barked. He turned on his heels and stalked out.

Irvin looked at me pensively and then, to my surprise, vanished into the water. His clothes were lying next to the pool.

"Come on, outsider," the peasant ordered grimly. "No more provoking the hjegg. There's nothing he likes more than when a maiden chatters in the water. Everyone knows that. Get out of the water. I'll turn around. You'll be sent to the inferno of Gorlohum. Then there will be countless misfortune. When the hjeggs are angry, it's better to get out of the way. The riar is furious — I can already see it."

The man had already turned his back to me and was muttering something else. I dragged myself up onto the burning stone. I peeled off my wet underwear, deciding it was no great loss, and rubbed myself with the linen trench coat I was wearing before. Then, without giving it a second thought, I pulled on Irvin's trousers and warm, sleeveless shirt. I rolled, tied, and wrapped everything in the trench coat with

The Charmed Fjords

the white fur.

The peasant cried out when he turned around and saw me. "Oh, outsider, you're wicked! You know wicked people don't live long, don't you?"

"They don't live long with pneumonia either," I said, tucking my feet into Irvin's boots. Of course they were huge, but it was better than going barefoot. "Or with inflammation of the lungs, without antibiotics. You don't have antibiotics here, do you? That's what I figured. I'll catch all those things if I walk around wet and naked. Where are you supposed to take me? Back to the storage room?"

"Hurry up," the man said in surprise. "You wicked girl, you say you won't catch anything, and to make things worse you're talkative. No matter. The talkative ones don't live long either."

"Is there anyone around here who actually does live? Or have they all been slaughtered?" I couldn't contain myself. The man didn't answer, but I noticed a smile creeping onto his lips.

Chapter 16. Olivia

"STOP!" I hung back when we arrived at the door to the dreaded storeroom. "Can I have some paper and a pen? Or even a little piece of coal to write with? And some coffee? Just a little cup, and I promise to sit here as quiet as a mouse!"

The man shook his head. "Oh, you wicked thing! Did the riar drop you when he was carrying you? I think he must have," he said. "Where do you think you are? We don't have any coffee! Come on, in you go."

I stepped inside and once again the door locked behind me. But at least this time I was clean, fed, and wearing warm clothes. Not bad, all things considered. Not only that, now I had a chamberpot and I could certainly lie down on the trunks and think things over.

I took stock of what I knew now. It looked like there was a second hjegg. So that meant Irvin wasn't human either. I was tired of shouting, "That's impossible." It was time I just reconciled myself to a different reality. Yes, it was illogical and incomprehensible, but that didn't mean it couldn't also be solid and tangible. My inner scientist smiled, gleeful at the prospect of learning more about the fjords. But on the outside, a frightened, disoriented woman hung her head. I shoved her away and told her to leave me in peace to think.

OK, so there were two hjeggs, and they were different.

The Charmed Fjords

Irvin, who has blond hair and blue eyes, transformed suddenly in the water. I also remembered that he shouted a command the day I saw the strange animal in the water. And the women from the tribe mentioned four hjeggs. One in the sky, one in the water, and one in the snow. Then there was the one who couldn't be named.

If I had to take a guess, I'd say that Sverr was the black fire-breathing dragon and Irvin was the water sprite. Or the water hjegg? Lagerhjegg and Njordhjegg — that's what the aborigine women had called them. Out of habit I jumped up to look for paper so I could write everything down. But then I remembered where I was and I settled back down on the trunk and scowled in irritation. There was no coffee here, and maybe there wasn't any paper either. I'd need to wait until I got home to drink coffee.

I bit my lip. When I got home, not if. Of course I would be going home.

SVERR

"So, Irvin, I don't think I've counted your teeth in a while, have I?"

"Did it bother you that I was paying attention to the outsider? Why? Anyway, why is she here? So the fish can eat her?"

I flew at him. Irvin was unrivaled in the water, but it was a different story on land. Here he always yielded to me, even in his human form. If he'd been wearing clothes I would have grabbed them and shaken him like he deserved. Then I would have bashed his face in to wipe off that smirk. But right now that bastard hadn't gotten dressed and he wasn't even dry yet. That meant he knew there was a possibility of a fight — it would be harder for me to catch a slippery body.

Book One: Beyond the Fog

But I wasn't planning on catching him or fighting with him at the moment even though I was so angry I couldn't see straight.

"Don't you dare go anywhere near her," I said softly, enunciating each word clearly to make my point.

Irvin narrowed his eyes and looked to the side, and like he always did, reached for the carafe of wine. Unable to contain myself, I seized it from him and sneered.

"If you touch what's mine, you'll regret it."

Irvin's smile faded.

"You never refused me anything before, riar. Not wine or..."

He trailed off. He obviously understood that I wasn't in the mood for fun right now and it would be better to hold off on the mockery. Admittedly, it was hard not to understand that. I knew that right now my eyes were starting to look like the animal's and the black shadow of my hjegg was so close that Irvin was uneasy. I used all my willpower to stop the merging and Irvin saw that and moved away from me. But he couldn't keep himself from saying sarcastically, "She's just a captive, Sverr. Isn't that right?" And with that, he took another step back. He shook his head and drops of water splashed from his hair. "By the way, I'm happy to see you too. I'm glad my riar came back alive and in one piece. How'd everything go?"

"Bad!" I barked. But the fury inside me died down a bit. I looked at the wine in my hand, downed a gulp, and put the carafe down a little farther away. I eyed Irvin. "Don't get near that girl, understand? Neroaldaf is full of girls you can swim with, Irvin. I didn't pull the maiden through the Fog so you could have a good time with her."

"You pulled her through the Fog?" Irvin frowned. "Hold on, Sverr. Are you saying you called your hjegg?"

"Yes." I rubbed my eyes wearily. "Irvin, I made a

The Charmed Fjords

mistake. And I merged with him before I came back to the fjords."

"How much time before?" Irvin asked tensely. I struggled to hold back a roar. My a-tem always asked the right questions.

"The humans saw the black beast," I answered curtly.

"Great Gorlohum!" Irvin bellowed. Red spots started breaking out on his face. He was getting angry. Or was he frightened? "But why? So you'd be torn to pieces? How could you let that happen? People in the Confederation saw the hjegg? Are you out of your mind, Sverr? And on top of that you took that girl with you? Damn!"

"It's too late to yell about this!" I screamed at him. "What's done is done. I'm responsible for my mistake and I'll fix it. Right now the most important thing is to secure the fjords. We've misjudged the situation with the Fog. The hole is in three places now, not just one. The humans showed the places where the Fog is dispersing. They're all in the free lands. Today we're going to send units to every hole with an order not to let anyone in. If anyone makes their way onto the fjords, we feed them to the wolves and fish. Today the Fog is thick again and no one will be able to pass through. I had to summon the hjegg's fury to outwit the humans and get back here. But who knows what will happen tomorrow? What if the Fog suddenly thins so much that the humans can come in on their own? If that happens, we'll be there to meet them."

"Do you know where the holes are?" Irvin asked, livening up.

I nodded and motioned to him to hand me a map. A couple of minutes later I was giving Irvin orders and indicating the places that the old researcher had pointed out at the council meeting. I tried not to think about what Irvin left unsaid, and about why I'd called the hjegg. Was it really impossible for me to tolerate the pain? No, I could. I tolerated

Book One: Beyond the Fog

more than that. That tiny lead pin couldn't break me. I'd been planning to leave the world of the humans imperceptibly — after all, the people of the Confederation liked to hide captives in iron or stone receptacles, but what iron or stone could hold me back? None. I was planning to learn everything I could and slip out of the city at night unnoticed. The Academy building was also stone, and that meant I'd easily disappear.

Damn it! May Gorlohum swallow all of them!

All that would have happened if only...

But the call had been spontaneous and I wasn't even aware of it. It was as though I hadn't summoned the hjegg, but instead he'd come on his own without my call. But that was impossible. I instinctively touched the black stone around my neck. The ring of Gorlohum gives the wearer power over the beast. That's how it's always been. And the beast doesn't come without being called by a human. But on the other side of the Fog, I didn't call him. I only felt my body transform and the beastly fury burn. But why?

I had to figure it out.

I needed to try to remember everything and understand, because deep down I knew that what had happened in that auditorium was very important.

But right now I had no idea what it meant.

Irvin walked out, yelling orders to bring him his clothes and weapons. I heaved a sigh and ran a hand over the bristles on my face. The girl was locked up again. I needed to decide what to do with her. And I somehow needed to cope with the fury that kept taking over me because of her. Just a few minutes ago I wanted to rip Irvin's throat out. Without the beast — just with my hands. And Irvin had seen that desire. That's why he'd stopped mocking me, and then stopped to think.

I didn't like any of this at all. He was angry, but I wasn't entitled to rage. That meant I needed to make a decision.

The Charmed Fjords

Neroaldaf depended on it.

OLIVIA

When I heard the door scrape, I jumped off the trunk I was lying on. The door flew open and Sverr entered the low-ceilinged room, ducking his head. He stopped and looked at me.

"I'm only going to say this once, Olivia Orway, so you'd better remember," he said. "Forget who you are. On my land you're an outsider, nothing more. If you want to live, don't make me angry."

"Talkative, wicked people don't live long. I got it." The words escaped me before I had a chance to think. Sverr narrowed his eyes in a way I didn't like.

"That's right."

"Well then, Sverr. What do I need to do now?"

Sverr looked at me unblinkingly, making me squirm. Here, on his own turf, Sverr was different. He was no longer an ilg wearing a hide, and he wasn't a savage stealing a pen with a smile. He hadn't just changed his clothes — it was as though he had cast off a sickeningly familiar role and become himself. But I didn't know who that was, and I had no clue how to behave with him. Memories surged through my head — his hands, words, caresses. It felt like a dream.

"You cause a lot of trouble, lilgan," Sverr mused, as if he were thinking out loud. "There's nowhere for you to run. Don't even bother thinking about it. Neroaldaf is surrounded by the ocean on three sides, and the water is full of wild hjeggs, in case you haven't figured that out yet. On the fourth side there are the cliffs, the forest, and wolves. There are a lot of animals here, Liv. There are animals you've never even heard of."

Book One: Beyond the Fog

"And?" I asked, frowning.

Sverr stepped closer to me, hooked his fingers under my chin, and lifted it.

"Why do I bother with you, Olivia Orway?" he asked in an odd voice. It was as though he were asking himself, not me. "Why should I feed you, shelter you, and chase away the people who want to take possession of you? Why should I fuss over a daughter of the Confederation if it would be easier to kill her and forget about her? Can you tell me that?"

I stared into his golden eyes without saying anything — those eyes in which the familiar flame of desire was already burning. Sverr's breath quickened. Worse than that, my body was already beginning to quiver in response.

"Yes, killing me would be easier. That's acceptable where you come from, right?" I exhaled and said quickly, "Did you put Maximilian in the coma, Sverr?"

"He behaved honorably," Sverr replied calmly. Apparently my resentment made no impression on him. "And I gave him the option of returning to the world of the living. If he can, if he finds the path, he'll return. Now it's all up to him. It's an honorable choice for someone who wanted to destroy my people and land."

"He was only a scientist. A researcher!" I yelled. "He never hurt anyone! What did you do to him? Did you poison him?"

"Only cowards and women use poison," Sverr smirked. "I just showed him what he wanted to see. The hjegg."

"You killed him," I whispered, staring into the golden eyes furiously. "He's just an old man. Max is still unconscious because of you."

Sverr only raised his eyebrows, showing me he couldn't care less about my accusations.

"So why should I preserve your life, lilgan?" He pulled me toward him powerfully and strongly, pinning me to his

The Charmed Fjords

tense body. "I see you like clothing that gives me an urge to rip it off. Only the maiden warrior is allowed to wear trousers. And you stole these from a hjegg. You should be fed to the fish for that. And because you tricked me to take my blood." His sinewy hand lay on my waist and pressed it. Unmistakable lust flashed in the gold of his eyes. Sverr bowed his head and his voice grew softer. "I don't hold it against you, Liv. You're a child of your own people. I'm only angry at the betrayal. And I don't know why I should protect you. But you could try to convince me. You could ask. You could surrender. Right now."

Sverr pushed me up against the wall, in a narrow space between two trunks. He pressed my back to the logs. With a smooth motion he tore off the trench coat and jerked the string on the pants that were too wide for me. The flame that bubbled inside me like lava clouded my brain and made me forget about everything. His callused fingers assertively touched my skin and he breathed heavily and laboriously.

"Silky lilgan. Everywhere you're like a flower petal. I never want to stop touching you."

He caressed me slowly and I sighed in contentment despite myself. I nearly surrendered to his hand, with its strong fingers. His call reverberated in me like a fire, and it filled my veins with a tantalizing, liquid flame and a foretaste of ecstasy.

"I want you to show me everything humans do," he whispered feverishly. "I want to do everything with you. But that will need to wait until next time. Right now just make peace with it, Liv. Accept it. I need your submission."

The order echoed inside me like a sweet pain. I wanted it. Oh, how I wanted it.

But what about Max? And my pride? And my promise to never kneel before anyone? Never! I'd sworn an oath to myself. Was there anything of Olivia Orway left, or had

Book One: Beyond the Fog

everything vanished into thin air?

My anger at myself brought me to my senses.

"No!" I shoved Sverr and held his arm away from me. "No!" Do you think I'll do that to save my own life?"

"Why wouldn't you?" He also got angry. I could see his jaw clench and his pupils begin to metamorphose. "Any woman with a brain would do it. She'd think it was an honor."

So, any woman?

"Go to hell, hjegg!" My rage was more powerful than Sverr's call. I was steaming so much I couldn't breathe. An irrational, feminine resentment began to boil inside me, and my head cleared. "Let go of me!"

"So you're refusing?" He grinned like an animal. "You're resisting me again? No one resists the riar of Neroaldaf. No captive, and not even a freeborn maiden."

"I'm not like any of the women from your world." My anger was building.

"But now you are one of them. And if you want to live, you'll get down on your knees, Olivia."

"No way in hell!"

Sverr took away his hand and slammed it on the log next to my ear.

"You didn't understand me," he said, drawing out every word. "Your world no longer exists. There's only mine. And here I decide who lives and how."

"You're proposing that I become your..." I faltered, swallowing the word that was rolling on my tongue. The word from my world that meant a woman who sold her body.

Anger mingled with pride and, for some reason, sadness. All my feelings were a hundred times sharper here on the fjords. Anger, resentment, bewilderment, hope, disillusionment... Something strange was happening to me, my reason was dissipating under the onslaught of instincts and feelings, and I couldn't deal with it. Now the emotions

The Charmed Fjords

that had been locked up for years were fermenting, taking away my ability to think clearly. I wanted to scream. Or hit him. I wanted to push him away. Become a submissive toy? No way! I knew very well that the role Sverr had in mind wouldn't work for me. "No! Let go of me!"

"So you're refusing?"

"Yes. Go to hell!" I spat furiously. "Anyone is better than you!"

Sverr's face suddenly turned to stone, and his eyes grew dull. "Very well. I guess that's how it'll be, lilgan."

He grabbed my elbow and pulled me outside. I gasped and pulled the string of the trousers, trying to hold on to the slipping fabric. Sverr dragged me all the way to the clearing, where soldiers were wielding weapons. He shouted, "Listen to the will of the riar! Today I am giving this outsider to whoever wants to take her. Is there even one soldier who wants this girl who is no longer innocent, and is willing to protect and feed her? Does anyone want to take her home?"

I looked around fearfully, nervously wrapping myself in the trench coat. The eyes of the stern, dark-haired men were filled with a familiar expression: desire. Lust, even. Was everything really connected to the riar's call? The dragon's call? What did he awaken in people? I'd seen the same expression in my colleagues' faces. At the time, the scientists had gone out of their minds. What would happen with these men who didn't know what it meant to be civilized?

The men looked at me with unconcealed interest and began to approach. The guy who had thrown me over his shoulder opened his mouth.

"I'll feed and protect this outsider, my riar. And I'll take her to my home."

The calm voice behind me made me tremble in surprise, and Sverr bared his teeth. Irvin was standing by the wall. He was dressed and wearing a trench coat now. The edge of a

Book One: Beyond the Fog

battleax behind him glinted in the sun, and his blue eyes looked like frigid ice.

"Irvin," Sverr said threateningly.

"Aren't I your solider, my riar?" Irvin raised his eyebrows. There wasn't a hint of sarcasm in his eyes, only apprehension. "I will take this outsider and protect her."

The two men with black rings around their necks locked eyes. Sverr looked furious. Irvin was pale but calm. The other men moved back — the strapping young guy even ran away. In the little area where the three of us were standing, the air began to smell like a storm and ash. The stone beneath my feet was heating up — I could feel it through the sole of the boots. I began to dread the hjegg's impending fury.

"You've made your choice," Sverr hissed. "As your riar, I order you to dance the dance of the shatiya."

Irvin pursed his lips and his pupils narrowed.

"What?" He faltered and jerked his chin up. "As you wish, my riar. When?"

"Today."

"All right," Irvin growled. He seemed to be having a hard time containing himself. "After the shatiya she'll enter my home and stay there. How many soldiers will you approve, outsider?"

"What?" I looked at each of them in bewilderment. The soldiers around us perked up and came closer. "How many soldiers?"

"For your shatiya." Irvin seemed to be losing patience. "How many?"

"What? I don't know."

"All who win the fight!" Sverr interrupted. He spun around and strode off.

I looked at the soldiers' expectant faces. I felt like the earth was dropping under my feet.

The Charmed Fjords

"Not many people have ever managed to get the riar of Neroaldaf so angry that he loses his head. You have a gift, outsider. Either that or a death wish," Irvin said pensively. He clearly also wanted to leave. I clenched my cold fingers around his trench coat.

"Wait! What's going on? What are you talking about?"

Irvin shook his head and looked meaningfully at my hand, which was balling up the thick fabric.

"What exactly don't you understand? The shatiya. For you. Get ready, outsider. I'll be the first in the circle. After that, I'll take you to my house."

With that, he pried my fingers from the coat and walked away. I was standing there blinking dumbly, trying to imagine the nightmare I'd gotten into, when two women came over to me and pulled me by the elbows.

"Let's go, girl," the one on my left said, sounding friendly enough. "There's not a lot of time, and you need to be worthy of the soldiers' fight in the circle. Come with us. We'll help you."

I pulled my arms free and broke into a run. I ran so fast the large men's boots fell off me. My scientific brain simply shut off the fear that had seized it. My head had been drained of reason, sound ideas, and logic. All I had left was the understanding that that night I'd be thrust into the circle toward the brutal ilgs, and they'd push me down on my knees. It would be better to die. If I could get to the water, I'd swim until I reached some place or drowned.

But I didn't even manage to run to the fortifying walls. The strong guy who had carried me on his shoulders took a few bounds and caught me, and easily dragged me to the doors of the fortress.

"Don't be afraid, outsider," he whispered, handing me over to the women by the door of the tower. "I'll also fight for you. My name is Virn. Remember that. If I can, I'll come in

Book One: Beyond the Fog

second at the shatiya. Obviously there's no way I can beat a hjegg."

He clicked his tongue in disappointment and walked off. The door slammed shut. So much for drowning myself.

Chapter 17. Olivia

THE ROOM THE WOMEN TOOK ME TO was larger than the little cage I was locked in before, but it was still small. That made sense — it's always much easier to heat a small room than a huge foyer.

The walls of this room were bare, but the floor was covered in fabrics and furs. The wooden furniture was unadorned and looked durable. Unlit candles stood in iron candleholders, and there were stone shelves scattered around the room. There was no fireplace or hearth, yet the room was warm. I reached out to touch the wall and was surprised to find that the stones were heated. No wonder the room was so comfortable.

"How can that be?" I said in amazement. "How do the walls get hot? Is there interior heating here? Or pipes with hot water, or steam?"

"The hjegg's fire flows in the wall," one of the women explained. She was stout and had a large nose and graying hair. Her light brown eyes were filled with surprise and curiosity, but her lips were pursed. "The flame pours between the stones, so Neroaldaf is warm all winter long. We're very lucky to live here."

My other escort, a young, ruddy woman with dark eyes, nodded cheerfully in agreement. "Yes, we are so lucky! You're right, Irga. We really couldn't be luckier. It's always warm

Book One: Beyond the Fog

here, and we always have enough to eat. You just need to make sure to get out of the way in time if the hjeggs get angry, and that's it."

"Exactly, Slenga."

I swallowed some saliva and they thrust a huge mug filled with a steaming liquid into my hands. It looked like mulled wine. I could smell the honey, herbs, and spices. It was delicious, and it eased my fear.

"Do they often get angry?" I asked as I exhaled, still standing in the middle of the room and trying to come to grips with this strange reality.

"The riar often does," the older woman said with a shrug. "But that's understandable. It's in his nature — his blood burns. When there's thunder and lightning inside you, you blow up. He's much calmer than his grandfather, though. When his grandfather got angry, all of Neroaldaf would have to sit in their shelters for ten days. That riar really got furious! But Sverr-hjegg almost always contains himself," she said, sounding especially proud.

I nodded grimly. So he contains himself. Not today, though, clearly. Even I couldn't contain myself. I was still seething. I was experiencing new emotions, and they terrified me. But why regret them now?

"Who is the riar anyway? Is he the leader here?" I asked carefully, and the women nodded.

"The riar is everything," Slenga answered with a sigh.

"And Irvin is the a-tem?"

"The a-tem is his twin. He's second most important after the riar. He protects the riar's life and sometimes subdues his fury. Water riars are a little calmer."

I nodded slowly. OK, that cleared some things up. I thought I should turn my attention to the shatiya. The women apparently had the same thought and remembered why they were here. They ran over to the trunks, started to

The Charmed Fjords

rummage around, and pulled out an ivory-colored garment. It was a sleeveless dress made up of two pieces of fabric connected on the sides, with high slits up the skirt. The whole thing was sewn with red thread, and the stitches were placed so skillfully that they looked like a watercolor on the silk. A wide piece of crimson fabric extended from the shoulders, forming a train.

Irga smoothed the fabric fondly. "This is so beautiful. What a shame that they'll tear it to pieces and destroy it. But that's the shatiya. All the clothes come off the maiden. Don't be afraid, outsider. My mother went through the shatiya. And my grandmother. But I didn't."

"Why is that?"

"It's unusual that she didn't," Slenga said with a shrug. "The shatiya only happens with the riar's consent, when he commands it. It's mainly for captive maidens, outsiders, or freeborn women who ask for it because they want to have a strong child. The old people say that's why their sons are weak. My great-grandmother remembered a time when there were ten hjeggs living in Neroaldaf, and before that there were even more. But now the call has become weak."

"Enough chitchat," Irga said in annoyance. "Get the maiden ready. Take off your clothes, outsider. We all have the same private parts. I've seen maidens in trousers. There have been women warriors from the islands. But it's obvious that you don't know how to hold a sword. Your hands are soft and you don't have a single callus. It's like you've never worked a day in your life. Are you a freeborn or something? Or a noblewoman? In that case, I can see why the twin will take you home."

As the women examined my hands in surprise, I tried to interrogate them some more. I also noticed they looked curious — I could tell they were dying to know who I was and from where, but they were afraid to ask.

Book One: Beyond the Fog

"You said I shouldn't be afraid of the shatiya. Why?"

"Don't you know? Your fear will disappear as soon as the hjegg puts out his call," Irga said, picking up my discarded clothes. "You'll forget everything. Everything will disappear. You'll just feel a bliss like you'll never feel again. Then everything will be clear and right, so don't be afraid."

A tremor passed through me. Yup, been there, done that. I'd die if I subjected myself to that.

"If you're lucky and the ancient hjeggs are benevolent, you'll conceive a strong son during the shatiya," Irga babbled like a river. "Then you'll immediately get everything even though you're an outsider — gold, dresses, honor, respect from everyone. Our riar will give a golden gift to every young person, then when they get a little older they'll be able to hold a sword from his armory. Giving birth to a child in Neroaldaf is every woman's dream. You won't be a wife because you were born in other lands, but what if you get lucky and have a son? There's no reason to be afraid. But I understand — stolen maidens often get the jitters and are scared the whole time."

"Stolen maidens?" I gave a start. "Does that mean there are often, er, outsiders here?"

"Yes, from time to time." As they talked the women pulled a narrow, short cotton underblouse on me. Then they put on the silk garment, which flowed coolly along my body. "Sometimes soldiers bring them back from raids and sometimes the riar and a-tem bring them back. Of course, we get all sorts of different girls here. Some of them don't speak our language at all — those are the captives who are from closer to the Fog. They're completely savage. Then there are the snow maidens, from the mountains. They're proud and snow white, with eyes like sapphires. They're so beautiful it hurts to look at them. Our warriors especially love them. But they also go to whoever the riar says. Last time the riar stole

The Charmed Fjords

a maiden from the master of the shining peak, Aurolhjoll. She was so pretty that half a dozen men gathered to admire her. But that dumb girl just cried and kept harping on her wedding. But now it's all OK. She got used to things and they say that she's already forgotten her icy chambers. And how do they even live there, in the ice? Those poor people."

The women exchanged sly glances.

"You're lucky, outsider, that you didn't end up just anywhere, but here in Neroaldaf. Our mighty riar rules over a million people. Do you know how many ships he and the a-tem have sunk? No one can defeat them. One of them scorches with his fire and the other smashes things with his wave. You can't imagine their strength. And then they bring all the gold and captives here. Warriors from all the fjords come to knock on the city gates every day asking to fight under the black flag of Neroaldaf."

I nodded, thinking all of this over. Well then. That meant that stealing women was commonplace here, along with the other goods like trunks. What wonderful company this riar and his twin were! Two bandits, what have you.

"Where do these snow-white maidens live, anyway?" It could be useful to figure out the geography of the fjords while I was asking all these questions.

"In the snowy lands!" Slenga threw up her arms and looked at me triumphantly. "And they froze to death there! But the ice hjeggs watch over them, and that's why they don't freeze in the snowbanks."

"Obviously they don't do a very good job watching over them since your riar brings them here," I muttered and the women laughed.

"Bringing things home is in their blood. And that's even more true for our riar — he's a child of Lagerhjegg. Both the fire-breathing and the gold hjeggs revered the black beast. The strongest hjegg is the black and gold one: he's the master

Book One: Beyond the Fog

of stone, iron, and heavenly fire. When he gets angry, the sky pitches thunder and lightning with him," Slenga said with a sigh. I gave her a sideways look. Now it was all clear — she had a hopeless, girlish infatuation with the hjegg. Her shining eyes and flaming cheeks gave her away. And yet, if I correctly understood what they were saying about this gold, fire-breathing being who stole anything that wasn't nailed down, or was sitting or running too slowly, then even Slenga could enjoy a bit of attention from him.

"We'll pray for you," Irga said solemnly. "We'll ask the firstborn hjeggs to bestow a worthy son on you. When so many warriors compete, there's a better chance that you'll get a little boy."

"Or a little girl," I added automatically, but the women winced.

"Giving birth to a girl after the shatiya is dishonorable. When men have fought for you and shed blood, and the hjegg has graced us with his call, what could be worse than giving birth to a girl?"

Wonderful, I also had to deal with sexism here. "What makes a girl bad?"

"The fact that she's not a boy," Irga said sagely. "Don't shake. Where one warrior doesn't succeed, there are ten who will. Just you wait, you'll have a little boy. The shatiya always helps with that."

"I don't want to. And I won't do it. Please give me a weapon."

"Of course we will," Slenga said to my surprise, straightening the dress on me. "You can choose one from the armory, whichever one you want. Or whichever one you can lift up."

"How will that work?" I was startled. "They give me a weapon?"

"You pick one out," the women said, also surprised.

The Charmed Fjords

They exchanged a look and shook their heads. "Fight with all your strength! The only way you can! Until the hjegg calls you, fight to the death."

"What?" I gave up trying to understand all of this.

"Hit them properly," Irga said, nodding in satisfaction. "I didn't have a shatiya. I just got married. But the first night I punched my husband in the nose and damaged his eye, before he dominated me and put me on my knees."

Both women burst out laughing and my head started to spin.

"What for?"

"What do you mean what for? So he'd understand that he didn't get a wife just like that, but that he won her in a fight and that she could stand up for herself, and that she was strong enough to give birth to strong children and raise warriors. Here we call intimate relations combat. And the fiercer she is, the sweeter the satisfaction will be. It isn't different where you come from, is it?"

I grunted. Um, yeah, it was different. Now I understood why the ilg didn't rush to kiss me. If their intimacy was combat, who knew what the stranger from beyond the Fog was capable of.

"Look, the fight's already begun!" Slenga cried out, rushing over to the narrow window.

I followed her, awkwardly dragging the long train behind me.

From the window I could see the expansive space next to the tower, and indeed, there were men fighting. There were around three dozen of them, all naked to the waist, clad in the same linen trousers. Their powerful torsos gleamed with oil. None of them had weapons. Apparently it was a fistfight, just like in the tribe. I saw the strapping Virn slam his fist into the jaw of his opponent, who wavered but regained his footing and rewarded Virn with a punch under the ribs. The

Book One: Beyond the Fog

men wheezed, yelled, roared, and thumped, trying to push one another outside the dueling line. A crowd surrounded them, cheering them on and whistling. Some men flew past the red string and spit in disappointment.

"Don't pay attention if they get beaten," Irga said matter-of-factly. "Our men are strong. Sometimes after a campaign they come back, and their cheeks are sunken, their eyes are intoxicated, and they're dirty and covered in their own and someone else's blood, but they'll catch you if... well, they'll love you so much it will be hard to stand later. It's because fire boils in their blood after the fight. Do you understand what I'm saying? It's from the riar's fury. Women don't feel that fury; we only hear the call. But with the men it's both. Look, now the warriors are enraged! Our firebreather isn't wicked in any other way. But this way it will only be sweeter for you."

I choked and looked at the jolly woman with an expression that made her stop talking and frown. Down below us Irvin was merrily throwing his opponents off.

"OK, enough of that," Irga said. "Slenga, stop staring at the warriors. This fight isn't for you. And you, outsider, sit here. We need to do something with your hair. It's a disgrace. Maidens need to have their hair to their waist so the warrior has something to grab and squeeze in his hand when he puts her on her knees. But what do you have? Nothing but a mess! You can't even put a crown on it."

They tried to pull me over to a bench but I snatched my arm away. The scene under the window had again filled me with horror. Damn, how many men were there? Even if most of them went outside the line, there'd still be quite a few left. What was I thinking?

My anger was so powerful I jumped up and started pacing quickly around the room. Of course talking was a distraction, but the time for the shatiya was still getting

The Charmed Fjords

closer. Shit! When it came to the shatiya my sense of humor failed me. The jokes here weren't funny at all. The women's lively encouragement wasn't helping either. I was so horrified I could barely breathe.

Then, as though I had willed it to happen, my lurking panic surged through me, knocking me to my knees. I doubled over, gasping for air. It was useless. My inhaler was back in the civilized world, beyond the impenetrable wall of Fog. I couldn't breathe without it.

It was a terrifying feeling. My mind understood that I was surrounded by nothing but oxygen, yet I couldn't take a single breath of it. I fell to the floor and vaguely heard Irga shouting. A circle of red spots appeared before my eyes.

The next thing I knew, a dry hand was lying on my forehead and a quiet voice was murmuring something. I caught the names of the ancient dragons. Was it a prayer? I would have burst out laughing, but I couldn't even breathe. Or could I? I carefully drew a breath. And another. It seemed that the attack had passed. I wiped the tears from my face and stared at the short man standing over me. He was dressed simply, like everyone else here, but he wasn't carrying a weapon. A bunch of little sacks filled with rustling herbs were knocking together on his leather belt.

"You're all set now," this man, who I supposed was a healer, said pleasantly with a smile. "Were you frightened, dear?"

"How did you do that?" I asked in astonishment. "I've been going to doctors for years and not a single one has ever been able to cure me. Nothing has ever helped me, just my inhaler with a strong prescription. And no one has ever been able to figure out what causes it. They said it was a psychosomatic condition, the kind you can die from."

Slenga and Irga looked apprehensively at the healer. Their expressions showed a mixture of gratitude and fear,

Book One: Beyond the Fog

which puzzled me.

"I asked the red hjegg to take your pain away, lilgan," the man said. "The shatiya is an important event. There's no use shaking in pain when you're there. Hellehjegg understands that, and that's why he cured you. But that's only for today. The pain will return later. You need to conquer it. Your illness isn't here," he said, placing a hand on my chest. "It's here," he said, putting his hand on my forehead. "Ask Hellehjegg to free you from it forever. Bring him gifts. He'll listen to you."

When they heard the dragon's name the women stepped back and began muttering. Were they praying again? Did they have some kind of protective charm? That's what it looked like.

"Who's Hellehjegg?"

"Where have you come from that you don't know about the red beast?" the healer asked in surprise.

"From far away. You said I should bring gifts. But where? Does the red hjegg have a temple or something?"

Slenga and Irga gasped in fear, but the man shook his head.

"You must be from very far away if you're asking that. I've never met anyone on the fjords who doesn't know where to find Hellehjegg. One temple belongs to the red beast. It's his home and fortress. It's called Gorlohum."

With that, the healer turned and walked off with a dignified air.

I opened my mouth to ask another question but Slenga and Irga withered and pushed me down on the bench. One woman began pulling at my hair with a comb while the other hastily smoothed the creases in my dress, placed a pair of soft leather shoes on my feet, and pulled ornaments out of a small box. The gold glinted in the sun. There was a wide leather belt sewn with a sparkling thread. Rows of hundreds

The Charmed Fjords

of round coins dangled from it, touching the ground. They placed a few heavy bracelets on my bare arms, and finally, a narrow crown on my head. The gold band had thin cords strung with precious beads that streamed down my shoulders and back.

The women stopped, looking at me rapturously.

"What a beauty you are! What a shame you're an outsider! Look at how the gold reflects in her eyes, what a lovely sight. We need to find the gold from the crown or belt after the shatiya. I hope I'll be lucky enough to find even one piece. Look! We have genuine ice glass. It was with that snow maiden on the ship. Now we have everything from that ship and we don't know where to put it. Take a look!"

I really didn't want to look, but they were talking about an object I wasn't familiar with, so I had to turn my head. At first I was just surprised: it seemed to be a piece of shining ice frozen by the wall. After a moment I saw my own reflection. I was stunned. I didn't recognize the girl in the bluish depths of the icy block. I was actually pretty — so pretty I caught my breath. I didn't look anything like myself. It was as though Olivia Orway had been wiped away and all that was left was this savagely dressed maiden with a faraway look in her big green eyes outlined in black and gold.

The sound of familiar music was drifting up into the room: the *din-shork*, the quivering strings that snaked around your soul.

"It's the song of the firstborn hjeggs! Can you hear it?" Slenga said in awe and began to sing. "Lagerhjegg rose up from the fire, iron, and stone. Njordhjegg floated up from the ocean depths and salty water. Ulehjegg descended from the snowy summit in the radiant sky. When Hellehjegg began to roar, Gorlohum cast his ash over the fjords. All because the Ancient Beasts saw the beautiful, pure maiden in the bloody garment. Each one claimed her as his. The Earth trembled

Book One: Beyond the Fog

for a thousand years before the beasts were defeated. Black and red, blue and white... fire and ash, water and snow... the beginning and the end. Only the ancient hjeggs know who caught the maiden." Slenga stopped singing and beamed. "It's time!"

"Now the warriors are speeding up," Irga said resentfully, pursing her lips. "They didn't let us prepare properly, and they're singing the song. What are they rushing for? I don't understand."

The door opened and two women walked in. The older one was holding a wide, dull chalice. I couldn't tell if it was made of gold. Before I had a chance to think any more, they came over to me, dipped their fingers in some viscous liquid, and drew them across my forehead. A sweetish odor wafted to my nose. I realized it was blood.

As I tried to process this, each woman continued dipping her fingers in the chalice and running them over my exposed skin. They covered my forehead, cheeks, shoulders, elbows, neck, and feet were covered in drops of this blood that came from who knew where.

"Merciful be the firstborn hjeggs... merciful and kind."

Irga was the last to mark me.

"Let's go, outsider. Come on, one foot in front of the other. We're not going to carry you."

"No!" I yelled. I began rushing around, looking for a way out. But the guards standing by the door caught me immediately, and again my servant-guardians grasped me. Men with weapons stood behind and in front of us.

"Don't! I beg you. I don't want to go!"

Slenga began mumbling some comforting words, Irga shouted something in annoyance, and they both pulled me toward the stairway. The guards accompanied us silently, but their threatening presence rankled me. There was no way I could run away.

The Charmed Fjords

I needed to come up with an idea. I was an educated, intelligent woman. It shouldn't be too hard, right? Primitive force couldn't possibly defeat reason.

I gave a jolt as I realized that of course it could, and it had already happened. Here, beyond the Fog, the rules were different, and here no one gave a damn about reason or my academic achievements. Clearly they didn't care about me either. The anthropologist Olivia Orway no longer existed. It was one thing to study a foreign civilization based on ancient fragments and papyrus, but it was totally different to be a part of it — and not just a part of it, but a captive, an outsider, a nameless maiden who was about to enter the circle of the shatiya. The terror practically immobilized me. I put one foot in front of the other like I was on autopilot. I felt like I was watching the scene happening to someone else. It was as though the real Liv were hiding, and had released the researcher, who was looking around like an indifferent, detached scientist. How many times had I hidden like that? Right now I was noticing what was happening but I didn't feel anything. The soft shoes were stepping on the paving stone, while the cool sea breeze made the coins hanging from my crown and belt jangle. Now the door to the armory was opening in front of me, and I went in and grabbed a knife with a smooth ivory handle. Now the row of warriors was parting. The men's eyes shone with rapture and hunger. I walked through the passageway of living people, the crimson train flowing behind me like a fiery river. The soles of my feet stepped on embers, which soiled the white dress.

And there were torches. In front of me, torches burned, illuminating the place of my fall.

The music wove a web and caught everyone's soul. Blistering lava coursed through me. And I heard the call of the dragon.

I lifted my head, instinctively confessing, and spotted

Book One: Beyond the Fog

Sverr. He was standing in one of the narrow windows, and I had the impression I could see the gold of his eyes — shining, enchanting, evil. But of course it was only my imagination.

Someone pushed me gently from behind and I took a few quick steps, nearly tripping in my silk gown. I turned and jumped up. My detached calm dissipated. I was surrounded by men on all sides. Their naked torsos were still gleaming with oil and they were smeared in blood and dirt. Here in Neroaldaf they didn't wear the halesveng skulls — but that didn't cheer me because the sight of their brown, black, and amber eyes gleaming with desire was intolerable. It would have been better if blood-smeared bones were grinning at me. But then again, in this situation nothing could help. No matter how you sliced it, it was vile.

Only I had a weapon, and I clutched the knife with the determination of a convicted criminal.

Chapter 18. Olivia

IRVIN'S BLOND HEAD was easy to spot among the darkhaired men. Irvin was also covered in blood, but I doubted it was his. He took a step toward me and I saw the fervor in his eyes. I jumped back, nearly losing my balance, and grasped the dragging train of my dress.

"Stay away from me!"

The music was spiraling through the air and drawing me in like a net. People pushed me from behind — gently and almost affectionately, but I pitched forward, right into Irvin's arms.

"I would have preferred to do this in the water, Ilgan, with no one else around," he rasped. "But it's better not to argue with the riar today."

He pressed me to him and tugged at my slippery silk dress. It snapped and hung in a shred on the bloodied embroidery. I swiveled and with all my might elbowed Irvin under his ribs, extricated myself from his embrace, and brandished my knife. A bloody scrape appeared on the ilg's body, and I felt a surprising satisfaction spark within me. I would not give in. I let out a ferocious, bestial roar as I surveyed the crowd. Everywhere I looked there were men with predatory eyes. I bared my teeth and slashed the knife through the train of my dress. It fell to the ground and I kicked it away. I looked into the crowd and saw a flicker of

Book One: Beyond the Fog

surprise.

"You're in that much of a hurry, outsider? Don't rush. All in due time."

"Suck it," I snapped and again stepped back, trying to remember everything I'd learned in my self-defense classes. I hadn't taken those classes for nothing, had I? After the trauma that left me covered in scars, I went to those classes like clockwork, never missing a single one. Another attack. I leaped aside and brought my knife down on my assailant. The steel slid along the ilg's greasy body, barely leaving a trace, and I nearly wailed in frustration. Were these people made of stone or something? Someone grabbed me from behind by the waist. My knees buckled and I crossed my arms over my head and tumbled down. In a split second I uncoiled and thrust out my knife without even looking at my target. To my surprise, I felt it penetrate flesh. An enormous man spluttered in pain and thrust me away. But I'd already sprung from him, turned, and stamped on someone's bare foot. The soft soles of my shoes were useless, though. I would have given anything for a pair of boots. I whirled around and cursed through clenched teeth. This damned dress. Had they gone out of their way to dress me in such uncomfortable clothes? Admittedly, part of it had already torn off and the rest was in tatters.

"Stubborn girl!" A ripple of amusement passed through the attackers, as though they didn't see the knife in my hand. "You're a feisty one!"

Someone else shoved me, and I was so focused on remaining upright that I didn't notice that another person had approached. I glanced up and saw it was Virn. He was no longer a goodhearted guy, but an animal coveting its prey. I stabbed him too — or I tried to, but he ducked out of the way. Another poke from behind, and I fell to my knees. I was jerked up, another piece of my dress ripped off, and I found

The Charmed Fjords

myself pressed against the burning chest of yet another ilg. Another stab, and then the bloodied blade, then a turn and a stab. My fist slid along an oil-smeared body. It dawned on me that I was too weak. I was prey being tossed from one predator to another. They were having fun. I fought, I hit, I bit, I stabbed, and I waved my knife around, but I didn't do more than scratch these battle-hardened warriors. They were all marked with scars. Each of them had surely killed. These men were in another league: strong, quick, and deadly dangerous. The difference between them and refined civilized beings was so striking that a fresh wave of panic overcame me.

I couldn't just give in that easily, though.

I staggered backward and sized up the situation. My dress was hanging on me in ribbons, and the gold coins were jangling with every movement I made, like bells on the sacrificial lamb. The circle of men was closing in on me, and I could see a flame in all of their eyes. Strangely, even though I was holding a knife, no one hit me back. The ilgs only bellowed and bared their teeth, chasing me, placing their bodies under the blade, waiting for me to run out of steam.

Someone pushed me by the shoulder and then a strong body pressed me from behind. It was an agitated body, and calloused hands squeezed my waist so hard I couldn't break away. I twitched and growled through my teeth. Now I was an animal too. Everything went dark before my eyes, and for a moment the real world disappeared and I was seventeen all over again, struggling to escape a man's clutches as he breathed hoarsely into my ear. I felt the same terror now as I had back then.

But I was no longer that girl, and I hated being afraid. I would not give in, not as long as I was alive. Above all, I couldn't lose my knife. The music soared and that cursed call grew stronger. Longing began to build weakly in my belly and

Book One: Beyond the Fog

then it faded, overwhelmed by my fury. Irvin's blue eyes shone in bewilderment, and I would have burst out laughing triumphantly but someone seized me by the hair. I hissed and flailed my arms, trying to break free. A moment later I did, and I plunged my knife into the body in front of me. I was in the center of a storm of prodding, foot stamping, punching, and the labored breathing of the hot-blooded men. It was a living nightmare.

Now my luxurious gown was a rag that barely covered me. Hysteria blinded me. I spun around wildly and punched everything in my path. Circles of lanterns floated in the misty darkness and I had the impression that all of Neroaldaf had drowned in the haze. My knife kept landing in my assailants' bodies, but the men just pushed me away. They didn't hurt me, but I could see their distorted faces all around. Gone were their tentative movements. Now they surged at me spitefully, sharply, and tensely. At the same time, they looked astonished, malicious, and even slightly ashamed. Apparently they'd all realized that the game was going to drag on, and the stubborn outsider didn't want to submit.

I felt a shove again, and from the impact I lurched forward onto my knees. A heavy body pressed me to the ground, a bare foot stepped on my unkempt hair so I couldn't get up, and a strong arm tossed aside the knife, which had fallen out of my hand. I screamed.

"Enough! You're a wild one. I wasn't expecting that."

At the sound of Irvin's voice I began to hiss and cower under him. He pressed my hips into the ground, leaning on me with his whole body.

"No!" I howled, looking around frantically for the knife.

"Stop!" Irvin yelled wrathfully, but then he sounded surprised. "Why are you still resisting? I'm calling you."

"Let me go!" I summoned all my strength and sank my teeth into Irvin's hand, making him cry out.

The Charmed Fjords

"Holy crap!"

His body slackened and something fell quietly behind me. I turned, squeezed my legs, and gasped. Sverr was standing in the shatiya circle. Fiery sparks were dispersing from his body. Without taking his eyes off me, he strode over, gathered me in his arms, and turned silently toward the tower. I sank my dirty, trembling hands into his shoulders, and Sverr breathed heavily, his pale face distorted.

"But, riar, the girl is ours!" screamed Virn, who had fallen under the intoxicating spell of the shatiya.

"Get away!" Sverr's bellowing voice was so imposing that the lanterns soared into the sky like fiery tornadoes and the crowd scuttled away in fear.

"That goes against the law of the shatiya, my riar," Irvin said, dexterously getting to his feet. "The captive is ours. You yourself made that law. So now she's mine. The fight was honest."

"Anyone who touches this girl will die. If you want to take the captive, you'll need to fight me — right now," Sverr spat. Silence descended on the square. Then a bolt of lightning struck and I realized that a strange, nature-defying storm was about to descend on Neroaldaf. There was no rain, just zigzagging flashes cleaving the sky. A violet, swollen storm cloud practically touched the roofs of the buildings, as though it were waiting to devour the stone and chimneys. The sky seemed to have gotten angry and was about to descend to Earth, burying the entire city.

"How can you do that?" one of the men grumbled as he wiped the blood off his face. They all seemed to have gotten a good beating from me. "That's not what the law says."

"You've forgotten the main law of the shatiya," the riar said as if talking to a slow child.

"She's not answering my call," Irvin said gloomily. He stared at me morosely. "That means we're not allowed to force

Book One: Beyond the Fog

her because we'll harm her if we do."

"What do you mean she's not responding?" the other men asked in astonishment. "That's impossible!"

Sverr seemed not to have heard them. We were staring into each other's eyes, and I saw melted gold in his. He stepped out of the circle. The warriors were panting and grinding their teeth, but they cleared a path for Sverr to walk through. Irvin watched us go, his face contorted. But for me, all the other people had disappeared. Sverr kicked open a massive door and carried me into the tower. He raced up the stairs, entered a room, and flung me onto the bed.

I leaped up and darted as far away as I could. "Stay away from me!"

But suddenly Sverr was beside me, and he clutched me to his body, which felt as frenzied as the gale blowing above Neroaldaf. His hands ran up and down me as he feverishly stroked and embraced me. We were both breathing like animals being chased. He pushed me back down on the bed.

"Don't touch me! I hate you!"

"Do you want to go back to the circle?" he growled. He grasped me by the shoulders and shook me. "Is it better there?"

I shook my head. He jerked my arms up and pinned me down.

"Speak up, girl! Where are you better off? Out there?"

"I hate you! Let go of me!"

He grinned. "You said it would be better with anyone other than me."

"But you handed me over to... them!" Fury and fear began to boil in me. I started to tremble and tried to break loose. It was hideous out there.

"You're defying me!" he bellowed, leaning down. "Do you think you're still on the other side of the Fog? You're in Neroaldaf now. You're a captive. You need to submit and

The Charmed Fjords

acknowledge my power."

"You handed me over to them!"

"Never," he breathed hoarsely. "I'm never going to give you up. Do you understand? Not to anyone." His golden eyes shone with fury and confusion. "You were wearing Irvin's clothes and you made me angry. I was too tired to hold back my fury. I'm not a human that heat can ruin, Liv. I can't help myself."

I caught my breath. I was totally lost now. I only sensed that I was about to burn in the flame the hjegg was scorching us with, or I'd die from the fear and fury he'd plunged me into. I wrenched my arms away and began to slap him and pummel his chest, shoulders, and face. All I could think about was hurting him. But he didn't lift a hand. He just let me rage on as he looked at me with his unearthly eyes and breathed haltingly, submitting to my blows. When I ran out of energy, he grasped my wrists and squeezed so hard I couldn't move.

"You just should have screamed, may Gorlohum take you," he said, his face distorted. "You should have called me, and asked for forgiveness and bowed your damned proud head. That's what any other woman would have done. Why the hell didn't you say anything? You didn't say a word the whole time."

He shook me and I blinked in bewilderment. Call him? That's what he wanted me to do? "I don't understand."

"Stop resisting me!"

He swiftly and ferociously ran a hand along my body, crushing me under him. The gold coins on my belt jangled. His hand stopped moving and he slowly pressed his lips to mine, and then licked me like an animal. He ran his tongue along my lower lip and poked it into my mouth ever so slightly. He bit me gently and then licked me again. His motions were awkward and strange. After a moment I realized

Book One: Beyond the Fog

he was trying to kiss me. What was it that I'd said to him when we were in my tiny apartment? I said that's what people do when they want to feel a different kind of satisfaction, and he responded that it was dangerous.

What was he trying to tell me now? That he trusted me? Or that I could bite off the damn tongue he'd used to issue the order to hand me over to the shatiya?

With a soft groan, I opened my lips and touched his tongue with mine. Sverr stopped for a moment and then resumed kissing me tentatively. He did so instinctively, moved by a desire that pulled us toward each other. The blundering kiss immediately sparked ardent arousal. Sverr pressed his hands on my hips and I gripped his shoulders, dissolving into ecstasy and an all-encompassing sense of safety that took me by surprise. After all, he was the one who had dragged me here to Neroaldaf and then sent me to the shatiya. He was the reason for all these problems. Yet he was also a source of warmth, strength, pleasure, and calm. He was the source of everything. A sea of feelings clouded my reason. This dragon had uncovered my instincts, ripped away the cover of civilization, and left me defenseless. I had no idea how to orient myself in this whirlwind of emotions. I felt like a different Liv — the stranger from the icy mirror. Sverr was right. How could I possibly study people if I didn't even know myself? Was Olivia Orway the anthropologist really capable of fighting like a furious savage, and then being consumed by desire?

He called me again. I could resist the call — I knew I could. I also knew that he'd retreat if I revolted against it.

Sverr squeezed his fingers over my hair. With a sigh, he opened his hand, then clenched it again.

"Get rid of the call," I gasped.

"I can't, damn it. Can't you see that?" He clenched my hair again. His burning lips met mine, which were swollen

The Charmed Fjords

from our ardor. When he tore away I saw his savage eyes.

He inhaled, then exhaled into my lips. Fear and desire... one must remain, that's what he'd told me. I wanted to remember this night differently, and etch different emotions and images in my soul. I wanted to drive the shatiya out of my head.

"Tell me what you want, Liv."

"I want to forget this," I whispered. "Make me forget. I know you can do it."

His body shuddered in understanding. "Yes," Sverr sighed.

He would be able to do it. He could do anything. That also scared me.

I screwed up my eyes. There was almost nothing left of my dress now. My body was streaked with dirt and other people's blood, my hands were trembling, and before my eyes a series of faces started swirling again.

Sverr let out a strangled grunt.

"Look at me!" he ordered me again, but this time I obeyed.

He pushed me deeper into the bed with one hand, as though he were afraid I'd run away. He pulled away for a moment and tore off his clothes. I stroked his muscular shoulders and dug my fingers into his dark hair, and like he had done with mine, squeezed it in my fist. I touched the ilg on the chest, pushing him gently onto his back. He frowned in confusion.

"You said you wanted to know what humans do," I said, placing my hand on his chest and feeling his heart beating. "Sometimes it's like this."

Of course I couldn't hold Sverr back, but he stopped moving, looking at me warily and giving me permission to do what I wanted. I ran my fingernails along his body, gently scratching his tanned skin. I traced his pecs, touched the

Book One: Beyond the Fog

iron bracelet on his forearm, and stroked his prominent ab muscles. I couldn't get enough of his perfectly toned body, which drove me wild. I flung out my leg and straddled his hips. His pupils were wide and the gold of his irises was nearly invisible. His eyes roamed ravenously over my face, chest, and legs. He began to hiss when I moved my hips. The wide belt with the cascading coins was still around my waist and the coins clanged softly with every movement I made. Clang! I circled my hips again, and Sverr groaned in response. Clang-clang! He raised himself up, greedily kissed my lips, and moaned when I lowered myself back onto him. The gold coins grated my skin every time I moved, but neither of us wanted to stop to take them off. His arms were so strong and his lips so soft. The unexpected feelings made my fear vanish and filled me with new, pleasurable memories.

When we were done, a languid contentment flowed through my body and erased all my thoughts. The riar was also lying still and breathing heavily. His golden eyes gleamed with bliss and sparks of abating passion. The black hjegg had calmed down. And the fury had been drained from me.

As I started thinking about that, Sverr raised himself up and shook me. "Don't go to sleep! You didn't say it!"

"I didn't say what?" I asked, aghast.

"That you belong to me!"

I emerged from my languor and clenched my teeth to keep myself from telling that dragon just where he could go. He flipped onto his side and pulled me under him, licking my cheek.

"You'll say it, lilgan" he said confidently. He smiled as he studied me. The ilg's eyes now looked like a pair of polished coins and I wondered how I'd ever thought they belonged to a human being.

Sverr touched my puffy lips again. He had a mocking, surprised look on his face.

The Charmed Fjords

"Who ever came up with the idea of putting your tongue in someone's mouth?" he said. "It's vicious."

He paused and took a breath. His eyes sparked as I could see him turning the idea over in his head.

"Well, maybe not the most vicious," he said in bewilderment. "But I'll try that with you later, lilgan. In the morning."

He clasped me to him and shut his eyes. Apparently he was just planning to go to sleep. What the hell? After all of that?

"I need to take a shower," I muttered, trying to extract myself from his arms. "I mean, I need, er, a washtub? A basin? A bowl with water?"

"No," Sverr interrupted me. "In the morning."

"I need to wash up now," I said petulantly. I shut my eyes wearily. The events of the day were spinning through my head like dancing, colored shreds of cloth: the council, the Academy, the flight, the storage room, the shatiya. And him. It was all too much for me to handle. My body and mind were screaming for a time out. There was no way I'd be able to fall asleep.

I jerked my body again, trying to wriggle out from under him.

"Tomorrow!" Sverr barked without opening his eyes.

"Now!" I shouted. I added quietly, "I need to wash everything off. And everyone."

"I already got the smells off you. Now you only smell like me." He opened his eyes and gave me an annoyed look. "You're a stubborn thing. You're not submissive. You don't let me sleep, outsider."

"And people like that don't live long, right?" I snickered. I saw Sverr try to conceal a smile. He abruptly rolled over, stood up, grabbed me by the hand, and began to pull me who knows where.

Book One: Beyond the Fog

For the first time I noticed the room we were in. It was large, round, and had sturdy furniture. There was a wide bed bigger than any bed I could imagine, now covered with a creased, dark blue bedspread, a massive table with dragon feet, armchairs, a filled bookcase, a fireplace with smoldering coals. It sure didn't look like a barbarian's lair. Admittedly, he wasn't exactly a barbarian, but he was certainly different.

"Not to the cave where Irvin almost drowned me!" I balked suddenly, guessing where he was taking me. Sverr shot me a mocking look and pushed away a piece of hanging cloth to reveal a door. Behind the door was another room, with a massive stone tub in the center.

The ilg pulled me into the middle of it and pushed back a lever. Warm water flowed over the stone.

"Wow!" I marveled.

"And there are no wild animals," Sverr said with a chuckle. "Except me, of course."

"How does the water heat up?" I couldn't hold back a laugh.

"There's a cauldron with the hjegg's flame under the tower. And a system of metal pipes," Sverr replied, pulling me toward him. The water slowly filled the tub, and Sverr squinted contentedly as he plucked the gold coins from the belt I was still wearing. I put my hands on his chest and raised myself up. Now Sverr seemed more relaxed and calm than I had ever seen him. He stroked my back, sending goosebumps up and down my spine.

"Here we say that a man is a cliff," he said slowly. "And he needs to stand upright, even in a gale or storm. And the woman is the water that flows around the cliff. It flows softly around all the sharp edges." He stopped speaking. "The woman needs to learn the flow of water, Liv. And you know" — his lips trembled in a smile — "I've never seen a cliff that water wouldn't hew off.

The Charmed Fjords

"But I don't know how to be water," I stammered. "I haven't had the kind of experience to learn that from. I've gotten in the habit of protecting myself, but not of flowing."

Sverr kept running his fingers along my spine. The tub had filled with water by now, and it felt incredibly soothing to lie in it. But it also felt strange, because it was something else I was experiencing for the first time. The emotional part of life always seemed too complicated for me to delve into, but here, on the fjords, everything was different. For a moment the thought even occurred to me that I could learn to be water. With him. Except it was impossible. My life was different, and I was different, and I didn't belong to the fjords. Here I was just an outsider. I couldn't forget that. And I couldn't allow myself to feel.

I looked at Sverr, whose eyes were clamped shut. I carefully touched the dark ring under his throat.

"So it's only the hjeggs who wear rings like this? Is that it? Do you call this the ring of Gorlohum?"

"It's his gift to people," Sverr muttered absently. His eyes were closed and his face looked drawn. Was he tired? I suddenly remembered how he'd been tormented at the Academy, how the guards had bombarded him with shots from their stun guns, and how the bullet had entered his chest. It hadn't happened that long ago even though it felt like a hundred years.

I gingerly fingered the red scar under his ribs.

"How is this possible? I thought you were dead. Any other person would be."

"I'm not a person, Olivia Orway. You yourself said that at the council. And to figure that out, you lured me to your bed and promised me bliss." His golden eyes blazed. Apparently he wasn't sleeping. No, he was lurking and watching me from under his downcast eyelashes. Like a snake, I realized.

Book One: Beyond the Fog

"Who are you, anyway?" I asked softly.

"If you yourself saw everything, why do you need words?" Sverr asked sarcastically, squinting.

"You're a hjegg. Where I come from we'd call you a dragon," I whispered. "But how?"

"Where I come from we don't talk about it," the ilg said, closing his eyes. His muscles relaxed. But his hand continued to stroke my back. "It's better not to talk about the hjeggs, Liv. Then you won't stir up trouble."

"What about the one you killed when we were with the tribe? Was that also a hjegg?"

"He was a wild, free one, without a ring around his neck."

I frowned. "What happens when you put the ring on?"

He shook his head again, smiling slightly.

"And the call of the hjegg? What's that?"

"You can feel it. My call. Every hjegg has his own call, Liv." The gold gleamed from under his drooping eyelids. "You didn't respond to Irvin's call and you resisted mine." The ilg frowned in annoyance. "That's very strange, outsider."

SVERR

I probed the protruding bones on Liv's back. She's so fragile. And small. And tender... and so headstrong I always want to smother her or fling her down on the bed again. Even now, when sleep was beckoning and my body was crying out for rest, I wanted to again submerge myself in the lilgan's heat. I wanted to move, look her in the eyes, and caress her tongue. It was so naughty, yet unbelievably enjoyable. Arousal began to creep up my spine. Liv blushed, sensing my desire. I smirked as I looked at her. She's fighting with me and herself. She's afraid, and getting angry, and resisting. The women of

The Charmed Fjords

the fjords would rejoice, but this one is asking herself questions again. She wants to know and understand. And she hopes to return to her home beyond the Fog to report everything to the people of the Confederation.

That makes me angry — so angry that it almost awakens the dormant savage fury. As I watched the shatiya from the tower window, I struggled to keep the beast at bay. He was so close that I started to breathe smoke on my own, with my human body that isn't meant to breathe fire. But I forgot about everything. I placed my people and city under threat. I only saw her — that fragile girl in the white dress who was madly fending off the warriors — and all I felt was an urge to kill. I wanted to kill anyone who touched her. All she had to do was yell out. And submit to me.

But Liv was silent. She fought like a man even though her strength was pitiful, and she didn't utter a word. I didn't know what was greater in me: admiration or fury.

My beast was raging nearby while I became aware of the most important things. First: pretty soon the black beast would annihilate Neroaldaf. Second: Liv wasn't going to call me. She wasn't going to ask for help or bow her head. She would perish there, in the circle of men and lanterns, but she wouldn't give in. Her pride was stronger than her will to live. Maybe it's ridiculous, but the fjords respect a proud, brave soul, no matter what body it comes in.

A fire blazed in me and bile scorched my throat. My hands tightened around Liv's body, and I wanted to overpower her again. Even our intimacy didn't appease the fury or that incomprehensible, painful hate that overcame me as I watched from the window. She's mine, only mine.

And she didn't respond to Irvin's call.

That consoled me, but not much. I didn't want to think about what I would have done if she had responded. My feelings were too irrational. There was no reason in them, no

Book One: Beyond the Fog

riar, just the dragon's instinct. And if today I tried to free myself from these abnormal feelings for the outsider, I would only make things worse.

Liv cried out softly and I loosened my hands, realizing I was squeezing her too hard. I cursed myself through my teeth and breathed in the steamy air. I need to calm down — I of all people should know how dangerous my fury is. Liv will remain here, in Neroaldaf. In my chambers. It's a done deal, but I won't tell her that just yet. If I do, she'll lash out again. Right now her head is too full of her past life and my world is too different for her. It's easier for me — I began reading about and studying the lands beyond the Great Fog when I was a kid, so I was prepared for the arrival of the humans. But for Liv, everything is different.

But she'll get used to it with time.

I'll just need to tame her differently. Liv isn't the water — she's the stone. She's a tiny, small, but hard stone, but if you hit the stone on the cliff, it will just disintegrate into dust.

The lilgan is asking about the hjeggs again, and about the ring around my neck.

Even though the last thing I want to do is talk, I answer her. She has that effect on me. I break off when I remember the call. I scowl.

OLIVIA

"I don't want you to respond to me now, lilgan," Sverr said suddenly, opening his eyes. "Got it?"

He waited for me to nod, and then resumed stroking my shoulders, his hands creeping lower. The familiar lava began to stir in me again. It was his call — the desire burning in me. The command to submit, accept, give, and receive ecstasy. I sighed and began to squirm, trying to slip from Sverr's firm

The Charmed Fjords

grasp. Apparently the ilg himself depended on this call. His muscles hardened and he began panting. I drew a deep breath and shook my head. When Sverr forced himself to unclasp his hands, I slid away to the opposite side of the tub. He breathed raspily and nodded.

"I don't even know if I should praise you or punish you. But you've confirmed what I suspected — you have an ability to resist the beast's call." Sverr frowned, as though this discovery puzzled him. "I don't understand how, though."

"So you're saying you've never met anyone who could resist this attraction?"

"Never," Sverr said. "And I can't exactly say I'm happy about that. Everyone submits to the call. No exceptions. Always."

He didn't look angry, though, just puzzled. This ilg was definitely unusual. Everything new and unfamiliar appealed to him, like me, an outsider who was able to resist him. I was a new, unexplored toy from beyond the Fog, like the gold-capped pen.

A feeling of sadness washed over me again.

I reached for a wide cup filled with something that looked like soap. I ran a bit of it along my body, trying not to look at him. I flinched when he stirred, slipped over to me, and pressed me against the side of the tub. The longing that had subsided now flared up again. "I thought you wanted to get some sleep?"

"Get out of here and come to bed, Liv. I'll be waiting for you."

He shook himself off, spraying water, and bounded out of the tub. He left the room, shutting the door softly behind him.

"Barbarian!" I muttered at his back, but it came out more laughingly than angrily. It was hard to get angry when my body was still basking in the afterglow of ecstasy, while

Book One: Beyond the Fog

inside my own volcano was dying down.

My feelings were too muddled for me to make sense of. I splashed some water on my body and decided to put the heavy thinking off until tomorrow. Right now, my body and my mind needed rest and a good night's sleep. Tomorrow I'd have a chance to think everything through and plan my next move.

I rinsed off, stepped out of the water, quickly dried off with a large piece of linen, and returned to the bedroom. The ilg was lying on the bed with his eyes closed. His tanned chest was rising and falling rhythmically. The fire was smoldering in the fireplace, and orange reflections created dancing spots on the floor. The storm outside had died down. I lay down on the edge of the bed, and immediately, without opening his eyes, Sverr pulled me to him and rolled on top of me.

I struggled to break free, but he didn't even budge, just pressed me closer. I resigned myself to the fact that I'd have to wait for him to fall asleep until I could move away. Staying put wasn't an option — I was used to sleeping alone and knew I'd never fall asleep in this position.

But my worn-out body had other ideas. It decided that sleeping in a man's arms was comfortable, so comfortable that in five minutes I fell into a deep, dreamless sleep.

Chapter 19. Confederation

THE EMERGENCY MEETING at the Academy of Progress began in deathly silence.

Instead of being held in the formal room usually reserved for such meetings, it was in a small room in the opposite wing of the building, mainly because the staggering and unthinkable damage done to the Academy wasn't visible from its windows.

Most of the people at this meeting weren't scientists, but rather men wearing the gray uniforms of the Confederation's security agency.

"Let's get started, everyone," the commanding officer boomed. "For those of you who don't know me, my name is Ethan Grey and I'm the chief of intelligence and national security for the Confederation."

Klin Ostrovsky snickered at the coincidence: the gray Grey. The soldier gave him a dirty look and he shrank back and stared down at his hands.

"We're not here to agonize over the missteps and mistakes of the Academy workers, who overlooked the danger and put the residents of the Confederation at risk."

"Overlooked?" Klin was unable to keep quiet. "Did you see who he was? We couldn't guess that."

"May I remind you that your colleague, Dr. Orway, did manage to guess that," Ethan Grey interrupted him icily.

Book One: Beyond the Fog

"That means that she had some basis for doing so."

"You don't understand!" The rector of the Academy couldn't stay silent either. He leaped up, mopping the perspiration from his forehead. "What happened is unreal and technically impossible. We don't know how to explain it. It defies the laws of physics, don't you realize that? What were we supposed to anticipate? A dragon?"

The scientists shivered and the soldiers responded with sullen looks. Ethan continued, "I'll say it again: we're not going to sit here discussing the reasons why that, er, creature appeared. Explaining his existence and his appearance inside the walls of the Academy is your problem. Mine is to eliminate the threat. And we can see for ourselves that it exists and on top of that, is completely real. All we need to do is look at the destroyed wing of this building." Grey gave everyone a barbed look. "We've now seen that our adversary has superior powers that we can't yet explain, and that we don't know how to fight. Our first task is to find out, understand, and disarm."

"Disarm?" Jean asked anxiously. "What do you mean exactly? This is a bombshell, a unique phenomenon we have to study. It's a life form we've never seen before. Do you know what a breakthrough that is?"

Ethan cut him off. "You can study this life form all you want after it stops threatening the Confederation. Gentlemen, I don't think you understand how serious this problem is, not that I'm asking you to understand. Right now I need something else from you. I need drawings, diagrams, and reports that will help us neutralize the threat. We'll start with you, Dr. Eriksen. You said you found three points where the Fog has dispersed? Right here?" Ethan pointed to a spot on the map.

"That's right. But one is in the ocean and one is on the mountain ridge. The Fog has nearly disappeared there, but

The Charmed Fjords

we may emerge into a gorge. We don't have a map of the location from the fjord side. The most accessible place to pass through is where the expedition entered the fjords."

"Most accessible doesn't mean best," Grey said. He looked at the map again and pointed at the outline of the cliffs. "What are the chances we'll be able to pass through here?"

"I can't tell you anything about our chances of passing through anywhere," Eriksen said grimly. "I'm inclined to say that the expedition was guided to the fjords by some sort of powers we don't yet understand. The dragon's power, if you will."

"But the Fog has practically dissipated here. Right?"

"Yes," Anders replied uneasily.

"Very well." Ethan nodded at his own thoughts. "We'll activate the plan for the armed incursion."

OLIVIA

Bam! Bam! Bam!

Damned alarm clock! Was it really time to get up?

I turned over, feeling vaguely that something was off, and opened my eyes. Everything came rushing back to me all at once: Neroaldaf, Sverr, the fjords, the dragons.

I jolted upright and jumped off the bed. Sverr was nowhere in sight. Outside the window, a bell chimed anxiously and jarringly: Bam! Bam!

The door slammed and Irga rushed in.

"Quick, get dressed!" she shouted from the doorway as she flung a few pieces of folded cloth onto a chair.

"What's going on?" I asked in bewilderment, hastily covering myself with the bedspread. "Where's Sverr?"

Irga grimaced at me. "The riar is at the shore. He

Book One: Beyond the Fog

ordered me to look after you, outsider. Get a move on, will you?"

"My name is Olivia." I let go of the bedspread and realized that getting dressed sounded like a good idea. I examined the clothes and grunted. Oh, well, what else did I expect? There was a white linen camisole and a dark green sleeveless dress made of thin wool with cutouts on the side seams. There were felt stockings and underwear that looked like short shorts. I guess it wasn't so bad on the whole. There were also soft leather ankle boots, a belt that circled my waist several times, and a broad, warm kerchief to go over my shoulders. Or was it supposed to cover my hair? I hadn't figured that out yet, but it appeared that the women here didn't cover their heads.

"What's that noise?" I asked as I pulled the clothes on.

"We've been attacked," Irga explained curtly. I dropped the boot I was holding. She raised her eyebrows in surprise. "Why are you so scared? Hasn't the place where you're from ever been attacked?"

"Who attacked?"

"I think it was Aurolhjoll again," Irga explained, but of course that meant nothing to me. "It's not far, no more than three days by sea from Neroaldaf. The white riar has had a grudge against our fortress for a long time."

The wind carried the sounds of shouting and clanging metal.

"How horrible," I gasped. "What's going on out there, a battle? What if they kill someone?"

"Anything can happen," Irga said philosophically as she briskly made the bed. "But don't be afraid. I'm taking you to a shelter. You'll stay there until the battle ends. Don't shake like that. Our riar can easily fight the snow people, especially when the a-tem is with him. But we need to hurry."

I quickly pulled on my shoes and bounded out of the

The Charmed Fjords

room behind Irga. She ran along the winding dark corridor, chattering along the way.

"I picked up a coin from the shatiya! It wasn't all by the rules, but it was a little piece of gold — thanks be to the firstborn hjeggs. It wasn't by the rules at all. I never saw one like it."

I clenched my teeth and kept my mouth shut, ignoring the avid interest in Irga's eyes. She pursed her mouth as though she were wounded, but then immediately chuckled playfully. "Judging by last night, by summertime we'll have lots of new babies. I can't remember ever hearing a call like that — no one can. Neroaldaf was awake all night."

"What do you mean?" I stopped in my tracks. "What are you talking about?"

"Why, the passion that seized everyone in the city," Irga said with a sly wink. "It was a good call, filled with fire. Everyone felt it and everyone obeyed. And now the children who are born will be strong, and we'll be healthy and strong. If there hadn't been an attack, Neroaldaf would be preparing a banquet."

"What?" I clutched my skirt. "Are you saying that everyone in the fortress feels the hjegg's call?"

"Well, you obviously felt it more than the others," Irga chuckled. "It was even frightening — the flame was strong enough to burn you. But of course the others feel it too. How could it be otherwise? The stronger the call, the stronger the children, so everyone was busy last night. Why are you looking at me like that? Did you really not know this? You are a strange one, outsider. What kind of a place are you from? They bring us a stranger and I need to explain everything to you."

Muttering under her breath, Irga led me down a staircase. Apparently the shelter was in the cellar. I anxiously tried to digest all this new information. OK, so the dragon's

Book One: Beyond the Fog

mental influence was important for the whole community, and everyone living close by felt it, and they all knew when he was calling someone. Super.

I ground my teeth. I bolted toward the other side of the room, away from the steps into the dark cellar.

"Stop! Where are you going? Outsider, come back!"

"I don't like basements," I said as I ran. I lifted my skirt and sped up, ignoring Irga's shrieking. Irga called to someone, but apparently all the warriors were busy fending off the attack and had more important things to do than play tag with the riar's captive.

I took full advantage of that. I darted around the corner, jumped out of the fortress, and ran under low awnings whose purpose I didn't know. People were scurrying along the cobbled lanes of Neroaldaf, but they didn't seem especially panicked. It looked more like they were moving with efficient composure. Women were herding livestock into barns, shutting the doors and shutters, and hiding inside. Some men were hastily dragging weapons and projectiles toward the wall while others, wearing leather armor with metal plates, were running toward the closed gates, weapons in hand. No one was shouting "We're going to die!" or "It's all over!" No one was even screaming in terror. They were all just doing their own thing, so I deduced that these sorts of attacks were common occurrences here.

I followed the men and rushed to the wall, trying not to call attention to myself. They clearly had other concerns and didn't so much as glance at me. Just one elderly ilg darted his eyes under his bushy eyebrows and thundered, "Where are you going, you wretched girl? The shelter is the other way!"

I nodded vigorously and when the man was out of sight, I darted toward the wall where soldiers were standing. Every twenty yards or so there was a short ladder positioned on the

The Charmed Fjords

wall. The huge jaws of the stone dragon's head slammed shut, so now the iron gates closed off the entrance to the city. Suddenly a wild roar shook Neroaldaf.

It sounded like what I always imagined a dragon would sound like.

I felt a twinge of fear and wondered if I should have crawled into the cellar after all, but then I was struck by a bold wave of scholarly enthusiasm and banal curiosity, which prompted me to scramble up one of the ladders, lie flat on the wall, and look down.

The broad expanse between the seashore and fortress gleamed like frost. I strained my eyes to look more closely and saw a white hoarfrost covering the grass, while a light snow blanketed the sand in places. The grass at the edge of the water was green, though. Where had this piece of winter come from?

Boom! Another shot hit the wall. Unfortunately, the wall was a circle and from my perch I couldn't see much. But I did see boats rocking by the shore and soldiers running on the sand. I looked more closely. It looked like the hair of nearly all the men had also been touched by frost, and bright layers of the same frost glinted on the leather armor. It looked silver, and I saw the same thing on their weapons: spears, short and long swords, battleaxes, and other terrifying axes.

"Bolts!" people from our side began to shout, and down below a downpour gushed from the round metallic artillery. I gasped enthusiastically, trying not to miss a single detail.

Another roar, and a gray-white tail hammered the wall. It was huge and covered with spikes. It slapped the brickwork, knocking out stone fragments. Then it drew itself up and disappeared behind the bend. There was a thud on the gates that was so strong it felt like the entire fortifying wall quivered. I craned my neck, hoping to see what was going on, but I didn't dare go any closer.

Book One: Beyond the Fog

The strikes and the roaring stopped, and then a yell rang out over the fortress: "Sverr! Are you going to sit there in your bunker or come out and show us what you're made of?"

"I was waiting for you to get tired of roaring and show your little white face, Danar." The mocking voice of the riar of Neroaldaf startled me. It sounded so close I tensed up, trying to blend in with the wall and listen more closely. "I think last time you also tried to break through my walls. But you never learn from your failure, do you, Danar?"

Laughter broke out on the wall. The soldiers down below began to hiss indignantly, brandishing their weapons.

"Get out here!" The voice of the invisible Danar was filled with fury.

That didn't seem to concern Sverr, who spoke in the same languid, mocking tone. "Why? To kick your snowy ass again?"

The laughter and angry shouts below resonated louder.

"When we come in you'll beg for mercy, you scoundrel!" Danar spat.

The soldiers below crouched down and covered their heads with their shields. I frowned. It indeed looked like we were being attacked now. How was that even possible?

The frozen enemy ship rocked in the distance, it shone white on the stern, and the vessel spat sparks. It sped past like a white clump, while a frozen lump struck the wall, making a hole.

I covered my head with my arms and scrambled down the ladder as bolts and stones rained down. The attackers let out a battle cry and the defenders bellowed back. The snow riar's soldiers scrambled through the hole, right into a mass of spears and swords. But somewhere on the ocean a white light flashed again and another block pelted our fortifications.

The Charmed Fjords

I crammed myself into a narrow space between a shed and a stairway, watching the battle in horror. The soldiers were destroying one another, tearing one another's armor and bodies with sharp edges. Thick crimson blood was spurting everywhere.

"How do you like this, Sverr?" A hoarse laugh echoed and then died out in a roar. A long shadow crept over Neroaldaf. I gasped and looked up. A black dragon soared up over the fortress.

"Sverr..."

The name escaped my lips and the dragon shook his head in my direction. Then a massive gray foot with jagged claws slammed against the wall and Sverr soared higher, spreading his wings. I jumped up and crept along the wall, keeping my head down and hoping to be inconspicuous. Nearby I heard metal clang threateningly, and behind me a soldier collapsed heavily. I slapped a hand to my mouth to keep from crying out, and looked out from behind the wooden planking. From there I spotted the snow riar. His white, frosty hair was smudged with fresh blood, and his light eyes looked unseeingly into the sky. Terror paralyzed me for a moment — terror and the realization that all of this was real, and that people were really killing each other. They were killing either people on their side or their enemies — it made no difference. Whose side was I on, anyway?

Looking around, I crept out of my hiding place and picked up a discarded weapon. The shiny blade blurrily reflected my frightened face, and I suddenly realized in astonishment that what I was holding in my hands wasn't metal. Instead, it looked like an icicle. It was slightly curved with a bone handle and leather sheath. It was the kind of weapon that penetrated the body rather than cutting with the tip. But how could it remain so hard and sharp? Not only that, the warmth of my hands didn't melt it.

Book One: Beyond the Fog

In any case, there was no time to ponder this. I was surrounded by chaos, shouts, noise, and a battle. And it was all happening against the trumpeting of two dragons. Something on the other side of the wall was struck. It dropped to the ground with a deafening clang.

Concealing myself behind the planking again, I crawled along the wall until I spotted an opening. It was a small opening where a stone had been knocked out. I clung to it. The sand on the shore boiled from the two monsters sinking their teeth into each other. One was a dirty white, with thick membranes on his sides, shining frost, and folded milky wings. The second monster was familiar: black with gold streaks under the scales.

They were so big they made the large beach seem tiny. The two monsters grappled and rocked, the pier splintered, and the water began to bubble when the hjeggs fell in. Their tails slammed on the water with such force that they created a wave that rocked the ships and scattered the puny boats.

The dragons' roars were so piercing I had an urge to clap my hands over my ears, or better yet, burrow into a hole. I was simultaneously enraptured and horrified. The feelings were so strong my body turned to stone and I couldn't tear myself away from the otherworldly spectacle of this battle. My blood was boiling, like the ocean. It took me a moment to realize I was gripping the trophy knife with an impulse to thrust it into an enemy soldier's body.

I came to with a shudder. That meant that people didn't feel only the dragon's arousal. They also felt his fury, ardor, and power. No wonder the soldiers were fighting like death didn't exist.

I grasped the opening in the stone harder. Now Sverr was flapping his wings, pressing the white dragon into the sand at the bottom of the sea. The black claws sank into the body of the white dragon, pinning him down. Danar bellowed

The Charmed Fjords

and furiously swung his tail, but he couldn't escape Sverr's grasp. One of the wings floated on the water like a faded rag while the snow hjegg pressed the other one under his belly. Sverr flexed his long neck and a flame blazed from his fanged mouth. The outstretched white wing turned black and the snow hjegg let out a howl and threw Sverr off him.

"Let's go!" The order echoed over the city.

Some soldiers were still fighting, but most of them ran toward the ocean. There were no boats, so the soldiers would need to swim to the ship. I had no idea how they'd do that with their weapons weighing them down.

Sverr heavily flapped his wings, lifted the snow dragon into the air, and carried him toward the water. A couple of slaps of the black wings, and the fire hjegg released his claws. Danar crashed down and the ocean heaved and splashed onto the shore. A red flame soared out of Sverr's mouth along with a roar, and the hjegg shot upward. The dark water frothed and became covered in frost where the snow dragon was trying to get away.

"Who's hiding there? A trophy!" A malignant voice made me jump. Someone behind me jerked me by the arm and grabbed me by the hair. I screamed and stared in horror at a scarred face. The light blue eyes looked like slivers of ice on a river. I realized it was the snow riar. The man sneered, revealing snow-white teeth.

"Hey, hands off!" I hissed and brought down my icicle knife. I missed. The blade slid along the armor, which turned out to be unexpectedly sturdy. The stranger exclaimed angrily and pushed me so hard I fell. I rolled along the moist ground and smashed my shoulder into a ladder. A heavy body pressed me to the wall and I yelled out.

Suddenly an enormous shadow blocked the sun and Sverr swooped down. The black claws made incisions in the stone, then seized the snow riar, and the dragon zoomed back

Book One: Beyond the Fog

into the sky. Almost immediately, a body dropped down onto the sand on the other side of the wall.

Clasping a hand over my mouth, I watched as a furious flame ignited the wooden planking and it sparked. Huge dragon feet grasped the edge of the fortifying wall, and the monster dipped his head. The bright golden eyes squinted and stared at me. The hjegg's mouth opened, and I got a close-up view of the spear-sized notched fangs. As though my brain were working in slow motion, it occurred to me that if Sverr suddenly decided to breathe fire on me, all that would remain would be my charred little head — that is, if anything remained at all. I tentatively stepped to the side and the dragon let out a roar, scalding me with his burning breath. Then he abruptly straightened his neck, scooped me up with his foot, and surged upward. The drop in air pressure made my vision dim and I nearly passed out. A few powerful flutters, a glide upward, a drop, and the feet opened and I fell onto dry grass. I got up onto my knees and looked around. It appeared that the dragon had carried me far from the fortifying walls, to a small plateau. I couldn't even hear the sounds of the battle from here. The ocean was no longer visible, so I must have been on the other side of Neroaldaf.

Spitefully breathing fire, Sverr made a circle and disappeared into the gathering clouds.

I rubbed my rear end where I'd landed and tried to get my bearings. There was a small, rocky projection blanketed in withered grass. It was about ten feet in diameter. There was no way to get down, and that realization irritated me. Apparently this was how Sverr had decided to punish me.

I pushed a clump of dry grass together, freeing up some earth, and picked up a pebble. I might as well make the most of my time and take stock, like any good scientist would. I could have used a strong cup of coffee and a warm muffin. I hadn't eaten since yesterday and the soup had long

The Charmed Fjords

evaporated out of my system. But there was no server keeping watch on this little cliff, so I'd need to manage without food.

Chapter 20. Sverr

MY WRATH WAS STILL SEETHING in my chest. I had to circle Neroaldaf twice to calm it. Otherwise, I would have killed everyone and sent them to Hellehjegg. The desire to burn my own people and everyone else bubbled in me, and fiery flashes branded my skin. I knew the people on the ground could see my fury, and that's why they were cowering in their shelters. It was shameful that it was their own riar, not the snow hjegg, who drove them to their hiding places.

    I breathed out some bitter-tasting fire, then dropped down on the grass behind the cliff, breaking up the ground with my claws. I made a few turns and spit black smoke and balls of flame. I glanced toward the sea and the fury began to roil inside me again. While I'd been dealing with that obstinate outsider, Danar had managed to climb back onto his ship. And where was Irvin? Why hadn't my a-tem demolished the vessel that carried these interlopers? Admittedly, it's hard to send the main *hjeggkar* to the bottom of the sea — the snow people have their secret defenses. I did try: I spit flames, but all I got in response was a hail of icy projectiles, which for me are repugnant. They burn my skin more strongly than acid. Those damned frost-backed vermin. May they freeze in their snowbanks up to their necks! It's impossible to reach their ships from above — the snow people

The Charmed Fjords

protect their hjeggkars so that I can't strike them. In theory I could have tried down below, from the underbelly, but Irvin is the only one who can do that. I can't travel in the sea.

Where the hell was that twin of mine?

I roared angrily, trying to decide whether to do another circle.

And what was my lilgan doing on the wall, where she easily could have been killed, wounded, or placed on her knees and taken? Sure, the snow people could be ripped apart and annihilated, but what if she ended up in the clutches of someone from Neroaldaf? My fury churns in the chest of every warrior, and the ardor of battle always spills over into lust. That's the instinct of the black hjegg. We're all built like that. And if I hadn't gotten to her in time, what would I have had to do later with her and with whoever took her?

I exhaled a flame and watched it char the edge of the cliff. A stone snapped and dropped into the sea. Fragments showered down after it. A few seconds later, an avalanche rolled down like stony foam, crumbling into the dark water. Fortunately, there were no houses on this side of the cliff — if there were, they would have been decimated.

I shook my head and sneered. The prospect of someone else taking Liv was enough to make me want to annihilate all of Neroaldaf, and especially all the men who were still agitated.

I scraped my claws on the granite ledge, trying to get my wits back. If I didn't let the hjegg go right now I'd cause mayhem.

I exhaled and when I opened my eyes, the world looked different. That's how it always was. Human eyes see differently. I knelt down in the twisted grooves my claws made. What really made my stomach churn was that even when I was in my human form, fury tore my chest and I had

Book One: Beyond the Fog

an urge to kill. The only difference was that instead of fire and fangs I wanted to use steel or my bare hands.

This was all the outsider's fault.

I spit on the grass and stood up. Liv needed to be punished. I should leave her on that ledge for a few days without water or food, so she'd understand that she couldn't disobey my orders, or crawl to where the warriors were skirmishing, or make me angry.

I spit again as the fury simmered. The hjegg's shadow covered me even though I hadn't called him.

I shut my eyes, trying to breathe evenly. No matter what, I couldn't merge with my hjegg, because then all hell would break loose.

The fury didn't die down completely, but it waned. I scowled at the cliffs. My human eyes were too weak to see the figure of the small woman from this distance. I was glad for that. I knew that if I saw her now, I'd immediately throw her into the dungeon and punish her.

Let her stay put for a couple of days and think things over. And then when she finally sees me, she'll greet me tearfully and she'll do anything I ask.

OLIVIA

The sun was beginning to set and I realized I was exhausted. I looked up from my scribblings on the ground and rubbed my stomach. I was hungry, but distracting myself with work was nothing new to me, so eventually I forgot about eating. What I really wanted was coffee, but I knew I wouldn't be seeing that. I stood up, kneaded my lower back, and examined my analysis skeptically. Drawing on the ground with a rock wasn't exactly the most convenient way of working, but I didn't really have much choice. Ideas had

The Charmed Fjords

started to take shape in my head and I was able to analyze what I'd seen, draw some broad conclusions, and map out a plan for what I'd do next.

On the whole, I thought I'd chosen the right path: study, remember, survive. The data I came up with wasn't just a discovery, but the breakthrough of the millennium. How I yearned to delve more deeply into the nature of these hjeggs. If only I could bring my lab here. Of course there were no science departments or civilized research methods on the fjords. But on the other hand, I'd gotten a unique opportunity to conduct research in the hjeggs' natural habitat.

Dragons, just think of that!

I still hadn't come up with any rational explanations, but I was so excited to be back in my element that I wanted to sing. Come to think of it, why not sing? The Academy's in-house psychologist always said that singing was excellent stress relief. Personally, I would have chosen chocolate, but here chocolate seemed about as easy to come by as coffee.

Nature hadn't graced me with a good voice or ear, so the sounds that came out of my mouth were pretty wretched. I was finishing an aria from a popular rock opera just as the cliff shook and a dark passageway appeared on the stone.

Suddenly Sverr appeared out of the hole. The expression on his face was a mixture of amusement and wrath. I raised my eyebrows and hastily wiped my scribblings away with my foot.

I was elated to see him but tried to bury the feeling, and I couldn't ignore the fact that I was also worried.

The ilg scowled and looked at me searchingly. I had no idea what he was hoping to find in my face, but I could see the malice building in his eyes.

"You're a terrible singer, lilgan," he finally said despondently. "And that song is horrible."

"Sorry," I said with a shrug. "Singing helps relieve

Book One: Beyond the Fog

stress and suppress hunger. At least that's what they say. But I've tried it and I think whoever says that is lying. I'm still hungry, and I'm even more thirsty than before. So based on my experience, this isn't a good way to get rid of your worries."

Sverr stared at me and let out a strange chuckle. He said, "I was sure I'd show up here and you'd be crying and in agony, lilgan."

"Really?" I asked, genuinely surprised. "What do I have to cry about? I'm alive and healthy, and the scenery is gorgeous. Sure, I'd like something to eat, but the situation isn't dire yet. But if I could get some coffee, I'd be willing to cry a little."

"For coffee?" The ilg narrowed his eyes.

"Yes." I shifted my weight and wiped away the rest of my drawings. "Coff-ee..."

"I'm starting to think you were foisted on me for no reason," the ilg said thoughtfully.

"You're the one who scooped me up in your legs," I corrected him. "No one asked you to. I'm sure of that."

"I scooped you up because you made me mad. I wanted to punish you," Sverr said, an odd expression on his face.

"I figured that out."

"Speaking of which, I haven't done that yet even though you deserve a whacking."

"I appreciate that. I have a low pain threshold."

The ilg stared at me unblinkingly. His golden eyes blazed and he took a step toward me.

"Enough! I'm going to punish you, Liv, because you ran away, defied my orders, and climbed onto the wall. Do you understand? If not, you'll stay here until you do. And don't expect to get any water or food."

"OK, I got it," I said quickly.

The ilg ground his teeth. Then he lunged forward,

The Charmed Fjords

grabbed my dress, and pulled me toward him. "Are you laughing? Are you mocking me? Do you think you're smarter than me, Liv?"

"My knowledge isn't comparable to yours," I answered calmly, trying not to shake. "Because it's different, Sverr. I know how and why a plane takes off. You know how a hjegg takes off. They're not comparable. And no, I'm not mocking you. I know I shouldn't have left the fortress, but I'm a scientist. It's my instinct to do things like that, just like it's your instinct to take possession of things, do you understand? I'm afraid it's stronger than me."

The ilg gulped greedily. "You must obey my orders."

"I'm not sure I can promise you that," I replied honestly.

Sverr's eyes flashed spitefully and then, to my surprise, he grinned. "I just don't know what to do with you, Liv. You confuse me. You make it hard for me to think. I look at you and there's only one thing I want."

A hot wave flowed from my head to my feet and I felt all my hair stand on end. Desire sparked for a moment and was reflected in his eyes, body, and words. I inhaled the air, which had become thick and sticky. I had the impression there were flashes of light sparking around me. Maybe there were. When it came to this ilg, nothing surprised me anymore.

He slowly pulled me to him.

"No," I said, pushing on his chest.

"Are you resisting?" he frowned. "Again?"

"I'm thirsty," I stammered hoarsely.

"I'll give you some water, however much you want."

Suddenly rain started to gush and I lifted my head in astonishment. A storm was gathering over the cliffs. Lightning bolts hissed and struck the rocks, leaving round depressions. A downpour assailed the fjord like a wall, instantly drenching my dress. Surprisingly, it was a warm, soothing rain. Sverr pressed his lips to my neck. A flaming

Book One: Beyond the Fog

arrow struck nearby, next to my foot, and I cried out. I instinctively jerked backward and cowered.

"Don't be afraid," the ilg said, placing his lips on mine. "Don't be afraid of anything with me, lilgan."

"Nothing?" I asked.

"Nothing. Except me."

The scientist went to hide somewhere in the back of my mind. She was trying to figure out this abnormal storm and the lightning that obeyed the ilg. But she quickly surrendered and disappeared, melting away from the scorching sensation. Sverr caught my quiet breath with his lips and smiled in satisfaction.

"This is how much I like you, Liv," he said, and another bolt of lightning struck the cliff, leaving a black, charred trace. It was as scalding as Sverr's lips and hands. "But I like you no matter what. And that's so strange. If I didn't know I was your first, I'd kill you. You're too desirable."

My mouth dropped. I was at a loss for words. He was a barbarian... I shook my head, shaking the drops of water out of my hair.

"What about your shatiya?" I asked.

"And don't you dare think about anyone else," the ilg said darkly. "Only me..."

After I finally nodded in agreement, he kissed me ardently. I felt the sparks burning my exposed skin. In a daze, it occurred to me that the lightning was still striking us, or maybe it was just my imagination.

When I came back to Earth and opened my eyes, the clouds were dissipating and the rain had stopped. Sverr's eyes were shining tenderly and contentedly. He let go of my dress and the damp fabric slapped my bare legs. I shivered. The ilg reached out as though he wanted to embrace me, but then he frowned. He stepped away and nodded at the opening in the cliff.

The Charmed Fjords

"Let's go, lilgan. You're frail. You might get sick." He took a step toward the wall and then glanced at me over his shoulder. A teasing chuckle gleamed in his golden eyes. "By the way, I also know how your planes take off. It's not very complicated."

He turned around and entered the cliff. My mouth agape, I stared after him. He knew that? So maybe I was the weak link here? Because I sure didn't understand a thing in this world of the extraordinary hjeggs.

Unable to restrain myself, I burst out laughing. At the same time, I was gripped by a feeling so powerful my heart contracted. Looking at Sverr's back, his broad shoulders, and his dark, wet hair, I realized that the feeling was an uncanny fear that shook me to my core. It was so strong I wanted to cling to him, but of course I couldn't do that. I bit my cheek, completely at a loss. Falling in love was the stupidest thing imaginable.

"Wake up, lilgan," Sverr called.

I shook my head and hurried to catch up with him.

Past the entrance, there were stone steps and a narrow, winding passageway. Burning-red streaks snaked along the dark walls, emitting a faint light. I ran my fingers over them and was surprised to find that they were warm.

"What's this? How did you make this passageway? Is this really the cliff rock? What did you use to break through it?"

Sverr snorted quietly and glanced back at me without stopping. His lips trembled in a smile. "You really haven't figured it out, Olivia Orway the anthropologist? Think about it. Or should I put you back on the cliff so you can doodle on the ground some more since you don't have your notebook here?" he asked mockingly. Turning away from me, he descended into the depths of the cave.

I stood stock-still on the stone ledge and contemplated

Book One: Beyond the Fog

all of this. I stroked the red snaking line, which was smooth, with no traces of clearing or cleavage. I couldn't forget the lightning that this ilg seemed to control, or the clouds. I gasped when a pebble stung my finger and left a little scratch. My foot slipped off the stone but before I crashed to the ground a strong hand pulled me up. Once again, the ilg burned me with his breath, and his lips ran down my cheek.

"Think and let me take care of Neroaldaf," he said with a chuckle and pulled back. "I can't get you out of my head, lilgan."

He thrust my cut finger into his mouth and licked it. I just stood there on the high step, feeling my throat catch again. What man in the Confederation would do that? After all, it wasn't hygienic. But this ilg — this dragon — couldn't care less about all of that.

My heart pounded against my ribs and I carefully extricated my hand from his mouth.

But Sverr pressed his fingers to my waist, making sure I wouldn't fall again. He encircled my arm with his fingers and I couldn't help laughing at the bracelet his fingers made — a barbarian bracelet.

We walked like that the whole way to the other opening. I was surprised to discover that the narrow passage in the cliff led straight to the tower that held the riar's chambers. When I looked back, trying to make a note of where the entrance was, all I saw was a dark wall with the same fiery streaks.

"I'll send the women to you," Sverr said distractedly. He frowned and harrumphed in annoyance. "No, it would be better if I sent a guard to you. Things will be calmer that way."

With that he strode off so quickly I didn't have a chance to respond.

I made a beeline for a table where I saw paper and a black ink holder. I grabbed the yellow sheet of paper, hastily

The Charmed Fjords

jotted down my observations, and wrote an arrow. I looked at my drawing. There was only one conclusion.

"That's impossible," I muttered grimly. Just like dragons didn't exist. No matter how many angles I looked at everything from, I reached the same conclusion: the fire hjegg controlled not only the storms but also the cliff rocks. And maybe he could move the stone just by looking at it, slap on steps inside, and open an entrance to wherever he wanted.

"It can't be!"

I could already almost imagine how I'd report back to the Academy about this. Everything defied the laws of physics, chemistry, and gravity, not to mention the world order. Humanity would need to reexamine everything — the laws, postulates, axioms, and theorems. All of them would become unthinkable and preposterous. I'd seen mountains that separated in obedience to a silent order, a dragon that soared into the sky, and the frontiers of a future that were unknown to us and that humans couldn't even dream of — new possibilities, discoveries, and breakthroughs.

I waved my arms helplessly and sat down on the edge of an armchair, thinking about what had happened at the Academy. I remembered how the soldiers had thrown themselves at Sverr. The image still put a bad taste in my mouth while feelings of guilt and confusion stung me. What would happen if I told everyone about what I'd seen here? The Confederation would put all its efforts into overcoming the Fog. And if Anders was right, the Fog was thinning.

But Sverr would never surrender his fjords, and none of the other ilgs would either. I was already sure of that. So what was I to do?

Understanding hit me like a slap in the face. My whole life was on the other side of the Fog: my work, my friends, the Academy, my small but cozy apartment. And this whole time I hadn't been afraid because I was sure I'd go back. It wasn't

Book One: Beyond the Fog

like I'd fallen into a time warp. There was an entrance, so I'd find the exit. And I wouldn't just return, but I'd return with a load of unique knowledge that would enrich the science of our world.

But now? Now I looked around the room in which everything was unfamiliar and strange, and I began to feel afraid, but not of the ilgs. No, I was afraid of myself because I no longer knew how I was supposed to behave. The people I'd always thought were reasonable had showered Sverr with bullets. Did people like that need science?

I buried my head in my hands. The contradictions were tearing me apart. I wanted to follow the path of knowledge, and I dreamed of discoveries — not for myself, but for the world, for a better future. But now everything seemed upside down. Was everything a lie?

Where was reality?

My anguish was interrupted by Slenga, who walked in carrying a tray. Weapons jangled behind the door and I caught sight of soldiers standing in the hall. Great. Now they were guarding me.

"I brought you some food," Slenga said with a smile, peering at me curiously. "The riar ordered you not to eat too much. We're having a celebration tonight. We fought off the attack and everyone's alive. Some people are injured, but it's OK, they'll live. We'll pray to Hellehjegg and he'll heal everyone."

I grabbed a bun with chopped meat and an egg, thrust it into my mouth, and smacked my lips in delight.

"Where did the riar go?" I asked with my mouth full.

"He's up there," Slenga said, pointing and leaning down. "He's yelling at the a-tem. What if they destroy something again! Last time they flattened the blacksmith's shop to the ground and they had to build a new one."

"Why's he yelling?"

The Charmed Fjords

"I don't know. We all went to hide as soon as we heard the roar. Better safe than sorry. But I wouldn't mind listening." I swallowed my food, moved closer to Slenga, and looked at her conspiratorially.

"Say, where do you get a ring like the one the riar and a-tem have? The ring of Gorlohum? Is that what you call it? Men become hjeggs because of it, is that it?"

"They plead for it," Slenga said, batting her eyes. "You really don't know about that? It's not like that where you come from?"

"There are no hjeggs where I live."

"Really?" Slenga was so surprised she nearly fell over. "What do you mean, there are no hjeggs? No protection? No call? You poor, unfortunate creatures! In that case, you should kiss the riar's feet for bringing you to Neroaldaf. He saved you from a terrible fate."

"Yeah, what a savior," I chuckled.

Up above there was a bang that made the tower shake and stones rain down from the ceiling.

"I'd better go," Slenga said nervously, jumping up. "I'll come back later for the tray."

She ran out, clearly frightened. I bounded toward the door, but when I got there the two guards pushed me back into the room.

"The outsider needs to stay here," the older one said firmly.

I went back in, deciding to look for another way out of the room. In any case, for starters I could get a good look at the riar's dwellings.

Book One: Beyond the Fog

SVERR

Irvin ducked out of the path of Sverr's fist, writhed like a slippery eel, and leaped aside.

"Stop yelling!" he snapped, panting. "Stop attacking me!"

"You haven't told me yet why I should stop and what you were doing with yourself while the fortress was being attacked," the riar spat.

"I came as soon as I heard!"

"Oh, come on!"

"Sverr, stop! OK, fine, it's my fault! And if you want, we can pull apart half the wall again," the a-tem said irately. "I wasn't expecting the attack. The sea was silent, and I was furious because of you — because of the shatiya and that outsider."

The riar stopped and looked at the a-tem distrustfully. Irvin bared his teeth. Sverr was already feeling the cold, wet shadow of his hjegg nearby.

"What's happening to you, my riar?" Irvin shook his head. "First you stage a show for the people from beyond the Fog, then you leave with them, and then you start to break our laws? What next? Will you spit on Gorlohum? Burn Neroaldaf to the ground? What'll it be, Sverr?"

The riar clenched his fists, itching to punch his a-tem again. He forced himself to calm down. "Do I need to explain it again, Irvin?" he said. "I'm doing all of this for the good of Neroaldaf and all the fjords."

"Are you? Or maybe you just can't tear yourself away from that maiden? I see how you look at her. You've been looking at her like that from the beginning."

Sverr reached the a-tem in a single leap and pinned him to the cold stone wall of the tower. He stared daggers at

The Charmed Fjords

Irvin.

"She's none of your damn business, Irvin. If you know what's good for you, you'll forget what that girl looks like."

The a-tem winced but didn't try to disentangle himself from the riar's grip. He knew it was useless to resist when they were in their human forms. Even when they were animals it was hard to fight him.

"Great Gorlohum! So I'm right. It's not for nothing that I took her to my cave. You have feelings for her, is that it? She's important to you. But she's just an outsider, Sverr, a daughter of the Confederation! You look her in the eyes when you take her, don't you? You've gotten attached to her and lost your mind. She's hell-bent on getting back to the other side of the Great Fog and gossiping about us."

"Yes, I know." The master of Neroaldaf loosened his hand and turned away. "But she's not going back. She's staying here."

"She'll end up hating you," the a-tem said to Sverr's back. "That girl isn't a prisoner from other fjords, Sverr. She's different. We all saw how she fought at the shatiya. She was ready to fight to the death. She was disobedient and stubborn. She'll never accept it, Sverr. Her life is different and she'll never understand the way we live. You and I both know that. To her, we're nothing but animals and our life is strange. As long as she consoles herself with the hope of returning, she'll keep acting nice to you. But as soon as she figures out your plan, she'll try to escape. She'll try to fight her way to the Fog, back to her people. We can't let that happen. So now what do we do? Hold her under lock and key? We'll never be able to trust her."

"I know that." Sverr's words fell like hunks of granite.

"But that's not the most frightening thing. You've gotten attached to her. That's unacceptable, Sverr. You don't have the right to do that. Your life is already bound to another

Book One: Beyond the Fog

woman, the one who will give birth to the heirs of Neroaldaf. Your bed is for maidens who don't look you in the eye and who turn their backs, and your call is for everyone. It's the law, Sverr. You knew that when you became the riar. The outsider has no place beside you."

Sverr didn't respond. He was no longer looking at Irvin, but Irvin saw his shoulders stiffen.

"It would be better if you gave her to me," Irvin said softly. "But it's already too late, isn't it? You look at her like you own her. You think of her as yours. What are you planning to do next, my riar? Are you going to wait for the day when she betrays you? If she has a choice between you and her own world, she'll choose the Confederation. Do you know that too?"

"If she does that I'll kill her," Sverr said calmly over his shoulder as he headed toward the stairway. "Now go perform your duties, my a-tem."

Irvin slammed a fist into the wall, bruising his knuckles. He gloomily watched Sverr leave.

"My main duty is to protect you, my riar," he said matter-of-factly.

Chapter 21. Olivia

THE DOOR SLAMMED as Sverr burst in. A scent of fire and ash trailed behind him. He was obviously enraged but trying not to show it.

He glanced at me sharply and ordered, "Come with me."

Of course I wanted to ask questions, but I kept my mouth shut. We walked to the end of the corridor and Sverr opened another door. When we stepped into the room I gasped. For a moment I thought I was back home — the room was crowded with objects I knew well but hadn't seen here. Unable to believe my eyes, I ran my fingers over a velvet armchair that some books were lying on. I even recognized the covers. There were novels I'd read when I was younger, adventure stories, historical reference books, and encyclopedias. A bulky floor lamp stood beside the chair, and behind it there was a dresser with bronze handles. There was polished wood covered with newspapers, photos, pads of paper, yellowing letters, boxes filled with pens, and two mugs with pictures of smiling fluffy cats. There was a round table that held board games, cell phones, and little gadgets. I was surrounded by so many familiar things my heart shook and fluttered.

There was a painting hanging on the wall that showed a familiar glade and houses. I smiled in spite of myself.

I looked at the ilg in bewilderment. He was standing

Book One: Beyond the Fog

still in the doorway and glowering at me.

"But how — where did all of this come from?" I asked.

"From the bottom of the ocean," he said blandly. "From the ships of humans who entered the Fog and disappeared. The metal sank to the bottom and the people died, but a lot of what was inside remained."

"From the ocean bed?" I asked in confusion. "But how did you salvage everything?"

I knew the answer before he told me — the sea hjegg. Of course.

"My ancestor, a former riar of Neroaldaf, began collecting objects from the Confederation. His name was Ragnar, and I also inherited his name. Like me, he had a twin, the sea hjegg. It's a tradition," Sverr said, still sounding indifferent. "My father didn't encourage this pastime — there are reasons for that — and he ordered that all the objects from the foreign world be hidden away deep in the cliff. The things here are what Irvin brought."

"Your father?" I asked.

"The previous riar. You can stay here, lilgan," the ilg said between clenched teeth. "There are a lot of things here you'll like. You'll be able to rest easy here. We're having a feast at the fortress tonight. Be ready for it."

I looked around in bewilderment. Thoughts tumbled around in my head. Conclusion number one: the ilgs, or at least Sverr, knew a lot about humans, and he'd obviously accumulated this knowledge from a huge amount of sources. He'd spent years studying us through books, encyclopedias, photos, and who knew what else. He'd held objects from another world and figured out what they were used for. If the sea dragon could raise ships, Sverr must have a lot of rooms like this one. How many vessels were counted as having disappeared without a trace in the vicinity of the mysterious Arvin Triangle, which wasn't far from the Fog? Between the

The Charmed Fjords

passenger ships and naval cruisers, there'd be a treasure trove of information.

That meant that the riar had been leading the expedition on from the start. Admittedly, I'd already figured that out.

Conclusion number two: I was never going to be released from the fjords. So the ilg decided to bring me here and show me this. It was like it was his way of saying, content yourself with this, Liv, and forget your past because now you know too much.

Lost in thought, I turned a phone around in my hands. Of course it was dead. There was no connection and the battery had long run out.

I wondered what Sverr would do if I tried to run away anyhow?

I was afraid to think about the answer.

"You wanted to go to the Academy council, didn't you?" I asked, lifting a thick iron nail. "So you orchestrated all of this. Did you find out what you wanted to, Sverr? And now what? What are you planning to do next?"

"Are you asking about yourself or the Confederation, Olivia?" The ilg came closer and studied me. He looked down at me mockingly and said, "You've already figured out what I'm planning to do with you. As for your world, I'm not interested in the people of your world as long as they stay on the other side of the Fog and don't stick their noses in over here."

"But why?" I couldn't contain myself. "We have so much to teach you. Progress..."

"Progress?" The golden eyes flashed menacingly. "Tell me honestly, anthropologist Olivia Orway, what do you think when you look at me? I'm capable of killing, wearing hides, eating raw meat, and dancing at the shatiya. I see superiority in your eyes. That's what you think. That's what all the people

Book One: Beyond the Fog

of the Confederation think. I know how your world was united. The Confederation just conquered the other peoples, and the ones that didn't go along with it were wiped off the face of the earth. You think you'll bring progress? The fjords don't need that kind of progress."

"But we have so many things that are useful and necessary," I cried out suddenly. "Tolerance, humanism, laws."

"There's no killing in your world? No atrocities, vileness, betrayal? Well?"

"There is, but — "

"Where did you get your scars?" he asked suddenly.

"What?"

"Where are they from? Tell me!"

"Burglars broke into my house," I whispered hoarsely. The words scratched my throat. "I was only seventeen. They thought I was somewhat attractive. They decided not just to rob the house, but also to bring me to my knees and take advantage of me."

I shuddered at the memory.

"What did you do?"

"I killed," I said. "I killed one of them. With a knife. I don't even know how I managed to grab it and stab him. I couldn't let them... the second guy pushed me out the window and I cut myself. Then and there I swore that no one would ever bring me to my knees, not in any sense of the word."

"And is that your law?" The riar exhaled furiously. "In Neroaldaf people are killed for trying to enter someone else's house or take someone else's woman. So here we don't shut the doors, and maidens aren't afraid to live in their own homes. We fight with our enemies but we don't make a mess in our own house." Sverr seized the nail I was rolling around in my hands and squeezed it. His eyes were burning and

The Charmed Fjords

hypnotizing me. I couldn't look away. "So why should we live like you? You think you're better for one reason only, Olivia: because you invented a bunch of metal machines that can kill. Your planes, your ships, your cars — you've lost yourselves but invented your damned progress."

"But..."

What about our achievements — science, medicine? I opened my mouth to speak, but then shut it again. Science? How could science explain the existence of the hjeggs? Or the fact that my asthma attack had been cured with words?

Sverr came closer, looming in front of me like a stone giant.

"So who do you see when you look at me, Liv? Tell me." His pupils elongated and for a moment I felt terror, knowing what that meant. "You see a barbarian, lilgan. That's just what the people at your Academy and in the expedition to the fjords saw. You look at the hides, our habits, and our customs, and arrogance burns in your eyes. You think you're superior. That savage, you think. An animal who looks like a man. But we just live differently. You measure development with your metal machines, isn't that so? That means that we'll always be barbarians to you, savages you won't allow to rule their own land."

He flung the piece of metal at my feet and stalked out of the room. I looked down slowly. The nail was gone — it was now a little iron bird lying on the floor. That ugly, crooked nail had become a graceful seagull in the ilg's hands.

SVERR

The soldiers enlisted to guard the holes in the Fog lined up behind the armory. I inspected each of them closely, looked into their eyes, and struck them with the hjegg's fury. The

Book One: Beyond the Fog

men bowed their heads and clenched their teeth but remained in formation. That meant they weren't concealing anything sinister and would serve loyally. But duty and honor are more durable than fear. Before settling in Neroaldaf, the soldiers had sworn an oath to me. But I didn't accept it in my human form. No one would bring themselves to lie to the hjegg in the lands of water and cliffs. Everyone knows that if you lie to the riar, the hjeggs' spirits will punish you with eternal torture in the afterlife. That's a fate worse than death.

A few dozen selected soldiers would be sent to the openings in the Fog in the morning.

"I have one order for you," I said. "Guard the fjords. Guard Neroaldaf. If people manage to get past the Fog, kill them. No discussion. No questions. Do not take any prisoners. Just kill anyone who wants to rule the fjords. You know that the people who will come want to take our land, women, gold, ships, and power away from us. For centuries they've been trying to penetrate the Fog that the mighty Gorlohum sent to protect us. If there's misfortune and people can pass through, kill them. Is that clear?"

"Yes, riar!" the soldiers barked. Their eyes burned with hate and the searing fury of the black beast. That was a good thing. I nodded.

"Tomorrow you will bid farewell to Neroaldaf, get into the hjeggkars, and go into the sea, to the lands I showed you. There are three points — three locations for you to guard. You'll be relieved in two weeks. The hjeggkars will be waiting for you tomorrow. Tonight we celebrate."

"Yes, riar!"

I dismissed the soldiers and headed into the armory. By evening I'd inspected the weapons, warehouses, and walls that had been damaged in the attack by the snow riar. The holes had already been patched; the part that had most

The Charmed Fjords

suffered was the northern section, where a ship could pass through. I examined the stones and decided it would be easier and faster to summon the mountains than to wait for the stonemasons to fix everything.

My soul was unsettled even though the sea was calm and didn't portend any danger. I was certain that my a-tem had learned his lesson and would now remember his duties and swim through the waters of the fjords to make sure the enemy wasn't in sight.

Yet I felt black inside, like the smoldering ruins after the hjegg's fire.

So before the feast I went out to the cliffs, stripped, and from the ledge submerged myself into the cold waters of the fjords. A wave stirred, carried me away, and closed down on my head like a frigid curtain. Here, in the depths, I was finally able to dispel the fury bubbling inside me. Of course, it would return — it always does. But in the evening, among the soldiers of Neroaldaf and their wives, I would be calm.

I'd be able to solve the main problem: what to do with the information I had learned. I couldn't keep it a secret, and unfortunately, that was a huge problem.

OLIVIA

It didn't take long to examine the photos, and I quickly got my fill of the cracked paintings and useless stun guns. My initial excitement dissolved and I began to feel like I was wandering through a cemetery. In a sense, that's exactly what this was, since everything came from a sunken ship.

So when there was a knock at the door and one of the guards entered, I was a little relieved.

"Let's go, lilgan. We've been ordered to escort you."

I nodded and we walked along corridors lit with lamps

Book One: Beyond the Fog

filled with the hjegg's living, eternal flame. I was led outside, past the place where my shatiya didn't happen the night before. I glanced at the square and felt a tremor run through me. It looked like the shatiya had never happened. Freshly washed paving stones sparkled, and there were no lanterns or crowds. We walked to a building near the riar's tower and entered a wide, brightly lit hall. Wooden tables were lined up along the walls. They were covered with linen cloths, and colorful needlework stood in the center of each table. It was an ornament depicting flowers, grass, runic symbols I couldn't read, and black dragons. It was easy to make out the long, winged shapes of the grinning dragons in the intertwined stitches. Behind the tables, against the walls, there were benches covered in fabric and hides, while girls deftly carrying trays scurried around the tables from the other side. The windows were high up — just below the ceiling — and the waning daylight mingled with the blazing torches.

The guards sat me at the end table, studied me for a moment, and went to join their friends. I settled down without complaint and examined the people coming in. Most of the soldiers weren't wearing armor, but they all had weapons. Evidently the people here took their weapons everywhere, even celebrations. They were wearing the same clothing: simple linen trousers, shirts, leather boots. Many of them wore fur-trimmed tunics that revealed strong arms with protruding muscles and bracelets on their forearms. Some of these bracelets were iron and some were gold. They had engraving on them, but I couldn't make out the details from where I was. I had a hunch that if I could look more closely, I'd see that familiar dragon motif.

The women were setting the tables, which I supposed made sense. Such work was always considered easy. They hastily covered the embroidered tablecloths with huge platters of meat, cheese, flatbread and rolls, mountains of

The Charmed Fjords

baked potatoes and carrots, chicken thighs, sausages, every type of fish and seafood imaginable, and mugs of hot beverages and wine. The savory, intoxicating fragrances of the hot food made me salivate and I felt dizzy. I realized I was starving, and I craved exactly this kind of food: unpretentious and cooked on an open flame or in ovens. I glanced around, furtively grabbed a little piece of cheese, stuffed it in my mouth, and looked around again. The front table had different utensils: golden goblets and platters gleamed on it. I supposed it was the riar's table.

The servants were wearing clothes like mine: the same sleeveless dresses made of thin wool, with high slits on the sides that revealed the underclothing, which was lighter and thinner. The comfortable midcalf-length skirt revealed knit stockings and sturdy, low-heeled shoes.

Well then, that's what caste I was lumped in with here, I thought with a chuckle. Of course, I'd figured out that it wasn't honorable to be a lilgan or an outsider here.

But then other women began appearing in the room. They were clearly the wives and daughters of the local elite. They were tall, brunette, amber-eyed beauties dressed in luxurious brocade and velvet. Their dresses also had patterns embroidered into them, but the thread gleamed like gold, and stones were woven into the fabric. My hands itched with a yearning not only to record a report about this beauty but also to draw it. The men led their companions to the benches, covered their knees with fur and velvet blankets, and retreated to the other soldiers. One of the last guests to arrive was a white-haired, blue-eyed wonder who seemed to float into the room. It was the snow girl, apparently. She was escorted by a colossal soldier whose eyes were darting around the room vigilantly. No emotions were visible on the coarse, tough face, but the fact that he was holding her by the hand spoke volumes. I peered in fascination at her intricate silk

Book One: Beyond the Fog

gown, which was different from what the other women wore. The dress looked too light for the cool evening, and the light blue fabric shone as though it were covered in frost. A crown with three stones gleamed on the girl's perfect white forehead and I nearly let out a whistle as I looked at it. It was made of diamonds. The girl surveyed the crowd haughtily and her exquisite eyes came to rest on me. Recoiling expressively, she turned away and whispered something to her escort. He leered, chuckled, and led her to the table next to the head table. They sat down. Then a few more beautiful women appeared, but they had different coloring, more blondish. Each of them felt compelled to cringe disdainfully when they looked at me and then proudly move away and sit down closer to the riar's table.

I grabbed another piece of food, this time a piece of flatbread, and curiously sized up the women's table. While the men looked at me with languid interest, the women all exhibited disapproval and condemnation. I wondered if they resented me because I was an outsider or if they were vexed because the shatiya had been cut short the night before.

Within a half hour the hall was full and all the tables were occupied. An old woman wearing a dark kerchief sat down next to me without giving me so much as a glance. The bench ended on my right.

Then I saw Irvin walk in, with Sverr close behind him. There was no thunderous announcement of the arrival of the riar and his a-tem — they simply walked in, glanced at the people who had bowed their heads on cue, and sat down at their table. The hum of voices resumed, until Sverr looked glumly around, found me, and said, "Come sit next to me, Olivia."

I stood up uncertainly, feeling hundreds of pairs of eyes boring into me. They were curious, mocking, judgmental, and spiteful.

The Charmed Fjords

"You're inviting the captive outsider to sit at your table, riar?" the soldier who had arrived with the blue-eyed girl asked disapprovingly. "That's against the rules."

"Am I supposed to always share meals with my twin?" Sverr answered mockingly. "Like you, Hasveng, I'd like to see a beautiful woman next to me, not Irvin's face, which I must say I'm tired of looking at."

Laughter rippled throughout the room before turning to chuckling. Even Hasveng laughed.

"So then," Sverr continued slowly, "I can decide for myself, without any help, who will share meat and wine with me. Come sit here, lilgan."

The white-haired girl's companion scowled but lowered his head. He eyed me as I walked among the tables. I ignored the other people and looked only at the riar, trying to figure out why he'd asked me to join him.

I sat down on the bench, which was covered with a soft fabric, and nodded to Irvin. He didn't respond. Apparently he wasn't pleased with me, or with the fact that I was now sitting between two men. I was taken aback when Sverr turned and spread a fur coverlet over my legs. A drawn-out, dangerous silence hung under the domes of the room. Irvin choked on his wine. I glanced at Sverr, feeling a strange lump in my throat. But he'd already turned away from me and was idly inspecting his people. A servant set a plate before me without raising her eyes.

"You're quiet, lilgan," Sverr said, pulling a tray of boar's meat toward him. He stuck a knife into a piece. "Don't you like our city?"

"I don't know yet," I replied. Irvin grunted contemptuously. I decided to ignore him. "Please tell me about these people."

"It looks like you've already met Hasveng," Sverr said, nodding at the soldier beside the snow girl. "He's..." Sverr

Book One: Beyond the Fog

paused, trying to find the right word. "The *konukm*. That means king. He leads Neroaldaf."

"What?" I was so surprised I dropped the piece of flatbread I'd pinched. "I thought you were the leader here."

"I'm the riar," Sverr explained calmly. "I protect Neroaldaf. Always. Hasveng deals with things that don't have to do with protection or war. Also, hjeggs occasionally die. Sometimes they go on campaigns to procure gold or prisoners. Sometimes they just disappear and don't come back. But the people shouldn't suffer for that. If one day I don't come back, a new riar will replace me."

"So then Hasveng is the deputy," I said, trying to clarify things for myself.

"You forgot to say that hjeggs occasionally lose their minds," Irvin retorted without looking up. "They have too many feelings and their mind fails. Then hjeggs try to be mere humans and want to take off the ring of Gorlohum. They die from that."

Sverr grumbled under his breath but then grinned. "My a-tem is moody today, Liv. He spent too much time chatting in the frozen waters of the fjords and his instinct for danger froze. So he's decided to make me angry."

"How do you take the ring of Gorlohum off?" I asked, looking closely at the solid black band around the riar's neck.

"There's only one way to do it," Irvin said, baring his teeth. "You need to take off the head. But occasionally hjeggs forget that."

He smirked as if that were funny for some reason.

"Why do hjeggs lose their mind? And why do they sometimes leave and not come back?"

"This gift is sometimes too much to bear," Sverr said indifferently.

"Where did you get the rings?"

"People forged them from stone they found by Great

The Charmed Fjords

Gorlohum, after the spouting fire cooled and the ash that blocked the sun for a few years fell. That's when Gorlohum, which had awakened, destroyed nearly all the people of the fjords. But those who survived received the gift of merging with a hjegg."

I scratched my nose absentmindedly. Myths and legends usually contained a kernel of truth, but what could that be in this case? In the Confederation we also knew about the eruption of the volcano. It was a historical fact. A massive region was covered in lava and buried under volcanic ash. The sea boiled and flooded the fjords, and the mountains moved. Then came the Fog, which cut the fjords off from the rest of the Earth. But the rings? The material looked like obsidian. I remembered that it was taboo to touch them. I wondered what they were made out of, and how they got around the neck.

All these puzzles about the ilgs made my head spin.

"Eat, Liv," Sverr ordered. "Your stomach is growling."

He smirked. I decided to follow his advice and happily filled my plate. I didn't skimp, and soon I had before me a small mountain of meat, vegetables, cheese, and all types of appetizers. I picked up a gold spoon and attacked the food with relish.

Sverr burst out laughing and it took me a moment to realize that the women's table was looking at me in near-horror. Well, of course — those charming women only had enough food on their plates to feed a bird.

"Your captive has a good appetite, my riar," Irvin commented acidly. "Has she been expending a lot of strength?"

"Oh, yes," I said after swallowing a delicious piece of hot meat.

"We got that impression," Irvin guffawed. "Apparently they also felt Sverr's call on the other side of the sea. No

Book One: Beyond the Fog

wonder Neroaldaf was overwhelmed."

"Overwhelmed?" I asked in confusion.

"Yes. That's the kind of passion you give to your wife on your first night together, not to a prisoner."

"Knock it off, Irvin."

"Why? I'm betting that the anthropologist Olivia Orway is dying to learn about our traditions, isn't she?" Irvin's eyes narrowed. "You do want to, don't you?"

I picked up an embroidered linen napkin and blotted my lips. "I'd love to know about the customs of Neroaldaf. After all, it's almost my home."

I smiled amiably at the furious ilg.

"I'll tell you, Olivia," Sverr said calmly. "My a-tem is dropping hints so desperately that I'm afraid he'll choke." Sverr swallowed a mouthful of wine from an enormous goblet. "Irvin is referring to the fact that captives can never become riars' wives. And according to tradition, the strongest call is given as a gift to the woman who enters into the lawful marriage bed." He stopped and spun the goblet around in his hand. "And also, I have a betrothed. The wedding will be in the spring."

I choked on the meat I had in my mouth. Clenching my teeth, I poured some wine as I felt my vision blur. "I see. So then, a wedding."

"The beautiful daughter of the black hjegg from Rovengard," Irvin nodded, looking pleased now. "Her beauty is legendary. And if you refuse a bride, the fjords are threatened with war, so who in their right mind would refuse such a maiden?"

"Irvin, you'd best shut up," Sverr said quietly but threateningly, and Irvin stopped talking.

"Eat, lilgan," Sverr said, glancing at me. "I like your appetite."

I shook my head and looked down at my plate. Why did

The Charmed Fjords

this ruin my mood? After all, I completely understood that I truly was an outsider, and of course I wasn't planning to spend the rest of my life in Neroaldaf. I didn't even allow myself to think I might. All of this was just research on a foreign world and material for my work.

So why did I feel so hurt? Was I upset by the mere thought that winter would end and Sverr would take some beautiful girl I didn't know as his wife? Then his call, his passion, and his tenderness would be for her. And the kisses he'd learn from me, and new ways to touch a woman — all of this would be for someone else and I'd just remain the outsider, a toy, an entertaining captive. I'd be just like that damned pen with the gold cap that the dragon had helped himself to and then forgotten.

I suddenly got a bitter taste in my mouth, and my throat contracted. Now I really understood the danger of my situation. I knew I couldn't remain aloof and not succumb to the magic of this man. I had to stop lying to myself. My interest stopped being purely professional on my very first morning with the tribe, when I opened my eyes and saw Sverr crouched beside me in my tent. When I was around him, everything was too sharp, ardent, and real to be just scientific work. It was what my life had become — a real life.

I clenched my fists under the table and became aware of Sverr's eyes on me. He was peering at me incisively. "Here, taste this wine," Sverr said, holding his goblet out to me. "It's made with juniper, pine nuts, honey, and dried herbs. We believe it can cure the body and soul."

"Sverr, what are you doing?" Irvin hissed. But the riar wasn't looking at him, only at me. Unsure of what was going on and why Irvin was so angry again, I took the cup and sipped some wine. I didn't feel any strength, just a bittersweet, spicy taste like mead filling my mouth.

"It's delicious," I muttered, realizing with surprise that

Book One: Beyond the Fog

my speech was slurred. I looked into the goblet. Whoa, had I drunk the whole thing?

The riar laughed quietly and suddenly pulled me to him. "I want Neroaldaf to become your home, Liv," he whispered in my ear, licking it slowly. "That's what I want..."

Longing flared in me so intensely that I nearly moaned. Damn, that ilg was making me tipsy, just like the wine. I felt Sverr's body tense up, and I saw hunger in his golden eyes. He took a deep breath, but then he abruptly pulled away.

I looked around wildly. I sensed that the atmosphere in the room had changed. I also smelled something I hadn't smelled before. It seemed like the odor of lust. I gasped with sudden understanding. It was the call of the hjegg that everyone felt. So if Sverr felt aroused all of Neroaldaf did too?

"What a nightmare," I muttered. "Do they all respond whenever you feel passion or fury? How do you live with that?"

"I know how to rein it in," Sverr snickered. In fact, he did seem calmer now. "Truth be told, before I met you I was able to do that better."

He shook his head, chuckling.

I pensively chewed a mint leaf and nodded toward the tables.

"That girl over there," I said, "next to Hasveng. Is that the snow girl?"

"Yes." To my surprise, it was Irvin who responded. "Sverr brought her here, too. He stole her right next to Aurolhjoll. She was a high-born prey."

"She's looking at me funny."

"Maybe she wants your seat?" the a-tem said in a spiteful tone that confused me. Irvin and Sverr locked eyes. Irvin was the first to turn his gaze away. Sverr shook his head in irritation.

Then he stood up. The noise in the room immediately

The Charmed Fjords

died down and everyone looked at him. He raised his goblet, and the flame from the torches gleamed on the gold.

"Today we again confronted our enemy and defeated him," he said, his voice resounding in the hall. "We cast him away from our walls and made him regret coming to Neroaldaf. The snow children of Ulhjegg took their vanquished brothers with them. And today we are going to eat, drink, dance, and thank the firstborn hjeggs for our victory and our lives."

He downed the wine and a hundred throats shouted his name.

The soldiers jumped up and cups and goblets soared into the air, scattering the thick wine. In response, music began to pour down from the upper story of the building. It wasn't music that yanked at the soul, like at the shatiya, but a lively and cheerful tune that made you want to laugh and have a good time.

With a yelp, people rushed to the center of the room. The men stamped their feet, danced away from one another, came together and slapped one another's backs, and then separated again. The dance was like everything else in Neroaldaf: wild, passionate, and uncomplicated. It was a battle dance. Then the women stood up and joined the men, and the music changed, becoming more fluid and slower.

"Come on," Sverr said, pulling me out from behind the table.

"Where?" I asked with trepidation. "Not that! I can't dance! I've always been a terrible dancer."

"If you trip I'll catch you," Sverr said calmly and I stung inside. He had said the exact same thing in a small apartment in another world.

The soldiers cleared a path for the riar but I barely saw them. I felt a buzz from the wine I'd drunk, the rich food, and Sverr's proximity. He pressed me to him and spun me

Book One: Beyond the Fog

expertly, leading me in a dance I'd never seen before. We must have been doing something odd because people were looking at us strangely. I decided to ignore them, and just allowed myself to float on the waves of bliss, feel the strong arms that were holding me, and look into the golden eyes. I gave myself permission to feel and to live — in the here and now, in the foreign world of the dragons. And to understand that inside me something was taking shape, something I was afraid to name, despite all my schooling.

The music suddenly broke off and Sverr stopped, with me pressed to his side.

"Velma, Velma," I heard voices murmur throughout the room.

The people shrank back, and an old woman walked past them. Her gray hair was plaited into two narrow braids that fell onto her sunken breast like piebald ropes. Her black garment seemed out of place among the colored clothing. Her blind eyes slowly scanned the room as though she were looking for a victim.

A sense of foreboding stung me below my ribs. I don't know exactly what the respected Professor Rindor proved, but for some time intuition had been my best counselor. I had an urge to hide under the table, and I might have done so, but Sverr didn't let go of me.

"I'm pleased to see the prophetic Velma at our feast," he said, looking point blank at the old woman. "It's an honor to have you here, seer. You're always an esteemed guest."

"And you're always wise, riar," the blind woman answered with a hoarse laugh. "And you know when it's best to hold back your fury. It has recently been tormenting you, isn't that so?"

"The beast's strength won't defeat man's reason," Sverr said.

"If he hasn't already lost his reason," the old woman

The Charmed Fjords

muttered, "if the man is cold like the waters of the fjords and isn't raving like Gorlohum. I see your ring is heavy, riar. You will be honored for your strength on all the fjords, but you yourself know that a stick always has two ends. The more strength there is, the more potent the spirit must be to pacify it."

Everyone in the room nodded. I saw that Irvin had come to stand nearby, and the expression on his face showed that he was not pleased to see this guest.

"I came because I had a prophetic dream," the old woman announced loudly. I suppressed an urge to roll my eyes. What else could happen here? Of course I respect the elderly and their gray braids, but prophetic dreams?

Well, this is Neroaldaf for you.

I stifled a laugh and tried to look attentive.

"And I saw death in my dream." The woman was now talking in a sinister whisper. "The death of a hjegg and the awakening of the red beast."

The crowd became agitated and started chattering. They looked afraid and alarmed. I turned my head, trying to understand. The red beast. Wasn't that Hellehjegg? His temple was Gorlohum. That meant that the old woman was talking about the volcano waking up. No wonder the celebratory mood of the banquet disappeared in an instant. A new eruption was threatening all the fjords. Volcanic ash, lava, tsunamis, earthquakes — yes, that was practically the end of the world.

"Did you see when the red beast will wake up, Velma?" Sverr's voice sounded even, and that calmed everyone else slightly.

"Before winter." The old woman lifted a gnarled finger. "I saw the crimson hjegg lift his head. I saw him open his mouth, and his tongue shone in it. It was red, like blood. I saw how sharp his spikes were — the color of fire. People of

Book One: Beyond the Fog

Neroaldaf, he will awaken soon. And he will awaken over the fjords and make them his own. His wings will open and his shadow will cover Varisfold. But before that, Aurolhjoll will be destroyed. Its shining towers will fall. Then the hjegg will rush to Gorlohum. And the cause of all of this is — her!"

Her finger unambiguously pointed at me. The soldiers began to grumble menacingly.

I heard a wail somewhere off to the side and the white-haired girl fainted. Fortunately, Hasveng managed to grab her before she hit the ground.

"Eilin, Eilin," he mumbled, hastening toward the door.

"This is bad news that you've brought us, Velma," Sverr said quietly. "But you're only a vessel, not the content. Please allow me to set a place for you at the table."

Velma bowed her head, turned around, and began to plod to the door.

The music started up again, but it didn't sound confident.

"Did you believe her?" I asked Sverr. "It was just a dream."

"It's Velma's dream," he said without meeting my eyes. "Let's go, Liv. The feast is over."

Chapter 22. Olivia

SVERR DIDN'T COME TO ME that night. I bitterly paced his spacious quarters, examined every inch of the furniture and the books, ran my fingers over every object, and touched the crossed swords on the stone wall. When I finally tired myself out, I lay down and fell asleep.

Slenga woke me in the morning. "Get up, outsider. I've brought you breakfast."

I yawned groggily and scowled at the empty spot next to me in the bed. "Where's the riar?"

"He ordered me to feed you and then show you Neroaldaf," she said, briskly setting the table as I climbed down from the bed.

"But where is he?"

Slenga gave me a surprised look, which I completely understood — after all, in this world I was just a lowly captive. I didn't have the right to ask questions like that. And of course I also didn't have the right to be jealous. Sverr didn't belong to me. This was a different world with different customs, and he was a foreign man, whom, incidentally, I'd kill if I found out he spent the night with a local maiden. And then I'd be burned on the town square, much to Irvin's delight. That would be the end of the inglorious life of this anthropologist.

I gulped down a nervous laugh.

Book One: Beyond the Fog

"Well, I probably shouldn't tell you this, but..." Slenga began softly. "Last night the riar was with his soldiers. They were drinking."

I nodded curtly and darted to the bathtub, not wanting Slenga to see how relieved I was. Yes, I'd sunk that low — I was jealous of an ilg. But what could I do? You can't stick your feelings in a test tube and lock them in a lab, no matter how hard you try.

When I emerged from the bathroom, Slenga had already stripped the bed. I invited her to share my breakfast, but that got me another surprised look and I ate alone. A short time later we were standing by the door of the tower, squinting in the morning sunshine. Two guards were standing silently behind me. This would make for an interesting walk, I thought.

"Where are we going?" I asked.

"Where do you want to go?" Slenga responded with a shrug. "The riar ordered me to show you everything you want to see."

"How generous of him," I muttered and started walking toward the square. When we got there I hesitated. "Slenga, did you hear what happened last night at the feast?"

"You mean when old Velma came?" She frowned. "Lots of people are talking about that."

"What are they saying, exactly?"

Slenga glanced at me and then looked away. She seemed annoyed that she had to answer my questions and go for a walk. But I also detected some pent-up fear in her. I didn't know what exactly she was afraid of — the riar or me after the witch's words.

"The prophetess Velma is never wrong."

"Really? Never?" I asked, starting to feel despair.

"Well..." Slenga hesitated. "There was this one time, when she had a dream about Irvin when he was a boy. She

The Charmed Fjords

said he wouldn't be able to bear the ring of Gorlohum and that he'd die. But he survived, vanquished the beast, and became the riar's twin and now protects him."

I was so relieved it felt like the sun started to shine more brightly. "There, you see? That means she makes mistakes, too. Every fact is potentially inaccurate. I mean, everyone makes mistakes."

"That's possible. But it's better if you don't walk around without protection, outsider."

"My name is Olivia," I muttered, looking back at the two silent soldiers. So they were protecting me?

I shook my head, deciding not to think about the old woman's prophecy for now. In any case, I didn't really believe it. How could I possibly awaken the volcano? There wasn't a single objective reason why I should consider her vision to be true. I decided to focus instead on more concrete things, such as my investigation of Neroaldaf.

I quickened my pace, looking all around with growing interest. On the other side of the square, the maze of lively streets began. Loaded wagons drove past, children chased each other around, rich women with servants ambled by, and soldiers stamped their feet. We walked up and down the hilly streets. When we got to the top of a hillock, I caught sight of the sea glittering in the distance and ships bobbing by the piers. Here the buildings were mostly one story tall, and Slenga explained that the waterfall divided the city into two sections. Craftsmen, tradesmen, and rank-and-file city residents lived on the left side. There were shops with every kind of good imaginable and dormitories for soldiers who didn't have families of their own. The rich people lived on the other side of Neroaldaf, where the buildings were two and three stories tall. On the stone walls of every house, next to the door, I noticed an iron cone that contained a vessel, which Slenga said was for a live flame.

Book One: Beyond the Fog

"When you want to light it, you take off the cover and the flame ignites," Slenga explained as though she were talking to a small child. Of course, she couldn't understand why the outsider didn't know such basic things. A live flame, just imagine that!

On the hill behind Neroaldaf the waterfall was thundering and I raised my head, looking at the system of pipes that supplied water to the city.

"It's freshwater," Slenga said, pointing. "You can't drink the water from the sea, but you can drink this water. Our fields start over there, beyond the cliff, and pipes go there too."

Being the scientist that I am, I bombarded her with questions, but she didn't know the answers to most of them. Slenga was a common servant and wasn't particularly interested in history, agricultural advances, or the economic issues in Neroaldaf. So I had to content myself with her narration of how many dishes are usually served at supper and what the riar liked to eat for breakfast.

Strangely, the riar's eating habits interested me just as much as the crops grown in Neroaldaf.

"Has the riar had a permanent, er, companion?" I asked.

"Like a concubine?" Slenga guessed. "He's not allowed to have a permanent one. It's forbidden. What, you didn't know that?"

"Why isn't it allowed?" I stopped in the middle of the street.

"Well, there's the call," Slenga explained patiently. "It's strong with a new maiden, but then it weakens. And that can't happen. That's why maidens only visit the riar once, then they turn their backs, and after that, they receive gifts and leave. He doesn't call them a second time."

"What about his wife?" This information made my

The Charmed Fjords

throat run dry.

"He needs a wife to give birth to an heir."

"But that doesn't cancel out the maidens who visit him once," I guessed. I looked morosely at Neroaldaf. Apparently Sverr was also bound by a bunch of obligations. And it didn't exactly sound pleasant.

"Sometimes he holds on to a girl a few times," Slenga said, frowning. "But I can't recall one."

"That's fantastic," I said through my teeth. "So I guess I've already exhausted the riar's attention span."

"What?"

"Nothing." I forced myself to smile and pointed at the closest building. It was long and had a red roof. "What's that over there?"

"The workshops," Slenga said. "Want to take a look? That's where we make dishware to export to other cities. Ships come here every summer to buy our goblets and platters. But as you can well imagine, the most valuable thing in Neroaldaf is the sword blades. There's nothing else like them on the fjords. Warriors would fight to the death for a sword forged by a skilled craftsman under our banner because everyone knows there's no sharper or more accurate weapon. Only men hammer the swords. You need the hjegg's fury for them." Slenga gazed proudly at the city from our perch on the hill. "Our dishware is also prized across the sea. Come on, outsider, you can see for yourself."

I followed Slenga through the open door, not expecting to see much.

The guards stayed behind the door. Slenga rushed over to a woman and whispered something to her, and I gingerly stepped into the room. Craftswomen were sitting behind long tables covered with wooden trowels, pestles, sticks, brushes, and other tools. Pieces of stone and iron were arranged in small piles. The young women behind the tables were

Book One: Beyond the Fog

pressing clay in their hands. Come to think of it, I wasn't sure it was actually clay.

I went closer to one of the women and leaned down to get a better look. "What are you making?"

"A plate," she answered, staring at me in bewilderment.

She continued rolling the soft substance around in her hands. I could have sworn it was iron, but that didn't seem possible. I picked up a heavy gray lump of a substance that was about the size of my fist. The girl was holding one just like it, only she was kneading it as if it were a piece of dough.

I couldn't believe my eyes. "May I see that?" I asked. The girl nodded and placed the object in my outstretched hand. I closed my fingers around it and turned it over. Yes, it was definitely iron. It was irregularly shaped, hard, and warm from the girl's touch, with a small fingerprint on the rough surface. My eyes hadn't deceived me — she had been kneading it. My jaw dropped.

"How can that be?" I stammered wistfully. "How do you knead it like that?"

"I just feel it," the girl explained guilelessly. "I feel every piece. It reacts in your hand if you're gentle and careful. Only people who are born from the call of Lagerhjegg's descendants have the ability to hear iron. Our riar is his descendant, and we all hear iron and stone. And gold, of course, but they work with that in a different workshop. The artisans there are more gifted. But people who have been living in Neroaldaf for a long time can acquire the ability. You just need to be patient — it takes years."

I gazed at the dull hunk of metal in my hand as though it were a charmed artifact. What did she mean, hear the iron and stone? And who did I think I was, trying to convince Sverr that he needed the Confederation?

I jumped up, reached into the leather pouch on my belt, and pulled out the shiny little bird Sverr had made out of the

The Charmed Fjords

nail.

"That's beautiful," the young artisan said when she saw the seagull in my palm. She looked distressed. "I can't make things like that. I can only roll out round plates, but look at this — you can see every little wing. It looks like it's alive."

The other women gathered around us to get a look at the trinket.

"That's meticulous work," the oldest woman said solemnly. "Even in Neroaldaf there aren't many people who can make that. And our craftspeople are celebrated on all the fjords. We make goblets, platters, spoons, and things like that, but to do this is amazing. The iron here is bad, almost dead, so to make something like that you need incredible strength. Like..." she broke off and looked at me sharply. *Like the riar's strength*, her face said clearly. Then she seemed to be struck by a realization. "I heard that an outsider from far away had appeared in the tower. And that old Velma predicted something bad."

The women started jabbering fearfully, like a group of chickadees. They gave me sidelong looks. The oldest one shushed them, handed the iron bird back to me, and frowned. "Get out of here. We have work to do."

"Why is this iron dead?" I asked, intrigued.

"What do you think? Because there's no life in it! Or the hjegg lying where it was mined has been asleep for a long time," the craftswoman snapped. "Enough of your questions. On your way, now."

I still had a million things I wanted to ask but instead I went back outside. I sat down on the steps and rested my chin on my hand. The iron they were kneading was like a piece of soft clay. It was alive. The stone statues that towered over the city, the tower, the walls, the impressive arches, the bridges without pylons spanning the river — no, slaves had not died to create all of that. It was simply that everything in

Book One: Beyond the Fog

Neroaldaf was different. And here the people could do things that we in the Confederation couldn't dream of. Change the structure of matter at its molecular level? Make something real, beautiful, and valuable from gray stone or useless ore? I became lightheaded as I processed this miracle.

I opened my hand and looked at the bird made from the nail. It looked ready to take flight to the place where the black dragon soared, to the place I couldn't reach.

"Hey, outsider, what are you screaming for?" Slenga ran over, looking alarmed. "Olivia, what happened? Did they insult you? Tell me. I'll take care of it right now."

I smiled at the militant servant and stood up. "I'm not yelling. I'm an old maid, the black sheep of the Academy of Progress, and an impractical fool who thinks she knows everything in the world. And I don't even know how to cry properly!"

"Of course you do." Slenga tactfully ignored most of my rant. "Let's go. It's time for lunch. You're just cranky because you're hungry. That happens a lot. We'll get you a nice bowl of hearty beef stew and you'll feel better right away."

I laughed in spite of myself. "You sure know how to make me feel better, Slenga."

"Oh, yes!" She laughed in delight and looked at me companionably. "You are strange. But that makes sense — you're an outsider. Not everyone is lucky enough to be born in Neroaldaf. That's not your fault."

"Uh-huh," I muttered, heading toward the riar's tower, which was visible from everywhere in the city.

Slenga looked at me and said suddenly, "I was also taken to the riar so he could give me the gift of a night and his call."

My heart turned into a piece of stone and fell out onto the pavement. "And then what?"

"Nothing," she grumbled. "He looked at me, yawned,

The Charmed Fjords

shut his eyes, and fell asleep. Then the next day he asked me to stay on as a servant. That was the gift." Slenga fiddled with a stone that was stuck in her sock and puffed her lips defiantly. Then she winked. "But I'm not insulted, and anyway, a soldier from the riar's personal guard wants to marry me. So everything is for the best. You know, Sverrhjegg has a powerful call, but no one's ever heard anything like what it is with you. The old people say that only the firstborn Lagerhjegg had a call like that."

I sighed, putting my heart back where it belonged. "Tell me about the hjeggs, Slenga."

❊ ❊ ❊

The black beast Lagerhjegg was born from iron and stone, in a golden egg. He is strong in the hills and in the sky, and the stormy weather responds to him. The black hjegg is the ruler of the heavens and mountains, and his call gives birth to the strongest warriors and hardiest maidens.

The white beast, Ulhjegg, was born from the union of ice and light, in a diamond egg. His eyes can see through the thickness of the ice. The crystal of the summits, the snow, and the northern wind respond to him. Ulhjegg's call gives birth to people who are not afraid of the cold or floating glass that is stronger than diamonds.

The gray beast, Njordhjegg, emerged from the depths of the sea, and his egg remained there forever. That's why it's easier for the water hjegg to live in the sea. This hjegg is free and his call is weak, so Njordhjegg's children prefer the freedom of the sea to dry land.

The egg of the red beast Hellehjegg cracked in the lava and fire. He awoke angry and treacherous because the burning coal has been scorching his skin since the beginning

Book One: Beyond the Fog

of time. This beast is so wrathful that people are afraid of his fury from the northern border all the way to the southern island. Every child of the fjords knows that if the red beast awakens he'll roar and death will come, because Fiery Gorlohum responds to the red hjegg's call.

We returned to the riar's tower just in time for lunch, but once again the riar himself was nowhere to be found. Slenga left me, and the soldiers only shrugged in response to my questions. So once again I set out to wander around the tower. The legend of the firstborn hjeggs still echoed in my head — it was melodic, peculiar, and intriguing. I could almost see the dragons born from the fjords, the creations of a different reality, and different laws of the universe. I had no idea how much of these stories was true, but I had other evidence of their truth.

I was torn from my musings by a tall figure that rose up in front of me so unexpectedly that I stumbled. Irvin — for that's who it was — didn't put out his hand to hold me up.

"Back in the day, spies were fed to the wild animals, and their heads were sent back to their masters so everyone would see how Neroaldaf treated such outsiders," Irvin drawled.

"Thank you, I'll keep that important information in mind," I said gratefully. Irvin turned scarlet and pursed his lips.

"Do you think you have the right to do more than other people, Olivia?" he said. "You're mistaken. In this world you're an outsider."

"If you think about it, I didn't really fit into my own world either," I replied thoughtfully. I lifted my head and looked Irvin in the eye. I was tired of his banter. "Look, I didn't choose to come here. That was Sverr's decision. I'm just trying to understand all of you. Why do you hate me so much? I haven't done anything bad to you or Neroaldaf."

The Charmed Fjords

Irvin smirked in a way I'd never seen before. "What makes you think I hate you, outsider?" His blue eyes shone and his lips creased.

He took a step and I recoiled, feverishly trying to read his behavior. All of this annoyance, spitefulness, desire to catch hold of me — could it be a sign of interest, not antipathy?

My back was pressed against the wall and Irvin's hand was propped against the stone. I glimpsed the unconcealed lust in his eyes.

"I can't forget how you splashed in the water, outsider. You were so soft and defenseless."

"Don't you dare touch me," I said, fixing him with a hard stare.

"I won't touch you," the hjegg agreed. "Not now, and not later. I'm not Sverr. I understand that you're dangerous, Olivia Orway. You arouse feelings, strong feelings, and you make me want to possess you. But that's bad. Women from beyond the Fog have a special magic. The riar is right about that. You all need to be annihilated without a glance." He bent lower and looked me straight in the eye. "At the feast the riar covered your legs with hides and let you drink from his cup. And everyone saw it. He's different now that you're here. But don't count on his feelings, outsider. Sverr is a warrior and if the choice is between you and Neroaldaf he'll always choose Neroaldaf. Not a single woman can be more valuable than the homeland. Remember that. Better yet, write it in your notebook. You're an outsider, you're a child of the Confederation, and you came from beyond the Fog. For that alone you could be torn to pieces if everyone knew. Neroaldaf will never accept you."

Irvin smirked and took a step back. "And after what the prophet Velma said, don't let down your guard, Olivia. The children of the fjords don't hesitate to inflict punishment."

Book One: Beyond the Fog

He turned on his heel and set off toward the stairway. I glanced at the guards, who were standing to the side and looking away. Fighting an urge to lash out and spit on the dark panels, I went in search of Slenga, hoping that the soup she'd promised would in fact cheer me up.

❉ ❉ ❉

I sat down to lunch in a small dining hall where the servants, cooks, and youngest soldiers — children, really — were eating. I took a place at the end of the table and thanked the servant for the bowl of hot soup and roll with cheese. As I began to eat, I heard friendly, enthusiastic cries of "riar," and when I looked up I saw Sverr walking across the room with his confident gait. He stopped in front of me.

"What are you doing here?" he asked curtly. "I told Irvin to take you upstairs."

"He must have forgotten," I grunted as I chewed my bread. I waved an arm and said, "They feed me well here, too."

The riar chuckled and sat down next to me.

"Give me a bowl of soup," he said to the cook. For a second she looked like she was about to faint, but then she recovered and rushed off to the kitchen. The young soldiers abandoned their food and stared at the riar as though he were a god, which he probably was for them.

When a huge, steaming bowl was placed before the ilg, everyone froze tensely. He took a spoonful of soup, swallowed it, and licked his lips. "Delicious."

The cook lit up and wiped the perspiration from her forehead. After a moment she went back to work, but she kept giving us sidelong looks. Sverr offered me a piece of golden flatbread with meat. I smiled and silently nibbled at it. We continued to eat, listening to the banging spoons and

The Charmed Fjords

crackling in the stove.

"I walked around the city today," I murmured. "Neroaldaf is beautiful. You were right."

Sverr nodded slowly. "It's the best place on Earth, Olivia. For us, it's an honor to give our lives for it."

If the choice is between you and Neroaldaf he'll always choose Neroaldaf. Irvin's words stung inside me and I screwed up my eyes. Some servants brought us heavy mugs filled with a berry-flavored infusion mixed with herbs. I happily took a few gulps.

"You love your home," I said.

"And you love yours," the ilg said, turning his head.

I nodded. Sverr didn't take his eyes off me, and then he reached out his hand, took the mug from me, and drank from it. A servant dropped the plates she was holding and they shattered.

"I'm sorry!" she muttered fearfully.

"Let's go, lilgan," Sverr ordered without looking at the servant. He got up and strode out of the room.

I obediently followed him, not that I really had a choice. The guards, at the riar's order, stayed behind the tables. Of course, we didn't go far. Behind the stairway Sverr turned me and pressed me to him, feverishly rubbing my body. Then he lifted me slightly and thrust his tongue between my lips, confidently running it through my mouth.

"I missed you," he said hoarsely. He started kissing me again, not giving me a chance to respond.

"Sverr!" I protested. "Stop! Don't!"

"Do you want me to bite you again?" He touched his teeth to my neck, tickling me with his tongue. A hot shiver rushed down my spine.

"We're in the hallway!"

"So?" He truly seemed surprised.

"Soldiers and servants pass through here!"

Book One: Beyond the Fog

"And?" He really didn't seem to understand.

"Sverr!" I grabbed his hand, which was fearlessly stroking my belly and inching its way lower. "Not here! Stop!"

"You're so naughty in bed and innocent everywhere else," he purred, caressing my chest through my clothes.

I licked my lips, trying to switch off the burning fire inside me. It was too hard to fight it and my own feelings. "You drank from my mug. That means something, doesn't it?"

The ilg stopped moving for a moment and then resumed nibbling my earlobe. "It means I was thirsty," he laughed. He sighed. "Come on, my modest lilgan. I want to show you something."

I straightened my dress, feeling both relieved and disappointed. Sverr noticed and looked at me quizzically.

"Let's go," I said. I smiled and held my hand out to him. He frowned and stared at it. I was sure he'd just turn and walk away, like before. But to my surprise, he reached out and squeezed my fingers, and his golden eyes melted from his inner fire. My breath caught. I sensed that here in this corridor, where it smelled of bread and beef stew, where the light was creeping in from the far window in narrow strips, something was happening between us.

But the feeling didn't last long, and Sverr scowled again, turned, and started up the stairs. He kept holding my hand as we climbed what felt like thousands of steps.

"Where are you taking me?"

"You'll see," Sverr assured me. Just as I was on the verge of plopping down to rest, he pushed open a door and we stepped out onto a sweeping platform. The clouds rambled along lazily beside us.

I looked down and gasped when I glimpsed Neroaldaf stretching out in the cavity of the cliffs and the sea lapping at the foot of the city.

"It's incredible," I whispered. The city was black, red,

The Charmed Fjords

and green. It looked like something out of a fairy tale with its bridges, houses, fortresses, and waterfalls. It was the most beautiful and captivating thing I had ever seen. The breeze lifted my skirt and ruffled my hair, and Sverr pulled me into his arms, warming me.

"I love looking at the city from above," he murmured. My back was to him, so I couldn't see his face, but I could hear the smile in his voice. "Sometimes I regret that I'm the only one who sees it like this."

"Neroaldaf is enchanting," I said sincerely. I settled into the ilg's arms. "Today I saw how they make dishware from iron and onyx. They told me that everyone in this city hears stone and metal. How is that even possible?" I turned to look at him. Sverr looked thoughtful.

"As I've already told you, you don't know anything about yourself, Olivia Orway. The people of the Confederation don't understand the world they live in. I don't know how to explain it to you."

He let go of me, took a step away, and picked up a pebble.

"Since the day we're born we know that the world around us is alive. The rocks, the iron, the sea, the land — everything has a soul, and it responds to us. It responds to some people with a shout and to other people with only a whisper." The ilg smoothed the pebble and I gasped when I saw the transformation. But I was even more surprised when Sverr cupped our hands together and placed the stone in my hands. "The problem with you people of the Confederation is that you long ago became deaf and believe that the world around you is dead. But we know otherwise. Listen, Olivia." I stared at the fragment in my hands. The warmth of Sverr's hands and his quiet voice mesmerized me. "You need to forget who you are. Forget your achievements, your experience, your knowledge. You need to stay here and now, with me and

Book One: Beyond the Fog

this stone. I can only show you that this is possible. I can't force you to believe."

He stopped talking and I tried to turn off my rational side, the anthropologist named Olivia Orway. I just wanted to become a nameless, newly born woman, and feel not the stone in my hand, but the particle of this world. Sverr was studying my face, but the stone in our hands was changing, taking on a different shape. It was like witchcraft.

"Try it," he whispered, taking his hands away.

I stared at the gray cobblestone that had begun to soften, about to become something new. How did that happen? Did the molecular structure change? What was I even supposed to do?

The stone hardened again, turning back into a cobblestone, and I was disappointed. It didn't want to change without Sverr. But I actually thought that a miracle would happen now and that I could make it happen.

"Not this time, I guess," I said with a sheepish smile, trying to hide my chagrin.

Sverr tossed the stone aside and in a quick movement pressed me to him.

"Look over there. Do you see the cliffs?" He pointed and I nodded. "There used to be a city there. It was called Salengvard. The riar was a black hjegg who wanted changes. He was also interested in humans and the Confederation, and he studied them — Irvin isn't the only one with the ability to reach your ships." He stopped talking and I tensed up, sensing he was going to tell me something unpleasant. "And the riar of Salengvard also believed in progress. They set up electricity in the city, they laid railroad tracks, and launched machines for transport. There was a lot of everything there, even things that didn't exist in the Confederation. Two centuries ago, Liv, there were things in Salengvard that the people in the Confederation had not yet dreamed of. The riar

The Charmed Fjords

of the city was very enlightened and innovative."

"So what happened to him?" I strained my eyes to see the city on the cliffs. I saw fragments of the towers, dark ramparts, and buildings. But I didn't see any movement or signs of life.

"The cliffs perished," Sverr said quietly. "The stone and iron stopped responding to the hjegg's call. As for the riar, he lost the connection with his black beast and went crazy. The city emptied out, and it became too hard for the children of the fjords to live among the dead stones. You asked why we don't accept the achievements of progress. It's because we remember Salengvard. You can't join two worlds. Our world is different. In your city, iron and stone are also almost dead, Liv. It would be hard to manipulate them even for me, the riar. And regular people wouldn't be able to change them at all."

I bit my lip, gazing into the distance. I could feel Sverr behind me along with the warmth of his hands, his light breathing, his heartbeat.

He spun me around to face him. "Liv, I..."

Boom! The bell in the fortress chimed its bronze clang over Neroaldaf.

"What's going on?" I asked nervously.

"Someone decided to try on the ring of Gorlohum," the riar said with a strange expression. He looked at me pityingly and mockingly. "Time's up, lilgan. We should have stayed in the hallway."

I ran after Sverr to the lower chamber of the tower.

People summoned by the bell had already gathered. A tense, expectant silence hung over the room.

Before I had a chance to interpret it or get scared, a stout woman walked slowly into the room. A pudgy child around ten years old tread beside her.

"The gift of Gorlohum!" The woman stopped in the

Book One: Beyond the Fog

middle of the room and thundered. "I am asking for the gift of Gorlohum, my riar!"

The voices and laughter died down, as though a black curtain had been lifted over a stage. Sverr nodded slowly. "Who is asking for the gift of Gorlohum?" he said, and his voice echoed off the walls. The fire in the vessel on the wall blazed more brightly.

"Garleta, daughter of Hansa! Ten years ago I gave birth to a son and today I am asking for the gift of Gorlohum. My Vilmar is strong and quick, and is already the best among his peers. He hits a squirrel in the eyes from a bow and throws a spear straight."

"Was he born after a shatiya?"

"No, my riar," the guest said, looking slightly embarrassed. She straightened up, puffing out her massive bust under her thick blue wool dress. "But he is a tenth-generation citizen of Neroaldaf. I am a widow. Vilmar's father was your warrior and he died in a campaign five years ago. I know he would have wished for such a fate for his son."

"You think you know?" Sverr asked quietly. I didn't understand what was happening. I could just see that the riar was getting angry. It was almost imperceptible, but I was standing close to him and I could see his pupils narrowing and I sensed his breath quickening.

What was setting him off?

The riar scanned the room, which had grown quiet.

"Well then," he said, with an edge in his voice. "You have the right to ask for the gift of Gorlohum, Garleta, daughter of Hansa."

He walked over to the wall. He stood there for a moment, then ran his hand along it and the stone separated, revealing a hollow. A dark ring gleamed, catching the red reflection of the fire. The riar raised it above his head.

"If your son is prepared to fight for the gift of Gorlohum,

The Charmed Fjords

then so be it."

"I'm prepared, my riar!" young Vilmar shouted in his child's voice.

"Do you know what you need to do?"

"Yes!"

"Very well." Sverr looked almost indifferent. Only the flame pulsing in his eyes gave him away. "You will only have a few minutes, Vilmar. Follow me."

The ilg walked past Garleta, who was standing motionlessly, and exited the tower. All the people in the room followed Sverr and the boy. Naturally, I ran after the crowd.

In the square in front of the fortress the soldiers had set up large torches that illuminated the entire area. The crowd formed a circle, staying away from the spot that was marked by the light. I shifted this way and that, trying to see between the people clustered together. The little boy was now standing in the circle, and his anxious, dark eyes shone in his pale face. He no longer looked as brave as when he was in the hall clinging to his mother's skirt. Now his hands were shaking and his shoulders were quivering uncontrollably.

"Think it over one more time, Vilmar, son of Garleta," Sverr said, stopping beside the boy. "Are you sure you want to try on Gorlohum's ring? Don't be afraid. Just say what you're thinking. No one can force you to do this. Not your mother and not me."

The little boy gulped but nodded again. "I'm sure, my riar. And I'm ready."

"This is what we'll do. I will give you the gift of Gorlohum. I hope you're strong enough to withstand this gift, Vilmar."

The chatter died down. It got so quiet on the square that if a feather fell it would have sounded like thunder. Everyone in the crowd stopped talking and gazed on solemnly. The men looked stern and approving, while the

Book One: Beyond the Fog

women wrung their hands.

I still had no clue what was going on and could only stand there and watch.

Two old men climbed down the wall onto the ground. They were holding the instruments I had already seen several times, and in a moment they started playing a drawn-out, anxious sound. *Din-shork, shor-di-i-in...*

Sverr raised the black ring in his outstretched arms and placed it on top of the boy's head. As I watched, the ring of Gorlohum flowed downward, as though it were made of a soft rubber or there was an invisible hand pulling it apart. It slammed down on Vilmar's shoulders and clamped around his neck. In an instant, the boy's legs buckled and he crashed down on the paving stone.

I yelped involuntarily and someone shushed me. I had to slap my hand over my mouth. Vilmar apparently regained consciousness and stopped struggling. He jumped up and looked around. Now his dark eyes were gleaming, and his face was distorted in such primitive horror that I had to press my hand to my mouth even harder. Suddenly Vilmar soared into the air, as though a clawed hand no one could see was carrying him. Then he dropped to the ground again. The crowd gasped tensely and shrank back. The boy got up again and spun around in place, roaring like an animal.

"He won't be able to do it," a familiar voice said beside me. I turned and my eyes fell on Sverr. He was looking at the boy, not at me. His forehead was creased morosely.

"What's going on with him?" I asked as Vilmar floated into the air again. "Tell me!"

"A young warrior is trying to catch the hjegg's soul," Sverr said evenly. "But he's too weak. He won't succeed."

"What?"

The boy's little face was now bleeding. Was he wounded? How was that even possible? Who had done it to

The Charmed Fjords

him? All I saw was the empty square. Yet I couldn't deny that Vilmar was battling an invisible adversary in the circle of light. This was the realest fight imaginable — a fight to the death.

"Stop this," I whispered, clenching my hands. "Stop it!"

"I'm not allowed to interfere." Fury exploded in the golden eyes. But I also saw regret. "Everyone who does this knows what they're risking."

Inside the circle of torches the boy flew up and fell again. Then he began to cry, pathetically, sounding like the child that he was. I also began to wail, forgetting that I wasn't supposed to interfere and that I didn't understand any of this.

I pushed the ilgs away and darted into the circle. The boy again started to rise into the air, as though gigantic claws were pulling him. I clutched the small body and jerked him downward, cushioning his fall. I pressed him to me and began to run away. But then some force tore Vilmar out of my arms even though I still couldn't see or sense anyone around.

"I won't let go!" Wheezing, I turned over, covering the boy with my body. He seemed to lose consciousness. "I won't let go. Go to hell!"

My shrieks destroyed the solemn silence in the square. Out of the corner of my eye I caught sight of distorted faces, resentment and anger, fury and confusion. But I had other things to worry about. Something was trying to tear my burden out of my arms. I didn't give him up, and I cursed as I pressed the boy into the ground.

Then a bellow flew over Neroaldaf. The flame of the torches shot upward, as though someone had poured gas on them. A black shadow covered the fortress. The women shrieked and the soldiers seized their weapons but didn't take them out. Beside me, two legs touched the ground. They

Book One: Beyond the Fog

were entirely real and even, sadly, familiar. They belonged to Sverr, in his dragon form.

Suddenly Vilmar's body stopped thrashing as he slid out of my arms and went limp. The thing that had been trying to pull him away disappeared.

I stood up shakily. I couldn't crawl to the edge of the circle. I looked into the golden eyes with the vertical pupils. Black smoke was pouring out of the hjegg's nostrils — clearly the riar was furious.

"I'm sorry," I said, feeling no regret.

The dragon breathed scorching air and flapped his wings. Tearing off the ground, he scooped me up with one of his feet, as I continued to clutch the boy to me.

Chapter 23. Olivia

THE DRAGON'S CLAWS opened over the familiar rocky ledge and dropped me onto the withered grass. I leaped up. The cliffs trembled from the dragon's roar and were illuminated by a red flame. Rain clouds began to mass, foreshadowing the storm that would soon batter Neroaldaf.

I laid the boy on the ground and gingerly ran my fingers over him, trying to see if he was wounded. His right arm was broken, and it felt like some of his ribs were, too. I bit my lip, willing myself to remain stoic. When the rock opened and Sverr emerged, I looked at him beseechingly.

"He needs help! Please! I don't care if you punish me — just help this boy!"

"I'll definitely punish you. You can count on that," the ilg spat at me. Seizing the boy, he disappeared into the cliff. I got up and ran after him. A narrow corridor wound downward, leading to a spacious cave that was filled from top to bottom with all kinds of rubbish. It looked to be the riar's storage space.

Sverr placed the boy on the ground and I raced over to him while the Sverr lit the lanterns.

"He needs a doctor! The healer! Right now!"

"No one is going to help him." I shuddered from the fury in the ilg's voice. "It's forbidden to touch someone who has fallen in combat against the hjegg's soul. It's forbidden to

Book One: Beyond the Fog

meddle in what you don't understand."
"But he's just a child!" I yelled.
"He's a warrior who chose his path."
"What path is that? To die?"
"He knew what he was getting into."
"But he's so young — he's only ten." I was ready to cry.
"He made this choice even though he saw his peers die," Sverr barked. He sat down beside the boy and carefully pulled at the black ring around Vilmar's neck. To my surprise, the ring of Gorlohum stretched again and then easily slid off. "Everyone has the right to this gift. And everyone knows what they're up against. Of the dozens who take a chance, only one has the ability to vanquish the hjegg's soul."

I joined my hands in supplication. "But, Sverr, he's nothing but a child! He's a little boy. I know I violated your traditions. I understand that. But I beg of you, please save him! Summon the healer!"

"No one's coming. Don't you get that?" the ilg snarled. His eyes turned red and his facial features sharpened. "What's worse is that I'm obligated to finish him off. It's my duty."

"No!" I shielded Vilmar with my body, covering him with my arms as though I were a bird spreading my wings over him. "Don't you dare touch him!"

The riar's eyes flashed and he scowled.

"Sverr, I beg you!" I pleaded. "You're not like that. You're different. You know so much, you study both worlds, you build houses and bridges and make birds out of steel. You're a scholar and protector, Sverr. You know very well that Vilmar is just a child and doesn't deserve to die. Please help him!"

The ilg sighed heavily. I could tell he was struggling — the gold of his eyes was melting and the tendons on his forearms and neck were protruding.

The Charmed Fjords

"Sverr..."

"Your medicines are over there, Liv," he said, to my surprise. "It's medicine from the Confederation."

I blinked, finally understanding him. I dashed to the pile of stuff he was pointing to and began to comb through the rubbish. Rags, pieces of furniture, a tabletop, dishes... finally, I found what I was looking for — a small case with familiar vials.

I went back over to Vilmar and dropped to my knees. Thankfully, he was still breathing. I scrutinized the contents of the first-aid kit. A lot of the bottles had expired, but I managed to find some that were still good. Acting fast and forcing myself not to think, I pulled Vilmar's torn, bloody shirt off. I touched his ribs again and made a mental list of what I would need: anesthetic, bandages, antibiotics, alcohol. A medicinal odor pierced the cave. My breath caught for a moment as images swam before my eyes. I was thrown back to another day, when I was lying on glass — that time, too, there was an unbearable scent of medicine and blood all around me. That day there was much more blood. Panic seized me and I opened my mouth, struggling to breathe.

Burning hands grasped my temples and I started. Sverr was looking into my eyes. His expression calmed and supported me. *If you trip I'll catch you.* Breathe in, breathe out. The attack subsided. No longer questioning myself, I pushed a needle into Vilmar's vein.

It wasn't until his breathing evened out and his chest was firmly bandaged that I allowed myself to briefly shut my eyes. When I opened them, I saw Sverr standing there, looking me up and down. I couldn't decipher his expression.

I flinched and slowly straightened up. I just stood there looking helplessly at Sverr, at a loss for words. On the one hand, the boy and I were still alive. On the other, would we live for long?

Book One: Beyond the Fog

"You'll stay here," the riar ordered brusquely. He wheeled around and started toward the wall. The stone separated in front of him. He slowed down as though he wanted to say something else, but he didn't. Without looking back, he walked into the cliff and the stone closed behind him.

"Thanks a lot," I muttered, kneading my stiff neck. I had no idea what was in store for me. Right now the most important thing was to take care of the boy. I dragged some hides and blankets across the cave and carefully tucked them around him.

Then I went to explore the cave. Patterns of red streaks twisted along the ceiling, emitting a dim light, enough for me to get a good look at the mountains of objects of every sort. The place reminded me of a storage room where someone had carelessly dumped a pile of unwanted belongings and forgotten about it. I was sure nothing else could possibly surprise me, but when I got to the other side of a piece of ship fuselage, I stopped in disbelief.

"What the — "

A mountain of gold stood before me. It was a few yards high and contained coins, assorted jewelry, goblets, platters, and even gold bars that weighed a few pounds. It looked like there was enough gold to buy a couple of countries beyond the Fog. I gazed at a coin that was shining next to my feet and smirked.

"Dragon's gold. Who would have imagined!" In fairy tales, only the beautiful princess could see gold like this. I must have ended up in the wrong fairy tale.

I went back to the other part of the cave, hoping to find something in all this stuff that would be useful for my little patient.

I had no idea how much time passed — there was nothing in this cave to help me tell time. But judging by the

The Charmed Fjords

fact that my eyes started to droop, apparently I'd been there a long time. During the long hours I managed to build something that resembled a dwelling. I pulled over a low table, on which I laid out medicine and vacuum packs of bandages. I placed more blankets under Vilmar and created a bed for myself. I even managed to find a notebook and pen and decided that later on I'd write down everything I had witnessed. I walked around the pile of gold again and found some boxes filled with bottles of water. That made me happier than the shiny baubles.

I sat down on the blankets and let out an exhausted breath.

"I bet there are even cans of food here," I muttered hoarsely. "I'll look for them tomorrow."

I checked Vilmar again to make sure he was still breathing, lay down on the blanket, and promptly fell asleep.

SVERR

"You have no right to do that, Sverr!" Irvin growled. The a-tem's bottomless blue eyes looked out of his pale face. "It's your duty to punish the outsider, in public! And..."

"And what?" The riar bared his teeth. "Kill the pup? I brought the ring of Gorlohum back. Enough of this!"

"Did you kill the boy?"

"Yes."

"I don't believe you." Irvin screwed up his eyes. "I think you managed to take off the ring of Gorlohum before it hardened."

"You're out of line, a-tem."

"But you're losing your mind! You're changing, Sverr, can't you see it? You're changing because of that girl. You were supposed to kill them both as soon as the girl entered

Book One: Beyond the Fog

the circle. But you didn't. Where are they? Tell me!"

"You're out of line, Irvin," Sverr repeated coldly. Irvin stopped talking. "And there are some things you should remember, like how you yourself fought with the hjegg's spirit, and how you lay there gushing blood. You couldn't vanquish it, a-tem. You and I both know that."

Irvin didn't respond. His anger had subsided. He unclenched his fists.

"That's why I don't believe that the kid is dead," Irvin croaked. "I know you already saved one person a long time ago. No one knows that, but I remember."

"I've always valued your advice, Irvin." Sverr calmly stopped Irvin's reminiscing. "And your protection, deep mind, and devastating blade. But don't you dare point it at me."

"You yourself mentioned protection. And that's what I do. You ordered me to tell you if I noticed any changes in you, my riar. And I am noticing them. You can't see that the outsider is having a disastrous influence on you. She's clouded your reason."

"There's absolutely nothing wrong with my reason," the riar shot back. Lightning blazed over Neroaldaf but the ilgs standing on the tower ignored it.

"No! You've never acted like this! How many of them have there been, Sverr — captives, local girls? You couldn't have cared less about them. But now? You take her out of the shatiya circle, seat her at our table, protect her. What's going on with you?"

"We need her! Liv knows about a lot of things."

"You're the one who needs her," Irvin roared. "Not us! Only you! And you're incapable of harming her even if she deserves it. She's important to you."

"You need to mind your own business, Irvin."

"You're the riar, Sverr. You're not entitled to have feelings." Irvin's eyes turned into black pools of water. "You

The Charmed Fjords

know that. We both do. Didn't you forbid me from taking that prisoner from Aurolhjoll, Eilin, into my home? But I asked..."

"I forbade you from doing that because Eilin is a freeborn daughter of Aurolhjoll," Sverr snapped. "She's entitled to have her own house and a husband and not serve as your plaything. I pulled that girl from her own wedding, Irvin. The hjegg doesn't know pity, but humans do. Eilin became Hasveng's wife by right of birth. She only would have been a toy for you. And anyway, she spent too much time thinking about gold and silk and didn't think about you for one second. An a-tem doesn't need a woman like that."

"And the riar?" Irvin spat. "You aren't entitled to any woman. Your call is for everyone, you know that, Sverr."

"I remember my duties."

Irvin grew silent, but Sverr was no longer waiting for a response. A moment passed, and the dragon dropped off the tower, throwing open his huge black wings.

OLIVIA

Sensing someone looking at me, I woke with a start. I opened my eyes and yawned sleepily. A man was crouching down next to my makeshift bed.

"Irvin?" I blinked in surprise. "Where's — ?"

"The riar is busy," the ilg grumbled. "He ordered me to look after you, outsider. Let's go."

"Where?" I asked in confusion. I jumped up, straightened my dress, and rushed over to Vilmar. He was breathing evenly and the feverish spots had disappeared from his face. I calmed down. I wanted to check the bandages, but Irvin grasped my arm.

"I'll take care of Vilmar. Let's go."

I frowned. Leave? Outside? Why hadn't Sverr come for

Book One: Beyond the Fog

me himself? I believed that the riar had a lot to do, but I didn't like any of this.

I sighed in resignation and set off behind Irvin, trying to keep up with him. He was walking confidently, as though he were familiar with this cave. We continued to descend farther into the cliff. It felt like we were going deeper and deeper into the earth. As we went along, there were fewer red streaks, and less light.

"Is this the way out?" I asked nervously. "You know, I'm not getting a good feeling about this."

Irvin turned and looked at me. His blue eyes shone in the semidarkness. "I warned you from the start, Olivia. But you didn't listen to me."

"Huh?" I asked. The ilg grabbed me by the arms and stepped away from the stone ledge. The dark water of a subterranean lake closed in above our heads. A dull tail swirled around me, as though a snake were embracing me. I wanted to scream but I just clenched my teeth. The transformed Irvin glided quickly through the water. When I opened my eyes I could make out the outline of the hjegg, but I couldn't distinguish the color. All I could see was an immense, smooth body, a crown of spikes along his spine, fins, and the end of the tail, which was squeezing me so hard I couldn't even disengage my arms.

I could tell that less oxygen was making its way into my lungs. I could no longer see anything. We were sliding through the deep water so fast that I didn't even want to risk opening my eyes. Red spots danced on my eyelids and I was unable to take in any air. When I was about to pass out, the tail flew upward and I was flung to the surface. I shot out of the water, but the snake seized me again and threw me onto his long body. I was spread-eagled between the spikes, coughing and spitting out water. Irvin let out a sound that was a cross between a snarl and a hiss and then began to

The Charmed Fjords

skate through the water. I knocked about on his back, trying not to fall off. The wind of the fjords was so cold that my teeth soon started chattering — or maybe that was from the sheer terror I was feeling. The day was fading over the fjords, and the red sun was dancing in the water, painting it crimson. But for a change I had more important things to do than bask in the local beauty. With trembling hands I clung to the protruding spikes on the sea serpent's body, trying to hold on to the slippery skin. The hjegg dove under a wave and plunged into the depths. I nearly choked again. My lungs were burning and my fingers were numb from tension. Then he surged up again so fast I got dizzy. He leaped, flew above the water, and dove in again. I tried to cry out a few times, but if Irvin heard me, he didn't slow down for a second or respond. I couldn't tell how long this wild swim lasted but just when I was sure I could no longer hold on, the hjegg dove, sprang up, tossed me as I was slipping, and hurled me up onto a high bank.

I lay splayed out on the ground, gasping for air and marveling that I was alive. Coughing and wheezing, I sat up and awkwardly got to my knees.

Then a wave gathered and washed ashore, nearly carrying me away, and the water dragon emerged from the depths. The serpent's body was at least ten yards long. There was a row of fins on each side, and blue-gray scales. His triangular head was crowned with broad, dark blue spikes. It was the kind of monster that showed up in nightmares. The dragon turned around in the air and entered the water without a splash. A massive shadow passed under the wave. The water sprayed on the shore. The undulating curves of the sea serpent were visible again. The long neck swung closer, and then the mouth opened, revealing sharp fangs, and the hjegg let out a blood-curdling roar.

"Explain!" I bellowed in response. "Irvin! Explain!"

Book One: Beyond the Fog

But the dragon only hissed and dove underwater, crossly slapping his tensile tail on the surface.

I staggered back, righted myself, and looked around. I had no idea where the a-tem had dragged me. The walls of Neroaldaf were nowhere in sight. The tiers of a cliff rose up behind me. It was overgrown with grass and shrubs. Something silvery flashed on the summit. I decided I wasn't about to stand around waiting on this little beach for someone to come rescue me. Cursing, I began to climb the cliff. Five minutes in, I realized that I wasn't cut out for rock climbing. My heavy, waterlogged dress didn't exactly help matters. My knees were quivering and my feet kept slipping off the rocks. Clutching the roots and blades of grass, I doggedly kept climbing, cursing Irvin the whole time.

"Long-tailed scoundrel!" I gasped. "Swimming worm! Mutant monster! Thick-skinned reptile! You dead end of evolution, that's who you are! I'd like to cut you up and put you in test tubes for experiments! Bastard, bastard, bastard! I hope you get the hiccups and choke, you vermin!"

When I got to the third ledge I started cursing at the top of my lungs, trying to suppress my fear of falling. When I finally made it to the top of the cliff, I fell down, throwing my arms out and burying my forehead in the moist earth.

Some men's feet, shod in boots, were right next to my head.

I lifted my head slowly and saw a pair of dark trousers with leather inserts, the hem of a trench coat lined with white fur, and a belt with a shiny buckle. I roused myself, sprang up, and stared into the man's silver eyes. He had a narrow face, prominent cheekbones, and thin lips. The sea breeze plucked his long white hair, which was plaited into dozens of braids and twisted behind his back. I realized I'd already seen this man — or more accurately, this hjegg. Danar was what Sverr had called him.

The Charmed Fjords

"Is this the outsider?" the snow riar asked over his shoulder, not taking his eyes off me.

"Yes, my riar!" the warrior standing beside him answered in his baritone. "I think she's from Neroaldaf. Hold on, I've seen her before. I'm sure I have. The black hjegg saved this maiden when we were storming his walls. I saw it happen."

"Are you sure?" Danar asked softly, as though I weren't right there.

"Yes, my riar. It's definitely her."

"Well, I'll be damned," Danar said, smiling. I got goosebumps.

I tentatively backed away a little, not that it mattered — there was nowhere for me to run to. The hjegg smiled even more broadly.

"Where were you trying to go, outsider?" Danar asked solicitously. "The only ways out of here are by sea or sky. I have a feeling you're not capable of that."

The soldiers behind the local riar snickered. I scowled, determined not to panic. "If you hurt me you'll regret it. I'm under the protection of the riar of Neroaldaf."

"More likely, you just warmed his bed," the hjegg snapped, his voice oozing with spite. "So you'll warm mine too, for a start. They've thrown you out, so clearly they don't care too much about you, maiden." He turned to his soldiers. "Take her to the fortress. And keep watch over the shore. If the sea serpent comes back, attack. The hjeggs of Neroaldaf take too many liberties."

He'd already turned away when he made his last comment. He walked off without giving me another glance. I didn't bother to dart from side to side — it was useless. I was an exhausted, frozen woman in a wet dress. Where could I possibly escape to, other than maybe the closest bush? So I just waited silently for the soldiers to approach me and

Book One: Beyond the Fog

nodded.

"The maiden is submissive!" crowed the soldier who had seen me in Neroaldaf. He was massive, like most of the ilgs, with white hair and a jagged scar across his left cheek. "She's already learned!"

The men smirked but I didn't say anything. All I did was jerk my elbow away when the ilg tried to grab hold of me.

"OK, then, bug off yourself," he said with a shrug. He spit a few steps later. "What a naughty maiden. She walks and water sloshes in her shoes."

"They got beauty but no brains," a soldier carrying an enormous ax said philosophically. "Why are you so surprised, Ulf? Maidens aren't for having scintillating conversation with. They only need to be soft and pretty. And submissive, like this one. You don't need anything else."

"Isn't that the truth, Riktor!"

I rolled my eyes. So now I had to listen to this baloney. Truth be told, there was one thing Ulf was right about. I should have dumped the water out of my shoes before climbing up the cliff. But after that ghastly swim on the sea serpent's back even now I wasn't thinking straight.

We walked deeper into the occasional undergrowth, and when the trees separated I gasped despite myself.

"You like it?" Ulf snickered in satisfaction. "I suppose you never saw anything like that in your Neroaldaf?"

I nodded. A staircase wended along the dark cliff overgrown in thick vegetation. The steps sparkled in the sun like frost, as though they were carved out of ice. There were at least a thousand steps. They scaled the mountain slope, higher and higher, all the way to the crest, where a snow-white fortress shone.

"Welcome to Aurolhjoll, maiden," the soldier said. "The only thing more beautiful is the palace of the hundred hjeggs. So you're lucky! Be thankful you ended up here. There's no

The Charmed Fjords

better place on Earth than Aurolhjoll."

I snickered to myself. Where had I heard that before? The name of the place was different, but the adulation and pride were exactly the same. I guess that was in the ilgs' blood: they praised their own home and thought it was the best. For the most part, they were right. Except...

"So, are we climbing up there?" I asked weakly. "By those stairs?"

"Of course," Ulf said in surprise. "Just don't shake and you won't don't fall. I'll hold on to you just in case."

"Thank you," I said reflexively.

"Oho, and you're polite! Were you beaten or something?"

"A little," I blurted, dumbfounded.

"I can tell. With a whip? Those fiery beasts! I was watching and saw you don't cry or scream, or walk along the shore like you're crazy, like others do. It looks like they squeezed out everything in that damned Neroaldaf, is that it?"

"Oh," I muttered indistinctly. The soldiers looked at me dourly.

"It's high time to lay them to waste," the ilg said indignantly. "You don't bully maidens like that. Animals! All right, let's go. You really should be glad. Of course, we have all types of people here, but no one whips maidens unless they commit an offense. See, you really are lucky."

I grunted. Yes, I certainly had uncommon luck. The only thing that cheered me was that now I'd bonded with the locals. Now all I had to do was haul myself up onto this staircase.

Someone shoved me in the back, so I had no choice but to go up. To my surprise, the steps weren't slippery, and in fact, from close up they looked more like stone than ice. But somewhere around the middle I was already cursing all the

Book One: Beyond the Fog

snow people, the hjeggs, the fjords, and these cheerful soldiers who were easily tramping up behind me. Apparently this sort of ascent was no chore for them. By the time we neared the top of what seemed like an endless staircase, I was huffing and puffing like an overworked horse and fantasizing about turning one of these men into an experiment.

When we stepped into the broad clearing, the snow-white fortress was standing before me in all its splendor. I found myself looking at ornamental arched windows, whorled grating, a few glowing spires, terraces, ice statues, and a sparkling mosaic. It wasn't a fortress — it was a castle, and a breathtaking one at that. Chuckling at my evident delight, the soldiers led me down a street and through massive gates decorated with a hoar frost pattern.

"How many hjeggs live here?"

"Three. The current riar and two of his brothers. For many years the ring of Gorlohum has gone to the riar's descendants, not to any random person. The next one will be Danar's son, if, of course..." He trailed off and the soldiers exchanged glances.

"If that son is born," Riktor said sullenly. "It's been a long time coming."

"Shut up," Ulf snapped.

"Where's the castle of a hundred hjeggs?" I tried to change the topic strategically when the men grew somber.

"Don't you know?" Ulf, who was walking beside me, asked in surprise. "It's south of Aurolhjoll, on the cliff of the victors, in Varisfold. The snow riars also built it, so it looks similar to this, just bigger. It's so big that they say that all one hundred of them could feast there when they're in their hjegg forms, can you imagine that?"

"Not really," I said honestly. "So there are a hundred hjeggs?"

The Charmed Fjords

"There used to be. But now, of course, there are fewer." Ulf's face darkened and he suddenly seemed to lose the urge to talk. He looked at me disapprovingly. "You know, you shouldn't talk so much. We say that when maidens make such a demand, they have a big mouth. But it's better to hold your tongue. Otherwise you get beaten again, and your brains won't help you. And the last one will beat you down."

"Why won't my brains help me?" I asked curiously.

"We heard you jabbering when you were climbing up the cliff," Ulf said, shrugging. "We immediately noticed the sea reptile. We saw him throw you onto the beach. Then we heard you yelling and realized right away that there was misfortune with a maiden. You kept talking about some Eva Lution. Is that your mother or something?"

"Ah. Yes indeed," I said, clasping a hand over my mouth to keep from laughing hysterically. He opened another door and pushed me into a small room, scoffed, and left.

I looked around curiously. While I was climbing the staircase my dress had nearly dried, but my camisole was plastered to me uncomfortably. My hair was stuck together and hanging like icicles, and water was still sloshing in my shoes. I pulled off my shoes and knit socks and then tiptoed into the room. Heavy dark blue curtains covered the windows, only letting in a sliver of light. In the dimness I examined the furnishings that seemed to be everywhere: a bed, table, and armchair. But unlike in Neroaldaf, here there were hides and fabric hanging on the walls and the white stone of the castle was cold to the touch. I pulled my hand away with a shiver.

There was a doorway hung with furs, and beyond that, a few more rooms. One of them had a round, empty tub in it.

"I hope they have hot water here," I muttered, returning to the first room. I pressed my shoes to my chest and stopped. Danar was standing next to the table. He was examining me,

Book One: Beyond the Fog

his white-haired head cocked.

He nodded to me to sit on the bed. "Take off your dress. You'll get everything dirty."

"What?" I asked in surprise.

"Your dress," the hjegg repeated, his silver eyes gleaming. "Let's see what the riar of Neroaldaf saw in you to make him save you and forget about the battle."

"This is a mistake," I said nervously, backing away. I had no idea what to do. "Let me go!"

"Why would I do that?" Danar asked. "You're my captive now, and I want to find out just how good you are in bed. Take off your rags."

I took a few more steps back, realizing with devastating clarity that there was nowhere for me to escape to. And it was no longer funny. Behind me there were adjoining rooms, while a hjegg was standing between me and the door. And he wasn't some sickly youth, but a six-foot-tall burly man who happened to be examining me unpleasantly and steadily.

"Look," I said, desperately trying to worm my way out. "You can't get near me. I..." I thrust a hand into the cutout of my dress, hoping I didn't have a weapon in it. My fingers closed around the plastic lighter I'd taken from Sverr's cave. But what if... I pulled out the knickknack and prayed that it would work. I struck the little wheel. Once, twice, and a flame came out, fluttering like a yellow tongue.

The snow riar lifted his white brows. "You think a flame you brought here from Neroaldaf scares me?" he asked with a laugh. "Idiot!"

Suddenly he seized my arm, jerked me toward the window, and threw open the curtain. "A knickknack like that doesn't scare me. I can decorate the entire sky with fire."

I looked up and my mouth dropped open in astonishment. Night was already falling over the castle, and multicolored glows were flashing over the spires, which were

The Charmed Fjords

gray in the darkness. It was like the northern lights.

I dropped the lighter in amazement. Obviously there was no way a tiny piece of plastic spewing a flame would impress anyone in the world of the hjeggs. Here a single individual could will the sky to turn into the colors of the rainbow.

"Have you had your fill?" Danar snickered. "Now take off your rags and get down on your knees. Greet your new riar like you're supposed to, outsider."

Danar agilely turned me around and kicked me under my knee. My legs buckled and I fell awkwardly to the floor. Before I knew what was happening, my face was being pressed into the hide.

"By the way, for the first time can you lift your skirt, like this?" The riar snickered and grasped the fabric of my dress.

I kicked, trying to get up or at least wriggle out from under his heavy body.

"My, you're squirming," Danar said in annoyance. His right hand grasped my hip while his left hand held my head down. He pushed on me with his knee. I exhaled, gathering my strength. I turned my head and sank my teeth into his fingers. He yelled, more in surprise than anything else, and jerked his hand away. All I needed was a split second to tear myself away and roll out from under him. I got into a sitting position, pressing my knees and pulling the dress over me. Danar, who was kneeling now, shook his head and scowled.

"You're a stubborn one, aren't you?" he said thoughtfully. "I don't like stubborn girls. They're nothing but a waste of time."

He looked me in the eyes and I saw the multicolored flashes spread in the pale irises. It was as though the northern lights also pulsed in his eyes. In the bottom of my stomach I felt a scratching sensation, as though ignited with

Book One: Beyond the Fog

cold. Then the sensation spread through my whole body. It was like plunging into icy wormwood after a run, when you feel cold and hot at the same time. My breathing came out like a moan.

"Now that's better, you stubborn girl," the riar said with a smile. "Now get on your knees."

The spite rose inside me, sweeping away the artificial desire. My knees? Why were all these ilgs so obsessed with this position of enslavement? They were the tyrants of the fjords, that's why.

I leaped up, dashed to the unlit fireplace, and pulled a poker out of a basket. I raised it threateningly, baring my teeth like a hjegg.

"If you get anywhere near me I'll push this stick into your you-know-what," I growled.

The flashes in the snow riar's eyes were shot with astonishment. He gawked at me as he stood up slowly.

"Who the hell are you?" he asked. "And why doesn't my call work on you?"

"I'm an erudite! I have special abilities. And that's why the riar of Neroaldaf valued me. Not because of what I do in bed."

"What kind of abilities could the maiden possibly have?" Danar smirked.

"I can find out why you haven't had a son," I blurted out.

The riar's face trembled and darkened. Up until then he'd been taking pleasure in our little swordplay, but now his cheekbones seemed to grow sharper and malice filled his eyes. Suddenly I was frightened.

"I can find out so you can fix that, my riar," I breathed out hastily, feeling anxious. In a split second I realized that neither a poker nor even a sword would stop the snow riar if he wanted to take me. Only a really good reason would make

The Charmed Fjords

him change his mind. "A woman should flow, like water," I heard in my head.

So I tossed aside my weapon, opened my hands, and bowed my head.

"I am under your power, my riar," I said quietly but firmly. I forced my muscles to relax. Submission, Liv, just demonstrate that. "I am aware of it. I'm grateful to the riar of Aurolhjoll for the life he has bestowed on me. And I want to show my gratitude. It's just that I'm not gifted in bed, and my body is disfigured with scars. What would you want such a maiden for? I'm sure you have many more maidens who are much more beautiful and snowy than me. But with your permission, I will find the reason and will explain why you are not fathering an heir. Allow me to do that."

"Show me," Danar ordered raspily. "Show me your body. Show me that you're not lying here at the very least."

I clenched my teeth but forced myself to relax. I resolutely opened the fasteners of the dress, and pulled the fabric from my shoulder along with my camisole. I stood still, trying not to squirm under Danar's gaze.

He gingerly approached and touched a welt under my chest.

"I've heard that the riar of Neroaldaf is worse than a wild animal, but I didn't know he was that awful."

He pulled his finger back. I held my breath.

"All right, outsider," he barked. "For now I won't touch you. But you must tell me before the half moon what to do so the heir to Aurolhjoll is born. You will be taken to other chambers and given everything you ask for."

With that, Danar turned and left the room.

With a sigh of relief I pulled my dress back on and smirked. Who would have thought that one day my scars would come in handy?

Chapter 24. Sverr

"**W**HERE IS SHE?" Irvin put down the ax he was polishing and stood up. Sverr was standing in the door to Irvin's quarters. He looked calm, but Irvin knew him well enough not to be fooled. "What are you talking about?"

Sverr glided toward Irvin.

"I'm asking you a question, Irvin. Answer me," the ilg said. He was speaking softly but Irvin detected the threat in his voice. "Well? Where is she?"

The a-tem glanced at his ax and sighed, "In the waters of the fjords."

The riar screwed up his eyes. "You're lying."

"It's the truth," Irvin said firmly. "You were changing because of her. She clouded your reason. I did what it is the a-tem's duty to do. I delivered her to the fish at the bottom of the ocean. I did what you were too weak to do."

Sverr took a swing at Irvin and the impact sent Irvin to the wall. He jumped up, wiped the blood from his mouth with the back of his hand, and jeered.

"How dare you?" Sverr hissed. He struck Irvin again, this time even harder. If Irvin didn't have the ring of Gorlohum around his neck, he would have been plastered to the floor for good. But he stood up again and lunged for his battleax.

The Charmed Fjords

"I did what I was supposed to do!" he repeated stubbornly. "Now you'll never have to worry about that outsider again. You're free of her."

Sverr let out a low, short growl, and his exposed sword gleamed in the narrow ray of light. He clanged his sword on Irvin's ax. The men grunted as they dueled, smashing everything around them. A blow from the riar sent Irvin crumbling against the door of the house, and he fell out onto the riverbank. He began to hiss when the dark shadow covered him. He couldn't contain his hjegg's call. The scaly sea serpent gored the transformed black beast and sank his poisonous fangs into him. The two hjeggs rolled, grappled, destroyed walls, pulled off roofs, and tore each other to shreds. The residents of Neroaldaf ran to take shelter, trying to hide from the fury of their rulers. The huge claws scratched the embankment and tore small trees up by the roots. Sverr squeezed the twisting sea serpent, lifted him up, and hurled him onto the stones. But at that moment the bell in the tower began to sound the alarm and the fire hjegg abandoned Irvin and took flight. Letting out a fire-filled roar, he sped to the fortifying wall.

The sea dragon sputtered, shook his head, and spit out poisonous saliva, which burned a hole in the wall of the house. He began to crawl after the riar. The gongs from the tower boomed and sounded the alarm signaling an attack.

SVERR

The inner rage clouds my eyes with a crimson shroud. It's hard to think, breathe, or live. I only want to kill. I would have torn the a-tem to pieces if Neroaldaf weren't under attack.

This time, there were three wild hjeggs, black ones — the malevolent, hungry ones that sense warm human bodies.

Book One: Beyond the Fog

The wild hjeggs are usually scared off by the fortified walls, statues, and my markings, but these three decided to feast.

And I was glad for that. I flew higher, beyond the edge of the clouds. The black shadows slid below, stretching out their long necks. I fell onto the one who was more powerful than the others, sank my fangs into him, and bit off his head. His thunderous roar made the cliffs shake. I buried my claws with gusto in the living flesh and tore it apart. The fog before my eyes lifted and my vision became clear and sharp. At the same time, my desires became clear. I wanted to kill, sink my teeth into things, lacerate, scorch, and rip out the meat — whatever it took to satisfy my rage.

The carcass fell into the water near Neroaldaf, and I saw the sea serpent entwine the wounded hjegg with his tail and drag him down into the ocean. There isn't a living being in the water that's more frightening than Irvin. I knew Irvin would pull the black beast down and down and down, and leave him there in the ocean depths. Just like he did with the outsider.

Liv.

Her name blazed in front of my eyes in a blinding, black-crimson flash. I cried out in pain. My savage roar rolled over Neroaldaf, setting off a storm in the sky. Why did it hurt so much? The hjeggs live in fury, not pain. The hjeggs are strong and evil, the hjeggs are free.

So why was I feeling this unbearable pain?

I clamped my claws onto the second beast, ignoring the damage to my own skin. The strong wings pulled me toward the wall, where we crashed together and rolled, shattering the stones. Destruction — that's our essence. Shouts, moans, cries, chaos — that's what we bring. We bumped against the side of the tower. The bell clanged and pitifully went silent. The spiked tail struck me horizontally, severing the armor of my scales. Before I could wriggle free, he struck me crosswise,

The Charmed Fjords

like with a steel lash. Blood spurted on the wall and I bellowed. I dodged, seized, and bit. Stones from the demolished signal tower showered down and smashed the bronze bell. With heavy strokes I rose into the air, dragging the carcass of the wild hjegg. I hit the ground and took off again.

Irvin was hissing in the water, winding around the third hjegg. The sea serpent's mouth was covered in blood, but I couldn't tell if it was his or the wild hjegg's.

A moment later I cast my prey into the crevice between the cliffs as I sped over a wave. The water was already calming down, and a finned silhouette was winding under the foamy peak.

Irvin was alive.

I wasn't sure I was happy about that.

Turning away, I scorched the frigid water and flapped my wings.

SVERR

I dug a hole in the pile of gold and covered my head with my tail. The yellow metal is stained with the blood gushing from my skin. I'm in pain, but it's not my skin that hurts. My skin will grow back.

Before tending to myself, I piled stones in the passage to the subterranean lake. I don't want Irvin to come. If he does, I know I'll kill him.

Time crawls. I shut my eyes. I still see only that crimson-black and feel the pain. Here in my cave I can smell the outsider. She was here. She stood beside the gold and looked at it. I can tell she didn't pick anything up. Not a single coin still holds the warmth of her fingers. My weak bellow bounces off the walls. They say that hjeggs can sleep for

Book One: Beyond the Fog

centuries. And that's what they do, when they're sick and tired of humans, or when they lose their minds.

Now I also know why that happens. The hjegg's fury gives humans strength. The call of the hjegg gives children and heals. Yet pain can annihilate everyone around it. I no longer remember why Neroaldaf is so important or why we need the fjords. I've forgotten everything. I only want to kill. I want to destroy the city Liv walked through. I want to fight Irvin to the death. I want to drown everyone in blood, including myself.

My human side barely manages to keep the beast at bay. With the shreds of reason I have left I force the hjegg to stay buried.

It's a struggle, and it hurts.

I wheeze, burrow into the gold, and wait.

I'll stay here until I feel just a bit better.

OLIVIA

Danar held up his end of the bargain. I was taken to a small room and a guard stood watch at the door. And as promised, he gave me everything I asked for. The first thing I wanted to do was trace the local riar's entire bloodline. I was given bundles of writing paper, pens, and ink, and even a boy whose job was to answer all my questions. Young Bjorn was considered a poet in Aurolhjoll — a clown and funnyman. This was all because he was born hunchbacked, which prevented him from being able to hold a spear or ax. But to make up for it, from childhood he proved himself a prodigy in the art of putting together letters and songs.

"The fjords don't pity people like me," he snickered. His light-gray hair protruded on his head in disheveled wisps and his fingers were ink stained. "They say that when someone is

The Charmed Fjords

born hunchbacked, it means that their kinsmen are being punished for angering the firstborn hjeggs. It's better to give those children to the sea as a sacrifice."

I shook my head. Humanity was clearly a foreign concept here.

In all honesty, Bjorn didn't look particularly disabled. He was a lively, cheerful, nosy adolescent who was intrigued by what I was doing. Unable to resist, I slowly showed him how to multiply and divide, and that filled him with so much glee you would have thought I'd given him a cookie. Accounting was a good skill to have in Aurolhjoll — accountants were respected and lived well.

"What's this for?" He again stuck his ink-spotted nose into my sketches.

"It's your riar's family tree," I said with a smile, dipping the quill into the inkwell. "Please stay focused. Now tell me about Vahendi, Danar's mother's mother."

He puffed out his cheeks self-importantly and began to talk. I listened and processed the information, and only wrote down things that were important to the family line. Strangely, ending up in Aurolhjoll was the greatest gift I could receive as a researcher. Under the pretext of studying the riar's family I could ask all the questions I wanted. But when it came to the basic questions — about the ring of Gorlohum, the hjeggs, and their abilities — Bjorn flatly refused to answer, instead skittishly babbling something about the fury of the firstborn. Still, I did have the opportunity to study the history of Aurolhjoll and the fjords.

"So the beautiful Vahendi was also a snowmaiden, right?" I asked.

"Yes. She was as white as the snow on the mountain peaks, with dark blue eyes like the night sky. She was one of the most beautiful maidens of the fjords, and the only thing as beautiful as her face was the moon."

Book One: Beyond the Fog

I winced. Sometimes in my search for a rational nugget of information I had to separate out the allegories Bjorn was so fond of. "I see. Who were her parents?"

After two hours, I stepped back and surveyed my diagram. "So the riar has no wife, right?"

"The riar of Neroaldaf kidnapped his bride," Bjorn said, throwing up his arms. "Damn that black beast! He snatched the beautiful Eilin and left our riar without a wife."

Now it all made sense. That's who the white-haired girl at Sverr's banquet was. The recollection stung and I shuddered. The only thing I was trying not to do was think about the golden-eyed ilg. I didn't want to remember his words, caresses, or laugh. But I was failing miserably. I'd begun to sleep fitfully because he was in every dream I had. But my thoughts kept returning me to the same question: why had he ordered Irvin to cast me out? To punish me for helping Vilmar?

Only Irvin and Sverr could answer these questions, but they weren't here.

I shook my grown-out curls and decisively clenched my teeth. I needed to focus on the task at hand and nothing else. It was a matter of life and death.

But inside me confusion and hurt were again pulsating. Had Sverr really handed me over? He had said he never would. But how much were the riar's words to an outsider worth?

"Tell me about the cliff of the hundred hjeggs," I said, turning back to Bjorn.

"Oh, I've seen it!" The boy's shining blue eyes sparked rapturously. "Just once, but I'll remember it as long as I live. That's where the great council of hjeggs gathers once every five years. During the banquet no one steals each other's maidens or drowns ships or fights. The hjeggs decide who they're going to enter into unions with, who they're going to

The Charmed Fjords

trade barley or textiles with, whose daughters they're going to marry. It's called the great gathering of riars. The next one is in three years. That's why our riar is so angry — it's the only place where he can bargain for a wife."

"Do you have a map?" I asked hopefully. "It would be great if I could see where this cliff is."

"We have lots of maps, but why should you need one, scholar?" A languid voice made my heart jump. Danar! How had I failed to notice him standing there? Then again, how was I supposed to notice someone who entered a room in a place where there was no door? That was an annoying ability of the riars: they got their possessions to bend to their will.

He approached me and looked disapprovingly at my papers. Bjorn looked despondent.

"It's just out of curiosity, my riar." I jumped up and bowed my head, like I was already used to doing, and like I would get used to. Damn. "I've never seen the cliff of the hundred hjeggs."

"And clearly you've never even heard of it," Danar said, studying me. "You haven't told me where you're from, Olivia."

"I'm from the tribe at the foot of Great Gorlohum," I said, looking honestly into the riar's eyes.

Danar glanced at my table, which was overflowing with papers. "How much longer do I need to wait for your answer?"

"I'm close to figuring it out, my riar," I answered meekly. "I just need a little more time."

"It's already been ten days. I gave you until the full moon. Hurry up. In the meantime you're eating the meat from my house and distracting my scribe."

"I understand, my riar. I thank you, my riar."

Danar left and Bjorn and I sank onto the bench.

"I'll show you a map," he said conspiratorially. "If you teach me to divide bigger numbers."

"I will," I murmured. Indeed, time was running out and

Book One: Beyond the Fog

I had to accomplish everything. I had long ago begun to suspect the reason why the riar was not siring an heir. I was willing to guess he couldn't have children at all, and when Bjorn told me a secret about the captives whom Danar made pregnant, I only became more confident in my hypothesis.

But all this time, it wasn't studying the riar that was occupying my days. Under the pretext of looking for reasons I was just dragging out time and studying the local customs. Fortunately, I was allowed to go wherever I wanted, but Danar had assigned me a guard, who trailed behind me indifferently, yawning every now and then. I also smiled at him and whenever we went somewhere I thanked him for the supervision since more often than not he spent his time looking not at me, but at the servant girls running past or the tall, thin maidens in dazzling clothing who walked the streets of Aurolhjoll.

In all honesty, the first time I saw these stunning girls, I froze in my tracks, my mouth agape. It was when a girl of captivating beauty walked past me. She had white hair and light eyes. Her luxurious, black velvet trench coat shone with countless spangles, and I realized in astonishment that they were diamonds. The precious stones also glistened in her hair and ears, on her neck, and on her fingers.

"That's the freeborn Argel," Bjorn whispered to me. "The riar's sister."

"She's gorgeous," I said sincerely. The maiden apparently heard me because she looked at me with a smile. She continued to float past.

"There's nothing the riar won't do for her. He's grown mountains of sparkles for her."

"Are you talking about the stones?" I asked, turning to look at him. "How did he make them grow?"

"You know, he just does," Bjorn said incredulously, raising his brows. "Like all Ulhjeggs. But our riar's sparkles

The Charmed Fjords

are the purest ones around, not like what those half-bloods from Gardoshel grow. Everyone knows you have to buy sparkles in Aurolhjoll and nowhere else. The riar has the purest blood, and so do the sparkles."

"Can I see how these sparkles grow?" I asked, intrigued.

Bjorn and I both started when we heard Danar's voice behind us. "You're very curious, outsider."

"Like all women, my riar," I said, bowing my head. But instead of appearing angry, the snow riar seemed to be in a good mood. He waved an arm at me.

"Well, why not. I'll show you the sparkles. That way you'll understand my strength and Aurolhjoll's power."

For some reason, when Danar said this Bjorn jerked his head up and darted away, and the guard raced for cover. I stood there alone and blinked hard as I saw the smirking Danar bend down toward the ground. A glowing shadow seemed to cover him, and when he raised his head, he was an animal. He was grayish-white, with specks on his scales, a long tail, and sharp needles running along his spine. The snow dragon was about the size of a small house. Although I'd already seen people metamorphose into hjeggs, I stood there gawking, unable to tear myself away from the incredible spectacle.

The beast shook his head, and the rainbow eyes with the vertical pupils looked at me. He opened his mouth, revealing a dark gray tongue and massive fangs. He slapped his spear-like tail on the paving stone, dislodging a stone right next to me. I recoiled, and out of the corner of my eye caught sight of a glinting sparkle. I was flabbergasted. Diamonds were hidden in the scales of the dragon's tail, shining behind the gray membranes and the armor covering his body. The impact of his tail made one drop out onto the dusty road.

I crouched down and picked it up. A transparent, light

Book One: Beyond the Fog

blue diamond winked at me in my ink-spotted hand.

"You can keep it," the riar said, now back in human form. "If you answer my question, you'll get ten more. And they'll be even bigger than that one. With a dowry like that, any warrior will take you into his home."

"Thank you, my riar," I answered automatically.

Danar nodded and I stared at his back as he walked away. I fell deep into thought. What would happen if the people of the Confederation found out about all that I had seen on the fjords? Sverr's caves filled with gold, the ordinary and unexplainable magic, the diamonds on the hjegg's hide, the submission of the sea, sky, and earth. Severity alongside sacrifice, men and women unlike the ones in the Confederation, as different as black and white.

Two worlds that couldn't mix.

And I, the anthropologist Olivia Orway, was already prepared to concede my utter powerlessness and the total failure of the research mission. Because here on the fjords I'd realized with complete clarity that I didn't know a thing about human nature. I was like a stupid, primitive old hag who sits in a cave, makes marks on the cooled embers, and thinks she's seen the world when in fact, all she's seen is her cave.

My mood turned dark. I clasped my head and wanted to wail in despair. Bjorn was looking at me pityingly, believing correctly that I'd gone mad from the sight of the diamonds.

But I'd realized that my world had changed so much that I could no longer go back to being the Olivia I was before. Everything I believed, everything that was significant in my life had crumbled into dust and there was nothing left.

At the same time, I couldn't stay here on the fjords. I understood that, too.

And now I needed a map so I could figure out how to leave Aurolhjoll. I had no alternative. No matter what I told Danar, everything would end with me needing to fulfill the

The Charmed Fjords

womanly duties. Things wouldn't turn out differently here. The fjords weren't yet ready for emancipation. But I wasn't willing to become a toy for someone's amusement.

"It's beautiful, isn't it?" Bjorn was still supporting me. "Our riar's sparkles are very expensive. You know, they're not just decoration. They also protect you from the cold. If you keep it on you you'll never freeze."

I opened my hand. The little stone was shining.

"I think there's something that could help you, Bjorn," I said, coming out of my reverie. I reached into my pocket and pulled out a scrap of paper and a pencil. "Do you really know how to carve wooden objects? Here's one you can make. Look, I'll draw it. Make a wooden frame like this, and put a stick in it and put little tiles on it. It's called an abacus. If you know how to use it, you'll be the best at adding numbers. That's what you wanted, isn't it? In return, I'd like you to get me a map. Can you do that?"

Bjorn grabbed the drawing from me and rushed off, and I headed to my chambers, under the gaze of the bored guard.

❀ ❀ ❀

Irvin looked at the girl sleeping beside him. The white hair was fanned out over the dark coverlet, and her naked body was exposed. What a beauty. The a-tem winced grimly. Sverr had been right. The alluring snowmaiden Eilin only wanted silk and jewels, and she was boring in bed. On top of that, she didn't need any prodding to abandon her husband for the hjegg. There was something repulsive about that. And he grew tired too quickly of admiring the ivory body. Irvin had already had his fill. And to think that at one point he thought that if he got hold of the maiden he wouldn't let her leave his bed for the entire winter. Winter hadn't even begun and he

Book One: Beyond the Fog

was already sated.

The maiden turned over in her sleep and smacked her lips unhappily. The a-tem suddenly felt irritated. He jerked Eilin by the arm.

"Wake up."

"What?" Eilin batted her long eyelashes inquiringly and looked at Irvin in confusion. His irritation mounted.

"Put your clothes on and get out of here," Irvin ordered, pushing the maiden off the bed. "Now!"

"What? But why?"

The a-tem grunted, not wanting to explain. "Go home, OK? Someone will escort you."

"But... what do you mean... I thought..."

"Get out of here," Irvin snarled.

The maiden leaped up and grabbed the silk dress and jewelry the a-tem had charitably given her. She pressed them to her chest as though she were afraid someone would steal them.

Irvin pulled a face and turned away. Yes, Sverr had been right. He always was.

His irritation turned into remorse, which had already been tormenting him for ten days. That was how much time had passed since the attack by the wild hjeggs, and since the riar hadn't been seen in Neroaldaf. The warriors were already asking questions. At the moment they were careful and timid, but soon they'd be bolder. And then a dozen or so of the strongest would come to him and ask if he was ready to become riar since the last one had disappeared.

The people needed a riar who would defend, protect, and lead them, someone they would go to with requests and complaints, someone they would go to battle for and who would give them the gift of his call.

It was just that Irvin had no desire whatsoever to become that hjegg. He'd always been at ease under Sverr's

The Charmed Fjords

wing. He could sink ships on Sverr's orders, fight with interlopers, pull enemies to the bottom of the sea, and kidnap maidens from other cities. And then he was happy to feast at a banquet, seated to the left of the black riar.

But now Sverr had disappeared and the opening to the cave was blocked off with gold. It was impossible to know whether the riar was there or somewhere deep in the cliffs. Meanwhile, Neroaldaf was silently being rebuilt, the destroyed tower was being raised, and the wall was being mended. For now the people were occupied, but that couldn't last forever.

Irvin hissed, chasing away his hjegg's shadow. He wanted to plunge down into the water like always, knowing that Sverr would make all the decisions and deal with everything. But now it was up to the a-tem to make the decisions. Irvin's head was already buzzing from the questions, complaints, and grievances.

Even the white-haired Eilin couldn't distract him. She was a dormant fish, not a maiden.

She was nothing like that outsider from beyond the Fog. That girl had the soul of a warrior — or of a hjegg. And Liv would never betray her husband. She would have scratched out his eyes if he made a proposition to her like he did to Eilin.

Maybe that was why he was so angry — because Liv always sparked such confusing feelings in him, and such interest. He had a yearning to figure her out and study her. He could have become infatuated with her just like Sverr, but he didn't want to admit that.

Irvin rubbed his stubbled chin and closed his eyes in exhaustion. He would have told the riar that the girl was alive. But where should he look for him now? On second thought, maybe it was better not to tell him. Something the riar would absolutely not forgive was someone else taking

Book One: Beyond the Fog

advantage of Liv. Not only that, Irvin had delivered her to the snow riar. No, Sverr definitely wouldn't tolerate that. Irvin had no doubt that Liv was already warming Danar's bed. He'd wanted to leave the girl on the bottom of the ocean, but he couldn't make himself do it. He thought she'd lose her grip and fall off him on the way to Aurolhjoll, but she managed to cling to his back as he twisted and turned through the ocean. Yet he just didn't have the heart to leave her on ocean bed. So he cast her down on the shore, furious at both himself and her.

He still had a bitter taste in his mouth. He swallowed it and screwed up his eyes. It was the taste of betrayal — his betrayal. It seemed like he had done everything right, so why did he feel so awful?

Irvin spat on the ground, trying to get rid of the bitterness. It didn't work. He had no idea what to do now.

Vexed, he snatched up his clothing and hastily pulled it on. He set off for the only place where lately he was able to find peace.

On the northern side of Neroaldaf, on a small patch of dry land in the ocean, there was a lone house. The salty breeze and spraying water covered the dark, tarred logs with a white coating, and the small windows were boarded up. But smoke rose out of the pipes, indicating that the dwelling was inhabited.

Irvin climbed ashore, shook himself off, returned to his human form, and straightened his wet clothes. He didn't feel cold, not even when he was standing on two legs and not crawling like a snake. The fabric dried out on him almost immediately. He pushed open the door and stared at the boy who jumped up off the bed. The boy gazed at Irvin with a combination of fear and adoration.

"Why are you up? It's early for you," Irvin grumbled. He dropped a waterproof parcel containing meat, boiled eggs,

The Charmed Fjords

bread, and cheese on a makeshift table. He wished he could have brought some thick soup with pieces of dough, like they cooked in the tribe where Irvin was born. Although the a-tem had been taken away from the tribe when he was a small boy, he'd never forgotten the taste of the stew. But for a sea serpent, transporting soup wasn't exactly convenient. In any case, it would freeze in the waters of the fjords. So the boy would need to be satisfied with cold and dry provisions.

"May the sea protect you, Irvin-hjegg," Vilmar said gratefully, bowing his head and stubbornly not sitting down on the narrow bed in the corner. Irvin snickered but looked approvingly at Vilmar. The boy had character and strength, which meant that he'd grow up to be a good warrior. Yet he'd never be a hjegg. No one ever managed to try on the ring of Gorlohum a second time, if only because in this duel there weren't people like Vilmar. The young boys either fought successfully against the spirit of the wild animal or — and more often — they perished.

As though he overheard Irvin's thoughts, Vilmar stepped closer and raised his head. He was pale and had circles under his eyes, but his lips were pursed in determination.

"Please tell me, what's going to happen to me, Irvin-hjegg? And how is it that I lived?" Vilmar touched his neck in bewilderment. "I'm not wearing the ring and my ribs are cracked. Doesn't that mean I lost? And doesn't it mean..." He trailed off, but his gaze remained dogged. "Doesn't that mean I have no right to live?"

Irvin snorted and sank down on the bench beside the wall.

"Are you in a hurry to die, Vilmar? First grow up, and then you'll have plenty of opportunities to go to eternity. It's too early for that now. You have nothing to tell the firstborn hjeggs in the afterlife and there's nothing for you to amuse

Book One: Beyond the Fog

yourself with. So today you're going to Sharondalhjoll."

"Where?" the boy asked in surprise.

"It's far away, on the other side of the ocean." Irvin looked stern and restrained a smile even though he wanted to burst out laughing as he looked at the child's wide eyes. But the a-tem recalled Sverr. Sverr knew how to put an expression on his face that made even the most skilled warriors tremble. And only Irvin knew that deep down Sverr both took pleasure in that fact and was irritated that people feared him so much.

But the memory served Irvin well and he remained serious.

"Yes. Consider this an order from your riar, Vilmar. You'll take a ship that is soon going to pass by the shores of Neroaldaf. You'll give this message to the man in command." He placed a wax-sealed scroll on the table. "And you'll do everything to become an honorable warrior. Forget about the ring of Gorlohum. Never tell anyone that you tried to put it on. Do you understand?"

The boy blinked rapidly and his light brown eyes gleamed. "But how..."

"Did I not make myself clear? What are you arguing with me for?" Irvin stood abruptly and looked down at Vilmar. He tried to channel Sverr again.

"Yes, I understand," Vilmar stammered in fear. He straightened up and tried to look brave. "I memorized everything you said, Irvin-hjegg. I'll do exactly what my riar and you order. "It's..." He licked his lips. "It's not easy, is it? You need me there, in Sharondalhjoll? Right?"

"Have something to eat," Irvin replied with a laugh. "And remember what I said. Become an honorable warrior."

Irvin chose not to tell the boy he would never see his mother or relatives ever again. In any case, Vilmar knew what he was getting into when he chose to try on the ring of

The Charmed Fjords

Gorlohum. By law, anyone who fails but survives the challenge is supposed to be sacrificed and thrown into the waters of the fjords to calm the wild hjeggs who have been roused.

That's what the a-tem would report that evening at the warriors' council.

Irvin scrutinized the boy, who was gathering up his meager belongings. Vilmar's movements were still tentative as he tried to protect his bound ribs, but the a-tem didn't offer to help him. It would only insult Vilmar, who was already bewildered to begin with. Only a mother or wife could help a warrior gather his things, never another warrior. Here it was every man for himself. So Irvin walked out and went to stand next to the boulders that were overgrown with moss and blocked the little house from the salty spray. On the horizon, Gorlohum protruded like a black tooth, and white smoke drifted over the summit of the volcano. In the other direction, the tower of Neroaldaf soared. Irvin looked at the glinting water, shading his eyes. There was a spot in the waves that a human eye wouldn't notice but that a hjegg could make out. It was a ship. It was time to go.

Vilmar emerged from the house in time, shut the door behind him, and looked at Irvin questioningly.

"You're going to get soaked," Irvin warned Vilmar crossly and grunted at the anticipation in the boy's eyes. Of course, who else could boast that he'd ridden on the scales of the sea serpent? Things like that didn't happen.

The a-tem shook his head, waving his long hair, and gave a running leap into the water. A moment later, a narrow, long mouth with snake eyes rose over the steep, craggy shore. The sun shone on his skin and illuminated the outstretched fins, making them look transparent.

Vilmar gasped in delight, tossed the parcel with his belongings onto the hjegg's back, and climbed on. The hjegg

Book One: Beyond the Fog

snorted, letting out a wisp of whitish smoke, and slid into the smooth water, trying not to soak his passenger.

A few hours later, after leaving the boy on the ship of his old friend, Irvin dived into the depths of the sea. He breezed through a wall of thousands of large, flat, silvery fish, opened his mouth, and swallowed a dozen of them in a single gulp. He growled in satisfaction, slapped his tail, and leaped out of the water. The a-tem was filled with joy. That was strange, seeing as how he had just violated a law of the fjords. And the *velv* soothsayers say that for a violation the ancient hjeggs get angry and punish the criminal. But Irvin felt calm. Let them be angry, he thought as he chased after a frightened, sharp-tailed fish. Instead, the boy would grow up, find himself a maiden, and produce children. Maybe that outsider Liv was right, too.

Chapter 25. Confederation

KLIN GAZED CHEERLESSLY at the cliffs, which looked impenetrable from here. Jean came over and stood next to him. He looked up, let out a whistle, and grasped his fur hat. The tops of the mountains were lost in the shroud of fog, which cut off the visibility like a wall.

"Do you think we'll be able to do it?" asked Klin, the expert in rare life forms.

Jean shrugged, but anticipation sparked in his eyes. Klin knew he had the same expression on his face. It was a burning anticipation, expectation, and hope. That's what was now flowing in their blood and pushing them forward.

"There's something strange about these fjords," Jean said in a muffled voice, looking at Klin with understanding. "It's like they're calling us."

"Yes, they're calling us," Klin agreed. He refrained from mentioning that they didn't just call, but also tortured his dreams, which were vivid, colorful, and three dimensional. His dreams were so realistic that he woke up with the taste of sea salt on his tongue and the sensation of the breeze on his skin. The fjords were a drug that seized the people from the Academy of Progress and didn't let them go.

Jean nodded toward the military vehicles and Yurgas, who was standing next to them. "They're also calling him."

"He's not coming with us because of the fjords," Klin

Book One: Beyond the Fog

said, with a surprising note of acrimony in his voice.

As though Yurgas heard Klin and Jean talking about him, he glanced up and then went to join them. He looked around.

"Do you remember your instructions?" he muttered gruffly. "Don't interfere and stay out of the way. Is that clear?"

"What's clear is that this thing alone could blow a small mountain to pieces," Klin replied heatedly, pointing at one of the nearby military vehicles. "Did you really need to bring that, Yurgas? We only wanted to go do research."

"Don't you get it?" Yurgas asked, flashing with anger. "Are you that much of a fool? Don't you ever take your nose out of your books? What research? From the very beginning the fjords have only been considered new territory full of new resources, including labor. But your research mission, your infiltration, is just a screen for unhappy people."

"What?" Jean asked, taken aback. "But how..." he clasped his arms over his head. "What do you mean? How can that be?"

"That's how it is," Yurgas said. He winced and spat on the ground. "I don't know what happened back there at the Academy, and I don't know what the barbarian turned into. But you can rest assured that whatever he was, he won't be able to fight off our vehicles. The beast is doomed. They've all been doomed for a long time. We've only been waiting for the right moment."

Klin let out a sharp wail, looking in horror at Yurgas's calm expression.

"So I advise you to just sit quietly and not meddle," Yurgas said and turned on his heel like a soldier leaving to carry out his orders.

"Is that why you're going there?" Klin asked him as he walked away. "You want to take revenge? For her sake?"

Yurgas stopped and clenched his fists. Without looking

The Charmed Fjords

around, he headed off toward the soldiers, who were examining a map spread out on the hood of an armored SUV.

Klin and Jean exchanged a glance, suddenly feeling superfluous and lost among the men in black-and-gray uniforms. They'd been included in this new expedition only because their experience passing through the fog might be helpful.

"Well, my friend, it looks like we've gotten into a jam," Klin said thoughtfully.

Jean nodded in agreement. "Do you think she's alive?"

Both men glanced toward the white swath of fog that was beckoning them to the mountains.

❊ ❊ ❊

Sverr sneezed and opened his eyes. He looked dully at the gold, the damp arches of the cave, and the thin, red streaks in the stone. He raised his head. The crimson veil had paled slightly and the murderous craving had receded. Yet the pain was still there. He just wanted to bury himself in the calming gold and fall back asleep. But he didn't allow himself to do that.

His roar ricocheted off the arches of the cave and the beast hauled himself up and turned in a circle, peevishly expelling black smoke from his nostrils. How long had he slept? Fear flowed through him like a cold wave. He had the impression that centuries had passed and outside there were no more fjords, Neroaldaf, or people. Sverr roared again, this time so loudly the cliffs trembled. He charged toward the obstruction in the cliff, dug it out, scratching his claws on the stone, and worked his way outside. He let out a sigh of relief: just like always, the black fortress tower loomed east of the cave. The hjegg took a running start and dropped off the cliff,

Book One: Beyond the Fog

spreading his stiff wings. The wind beat against his hide. His old friend, the scattered lightning, lit up the sky. The warriors of Neroaldaf began to shout joyously and wave their swords when they caught sight of their riar overhead.

Sverr circled the city, closely taking stock of the changes.

He landed on the platform of the tower, adding a few fresh grooves to the granite. He stood up on his human legs and nodded at the guards, who had shrunk against the wall.

"How long was I gone?"

"Twelve days, my riar."

"Where's Irvin?"

"In the fortress, riar."

The soldiers exchanged glances and Sverr barked, "Why are you looking at each other like that? What else has happened?"

"This morning one of the soldiers you sent to the Fog came back," the older guard said hoarsely, stepping forward. "He had news, my riar. He's waiting downstairs."

Sverr nodded and went inside. Thoughts were pounding feverishly in his head, and his intestines were cramped from hunger. He wanted to eat and drink, and then change his clothes, which were full of the musty odor of the cave. But all of that would have to wait. First he needed to deal with this news from his messenger.

The riar raced so fast into the long room decorated with weapons and the seal of Neroaldaf that the guards barely had time to open the door.

"Speak up!" he ordered the worn-out soldier who leaped up from behind the table. A goblet of wine toppled over, and a red spot seeped over the embroidered tablecloth.

That was a bad sign, and an alarm went off in his head.

Irvin, who was sitting next to the messenger, also stood up and greeted Sverr. A happy look flickered across his face

The Charmed Fjords

before inexplicably turning to fear. Sverr had no time to try to decipher his a-tem's reactions and turned to the pale man standing next to him. The soldier bowed his head and shifted heavily from one foot to the other. The awkward movement indicated he was injured. Sverr pointed at the bench and ordered him to sit down.

"There's trouble, my riar," the messenger croaked. "Like you said, the people from beyond the Fog have come. We didn't have time to do anything. Iron monsters crept out of the haze. They were spitting fire, almost like you, my riar, when you fly in the sky. But these monsters aren't alive. And they're carrying death. Out of the whole unit, I'm the only one left. I wasn't a coward. Don't think that. I was thrown into the crevices of the cliff, and I hit my head on a stone. When I regained consciousness, there was no one around. I buried whoever I could and then came back to Neroaldaf as fast as I could with the news."

He swallowed hard and glanced at the puddle of wine.

"Where did they go?" Sverr asked.

"Toward Aurolhjoll," the messenger said. "The snow people are the closest in that direction. They've probably already arrived there. We don't need to pity the snow people, we just need to avenge the deaths of our people, my riar. We can't accept this."

The color drained from Irvin's face and he jumped up. Sverr frowned and looked at Irvin critically. A premonition stung him.

"Speak, a-tem," the riar said.

"The outsider is in Aurolhjoll," Irvin blurted.

Sverr blinked in confusion. Heat flared up in him, and his heart jumped, finally waking up and throwing off the shackles of pain.

"What did you say?" Sverr's voice was dangerously soft.

"The outsider is in Aurolhjoll. Liv." Irvin grit his teeth

Book One: Beyond the Fog

as he looked defiantly into the riar's red eyes. The messenger slid sideways off the bench and headed toward the door, sensing that the hjeggs would soon destroy this room, too.

The a-tem nervously sawed his hand along the table. "Yes, I lied to you before. She's alive. At least, she was alive when I threw her down on the beach by Aurolhjoll. I'm not going to justify myself. I'll accept whatever punishment you give me."

"You're not?" Sverr hissed in his face. He said nothing else, just took a step back. The only telltale sign of his anger was his livid cheekbones. "Did you betray me, Irvin? Did you sell out to the snow hjegg?"

"No, it's not like that!" Irvin yelled. "I only wanted to protect you. You've changed since that girl has been here, Sverr. You fell in love, may Hellehjegg take you! You fell in love with the outsider! I was just trying to save you. You're not allowed to fall in love with the enemy. What else was I supposed to do?"

"For starters, you could have just wished me happiness!" Sverr bellowed.

"But she's a girl from the Confederation."

Sverr started moving toward Irvin, and when Irvin looked at Sverr's face, he realized with hopeless clarity that Sverr was going to kill him. But the riar stopped, sighed heavily, and turned away.

"I can't punish you now, Irvin," he said blankly, avoiding Irvin's eyes. "Neroaldaf is in danger. All the fjords are in danger. But after that..." he turned his head and Irvin saw how his eyes burned with scorn. "You've let me down."

With that, he pivoted and walked out of the room.

Irvin placed his fists on the table and lowered his head. The bitter taste in his mouth choked him like bile. But it was all true, and Sverr was entitled to be furious. Still, Irvin had only wanted to protect his twin. He became frightened when

The Charmed Fjords

he saw the fire that the outsider ignited in the riar's soul. This fire was so strong it could burn not just Neroaldaf, but all the fjords. The a-tem had never seen Sverr like that. His friend could try to lie to himself and say that the girl didn't mean anything to him, but Irvin knew the truth. Sverr had begun to love like the ancient hjeggs had loved — for all eternity.

The worst part was that Liv had not just irritated the a-tem; she also attracted him. She'd stirred something in him. She'd awakened dangerous thoughts and desires he shouldn't have. It wasn't for nothing that he'd wanted to take her in the shatiya circle. He'd wanted to make her his and take possession of her, just like it was in the hjeggs' nature to do. The hjeggs always took whatever struck their fancy. It was their essence. Maybe it was because hjeggs ran away from feelings — it was too painful for them to lose things. But it was forbidden to take things from Sverr — Irvin had no delusions about that.

He clenched his fists. He should have left the girl in the waters of the fjords. But he knew he couldn't do that.

OLIVIA

I spread the map out on the table and when I figured out what was before me I smiled jubilantly to myself. The names were written in symbols I had never seen before. They looked like ancient runes.

Bjorn leaned over the map beside me, resting his elbows on the table.

"OK, here's Aurolhjoll," he said, pointing at a white mountain with an intricately drawn castle on it. I could even make out the staircase that wound from the shore along the slope of the mountain. "It's surrounded on three sides by the ocean, and on the fourth there are the mountains and gorge.

Book One: Beyond the Fog

If you travel two days from here by ship, you'll get to Grindar, and if you keep going, you'll reach the islands of the maiden warriors. You don't want to mess with them. And here's the fjord where you were saved from, Neroaldaf. This is Great Gorlohum, and here's Varisfold, where the hall of the hundred hjeggs is."

I carefully smoothed the rough sheets of paper, which were bound by a thread and on which someone had meticulously drawn images and detailed inscriptions.

"What does Neroaldaf mean?" I asked suddenly.

"Don't you know?" Bjorn asked in surprise. "It means nest on the cliff. Aurolhjoll is the Shining Summit. That's a much more beautiful name, isn't it?"

"Nest on the cliff." My throat constricted and I screwed up my eyes. The feelings I'd been holding in all these days now distilled into stinging tears. I leaned down closer, trying to look like I was examining the drawings rather than screaming like a fool. Nest on the cliff. And the room with the soft blanket, warm walls, and fireplace with a dancing flame. And the man whom I'd taught to kiss and touch indiscreetly. The flecks of light in the golden irises, the laugh on the stern lips.

I longed for him desperately and with every ounce of my being. And it wasn't because he was the first, the best, and the most impossible. It was because he was the only one.

Except that I had no clue what I was supposed to do with that feeling. It was stupid and useless. It didn't fit into any of my plans. It bothered me, pricked me, and made me dream. It forced me to wait. To call.

What Sverr had said in my little apartment was true. Love is a bad feeling. It makes the man vulnerable, and it causes the woman pain. And yet I wouldn't give up the opportunity to experience it, not for anything in the world. Not even the Confederation's Viry Prize, the most prestigious

The Charmed Fjords

science award.

"Liv, are you crying?" Bjorn asked in astonishment when he saw my tears drop onto the paper despite my efforts to hold them in. I hurriedly wiped them off with my sleeve.

"I was touched by the beautiful names," I lied. "What's this here?"

Bjorn began describing the landmarks and I stared at the snowy mountain chain that stretched alongside Aurolhjoll. If my memory was correct — and it pretty much always was — it was exactly where there was a spot where the Fog had nearly disappeared. It was very close to where I was now.

My heart pounded against my ribs. There, beyond the Fog, was my life: people, civilization, the Academy, and everything else. It was time to go home.

※ ※ ※

I threw on a warm trench coat padded with fox fur and chuckled. What do you know, I'd almost gotten used to the clothing of the fjords. Still, I would have been more comfortable in my jumpsuit and parka than in a wool dress.

But I was grateful to the hjeggs for the clothes. Bjorn went home, and I reread the letter I was going to leave for Danar. Although the snow riar had plans for me that I didn't care for, he was basically a good guy. And I'd promised to figure out why he wasn't siring an heir. But I knew it would be better for him to read the reason in a letter rather than hear it from me. I grabbed my knapsack filled with a knife, some meat, cheese, and bread, a mysterious fragment of coal that could be lit on a tree or wood shavings, a rope, map, and the diamond, which would ensure that I'd never freeze. Yet more examples of the magic of the fjords, which I was unable

Book One: Beyond the Fog

to explain and would never be able to explain. Even my scientific training had its limits.

Out of habit, I stroked the iron bird for a moment and then put it back in the leather pouch on my belt. It was time to leave.

My continual smiling and constant delight had paid off: the guard in charge of me became a little less vigilant and in the last few days ambled around after me lazily and with an expression of obvious confusion on his round face. He didn't understand why he needed to guard this girl who with every step she took admired Aurolhjoll's wonders and praised the snow hjeggs. I thanked everyone around me for life in this stunning place so many times that they believed me. Even Danar looked on with an indulgent chuckle and idle interest. Yet I didn't want that interest to grow.

Now, in the predawn hour, the guard was blithely snoring by the door to my room. The door latches I'd smeared with oil didn't make a sound when I crept out.

Aurolhjoll was still sleeping as I made my way like a shadow along the bright corridors and exited through a small door behind the kitchens. The slowly burning light of dawn painted the crystal peaks of the towers in pink and gold and I stopped for a moment, in awe of the beauty. I jolted myself from my reverie and set off in the opposite direction of the main gate. Any typical runaway would rush toward the sea and try to pull away one of the boats. Instead, I hurried eastward, where the snowy mountains rose up and the murky strip of Fog was visible. None of the children of the fjords would go voluntarily in that direction — I was counting on that. Originally I'd planned to steal a horse, but I quickly abandoned that idea. I doubted an animal would be happy about carrying a rider who was trembling with fear. Also, I had no idea how to secure a saddle, and I knew I wouldn't be able to hold on to the croup without one. So I'd need to travel

The Charmed Fjords

on my own two feet.

The fortress wall ended behind the towers, so after an hour of brisk walking I found myself on a snow-dusted plateau. The Shining Summit remained behind me, and the colors of its tower faded in the daylight and again became diamond-silver. The cold was bracing but I didn't notice it. The plateau was picturesque, with soft blue edelweiss peeking through the thin blanket of snow, but I stopped myself from reveling in it and trod on.

After a couple of hours I began to see the side of the cliff and the edge of the Fog next to it. The most important thing was to not make a mistake. If I was correctly remembering the spot Anders Eriksen had pointed to, this was where the curtain between the fjords and the Confederation had practically disappeared. I needed to believe Eriksen and find that rupture. This was no time to think about potential inaccuracies. I would find that damned rupture, come hell or high water.

The Fog was already close by when I heard a heavy, muffled din and then the anxious tolling of a bell behind me. It was coming from Aurolhjoll. I jumped. What was it for? Had they really noticed I'd escaped, and now they were summoning the people to catch the runaway?

The bell sounded again. I turned around and shaded my eyes, trying to figure out why the northern tower, which an hour ago had been turning pink in the rising sun, was shaking. It quivered, and then melted away and began to crumble, as though it had been sawed in half by a gigantic beam.

My throat closed in horror and panic seized me in its familiar embrace. From where I stood on the cliff, I could see the top of the tower crash down. There was only one weapon I knew of that could do that: the lasers of the Confederation.

But how could that be, just as I was planning to cross

Book One: Beyond the Fog

to the other side?

I began to gasp. My asthma knocked me down onto the snow, and it felt like a noose was tightening around my neck. My vision dimmed, but not before I caught sight of a shadow ascending over Aurolhjoll: a colossal, long silhouette spreading its black wings in flight, disgorging a flame from its fanged mouth.

Sverr. Over there, above the glowing spires, there was Sverr. I'd recognize him in any guise.

I got to my knees, breathing carefully. One, two, one, two. What had the healer told me to do?

"Hellehjegg, born in the flame of Gorlohum, take away my pain, help me," I began to mutter, gasping. I wasn't thinking of how primitive and even stupid the thing I was trying to do was. To hell with science! I'd left science behind on the other side of the Fog. In the here and now, Sverr was circling above Aurolhjoll and he was being shot at. "I beg you, Hellehjegg!" I prayed. "I need to help him!"

I began to breathe more evenly, carefully drawing in the snowy air. The asthma attack passed, without my inhaler and medicine.

But I couldn't waste time thinking about it. I jumped up and rushed back toward the city. This time I no longer saw the beauty of the mountains or the edelweiss I was trampling with my boots.

SVERR

I separated from my beast, lost my balance, and collapsed onto the snow. Then Irvin let out a trumpeting roar, spit burning acid, and metamorphosed.

"What are you doing, Sverr?" he yelled, looking around in alarm. "Summon your hjegg! It's too dangerous here as a

The Charmed Fjords

human."

"Go back to Neroaldaf!" I bellowed at the a-tem. Irvin clenched his jaw stubbornly. I knew my twin wouldn't leave. He ignored my direct order.

"Sverr, listen to me..."

"Go!"

He shouted something at my back but I didn't pay attention. I pivoted around and swung my battleaxe at the snow warrior who had tried to chop off my head. People were screaming all around us. The inhabitants of Aurolhjoll were running to hide in their shelters. No one knew what was happening or where this trouble had come from. I turned around, trying to orient myself.

Aurolhjoll shook again, like a living, wounded animal, and all seven towers chimed mournfully. Then a thin, light blue beam rose out of nowhere and struck the eastern tower. The severed top fell in slow motion and the white stones showered down like an avalanche. I could hear more people shouting and crying.

"Sverr!" Irvin shouted again. "Sverr, merge with your beast!"

"I need to find her!"

"I'll help you..."

"You've already helped enough," I said, thrusting a fist into the stomach of a warrior who had charged at me. I ducked, raised my white steel weapon over my head, and struck.

"Hey, blackie!" It was Danar's voice, filled with spite and hate, that I heard through the din of the battle. I turned toward it. The riar of Aurolhjoll was standing in a narrow window of the fortress. He was still in his human form. Perfect — I needed him to remain human for just a little longer.

I fended off the soldiers standing in my path and set off

Book One: Beyond the Fog

on a run, squeezing my weapon in my hand. Danar leaped down and righted himself easily. An icy steel weapon glinted in his hand.

"You've brought misery to my home!" the snow riar began to yell. "Die, you wretch!"

"It's not me, you idiot!" I roared when the northeast tower also shook and tumbled down. "It's the Confederation! The people from beyond the Fog! Just look!"

Danar looked incredulous.

"I sent you a warning, you frozen fool! The birds!"

"I fed your birds to the dogs, you monster!" the white riar thundered. But his white eyes began to shine with understanding. Danar saw the beam that sliced the stone buildings like a scorching knife. He knew there was no weapon like that on the fjords.

A burst of cold air struck me, signaling that Danar's snow beast was nearby.

"Stop! Where is she?"

"Who?" The riar of Aurolhjoll had already merged with his hjegg.

"Olivia! Where is she?"

The snow hjegg stopped and his white eyes suddenly flashed with understanding. He snorted. "In Aurolhjoll, blackie. In Aurolhjoll..."

The echo bounced off the walls and brought me the words as the snow hjegg beat his wings, soaring upward. Behind me, Irvin cried out and I also started to slow down. I summoned my beast and a moment later exhaled a long stream of smoke as I lifted into the sky over the Shining Summit.

I filled the sky with hateful roaring and fire. Next to the wall, ghastly iron monsters were standing on the snowy plateau. There were two dozen Confederation vehicles, and each one held a killing apparatus. The light blue beam surged

The Charmed Fjords

again and struck the stone wall, boring a massive hole.

Danar began to bellow, and two of his brothers — smaller snow beasts — shot into the sky. For a moment I caught the riar's eyes: the icy eyes with the extended pupils looked at me inquisitively. I shook my head and let out a stream of fire toward the vehicles. Danar nodded and sped toward them.

OLIVIA

I began sprinting back to the city. I ran so fast it was like I'd sprouted wings. I was struck by terror and the understanding of the finality of what was happening. When the military vehicles appeared before me, I started to gasp again — this time from exertion.

"Stop, stop!" I began to yell, waving my arms and trying to attract attention. "Stop! Don't! I'm here! It's me, Olivia Orway! Don't!"

A bulky, heavy vehicle turned and a laser pierced a hole in the city wall. Damn! The wall crumbled, creating an opening for the equipment. I didn't see any people, but that wasn't surprising — they were concealed behind the iron armor.

"Stop, stop! Please don't! Don't touch them!" Continuing to scream and wave my arms, I set out at a run, desperate to stop the assault.

But between the mayhem and booming of the vehicles and the dragons circling overhead, no one could hear me, and no one saw the small, human figure running from the cliffs. I was totally confused. I only saw the walls being destroyed, the people of the Confederation shooting, and a throng of armed snow warriors running out of Aurolhjoll. They were wearing icy armor and clutching swords. These were soldiers

Book One: Beyond the Fog

who would die before even reaching the men in the military equipment.

But as soon as I thought this, Danar gave out a drawn-out cry. A snowy vortex suddenly flew down in a thick, compact curtain that covered the warriors. Their white armor, hair, and clothing dissolved and became invisible. At the same time, the mottled vehicles stood out prominently against the backdrop of the plateau. Sverr descended and breathed out a flame. The nearest vehicle melted away. I could hear people shrieking inside, and I slapped a hand over my mouth, unable to contain an exclamation of horror. What the hell?

In the haze of gathering ice I saw Confederation soldiers fall onto the snow and fighters from Aurolhjoll drag them away. But the Confederation soldiers had stun guns and other weapons of progress, and they got their bearings and went on the offense. When a green smoke rose over the walls, the tower guards fell, grabbing their throats. I managed to get to the battle site. I searched frantically for our commander. Our commander? Shit, I no longer knew who "my" people were. The attackers or the defenders? The Confederation or the fjords? Whose side was I, the anthropologist Olivia Orway, on?

"I need to stop this," I muttered, frantically trying to come up with an idea. Through the snow, hubbub, and mass of people I spotted a familiar face. "Yurgas? Yurgas! It's me, Olivia!"

But Yurgas didn't hear me. He was shooting aggressively, trying to hit the dragon circling above. With obvious annoyance, he tossed aside the useless pistol and jumped into the vehicle. I saw him unroll the barrel of the device.

"No!" I screamed. I was worried that even a hjegg wouldn't survive being hit with a laser.

The Charmed Fjords

Someone pushed me by the shoulder and I flew onto the snow.

"Get out of here, girl!" a soldier from Aurolhjoll I didn't know barked at me without malice. He turned around and came face to face with a Confederation soldier. I crawled out of the way and then sprang back up. A light blue beam shot into the sky and, mercifully, flew past the closest hjegg.

The hjeggs roared in unison and the northern lights and flashes of lightning simultaneously illuminated the sky. Another deadly beam was released. I cried out and the black hjegg's head jerked and his golden eyes narrowed. The iron vehicle again spit death and the beam landed on the hjegg's wing. The black hjegg's side twitched and he arched his body and then collapsed onto the snowy ground.

"No..." I murmured, rooted to the spot and unable to believe my eyes. Not this. Anything but this.

Sverr raised his head and blinked. He tried to get up, sinking his claws into the ground. His massive, spiked tail slapped the nearest vehicle, which tipped onto its side. Danar hooked his immense legs onto another one and began to thrash it with his wings, wrenching the vehicle from the snow and lifting it into the air. He opened his legs and the iron crashed onto the frozen ground and shattered.

But then Yurgas again trained the laser on Sverr.

Without thinking, I raced forward. I pushed someone aside, slipped, got up, and kept running. My fur trench coat fell off somewhere among the stones, along with my knapsack. I kept running until the black dragon loomed before me. I didn't stop until I reached him. I turned toward the Confederation vehicles.

"Don't you dare!" I hollered so loudly that the skirmish actually died down. Behind me, Sverr was trying to get up. His left wing was almost completely burned. He roared and butted me with his head. No words were needed for me to

Book One: Beyond the Fog

understand that he was ordering me to get away. But I only grabbed him by the leg, staring into the barrel of the weapon being controlled by people from the Confederation. I waited for the next deadly beam.

The brief moment stretched into eternity.

When I had already said goodbye to my life, the hatch of the vehicle swung open and Yurgas's pale face appeared.

"Olivia? Is that you?"

The last vehicle in the convoy from beyond the Fog suddenly shuddered, let out a puff of steam, and stopped. Klin climbed out.

"Liv! We stunned the soldiers and tied them up. I knew you were still alive! Liv, we've come back!"

With a sigh I unclasped my sore hands, which had been gripping Sverr. The giant hjegg suddenly blurred, as though he were evaporating, and in a moment a man was lying beside me. His entire left side was blackish-red from the ghastly burn. I willed myself not to cry. Sverr tried to stand, but he kept falling back to the ground. Behind me, the soldiers of Aurolhjoll tied up the people of the Confederation.

"It's nothing. It'll heal, right?" I muttered, kneeling down next to Sverr, afraid to touch the burn. He looked at me foggily and clenched his teeth.

"Lilgan," he said softly and pushed away my hands. "Please don't."

He pulled himself up and clasped me to him. "If you ever do that again, I'll kill you with my own hands," he said hoarsely.

"Sverr." Danar's voice made us turn. He was also wounded, and the blood on his pale face and white hair seemed too bright. And his eyes seemed too calm. "Your twin, blackie..."

"What about him?" I asked anxiously. Danar didn't answer. He looked at his archenemy, but this time his eyes

The Charmed Fjords

held no animosity, just an ancient, silent understanding. And pity. The two snow hjeggs, Danar's brothers, circled above, filling the sky with vicious roars.

Sverr released me and stumbled past the soldiers standing there. I followed him, holding back tears. I already knew what I was going to see.

Irvin was lying in the snow. He looked like he'd just laid down for a nap. His light blue eyes were gazing at the sky with a slight look of surprise in them. The defenders of Aurolhjoll silently gathered around us in a circle. Each of them raised his blood-dipped weapon, a tribute of honor and respect.

"We need to take off the ring of Gorlohum," Danar said in a strained voice. "I can..."

"No. I'll do it," Sverr said sharply. He stood over Irvin's body. Irvin's eyes looked like two black holes.

"Of course, riar of Neroaldaf," Danar said calmly.

The soldiers lowered their weapons and beat the freezing earth. Bang-bang-bang... a heavy, hollow rhythm. Those pale faces. I shut my eyes for a moment. I also stayed standing there, understanding that Irvin merited this sign of respect.

When I opened my eyes, Sverr was holding the black stone ring. Blood dripped from it onto the snow.

I bit my cheek to keep from crying. I knew that until the end of my days I'd never forget the empty, despairing look in the eyes of the riar who had lost his twin — the woe that could not be expressed in words and was impossible to forget. It would dull with time, but it would never disappear completely.

"Riar," the soldiers breathed, slowly kneeling down. Danar remained standing and bowed his head.

"My riar," I said quietly and also knelt down on the snow. Sverr raised his head abruptly when he heard my

Book One: Beyond the Fog

voice. I carefully lifted my eyes and looked up at him. In that moment, in that position, on the chunks of melting snow, I realized I had chosen my allegiance, and the riar. Sverr realized it too. He blinked and turned away. The soldiers stood up. People had already begun to run toward us from Aurolhjoll.

Within an hour the casualties were buried and the captives were tied up securely. I clenched my teeth so hard they almost cracked. The stubborn Sverr insisted on being the one to carry Irvin to the water. He placed Irvin in the ritual boat and set fire to it, pushing it out to sea, to the place where the sea dragon would find eternal freedom and peace. I held back, sensing that Sverr wanted to be alone. Except that when everything was over, the riar of Neroaldaf dropped to the sand and didn't get up.

"He needs to go to his place of strength," Danar said grimly, crouching down beside me, "or else he'll die from his wounds."

"Take him there," I whispered. "He helped you."

"He didn't come to help. He came to find you," Danar interrupted. "I've already paid my respects to the hjegg. Now —"

"Help him!" I grasped Danar's sleeve and he looked at me in astonishment. "Everything has changed, don't you see that, riar of Aurolhjoll? The Great Fog is dissipating and the people of the Confederation are reaching the fjords. What you saw today is just a drop in the ocean. The Confederation has a lot of vehicles like that," I said, pointing behind me at the overturned equipment. "You have no idea how many! And soon they'll come here! Who will fight, Danar? You can't even imagine what the Confederation is capable of. This isn't the time for grudges. Help him!"

"Who are you, anyway?" he barked. "You're one of them, aren't you? You came from beyond the Fog. I knew

The Charmed Fjords

immediately that you were different."

"Yes, I did come from there. But I'm on your side. I think I've already proven that." I raised my head and stared into the ilg's crystal eyes. "Now it's your turn to figure out who you're fighting for — just yourself or all the fjords."

Danar cocked his head, studying me.

"Interesting. Now I understand." He shook his head and his long silver braids danced on his back. Without answering me, he walked away.

I wanted to cry out and try to persuade him, but at that moment the snow hjegg bent down and a white haze enveloped his body. I darted away, knowing from experience that it was better to keep my distance from a metamorphosing dragon. But as I tried to escape a gigantic leg seized me. Danar held Sverr in his other leg.

Chapter 26. Olivia

WHEN WE LANDED in Neroaldaf, the city's warriors were gathered to meet us. Danar let out one last roar, dropped us down by the wall, and soared back into the air.

"The riar is wounded!" I yelled. "Please hurry!"

"What happened?" Hasveng ran over and some ilgs carefully lifted Sverr and laid him on a trench coat serving as a makeshift stretcher. I told them briefly what had happened and the men erupted in alarmed, enraged screams. The people of the Confederation... the Fog... the hole... the attack... they tried to wrap their minds around the changes happening in their familiar world.

"You can crack up later!" Hasveng barked, breaking up the chatter. "Right now we need to save the riar. Take him to his place of strength. Come on, get going!"

He didn't ask about Irvin, and I quickly figured out why: Sverr was still clasping the ring of Gorlohum, which he had pulled off his a-tem's neck. The soldiers also saw it, bowed their heads, and observed a moment of silence. As we approached the cliff, the clanging of the bell announcing the sad news floated over Neroaldaf.

Gritting his teeth, Hasveng laid a hand on the smooth stone. It dawned on me that he was separating the cliff to create a passageway.

The Charmed Fjords

"Hurry up, I can't hold the passage open for long," he said. He wiped the sweat from his forehead and motioned toward the narrow tunnel. "Come on, take him. I can't hold it anymore. I'm not a hjegg."

The soldiers edged into the narrow passageway, carrying Sverr carefully.

"Where do you think you're going?" Hasveng asked me.

"With him," I snapped, not looking at him. Before anyone could stop me, I slithered into the crack in the rock.

"Fool!" Hasveng yelled angrily. "He's going to turn into his beast. He won't have any reason at all."

I didn't respond, and instead went deeper into the cliff.

"May Hellehjegg protect her," one of the soldiers said, straining under his burden. "The riar will burn her if he's hungry and then gobble her up."

We continued on silently until the cliffs separated and opened up into the cave that held the gold. The men gingerly placed Sverr on the pile of gold, looked at me somberly, and left. The cliff closed behind them. I stayed there, in the semidarkness of the cave, which was illuminated by the shining gold and the dimly glowing red streaks. I stayed there with the mountain of gold and the dying Sverr.

I knelt down next to him. In my fearful state I had the impression he was no longer breathing. Had we been too late?

"Live!" I pressed my fingers to his neck in despair, trying to feel for a pulse. Once again I didn't feel anything. But Danar had said that the riar needed his place of strength. Was this it, the pile of gold? This is where the hjegg would recover? I carefully pulled the remains of Sverr's shirt and trousers off him.

"Maybe you need to touch the gold more?" I muttered desperately, piling coins on the ilg's body. "With all your skin? Why aren't you breathing? That damned Hasveng, he didn't tell me anything, and I don't understand! We need to clean

Book One: Beyond the Fog

your wound and find antibiotics. It doesn't look like your place of strength is working. The hell with it, and all of you. Don't die, do you hear me? You can't die! Don't you dare! I can't live without you."

I was determined to clean Sverr's wounds, so biting my lips, I raced over to where I'd seen the water bottles, grabbed a few, and ran back to Sverr. But when I got back to the pile of gold, there was no man lying on top of it. Instead there was the black dragon, burrowed into a little cavity. His tail covered his face, and the burned wing was stretched out like a charred rag.

I stared at him, opened one of the bottles of water, and gulped some greedily. Then I poured the rest over my head. I was about to turn around and look for a quiet corner to settle in when the dragon opened his eyes. They were golden and misty. As he stared at me, he drew air in through his nostrils.

"Sverr, I'm going over there," I stammered, stepping back. "Everything is all right."

The hjegg hissed petulantly. I took another step and the cave shook with his hostile roar. I stood rooted to the spot, and the dragon was also motionless. Then he shook his head.

"What?" I asked. I approached him incredulously. The dragon shook his massive head again without taking his eyes off me. I took another step. And another. And then a few more. The dragon watched me intently until I sat down on the gold. Then he snorted, lifted himself up laboriously, pushed some of the gold aside, and lay back down. His head dropped down next to me and his eyes closed.

"Well, OK, if you say so," I muttered. I cautiously leaned on his black scales. They were warm. "Despot," I chuckled.

The dragon didn't respond — he'd already fallen asleep. I also yawned and leaned on his side. The gold pieces and the hjegg's scales were an inadequate substitute for my comfy couch, but at this point I was too wiped out to be picky. In

The Charmed Fjords

any case, as soon as I shut my eyes, I fell into a heavy, fitful sleep.

I had no idea how much time passed. I woke up a few times to answer the call of nature, eat something from the reserves I found in the cave, or splash some water on myself. A few times I looked into the corner where I'd tended to Vilmar not so long ago. I wondered what had happened to him and if he was even still alive. But right now there was no one for me to ask. Whenever he couldn't bear it any longer, the dragon would wake up and let out a mournful roar that shook the walls. So I would go back to the pile of gold and arrange myself in the ring his legs formed, on fur blankets I hauled over. Only then would the hjegg shut his misty eyes and fall back asleep. Resting on the snoozing dragon, I had a hard time keeping my eyes open, and I too fell into deep slumber. In the semidarkness of the cave with the shining gold, neither time nor the outside world existed.

I had no idea if it was day or night, but every time I woke up I felt like I was getting enough sleep to last a whole year. I decided to read to help make the time pass. Arranging myself comfortably on a blanket, I chewed a slightly dried-out chocolate bar I'd found in the cupboard and tried to immerse myself in a romance novel. I'd just about managed to do it, but then the sleeping dragon quivered and his silhouette began to blur. After another moment, the dragon was gone and replaced by a man. Sverr opened his eyes and the melted gold of his irises seared me. I gasped and smiled timidly.

"Hi," I said, unable to think of anything more intelligent. He didn't say anything, and I nervously licked my lips. "Your wounds... have they healed?"

Sverr raised his hand and ran his fingers along my lips, which still had chocolate on them.

"I'm starving," he said hoarsely.

Book One: Beyond the Fog

"There's some canned food over there," I began, but stopped when I saw the amused look on his face.

SVERR

She was sitting cross-legged on a fur, chewing a piece of chocolate and lazily leafing through a book. Her dark hair was disheveled and the plain dress was clinging to her thin body. My hunger mounted. Desire bubbled in my blood along with the strength the gold had given me. I propped myself on an elbow and ran my fingers over Liv's lips, rubbing off the pieces of chocolate stuck to them. I leaned in and began to lick her, not taking my eyes off her. As I'd expected, she blushed and I almost cursed. Oh, hell of Gorlohum! How I wanted her — that entire sweet, tender, passionate girl. I shifted my weight and pressed Liv into the hide. She opened her mouth and our tongues met in a wanton kiss that made me groan in ecstasy. I tugged at her clothes, annoyed that there was fabric between me and my Liv. All I could think about was making her mine, right here in my place of strength. My desire was so overpowering I was ready to just turn her over and enter her, but I wanted to take my time and exult in her body. I pulled Liv's dress off and slowly ran my tongue over her soft skin. The sight of her face, neck, chest, concave stomach, and smooth, hairless private parts sparked the scorching volcano of lust inside me. Liv's breath quickened. My arousal peaked. At least, that's what I thought. But then Liv grasped my back. I panted as I gazed at her. She smiled mischievously and then lowered her head, and I felt her mouth creep down my body. My throat went dry and I moaned like an animal as all my sensations gathered in my manhood. It was so wild and so erotic that I felt delirious. She kept teasing me with her tongue and the

The Charmed Fjords

anticipation tortured me. Holy hell! At the mere thought of what she was doing I clenched my fists and prayed to the firstborn hjeggs to give me strength. I could no longer look at her. The pleasure was too staggering. I threw my head back, looking unseeingly into the dark arches of the cave. But that only aroused me more. Then my body shook like I'd just won a deadly battle, and I was glad I was lying down. The blood pounded in my ears and I screamed, flipped Liv over, and pressed her into the hide. She cried out and arched her body to meet mine. I couldn't resist biting her shoulder — I needed to feel her entire body. The unexpected, all-encompassing desire no longer made me angry. Instead, I wanted more. I wanted everything. I wanted to take possession of her, spirit her away, and hide her from the world. I wanted her all for myself.

I wanted it, and my hjegg wanted it.

But my human side knew it was impossible. Our proximity made me feel greedy and savage. I did all I could to make her mine, while I still could.

OLIVIA

When we stepped outside the cave, I found myself squinting in the sun — I'd grown unaccustomed to sunlight after all that time inside. Sverr grabbed me by the hand and we set out for the fortress, practically at a run. As soon as people noticed us, a din rose over Neroaldaf: "The riar! The riar is back!" This time the bell chimed to announce joyful news.

"How many days have passed?" the hjegg shouted to the soldiers from his personal unit who were hurrying toward him.

"Eight, riar!"

Sverr winced.

Book One: Beyond the Fog

"Prepare the ship," he said, tossing off orders as we walked. "Load it with food, equipment, and weapons. We're leaving for Varisfold in an hour. Where are the prisoners from the Confederation?"

"The snow riar sent a ship with them. They're all in the dungeons. The snow people's ships have been waiting by Neroaldaf for a few days, my riar. They were waiting for you to wake up. Danar-hjegg ordered us to tell him when you're ready."

"Give me an hour. I want to talk to the prisoners first," Sverr said dryly. He shot me a look.

"I'll go with you," I said, clutching his hand, but he shook his head.

"No. You shouldn't see this."

"But Klin is there!" I pleaded. "And Jean! They stunned the soldiers in one of the vehicles. They didn't want a war, Sverr. They're scientists who only dreamed of studying the fjords. Don't punish them for that!"

"The dreams of the people from beyond the Fog come at a high price for us," the riar said sharply. "I'll handle it, Olivia."

"Sverr!"

"I'll handle it," he said in a tone that let me know there was no room for discussion. I backed off. My tender, passionate lover from the gold-filled cave was now a strict commander, and he alone would decide the captives' fate. I bit my lip, fighting back the urge to beg and run after him.

"Yes, my riar," I said tightly, bowing my head humbly. I saw his golden eyes flash.

"Take my *shelli* to my chambers. Go rest, Liv."

Two soldiers obediently came to stand by my side. With a sigh I watched Sverr walk away, and the soldiers led me to the riar's tower. When we reached the door to the chambers, I finally remembered to ask a question:

The Charmed Fjords

"What does shelli mean?"

The guards exchanged a look.

"You don't know?" one of them asked respectfully. "It's the one the riar is indebted to. The one who shed blood to save his life."

"I see," I said with a smile. "The lilgan has become a shelli."

When I got inside the chambers I made a beeline to the tub. I was too anxious to just sit around and wait for Sverr. I ducked under the hot water and washed myself until I squeaked. When I emerged from the bathroom, Slenga was jumping around impatiently and waiting for me with a clean dress.

"The riar's most beautiful shelli!" she cried gleefully, bowing to me. I cringed.

"Stop that and tell me what happened while we were gone," I commanded her as I looked over the clothing. "Wait. First bring me trousers and a shirt. And boots. I don't think this dress will be comfortable when I'm sitting on the ship."

Slenga opened her eyes wide, but she darted off without arguing. I marveled at the new status I seemed to have — clearly it was more honorable to be a shelli than a captive or lilgan.

Fifteen minutes later I was chewing a meat roll slathered in butter and cheese and admiring my new outfit: linen trousers, a shirt, a wide belt that encircled my waist a few times and buckled in the front, a trench coat made of warm wool with a fur lining, and soft boots. Slenga stopped staring at me and arranged my grown-out hair into side braids that she then tied at my neck.

"I know who you are!" she said, appraising me. "You're a maiden soldier! Only the maiden soldier can save the riar."

I snickered and took a big swallow of the mead wine.

"Since I'm a maiden soldier, it would be nice to get hold

Book One: Beyond the Fog

of a weapon," I mumbled.

"I don't think that's too hard in Neroaldaf," Sverr said with a chuckle, making Slenga and me jump. The ilg scrutinized me, nodded, and raised his brows. "Just where were you planning to go, my shelli?"

"To Varisfold," I said firmly, looking into the dragon's eyes.

"Why?"

"I've decided I want to see the legendary hall of the hundred hjeggs. I've heard it's the most beautiful thing on all the fjords, but I don't believe that. What could really be more beautiful than Neroaldaf? So I want to see for myself. You're not going to deny me that, are you, my riar?"

"I have the impression that the curious anthropologist has learned to use her cunning." He crossed the room and lifted my chin.

"I was telling the truth, my riar," I said, allowing myself to smile.

"Is that so," he said, stroking my lips. He leaned down and kissed me greedily. Somewhere in another dimension Slenga squealed and dropped something.

"Let's go, Liv," Sverr said, pulling away regretfully. "Very well. You'll see Varisfold."

I grabbed the bag I'd thrown my belongings into. As we walked through Neroaldaf, everyone stared at us. People gathered on the square and leaped up when they caught sight of Sverr.

"Riar..." The word echoed along the sidewalk and reverberated off the walls. The single word held so many emotions: hope, despair, fear. The people of Neroaldaf were aware that disaster had come to the fjords.

Sverr stopped and raised his arm, calling everyone to silence. The chattering instantly died down. Even the wind seemed to stop.

The Charmed Fjords

I stood there looking at the solemn faces — the severe and weather-beaten ones of the soldiers, the well-groomed and beautiful ones of the maidens, the puffy-cheeked ones of the cooks, the bearded ones of the craftsmen and blacksmiths. How many of them were there here? Thousands. And every one of them was waiting for their riar to speak. Hasveng stood in front as the white-haired Eilin lingered behind his shoulder.

"Neroaldaf!" Sverr began. "Misfortune has come to the fjords. The shining towers of Aurolhjoll fell several days ago. The people from beyond the Great Fog are to blame." An outraged murmur rumbled over the square and then died down when the riar looked at them. "My brother, Irvin-hjegg, died in this battle." The heavy silence was louder than a shout. "Neroaldaf! We will not allow the foreigners to take possession of what belongs to us. I'm going to Varisfold so the council of hjeggs can decide the future of the fjords. But first..." Sverr pulled a black blade out of a sheath and turned to me. "First I would like to announce that this woman, who I stole in the distant lands and who was born on foreign shores, is now a freeborn maiden of Neroaldaf. She is a part of it and it is a part of her." The ilg slashed his palm with the knife and ran it over my face, drawing a red stripe from my forehead to my eyes and down to my chin. So that's what those marks meant: belonging to the land and the riar. "I rule you with the hjegg's strength and blood. Olivia, daughter of Neroaldaf! The stones of Neroaldaf will always wait for you, maiden, and the iron of Neroaldaf is now with you forever."

I squeezed the narrow knife Sverr held out to me. He glanced at the ground and I knelt down.

"My riar," I whispered.

He pulled me up swiftly and I saw the admiration in his golden eyes. "There's no fear left in you, Olivia."

"Not a drop," I said with a smile. It was the truth. After

Book One: Beyond the Fog

all, here kneeling down signified becoming worthy of such honor.

"Daughter of Neroaldaf!" hundreds of throats shouted. I struggled to swallow the lump in my throat.

Even as we climbed the gangway to the deck of the ship, Sverr's words continued to echo in my head: "Olivia, daughter of Neroaldaf."

Chapter 27. Olivia

WHEN WE GOT ABOARD the ship, Sverr went to join his soldiers and I was taken below deck to a small room where I could leave my things and rest. I stashed my bag in the corner and decided to go for a walk. The first place I went was to check on the prisoners. Sverr said they'd be taken to the council of hjeggs.

Most of the survivors from the Confederation were kept back in Neroaldaf and I didn't know what would happen to them. There were five men on the ship, and I was delighted to see Klin and Jean among them. When I walked in, they leaped up from the floor.

"Liv!" Jean shouted. He tried to rush at me but was jerked back by the chain around his hands. He winced in pain and smiled in embarrassment. "I'm so happy to see you! I wish I could hug you!"

"We were sure you were alive!" Klin said, nodding happily.

"Not only alive, but she's managed to betray the Confederation," Yurgas said dryly from his spot away from the other prisoners. He shot me a look filled with spite and hostility and then turned away.

"I haven't betrayed the Confederation, Captain Lith," I said softly. "But I want nothing to do with killing innocent people."

Book One: Beyond the Fog

"Is your beast innocent?" Yurgas spat on the floor. "The one you so touchingly shielded? I should have shot him, it was all for nothing that I..."

"You're an idiot, Yurgas," a blond giant muttered from the other corner of the room. "I'm glad to see you, Dr. Orway." I smiled at Anders Eriksen. The renowned researcher looked exhilarated, and his blue eyes shone with scientific enthusiasm. He didn't even look bothered by the chains binding him to the wall of the ship. Giving me an ingratiating smile, Anders added, "I never dreamed I'd end up here! After I heard all about the expedition from Klin and Jean, I was desperate to see the fjords with my own eyes."

"You'll definitely see them," Yurgas muttered. "You'll watch while these barbarians burn you, or do whatever they do here in their rituals."

"You attacked a peaceful city!" I burst out. "What gave you the right to do that?"

"We've already told your scaly lover everything," Yurgas barked. He nodded toward the others and said, "At least, they did. They're traitors just like you, Dr. Orway."

I didn't reply. There was no point arguing with a soldier. I crouched down next to Klin.

"How's Maximilian doing? Have you heard anything?"

"He regained consciousness," Klin said brightly. "You know what the first thing he said was? 'Dragon! I saw a dragon!' We had to break it to him that we also saw it and he was giving us old news." Klin smirked impishly but then his face clouded. "What are they going to do with us, Liv?"

"I don't know. We're going to the council of the hundred hjeggs and they'll decide your fate."

A heavy silence hung over the prison. Everyone understood that the decision was unlikely to be humane.

"I'll do whatever I can," I promised, hoping despairingly that I really would be able to do something. But what? I was

The Charmed Fjords

an outsider, a former captive, and on top of that, a woman. In both worlds — here and on the other side of the Fog — women's opinions didn't count for much. But I clenched my fists and repeated stubbornly, "I'll do whatever I can."

"Thank you, Liv." Jean sighed quietly.

I nodded and walked out, suddenly feeling empty inside. Despite everything, Yurgas's words about betrayal stung me. But could I really have done things differently?

Up on deck, a cold sea wind was blowing and the black towers of Neroaldaf were fading behind the mist. I walked a little farther and stopped, staring vacantly at the water. White froth streamed from each side of the ship, and the waves glinted and spewed salty spray. I didn't hear Sverr approach and I started when he came to stand beside me.

"Did you talk to them?" Naturally I couldn't keep my visit to the prison secret from the riar.

"What will happen to them?"

Sverr shrugged as he gazed at the water.

"Is that why you called me the daughter of Neroaldaf?" I asked slowly. "To protect me? You're always looking a few steps ahead and you know what's going to happen."

"I don't know anything now," Sverr said. "But you'll walk into the hall of the hundred hjeggs as a free maiden of Neroaldaf and no matter what happens, no one will touch you."

"No matter what happens?" I asked, frowning.

"Even if Neroaldaf gets a different riar," Sverr said blandly.

My veins ran cold. "Is that even possible?"

"Yes. The council could decide that Neroaldaf will be better under the leadership of a different hjegg. That sort of thing has already happened."

"And you'll accept that?" I almost shouted.

Sverr turned to look at me and smirked. "Do you think

Book One: Beyond the Fog

I should gather my troops and lead them into a battle that's lost before it even starts? It's impossible to convince the combined forces of the council, Liv. Twenty-three hjeggs are now gathering in Varisfold. Not a hundred, as it was in the beginning. Just twenty-three. But that will be enough to cut off my head. There's no doubt I'd risk my own head, but I see no point in sacrificing all the men who have served me all these years. No one else should suffer for my mistakes." Lost in thought, he stroked the wooden handrail. "Don't think about it, Liv. You'll be taken care of."

I shook my head angrily. I'd be taken care of? How, exactly?

"You're a true warrior, Liv," Sverr said without meeting my eyes. I could hear a smile in his voice. "The second I saw you, I knew you'd always fight for what you believe in."

"It's just that my ideals turned out to be a lie," I muttered. "You were right, Sverr. I always thought the people of the Confederation were civilized, but that was wrong. We couldn't conquer greed or brutality. We didn't become more human or humane. A society's level of civilization shouldn't be measured by its killing machines. If our progress just boils down to more and more devious ways to fight and destroy, that's no kind of progress, and we're nothing more than barbarians."

"Not bad, Olivia Orway," Sverr said with a chuckle.

He turned his head and looked me up and down. Something savage and anxious, real and deep swam in his golden eyes, but I was afraid to ask about it.

I turned away.

"I'm sorry to say that you children of the fjords, with your shatiya and other traditions, don't exactly seem civilized either," I muttered. "But if I have to choose between those who attack and those who only want to defend what's theirs, the choice is obvious." I sighed, calming down.

The Charmed Fjords

I ran my hand along the polished railing.

"This is a beautiful ship," I said. "This is the first time I've been so far out to sea."

"Irvin built it," Sverr said emotionlessly. "Did you know that water, salt, and wood respond to the sea hjeggs? South of Neroaldaf there's a grove where the trees are frozen in obscene positions." Sverr snickered. "That's how Irvin got back at me once after I locked him in a closet. I think we were around fifteen."

Sverr went silent and for a moment his face contorted as if he wanted to cry. He turned away again and stared unseeingly at the ocean.

"Irvin loved this boat. It's the fastest one on the fjords. He gave it to me three years ago as a gift. And the last words my a-tem heard from me were words of hate."

My heart constricted because I could guess the reason for those words.

"He loved you," I said quietly, not knowing how to ease the pain of this man beside me looking at the boundless sea. There wasn't a single word that could soothe the pain. Only time would help. It wouldn't help him forget, but it would calm him. "And he knew you loved him too."

Sverr nodded. "Don't stand here too long, Liv. This sea breeze is deceptive."

With that, he turned and went back to the soldiers. I stood there for a while longer, wrapping my arms around myself and peering into the glinting waves. I imagined I saw the long body of the sea serpent flickering in the depths.

❅ ❅ ❅

The shore came into view after three days of sailing. I rarely saw Sverr during the trip — he spent most of his time with

Book One: Beyond the Fog

his soldiers, almost as though he were trying to avoid me. I felt a strange melancholy as I drifted off to sleep on the narrow bed in the cramped room. It wasn't until the last night that the ilg woke me with greedy kisses, but when I opened my mouth, his hand clamped over it.

"No," the riar ordered so quietly I almost couldn't hear him. He didn't want any words. His body burned and beckoned, submerging me in the boiling lava of desire. And on that night, on the rocking ship, we joined together as if it were our last night together. And maybe it was. Sverr hurried, kissed me so hard I nearly ached, licked my body, and quietly growled. He was clearly using all his willpower to suppress his call. That made sense to me, because if he called on a ship full of men without women, that would be vulgar. Our intimacy felt ragged, savage, burning, and out of this world.

I nearly cried out. Sverr clamped his lips over mine to keep me silent. When it was all over, he went back up onto the deck, leaving me on the blanket that still held his warmth and smell. I burrowed my nose into it, shut my eyes, and tried to imagine that he was still beside me. How I longed for that.

But then I snapped out of it, forcing myself to clear my head.

In the morning I spotted the narrow shore and the cliff on which Varisfold perched. The hall of the hundred hjeggs.

Even the stoic soldiers paused to watch the armada approach. I saw the majestic peaks of thirty towers, white stone and black ornamentation, iron arches, and gleaming glass and crystal. The banks of a narrow canal that led to dry land joined the feet of a giant warrior who held a raised sword in his hands. The black iron tip pointed down menacingly, and I shuddered when the ship passed under it.

"That's Haros the First. He was the first to merge with a hjegg," said one of the men guarding me. "Legend has it that his sword strikes down anyone who comes to Varisfold

The Charmed Fjords

with bad intentions."

Danar's hjeggkar, which had been nearby the whole trip, entered the harbor after us. The snow people's ship looked like a fragment of ice on the water.

"That's unbelievable," I heard Anders say in awe. The prisoners had also been brought out to the deck, and they were now blinking and swiveling their heads, trying to take in all the beauty of the approaching city. I was so anxious about the upcoming council that even the impressive buildings, streets, and bridges couldn't distract me. I remembered how I'd taken Sverr to the Academy. Had he been nervous just like I was? I looked around for him and snickered when I caught sight of his calm, concentrated face. Nope, not Sverr. I couldn't imagine him ever getting nervous.

At least twenty ships were bobbing in the harbor, so I supposed nearly everyone had arrived. Sverr had once told me that the law was that you could only enter the hall on human legs. A marble staircase with at least a hundred steps led up to a round building that looked like an amphitheater. A massive door opened as we approached and we could finally see the hall of the hundred hjeggs. With a smirk I remembered the image of Sverr standing in the auditorium of the Academy of Progress. We thought the savage was awestruck by the splendor and size. But after seeing Varisfold, I knew I'd never be impressed by any building in the Confederation. Without a doubt, this was a Hall with a capital *H*. It was an expansive space built of marble, gold, crystal, stones, and iron. Standing under the cupola with a round opening in the middle, I felt like a bug that dared to appear in a temple. Dragons stared down at me from all the walls. There were black ones with outspread wings, white ones with rearing spikes, sea ones rising up from the depths of the water, and dark crimson ones flying up out of boiling lava. A hundred hjeggs surrounded us: they emerged as bas

Book One: Beyond the Fog

relief from the walls, bared their iron fangs, stared with their crystal and diamond eyes. They were so terrifyingly realistic I had a sudden urge to pray — anything to keep them from attacking me. The cupola shone with stars, and it occurred to me that at night it would be hard to tell which of the stars visible through the opening of the roof were artificial and which were real.

Behind me I could hear Klin quietly and admiringly curse under his breath, as Jean gasped and Anders oohed and aahed. We instinctively huddled together as though the beasts would jump out of the walls and ceiling and land on the marble floor at any moment. A white-stone table dominated the center of the room. Twenty-one riars were already seated around it: the masters and protectors of the mightiest cities of the fjords. Sverr nodded at them and silently took his place. We crowded together behind him. Danar sat down across from Sverr without looking at anyone. I furtively looked at the riars who would decide not just the fjords' fate but also mine. Most of them were sea hjeggs — I counted eleven. They all smelled like salt and the sea breeze, and their faces were sullen and worried. It was as though these children of the depths couldn't wait to leave Varisfold.

There were seven snow hjeggs. They were easy to recognize by their white manes and icy, almost transparent, eyes. There were four descendants of Lagerhjegg, including Sverr. I stared curiously at a huge man with a battleax. He had dozens of small black braids on his head and a scraggly beard into which animal fangs and bones protruded. His savage appearance made me shiver. His leather clothing seemed to have stiffened on him from dirt and sweat. His huge boots were covered in clots of earth, while his single amber eye looked around with a cheerful animosity.

"That's Bengt, the riar of Karnoherm," Virn whispered. "I recommend you don't look at him. The lands of Karnoherm

The Charmed Fjords

are wild and dark, and their riar is the same. The only one worse is Tjarvenshil, but thank the firstborn their riar didn't show up." I quickly averted my gaze because Bengt had jerked his head and turned toward us, as though he sensed me looking at him. A young guy sat next to him with an indifferent look on his face. His long, black hair fell down his back like a wave, and the chiseled facial features didn't seem to match the aggressive expression in his yellow eyes.

"That's Melvin from Garaskon. He's strong even though he looks like a girl," Virn said so quietly I had to strain to hear him. I nodded gratefully. The sea hjeggs were talking and joking with each other while the snow hjeggs were sitting quietly. Soldiers and entourages stood behind all the chairs. Only the one-eyed riar was alone.

"Why isn't there a single red hjegg?" I asked, suddenly registering the absence. Virn looked at me in surprise.

"Who would go to something like this voluntarily?" he hissed. "Be quiet now. Magnus the elder is coming."

Booming steps echoed through the room and the chatting stopped. Marching in lockstep, a grizzled old man approached the table and surveyed the council with yellow lupine eyes. His hair was white and for a moment I thought he was a snow hjegg, but then I realized he was just gray with age. He was also a descendant of Lagerhjegg, the black dragon. He leaned his arms on the high back of the chair but didn't sit down.

"I can't say I'm happy to see you today, riars," he said sharply. "The council has gathered because misfortune has come to the fjords. So let's dispense with the pleasantries and decide what to do now." The sea hjeggs nodded approvingly while the long-haired Melvin rolled his eyes. But no one was about to argue with the elder. "Danar, you go first. What's happening with Aurolhjoll?"

Danar quickly and clinically described the attack by the

Book One: Beyond the Fog

people from beyond the Fog. At first the other hjeggs looked incredulous, but then their expressions turned to fury and outrage.

"How can that be?" One of the sea hjeggs was unable to restrain himself. "The Fog has always protected the fjords."

"The Fog started dissipating two winters ago," Sverr replied. "At that time I proposed dispatching soldiers to keep watch, but you thought my idea was crazy and there was no threat. Danar was the first one to say that, if I remember correctly. Now this nonexistent threat is capable of destroying the fjords."

Danar winced. "I know how to admit when I'm wrong," he said peevishly.

"If you knew how to listen, your soldiers would be alive," Sverr shot back.

Danar clenched his teeth so hard his pale cheeks blanched even more.

"I think today we'd accept your proposal," Magnus said, putting an end to the discussion. "Every riar will allocate troops that will keep watch over the Fog next to their lands. If the enemy comes back onto our territory, they'll be noticed and destroyed."

"Our troops will be destroyed," Sverr said emotionlessly. "I don't think any of you understand the magnitude of the problem. I interrogated the people from the Confederation who survived. The vehicles that came to Aurolhjoll are just a drop in the bucket. Soon there will be a deluge — thousands of vehicles equipped with apparatus that can destroy our cities."

"We're riars!" Melvin cried, leaping up. "One hjegg is worth a hundred of those idiots, no matter what they're riding on. My beast's fire can liquidate not only iron, but also stone. They won't be able to resist."

"There are too many of them," Sverr said, and I could

The Charmed Fjords

hear the fatigue in his voice. "If the soldiers from the Confederation come here, that's the end of the fjords. They have too many weapons. They have vehicles, planes, missiles that fly through the air. We're strong, but not immortal. If the Confederation comes here, they'll start a war that will cost thousands of lives. The fjords will lose too much."

"What makes you say that?" one of the snow hjeggs asked indignantly.

"I was there. I was in the capital of the Confederation. I saw their city and felt their weapons. The iron... there's so much there, and almost all of it is dead. Both the iron and the stones. The call doesn't arouse them, so we can't stop them."

"Dead?" The riars exchanged disbelieving looks. "Why?"

"I don't know. I didn't spend enough time there."

"You crossed through the Fog without the council's permission, Sverr?" Magnus asked menacingly. "That's unacceptable."

"That's not important now," Sverr said gloomily. "I did it to find out what the people knew about the holes in the Fog. But they don't know any more than we do. They don't understand why it's dissipating either. Meanwhile, putting up a barrier between us and the Confederation is the only way to safeguard the fjords."

"We've been looking for the answer," the elder said heavily. "We've all done everything to try to understand what's happening to the Fog. We've gone to the *elvs* in the south, the *jötunn* at the tops of the mountains, the soothsayers, and the sea fish, who remember the world since it was created. But we didn't learn anything. Not a single myth or tale holds the answer." Magnus lowered his head and took his seat. I realized that this hjegg was very old. "You're right, Sverr. War awaits us. I'm not sure the hjeggs will be able to win it. The only choice we have is to fight."

Book One: Beyond the Fog

Before any of the riars could respond, I spoke up. "I have a theory," I said.

Magnus raised his head in surprise and the other hjeggs scowled. Sverr raised his eyebrows warningly but I'd already stepped forward.

"A woman?" the elder snickered. "Women are forbidden to speak in the hall of the hundred hjeggs."

"Maybe that's why the fjords are on the brink of a war that will destroy them," I retorted.

"Olivia," Sverr snapped.

"Take her away," the snow hjeggs said, wincing. Danar didn't say anything.

"Sverr, did you bring your bed maiden here?"

The riar of Neroaldaf jumped up and his eyes narrowed threateningly. "Shut up, Jons."

"Get her out of here."

"She's going to tell us what the problem is," Sverr said.

"That's true, let the girl talk," the one-eyed Bengt said suddenly. "I'm sick of listening to your shrieking. Let a woman's voice soothe the ear."

The snow hjeggs winced again but stopped talking. The elder's eyes bored into me. "Go on, speak then. Who are you?"

"My name is Olivia Orway," I said quietly. "I was born in the capital of the Confederation."

"She's one of them! Why isn't this girl in shackles?"

"Let her speak!" Sverr said angrily. He was standing now, looking at the other hjeggs warily. The soldiers of Neroaldaf tensed up, ready to draw their swords. But that didn't mean much — all the hjeggs had armed retinues. I took a deep breath.

"What I'm about to tell you is going to sound strange, but it could be the cause of all the misfortunes on the fjords, and the reason why the Fog is dispersing."

A thick, heavy silence fell over the room. But the hjeggs

The Charmed Fjords

were listening. They were listening to me!

"In my world I was a scientist. I used to study human nature, and the path of humans from the beginning up to today. I was considered a decent scientist. I recently ended up in Aurolhjoll." I nodded at Danar, who was frowning. "And the snow riar asked me — or rather, instructed me — to study his bloodline." When I saw Danar's eyes shining, I decided to omit the details. "I carried out the order and researched all the generations of the great riars of Aurolhjoll."

"Why is that important?" Jons asked, jumping up.

"Silence!" the elder ordered. He looked interested and that emboldened me.

"The problem of the Fog isn't the only problem, great riars. The problems are much worse, and they go deeper. This place is called the hall of the hundred hjeggs because at one point the hundred strongest warriors of the fjords sat at this table — not all the warriors who could merge with a beast, but the strongest ones. Today there are only twenty-three of you. Tell me, which animal is considered the most wrathful and powerful one?"

"Lagerhjegg," Bengt chuckled.

I bowed my head and corrected him: "The strongest is Hellehjegg, riars. But there's no red beast here. The second strongest is the one who commands iron and stone. And only four of you merge with that beast. The third strongest is the snow hjegg. But here most of you are sea hjeggs, who on the fjords are considered the weakest."

"So what?"

"Degeneration. That's what's happening to you. You're losing your strength. With every passing generation, there are fewer and fewer young boys who are capable of putting on the ring of Gorlohum and catching the strong beast. That's degeneration. There will come a day when not a single new riar appears on the fjords. Not a single boy will be able to

Book One: Beyond the Fog

merge with a dragon."

Several sea hjeggs jumped up, unable to contain themselves, but they sat back down when the elder glared at them.

"Do you know what's making that happen, woman?"

"Yes," I answered firmly. I looked at Sverr. His eyes shone like two suns — my lodestars. "I do. There are a few reasons. But everything in nature is interconnected and every reason is just a continuation of the previous one. But I digressed. Your race is degenerating because it needs new blood. Tell me, why do you steal women?"

"It's the hjeggs' instinct."

"Exactly. The hjeggs' instinct is smarter than human reason. The beasts have sensed that to have strong descendants they need fresh blood, and the beast makes you kidnap girls. That's also why your ancestors danced at the shatiya. After the volcano erupted, the fjords were thinly populated, and rituals to mix blood were created. The children belonged to everyone, and these were strong children. But after a while you began to change." I smiled bitterly. "The tribes at the foot of Gorlohum don't know what civilization is. The first sign of civilization is the possession of property. In the tribes everything is shared: dishes, tents, women, children. But cities, castles, and fortresses came into being, and the riars wanted to pass those on to their children." I glanced at Danar. He was as pale as a piece of ice from Aurolhjoll. "For centuries the riars of Aurolhjoll only married the high-born and freeborn maidens of their own city. They kept mixing the same blood until it stopped creating offspring. Children are no longer born from the union of two snow people, isn't that so? Riars aren't exactly people. The ring of Gorlohum changes you, and merges you with the beast, but inside it senses the abnormality and doesn't allow children to be born. The dragon keeps making

The Charmed Fjords

you steal women from other cities, but you're not getting the message. Unfortunately, humans have always overestimated their own rationality."

Ulhjegg's descendants jumped up, losing their frozen restraint.

"That's impossible!"

"What is she saying?"

"What are we supposed to do, marry maidens with dark hair? We may as well marry the savages."

"She's right." Danar's voice reverberated wanly. "Servants and captives in Aurolhjoll give me children, but not maidens with white hair. Not a single one of them."

The snow hjeggs sat down and exchanged bewildered looks. The other hjeggs were frowning, trying to process all this information.

"I think you've disrupted the equilibrium," I said thoughtfully. "Sverr is right, the Confederation doesn't know where the Fog came from. But I think it's something like protection. The Fog split the planet into two parts and in each part, civilization followed its own path. But you, respected riars of the fjords, disrupted the equilibrium and the Fog began to dissipate. The children of the fjords need new blood. New people. And women who can resist the call."

"There are no such women!" someone shouted.

"Yes, there are," Sverr said. "Olivia can resist mine. And she barely felt Irvin's."

I nodded. "That's true. The women of the fjords became weak, and the generations that grew up on the hjeggs' calls have completely lost the ability to resist it. That has also affected you. The most reliable sign of degeneration is weak or unattractive females. I saw that in the tribe at the foot of Gorlohum. Mixing blood too frequently within a small population leads to extinction."

"Are you saying that the Fog started to dissipate

Book One: Beyond the Fog

because the riars only married women from their own cities, and that they were preserving the purity of the blood?" Magnus asked, slightly confused.

"Exactly. Each of them wanted to preserve his, you could say, color. And they wanted to produce a child who could catch the same beast as the father. It turned out that they were marrying their distant relatives — first, second, or even fourth cousins. The result was that each generation became weaker than the last."

"Even if all of this is true..." the elder began. "Even if this is true, it won't help us stop the catastrophe. Do you know how to make the Fog come together again?"

"I think the fjords need the people of the Confederation. And that's why the barrier opened. The most important thing — " I drew a deep breath and glimpsed Klin's and Jean's rapturous eyes, Anders's anxious ones, and Sverr's blazing ones. I took a few steps back, toward the empty space behind me. "The most important thing is that you need to do more than let the people of the Confederation in. You need to..."

"What?" Bengt asked impatiently.

"You need to restore the equilibrium. Respected riars, there were four firstborn hjeggs, not three. If you follow the logic, the red beast, the firstborn Hellehjegg, was female."

Now everyone leaped up. But it was too late. The black ring Sverr had removed from Irvin's neck was already glistening in my hands. This whole time it had been hidden in my bag, and then under my shirt. Without another thought, I placed it on my head. I was surprised to feel it become as soft as butter and easily flow down until it encircled my neck.

"Liv!" Sverr shouted.

By now I could hardly hear him. The figures of the riars became murky. Reality turned into a smoky illusion, opening up a completely different world. For a moment it seemed like

The Charmed Fjords

I was alone in this cavernous hall and the riars were shadows. Then the head of one of the riars on the wall shook. The black obsidian eyes opened wide and looked at me. The dragon opened his tusky mouth and let out a roar. He climbed out of the stone, took a breath, and darted at me. In a split second I bent down, dropped onto the marble, and rolled away. Out of the corner of my eye I spotted a second beast — a snow dragon this time — disengage from the ceiling. I sprang up and sprinted toward the walls, hoping to be able to hide. With each passing moment the number of dragons multiplied and I got completely lost in the crowd of fanged predators. They were everywhere — they were shaking their wings, bellowing, baring their teeth, dive-bombing, and slithering along the ground.

The riars' shadows faded and became transparent until I could almost no longer see them. All I could see were dragons everywhere. One of the snow dragons breathed out, blanketing me with snow that pierced me like needles. I doubled over in pain and laid my head on the stone.

"Get up!" a familiar voice shouted next to me, and I leaped up in astonishment.

"Irvin? Is that you? But you..."

"Duck!" he interrupted me angrily. I dropped down obediently and again jumped up. "And stop talking! Is that why you put my ring on, outsider?"

"But how..." huffing and puffing, I rolled over, dodging the claws of a black beast.

"Just like the hjeggs' spirits," Irvin grumbled, annoyed at my confusion. "I'm not staying long. I need to go. I'm just going to see what you can do."

I leaped up, oblivious to my battered elbows and knees. All I noticed were the dragons that were suddenly everywhere: black ones, white ones, water ones. How many of them were there? I decided not to count.

Book One: Beyond the Fog

"Don't stand there like a dummy!" Irvin yelled. "You don't have much time, outsider! Catch the hjegg!"

"These aren't the right one!" I erupted, looking around. "I need a different one! The red one!"

"What?" The ilg stared at me like I was a madwoman. "Are you crazy?"

I waved my arm. There was no time to explain. A sea hjegg poked me with the end of his tail, as though he were playing. But then a second one pushed me back and I hit the ground and somersaulted. A black hjegg growled up above me and I managed to escape in time, right before his fiery breath singed the marble. Now I was sure of it — my body was in two worlds at once.

"Crazy fool," Irvin said after materializing beside me again. I didn't respond — I was too busy dodging dragon legs, fangs, and spikes. Then I saw a ruby-red hjegg flash behind a snow hjegg.

"You're going to die!" Irvin shouted wildly as I tore off toward the red hjegg. "That's the red hjegg! No one catches the red hjegg!"

"But that's the one I need!" I blew up at him.

The crimson beast turned her narrow muzzle toward me. I stumbled, doubting myself for a moment. This dragon was different — she seemed to be made of smoldering coal. Burning lava rolled under the scales like a dangerous heat. The vermilion eyes looked at me attentively, not at all like an animal.

Suddenly the legs of a black dragon seized me and jerked me into the air. Irvin began to holler down below. I did too. Then I thrust my knife — the one Sverr had given me — into the top of the dragon's claw. A flame tore out of his mouth, the leg opened, and I flew down from a height of three stories right onto the marble floor.

I saw a flash of red and then landed between two

The Charmed Fjords

spikes. The long neck arched and I again saw the vermilion eyes, right next to me this time. The red beast was looking at me sharply and intently, right into my soul. Or more accurately, at my soul. And I looked at the beast who had placed her spinal column under my weak body. At the beast who had caught me. Not the opposite. For perhaps the first time in the history of the fjords, a dragon had caught a human and allowed the merging to occur. The red beast had been waiting too long for the reckless girl who dared to come find her.

Chapter 28. Sverr

"**K**ILL HER! Chop off her head and take off the ring! Now!"

I rushed to stand between the fallen girl and the riars. I drew my sword even though I knew that was sacrilegious in the hall of the hundred hjeggs. But to hell with the laws. I couldn't let anyone get near Liv.

"Don't you dare get near her," I snarled, glaring at them. I wanted to check to see how Liv was faring but I knew if I took my eyes off the riars they'd fly at me.

"Do you have any idea what you're doing, Sverr?" Magnus asked, getting up. "A maiden can't put on the ring of Gorlohum. It's unheard of, especially in this holy place. Get away and give us — "

"Stay away," I said firmly. I heard Olivia let out a muffled cry. It sounded like she fell down. I grit my teeth until they almost cracked.

"At this rate they'll be wiping the floor with her before you know it," one of the snow hjeggs said. "You want to let a maiden defeat a hjegg? That's madness."

I gave out a strangled hiss. The riars exchanged glances. Most of them were also already flashing their weapons, but they hadn't yet made up their minds to attack. They knew that not only was my hjegg strong, but that in human form I could take a lot of them with me into the next

The Charmed Fjords

world.

"Sverr, let us help her," Magnus said, sounding almost calm. "The girl is doomed. You know that. We can take the ring off before it hardens on her body."

I heaved a big sigh. It was true that soon the ring would harden like a stone yet be light as a feather. Sometimes this took an hour, and sometimes a whole day. It was always different. I had no idea how much time Liv had. The elder's words made sense, and maybe I could still save my lilgan, my shelli... my everything.

"Come now, Sverr. Put away your sword. We understand that you have too much of the black beast's fire in your blood and you're quick tempered. It's been a rough day. Put away your weapon and the girl will live."

I looked into the old man's eyes and squeezed the handle of my sword harder. "No. Liv will do it. And all of you, stay away from her."

"She'll die..."

"She will!"

"It's the law!"

"It's unheard of..."

"This is unacceptable."

I heard a woman scream behind me again. It was somewhere above me. That meant some animal's claws had caught hold of Olivia. The scream was plaintive and frightened, but brief.

It took all my willpower not to turn around and also to keep myself from attacking the other riars. My hjegg's shadow was already covering me, demanding that we merge. It came out of nowhere, without my summoning him. That was what had happened at the Academy of Progress when Liv needed help, and when she was fighting for the boy in Neroaldaf. And it almost happened now. My need to turn into my beast was as much a part of me as my need to breathe. I had an intense

Book One: Beyond the Fog

need to become bigger, stronger, and more wrathful to protect her and shroud her, but I wasn't the only one feeling this need. So was my hjegg — the dragon I had been inextricably bound to since I was seven years old. Now this dragon was growling and spitting fire, trying to break through the barrier of my mind and protect Liv. But now, more than ever, I needed my reason because I wanted to knock all these riars down and rush to the girl and pull the ring of Gorlohum off her, praying to the ancient ones that it wasn't too late. But I couldn't do that. Liv knew what she was doing, and it was my duty to grant her what she had chosen. I needed to allow it and hold back my fury and fear. I needed to believe in her.

My dragon knew that too. Even if I didn't know it at the time, there was a reason why I had pulled her through the Great Fog. The beast knew from the start that the fjords needed this woman.

I had to believe in both of them.

All these thoughts flashed in my head in a heartbeat, but it felt like an eternity.

"Stop!" Yelled Shenk, the riar of Halmung. "Stop your vileness!"

He brandished his sword fiercely. I fended him off, dodged, and punched him with my left fist. Shenk teetered but didn't fall down. But by then I was already fighting off the riar of Moralhun. Behind me an immense silhouette rose and I turned and lifted my sword.

"On your left," Bengt said calmly. He was standing beside me and grappling with three snow riars at once. "I've never liked the council. What wimps."

I gave him a quick, grateful nod — there was no time for anything more than that. Suddenly, ten riars were attacking Bengt and me. Each of them was a seasoned warrior who could expertly wield a sword, battleax, or two blades. There were no weaklings among the riars. It would be

The Charmed Fjords

hard to repel them. Only the firstborn hjeggs knew why Bengt had decided to help me, but he'd always been different from everyone else.

Stab, stab, duck, whack, stab. My black sword whistled in the air and managed to draw blood, routing the attackers.

Olivia's faint cries were drowned out by the clanging iron and yelping riars.

"I don't believe this," Melvin gasped. I couldn't restrain myself. I spun and hacked with my sword, snarling the whole time. I hazarded a quick glance behind me.

Olivia was suspended between the ceiling and floor. Then she squawked and crumbled down. I shrieked, my mind went dark for a moment, and despite myself I merged with my beast. I began to roar with all my might and struggled to hold in my flame. Then Bengt metamorphosed, and then Danar. But I could no longer see anything. My wings spread, catching a gust of air, and I raced toward the thin figure hanging like a marionette. Before I could get to her, I froze in disbelief.

Olivia was nowhere in sight. For a moment I thought I saw Irvin standing by the wall laughing and giving the thumbs-up. He turned to look at me and smiled in amusement. Then he disappeared.

I shook my head, let out a puff of black smoke, and scratched the holy marble with my claws. Where the hell was she? I spun around and roared. Where had she gone?

I stopped again. Right smack in the middle of the hall of the hundred hjeggs there was a red dragon. It had skin blazing like fire, a pair of short wings, and a long, thin tail. It was the beast the fjords hadn't seen for a century. The ruby eyes were gazing at me pensively. Its triangular head cocked in a way that seemed familiar. Then it snorted in amusement.

I sat down on my rear legs and opened my snout. Holy Gorlohum. Was that Liv?

Book One: Beyond the Fog

The ruby hjegg breathed, and blazing embers flew out of its mouth and immediately singed the marble. Olivia turned around in place, examining herself. I started to laugh — roar was more like it. When I returned to my human form, I was still grinning. The riars had long stepped away, and they were now staring slack-jawed at the red beast.

It shifted its feet, scraping the marble with its claws. It looked at us and guiltily pulled its leg back. Then there was a spatter of red and all that remained on the ground was a girl wearing trousers and a tunic — and a black ring around her neck. She stood up in seeming disbelief and teetered. She thrust out her chin and stared at the dumbstruck riars.

No one said a word. Finally Magnus, the elder, stepped forward and peered at Olivia's face. I gripped my sword, girding for another skirmish.

"I think we need to put out another chair, riars," Magnus said gruffly. "We can't allow the first person to catch the spirit of the child Hellehjegg to stand. And she's a lady."

"Maybe I'll stay awake during these councils now," Bengt quipped.

In the stunning quiet, a servant pulled over a chair and triumphantly placed it at the table. Olivia blushed but I noticed that she lifted her chin a little higher. I tried to hide my admiration as I looked at her. She was the maiden warrior, proud and strong. And genuine. I saw the growing admiration in the riars' eyes, and their burning desire to possess her. A feeling of murderous envy flickered in me. I didn't want any of them to even dare to look at her. I wanted to abscond with her to the cave and hide her there. My hjegg growled and beat at me, again demanding that I merge with him and seek flesh to destroy.

I suppressed him. Liv was no longer my lilgan or shelli. She was a hjegg. She was the one who had caught the soul of the red beast. Now what was I supposed to do?

The Charmed Fjords

OLIVIA

The riars looked stunned to have witnessed my battle for the hjegg's soul. Then again, I wasn't sure how to react either. My adrenaline rush had begun to subside and now I only felt a quiet contentment and fatigue. It was a strange sensation, because even now I could still feel my hjegg. It was as though our souls were connected by an invisible thread. It was a connection formed by an image I didn't comprehend even though I knew it was completely real and alive. I couldn't depend on my beloved science to explain anything, and anyway, I'd realized long ago that there are things we simply don't know. We just need to accept them, for a start. It's impossible to grasp a huge swath of another world, its magic, witchcraft, or dragons in one fell swoop. It takes time.

Somewhere in the unearthly world my beast bellowed. I smiled inwardly and continued to tune into the roaring only I heard as I walked past the riars. They were all standing and staring at me. They stepped aside when I moved toward them. They were looking at me, appraising me, and practically sniffing me. I saw different expressions in their gazes: indignant, interested, astonished, hungry. In a world where strength was prized, I had just offered the highest display of it. The masters of the fjords had no choice but to accept it.

In the deafening silence I reached my chair and sat down, straightening my spine. The men took their places, staring at me the whole time.

"Please allow me to speak, elder," I said, turning to Magnus. He nodded benignly. "I'd like to apologize for my behavior. It was the only way to prove I was right. I'm only a woman and you wouldn't have listened to me otherwise."

"You could have died," the old man pointed out.

"I know. I thought that was what would probably

Book One: Beyond the Fog

happen. But desperate times call for desperate measures, riars." I took a breath and looked around at the men. "I believe that the fjords need new blood. They need people from the Confederation — people who will want to live here, produce children, or try on the ring of Gorlohum. Otherwise we may become extinct."

"*We?*" the elder smirked.

"I'm a freeborn daughter of Neroaldaf," I said firmly. "So yes, we may become extinct."

"I'd like to try to put that ring on!" a voice called out from among the soldiers. I smiled at Anders Ericksen. His eyes were gleaming with anticipation and the enthusiasm of a scholar.

"It's impossible! We can't allow that!" The snow riars became agitated again, but not as vigorously as before. Many of them were sitting silently, frowning and clearly lost in thought.

"Riars, I think the time for changes is upon us," the elder said firmly. "And we all need to prepare ourselves for that."

"A word, please," Melvin said, raising his hand. "As far as I understand it, the council is where the riars solve issues that affect not just their own territory but also the continuation of the dynasty. If that's the case, I'd like to declare my right to take a wife." He winked at me. "I'd like to take you as my wife, Olivia. You don't have any land, so Garaskon will become your home and protection."

"But riars don't marry those who have put on the ring of Gorlohum," Magnus said incredulously.

"You yourself said the time has come for changes," Melvin interrupted him with a smirk. "So it's time to change that custom, too."

"Go to hell, Melvin!" one of the sea riars boomed. "I'm also declaring my right to take a wife. So what will happen —

The Charmed Fjords

we can both have a double call?"

"Both of you go to hell! I'm declaring my right..."

Trying not to burst out laughing, I listened in shock to eleven suggestions to go to hell and the same number of marriage proposals. Of course, the suggestions to go to hell were meant for the riars while the marriage proposals were directed at me. The riars who already had a wife or bride-to-be kept quiet. Then there were the elder, Danar, and Sverr. Sverr sat with such a distant look on his face that my exhilaration dissipated like the wind.

"Olivia... er, Olivia-hjegg?" Magnus cleared his throat and turned to me. "Are you willing to be united with one of these riars?

I looked again at Sverr, who was silent.

"I'll think it over. Thank you for the proposals."

"I think we could all probably use some rest and time to think," the elder announced, heaving himself from his chair. "That's all for today, riars. We'll reconvene here tomorrow, and I hope the night clears your minds and brings you positive thoughts."

Everyone followed Magnus to the door. I went over to the people of the Confederation, who were staring at me with a mixture of fear and rapture.

"This will do Maximilian in when he finds out he missed this," Klin said. "You were always an odd one, Liv."

There were crimson spots on Yurgas's face. I couldn't tell if they were from anger or other feelings. In any case, he was trying not to look at me.

"What does that merging feel like?" Anders asked eagerly.

"It feels strange," I muttered, darting my eyes around looking for Sverr. I didn't see him behind the soldiers or servants. Why hadn't he come over to me yet? Where on earth was he?

Book One: Beyond the Fog

The guards took the prisoners to their rooms, promising to treat them decently until the council announced its decision. When they had all gone, Virn touched my shoulder.

"Let's go, Olivia-hjegg," he stammered. "I'll take you to your chambers. You might get lost because you've never been here."

"Where's Sverr?" I snapped, beginning to lose patience.

"He already left," Virn said, blinking. "He left before everyone."

He left? I opened my mouth to grouse, but there were still too many people and hjeggs around. So I shut my mouth, drew up my spine, lifted my head so high I could see the drawings on the cupola, and headed toward the door. Virn followed me in bewilderment.

OLIVIA

The chambers I was given were huge. There were several rooms, a tub filled with warm water, and a private garden at the foot of a staircase decorated with ornate drawings. But I couldn't focus on the beauties of Varisfold. I was too preoccupied with all the strange things that had happened to me. Happiness and fear were throbbing inside me and I wanted to talk everything through with someone.

I looked up at the darkening sky. So all of this meant I could fly? I'd feel the sky, see the stars close up, and touch the clouds? I wondered what it was like to fly, and to be something different, something not human. In the brief moment of uniting with the dragon I didn't have a chance to figure that out.

I wanted to start learning immediately: to run around, jump, and summon the beast. But I didn't. For now I thought

The Charmed Fjords

it would be best to remain human because I needed all my wits about me. Being in the dragon's body affected my mind — even in the brief moment of merging I grasped that. Instincts took over and dictated all my actions. I would need to learn how to manage that.

SVERR

I'll think about your proposals?
　　I was so livid I punched the wall, sending a stone fragment to the ground. I had an urge to kill someone. I wanted to tear flesh with my teeth, torment, knock out someone's kidneys. I wanted to rip everyone at that council to pieces, even old Magnus. My beast roared and spit fire, expressing my inner pain. I'd long ago realized that my feelings weren't just inside me, the human Sverr. My hjegg also thought of Olivia as his own.
　　And now the beast was enraged because he saw that there were other people staking a claim to Liv, and he wanted me to destroy them and make sure they drowned in the waters of the fjords. I agreed with my hjegg. I landed another punch and winced in pain.
　　It was just that Olivia had changed. She was a woman who could unite the two worlds and become a part of both. She was no longer a captive outsider, but the first red dragon in many centuries. Her words continued to send chills down my spine. But she'd been victorious. She stood her ground. I doubted she'd allow me to shut her up in the cave, as I yearned to with all my being.
　　I punched the wall again and this time it cracked.
　　Damn it! The hell with her changes. I'd take her, shut her away, and not let her out. My dragon's instinct was blurring my reason and inhibiting my thinking. She's mine.

Book One: Beyond the Fog

I'm not giving her up. I'll hide her. *I'll think about it?* I also wouldn't let her think. To hell with what she wanted. To hell with everything. She's mine!

I shook my head, trying to clear away the bloodthirsty haze so I could think straight. I needed to find Liv. And stay human.

OLIVIA

I looked perplexedly at the trunks the servants hastily brought in.

"What are those?" I asked.

"Gifts for the maiden," Virn told me. "From the riars."

As if to console me, he added, "Don't worry, you'll get to keep the gifts no matter who you choose. Men don't take their presents back."

"You mean I'm supposed to choose someone?" I ran my fingers across a soft blue piece of silk that had stones and pieces of silver sewn into it.

"Yes," Virn muttered, sounding vexed. "Otherwise there will be fights — you can count on that. And when riars fight, it always ends badly. I heard that around twenty years ago there was a squabble over one maiden. The city where the fight happened no longer exists."

I hurled the fabric away like it was a poisonous snake. "What if I don't want to choose anyone?"

"Then they'll steal you," Virn responded sadly. "But you're a hjegg now," he said, rubbing his neck and looking like he was trying to solve a riddle that was too hard for him. Finally solving it, he nodded and said, "They'll still steal you, even if you are a hjegg. They'll take you away and stash you in a big cave. That's what riars do — it's in their blood."

"Magpies also drag shiny things to their nests," I

The Charmed Fjords

erupted. "What am I, a souvenir they can hide? I don't want to choose anyone!"

"You'll have to," Virn said with a shrug. "By the way, if I were you I wouldn't go anywhere alone. Actually, don't go anywhere at all."

I stared at Virn furiously. Fantastic. Now I was supposed to sit here under lock and key so I wouldn't be kidnapped?

"You should probably hide in a trunk tonight," he added. "In case they sneak in."

"Damned riars!" I muttered. "Those executioners and robbers. I wish they were all dead."

And one of them in particular, the one with golden eyes. I shuddered at the recollection of Sverr sitting at the council silently. When the other riars extolled the beauty of their lands and proposed marriage to me, Sverr was silent. Admittedly, he already had a bride, and it had been arranged long ago. Of course that ilg was so damned honorable he couldn't allow himself to go back on his word. A high-born bride was going to enter Neroaldaf as his wife, while I was nothing more than an outsider from the Confederation. I couldn't care less about this ring around my neck.

Let him kiss me on the pile of gold, let him press me to the bed as though he were going to suffocate me if he didn't take me, let him look at me ardently and yearningly, but another woman would become his wife. I hated him.

Fury sparked inside me and Virn darted away.

"Your eyes," he whispered hoarsely. "And your hair! You're changing."

I looked at him quizzically and went into the bathroom, where a silver mirror gleamed. I gasped. My reflection looked at the world through dark red eyes, and my hair had taken on a distinct scarlet tint.

"What's going on?" I asked fearfully. "What's happening

Book One: Beyond the Fog

to me?"

"You're changing color," I heard a voice say gruffly from the doorway. I jumped and turned around. Sverr was standing there looking at me searingly, but he didn't approach. "You're becoming the reflection of your beast. That happens to everyone who manages to put on the ring of Gorlohum."

I gulped and felt clammy with fear. As though I didn't have enough scars, now I was becoming a red-eyed creature? It hadn't occurred to me that these would be the consequences. I touched my hair. Even that seemed to feel different now — it was smooth. "Is my hair going to change too?"

"Yes."

"What else is going to change?" Shit, I couldn't keep my voice from trembling. "Am I going to grow spikes? Or fangs?"

"Just your color will change," Sverr smirked. "But the fjords haven't seen the red beast in a really long time, Liv."

He grew silent and we both stood there, looking at each other through the silky water in the tub. Sverr heaved a sigh. His gaze touched me, caressed me, took possession of me. The mutual attraction made my head spin and I couldn't think clearly. We yearned for each other so strongly we had to force ourselves not to move. Everything had changed. I had changed.

"I see that the riars are already sending you gifts," Sverr said. His voice held a note of malice. I raised my head defiantly.

"Yes. They're very generous. I've never seen fabrics like these. Or jewelry. Or any of it."

"I didn't know you were interested in fabrics and jewelry." His tone grew even more spiteful. "I thought science was the only thing that concerned you. And sometimes my tongue in your mouth."

The Charmed Fjords

I instantly flared up like sulfur soaked in gas. I almost felt like I was expelling smoke. "Maybe I just haven't tried any other ones, Sverr."

He crossed the space between us in a split second. He swiftly pushed me up against the cold mirror and pressed my body in a vice.

"And are you hoping to try other ones?" His face was distorted in anger. "Don't you dare, Liv. Don't you dare, you hear me?"

"Why not? I'm getting offers to become a wife and mistress. Why shouldn't I agree? You haven't offered me anything." By the time I finished I was shouting, and my burning fingers were clutching his arms. "You just sat there and didn't say anything, you damned ilg! Nothing!"

"I've sworn an oath! Even though I only saw my bride once, I gave my word!"

"So keep it!" I yelled. "And don't touch me!"

He seized my hands and suddenly pressed them to his lips — it was painful, agonizing, and affectionate all at once.

"Liv, I..."

Suddenly the bell chimed in the tower, cutting Sverr off. He let go of me. I wanted to wail and take shelter in his warm body again, but I restrained myself. The fjords were in danger. By now I recognized the sound of the alarm bell.

Virn raced through the door, panting, and stopped when he saw us.

"We're being invaded, my riar! Next to the mountain ridge, near Gorlohum. There are too many people from the Confederation to count."

Sverr clenched his teeth and threw me a look. "Stay here, Olivia. Do you understand?"

I shook my head. There was no way I could just sit here and enjoy the view of the city while the fjords were in danger. Of course Sverr knew that.

Book One: Beyond the Fog

"I'm a hjegg now," I said quietly. "And a daughter of Neroaldaf. You said that yourself."

"At least try to stay out of the battle, OK?" Sverr said grimly on his way out.

A few minutes later we were standing on an open terrace with a stunning view of the city. The other riars were also there, gloomily discussing the news.

"Svenn saw Confederation people pass through the Fog," Magnus said, nodding at a young guy with a ring around his neck. He was a hjegg — a very young snow hjegg. "He was hunting near the mountain ridge. What else did you see, Svenn?"

"The Fog between the twin peaks has disappeared, elder," Svenn said shakily. "There's nothing left. It's empty. And I saw a lot of iron vehicles beyond the cliffs. They're headed toward Gorlohum."

I suppressed a cry of indignation and tried to picture the map of the fjords. If the Confederation was going away from the mountain ridge, then next...

"They're headed toward Neroaldaf," Svenn concluded.

"I was hoping we'd have time to prepare, but I guess not," Magnus said heavily. He straightened up and his aged eyes flashed gold. "It's time to summon everyone who wears the ring of Gorlohum. From the young ones who have hardly seen thirteen springs to the oldest. The fjords need everyone who can fly, burn, and tear apart the enemy. May the firstborn hjeggs give us their blessing for this battle. Onward!"

The men let out a roar and the terrace became crowded with metamorphosing hjeggs. The situation was so dire that for once the riars were allowed to merge with their hjeggs in Varisfold. The sky thundered with the bestial roars, and down below the city residents stopped in their tracks, fearfully watching the dragons take flight. I threw back my

The Charmed Fjords

head and looked up at them — the black and white ones, who commanded storms and light. The sea hjeggs departed by water, and would meet us next to Gorlohum.

Only Sverr and I were left standing on the terrace. I looked at him in confusion.

"You're not really staying here to keep safe, are you?" he asked somberly. I shook my head. I again looked down from atop our post.

"Then call him, Liv. Call your beast," Sverr said hoarsely. "Call him!"

I took a deep breath, already able to feel the transformation. At the last second, right before my body disappeared and was replaced with the dragon, I managed to say, "It's not a him, Sverr. It's a her."

I saw a flash of astonishment in his golden eyes. Then I stepped from foot to foot and stretched blissfully. Power, strength, and grace — I was fire and wind, instinct and savagery. I was the descendant of Hellehjegg! I was the one in whose body the original fire burned.

I spread my wings, dropped down, adroitly caught a gust of air, and soared up over the eternal city. The people below were shouting. They were both marveling at the sight of me and afraid of me. They were bowing to me. I was the red beast, I was the one they only whispered about. I was fury itself.

I let out an enthusiastic roar along with a black, destructive flame. The white wall of the castle melted away, forming a hole through which a little girl stared at me. She threw up her hands, gazing at the creature in the sky, and her little mouth opened into a soundless scream.

I abruptly came to my senses. For a moment the dragon's mind had overtaken the human one and I'd completely forgotten who I was. I'd almost just killed a child. The terror immobilized me and my wings began to flap half-

Book One: Beyond the Fog

heartedly, forgetting how to keep my huge dragon's body in the air. I felt myself falling. But then I lifted myself up, and headed straight toward the sharp peaks of the border. Panic swept through me. I had no idea what was happening and I couldn't orient myself in the chaotically changing landscape.

When I was sure I would fall, two powerful legs seized me, squeezed me in their claws, and jerked me upward. The golden eyes on the narrow dragon snout looked furious. I cheeped and blinked. Sverr lifted me into the sky and began to roar warningly. He opened his claws. I again crumbled downward. I spread my wings and yanked them like arms. Once, twice, three times. I wasn't exactly flying, but at least I wasn't falling. The black dragon was circling close by, snorting smoke and warily keeping an eye on my inept flight. I kept slapping, trying to figure out how to move in this new body of mine. Out of the corner of my eye I spotted Sverr. He was soaring, practically not even moving his wings, just gliding on the air currents. He was massive and black. For a moment I felt insulted — his hjegg was three times as big as mine, and his wings were huge while mine were small and weak. I hissed in annoyance and spread out on my celestial pillow, trying not to think of falling and to just copy my teacher's movements. Sverr snorted again, but this time approvingly. I was surprised that even in our dragon forms I understood him easily. I saw the familiar chuckle in his golden eyes and was smitten.

The wind stopped seeming like an enemy and started to feel like a true friend that reliably kept me up in the air. I flexed my tail and neck, dove under an air wave, caught the current, and soared upward. I began to roar in delight. Beside me Sverr let out an answering roar that held a man's laughter. He made another circle around me and then set off toward the east, where the peak of Gorlohum towered.

I followed him.

Chapter 29. Olivia

AFTER A FEW HOURS I got the hang of flying and could nearly hold back my dragon, who kept trying to chase ducks or plunge into the water after spotting a school of silvery fish under a wave. Sometimes she seemed to get tired and wanted to turn toward the cliffs and go take a nap. Sverr roared at me from time to time, warning me not to do this or that or go somewhere, and my red beast obeyed even though she grumbled about it. A few times the black hjegg caught me and lifted me back up as I lost an air current and was about to crash to the ground. He guided and supported me, and made me thrash my wings and fly by myself.

If you trip, I'll catch you. And if you lose your support, bearings, and reason, I'll also catch you.

When the peak of Gorlohum loomed ahead of us, I spotted a procession of iron vehicles creeping along on the ground. They were like evil, stinging insects marching toward the fjords. The young scout had been telling the truth: the Fog had disappeared between the cliffs, opening areas a few miles wide. It was no narrow tunnel, but a channel big enough for an army to pass through.

Sverr and I landed on a rocky ledge. The black dragon let out a roar and then metamorphosed.

"We need to wait for the others," the ilg said.

I roared weakly, turned in place, and shed my dragon.

Book One: Beyond the Fog

Unaccustomed to the process, I staggered from the force, fell down, and stayed there for a moment to catch my breath. I stood up and clenched my fists, feeling a rage I'd never felt before the black ring encircled my neck.

"Careful," Sverr said, understanding everything like he always did. "Keep your beast in check, Liv. Otherwise things will end badly for both of you. Hjeggs have a different mind. They're not familiar with our human concepts, especially morality. Honor, virtue, and compassion are things humans need, but dragons don't. Remember that the human and the hjegg are distinct but you're more important."

"This is complicated," I said with a sigh. I looked at Sverr. "I didn't know it was so complicated."

"You'll be fine," Sverr said confidently.

We walked over to the edge and looked down. From here we could see a convoy of vehicles plastered with the Confederation's insignia. The heavy-duty apparatus on the military equipment was certainly intimidating. Examining them, Sverr said, "But now I'm not even confident in myself. I have an urge to burn everything. All of them."

"There are too many of them. But that's not the worst part, Sverr." I motioned toward the twin peaks. "The Fog is gone! That means that new troops will come to the fjords. We need to think of something. We have to stop them."

"If only I knew how," Sverr said vehemently.

Suddenly a few snow hjeggs landed on the ledge, followed by Bengt, Melvin, Magnus, and the others. Altogether there were around fifty hjeggs — riars, their a-tems, young sons, and old ones with worn-out wings. Most of them were sea dragons who had limited capabilities on dry land. The dragons had a destructive strength, but I knew plenty about the might of the Confederation. I had seen how Sverr fell when he was hit with a heavy-duty laser. The hjeggs weren't immortal; they died just like any other living creature.

The Charmed Fjords

And in this battle too many of them would die — everyone knew that.

The men spread maps on a flat stone and while they had a heated discussion I stepped aside. The imposing Gorlohum stood nearby.

I gazed at it, at the sky with the lazily floating clouds, at the silent volcano, at the vehicles from the Confederation, at the men trying to figure out how to save their home. Those men turned into beasts every day but never stopped being human. I ached for them. I didn't want to see them perish.

Maximilian had once said that I was a degenerate species and reckless idealist because I believed in good, fairness, and the ability to change this world for the better. Then he smiled and added: but strangely, it's only such people who can change it. I was eighteen at the time, and if I could see the professor again, I'd tell him that even all these years later I still believed that. And I swore on Gorlohum that I would believe it until my very last breath.

I reached into the leather pouch on my belt and pulled out a flattened sheet of paper and pen. The pen was thin and had a gold cap. I grinned as I looked at it. It was the one Sverr had filched from the Academy of Progress. How much time had passed since that day when the evil dragon abducted the girl who wasn't a princess? It felt like a century ago. So many things had happened to the anthropologist Olivia Orway since then. I had seen and come to understand so much — about people, but most important, about myself. I smiled slightly. I hastily jotted down a note and laid the paper down. I stroked the little iron bird that was now hanging from a leather string around my neck.

As I approached the group of men, Sverr glanced up at me absently from the war plans. I beckoned to him and he came over.

"What's going on, Liv? Are you OK?"

Book One: Beyond the Fog

"Everything's fine," I said with a smile. "I was just getting bored."

The ilg frowned and looked at me intently. He sighed and brought his fingers to my face and traced it. "I need to tell you something important, Liv," he murmured. "But there's no time now, and this isn't the right moment."

My heart skipped a beat. "You can tell me when it's all over," I said.

Sverr nodded slowly, and his golden irises caressed me. "All right," he smirked. "When it's all over. Will you wait for me?"

"Yes." I looked at him, drinking in his manly face, the sweep of his broad shoulders, and the smoldering look he always gave me, from the very first time we met. And I realized that I needed all of that. I never wanted Sverr to stop rising into the sky, roaring, flying, and living. I wanted his shadow to float over Neroaldaf again, and I wanted the gold that gave strength to the black dragon to multiply in the caves. I longed for all of this.

"Why are you looking at me like that?" the ilg asked with a frown.

I shrugged. "Go. The elder is calling you."

Sverr peered at me, and for a second I thought that now he'd understand everything, but the hjeggs had begun to shout and Sverr turned and went back to them. I waved over one of the boys, thrust the note into his hand, and told him to give it to the riar of Neroaldaf when the sun touched Gorlohum.

Forcing myself not to turn back, I stepped to the end of the ledge and dropped down. A moment later the red dragon opened her wings over the fjords and set off for Gorlohum.

The Charmed Fjords

SVERR

You can tell me when it's all over...
I tossed the map aside and straightened up. A bad premonition nagged at me, but that wasn't really surprising. Perhaps it had nothing to do with the looming battle. I turned my head, rubbing my neck and looking around for Olivia. I didn't see her thin figure anywhere. Had she gone to the other side of the cliff? Was she tired?

"If you're looking for Olivia-hjegg, she told me to give you this." I glanced sideways at the young snow hjegg and took the piece of paper he was holding out to me. What the hell was this? I opened the paper and read:

I know you wouldn't have allowed me to do what I'm about to do, so I'm writing. Sverr, we both know the fjords are doomed. The only way to save them is to restore the Fog. But I have another theory. It's yet another crazy theory, but it's better than nothing, right? I'm the only red hjegg, Sverr. That means that Gorlohum will only respond to me. My idea might be ridiculous, but I want to try. At one point the Fog formed because of the volcano. Maybe that will also help now.

And one more thing. I really want to hear what you were planning to tell me, Sverr.

Liv

"No!" I yelled. All the riars looked up and Magnus raised his white brows. But I was so blinded by rage they may as well have been on another planet.

"When did she give this to you?" I grabbed the messenger boy so forcefully he whimpered like a puppy. "When?"

"An hour ago, riar of Neroaldaf! She didn't say anything else!"

A whole hour! That was plenty of time to fly to the

Book One: Beyond the Fog

volcano. I cursed at the boy so violently his light eyes popped out and he snapped to attention. The other snow hjeggs scowled.

"Sverr, stop yelling at my son. What's going on?"

I struggled to hold back another surge of fury. I turned to the mountain peak behind me. The Confederation forces were already approaching the border of the mountain ridge beyond which the territory of the fjords began. The riars were already merging with their beasts and growling. I was torn between my sense of duty and my feelings. But when the shadow of the black dragon covered me, I made my choice.

OLIVIA

From close up Gorlohum seemed to be a forbidding cliff whose summit got lost in the clouds. I kept going higher, toward the narrowing crater, trying not to think about what awaited me inside. When I reached the edge of the crater, I grasped it with my claws and peered into the darkness. Way down below, embers were slowly smoldering and magma was bubbling. The sleeping funnel was breathing poisonous steam and acid, occasionally shooting out thin burning plumes. I wasn't about to risk flying in with my weak little wings. I breathed in the heavy air and climbed down, gripping the rough stones. The magma, which was covered in a layer of embers, was sleeping, but I sensed its movement inside me. I felt it — an unbelievable heat, hidden behind a shell, a fire that was ready to erupt at any moment and kill everything living. It was quiet inside the volcano. Occasionally a liquid flame would gurgle and gas would spurt out, creating small sputtering fountains. Irregular black ledges inside the crater protruded like stairs, and I fell down on one of them. I took a moment to get my bearings. Human consciousness pulsed

The Charmed Fjords

inside my dragon body, while my instinct for self-preservation screamed at me to get as far away from here as fast as possible. But I just breathed steam out of my nostrils and climbed toward the edge of the projection.

I wished my beast had some memory that would help me figure out how to wake the volcano. How was I supposed to do it? I pulled my foot up, out of habit trying to touch the iron bird on the string. But the bird and my body were both in another world, while here I was just a dragon. But still...

The bird!

I concentrated, conjuring up an image of the tower in Neroaldaf and of Sverr when he taught me to listen to the iron. *You have to understand, feel, and become part of it.* I stood still, looking into the shell of ash on top of the magma. It was alive. It was breathing, and gurgling, and churning heavily deep down. I slapped my tail and also gurgled, and then began to roar with all my might. My roar echoed off the volcano walls and then went silent, muffled by the stone.

Nothing happened. Gorlohum continued to sleep. Maybe I needed to go down lower?

I shook my head in puzzlement and crept closer to the magma, leaving grooves on the ledges with my claws. Closer, closer, and closer. The volcano's breath was beginning to singe my nostrils and tickle me with poisonous gases. A tiny ledge — the last one — hung over the lazily flowing lava. The only thing that lay below it was an endless expanse of heat and fire. I arranged myself on the step and drew in my tail like a puppy. My feet slipped. The poisonous air scratched my throat. I felt somehow unsettled — because of what I was doing and because of what I wanted to do. What if I was wrong? I needed to talk to Anders Ericksen and get his advice. But the Fog expert was back in Varisfold. Here I was all alone.

I stretched out my neck and roared again. I screwed up my eyes and braced myself. When I opened them I thought I

Book One: Beyond the Fog

was seeing things. But no, the shell on the lava had really fractured. I took in a little more air and began to bellow at the top of my dragon's lungs. The insides of the volcano inflated like rising dough and trembled. The magma began to sway, and in its core I could see a hole with a web of cracks running out of it. Gas spurted out of the hole in the volcano, and somewhere deep down something heavy and powerful soared up, presaging the fiery avalanche to come. I darted off the ledge and began to flap my wings, feeling the bursts of heat down below. The volcano was enraged. Its funnel was shaking and seemed alive. I hammered my wings with all my might but still wasn't fast enough. Gorlohum quaked and suddenly spewed a fountain of scorching lava. The blazing air flung me aside as though I were a small bird. The impact plastered me to the ledge. I lost my balance, and circled like a maple seed helicopter. Down below the fiery elements were raging. They bubbled and then shot another fountain. I began to wail and surged upward. But my left wing was working poorly and I was too weak, even in my dragon form.

Floundering in the scorching air, I tried to level off, but I realized I couldn't do it. When I was nearly ready to give up in despair, familiar claws latched onto my tail and with a fierce strength yanked me upward. I began to hiss and Sverr responded with a dull growl. He tossed me up and then grabbed me again, this time across my torso. His wings stirred the fiery air with such power they created a mighty tornado under us. We careened, racing with the stream of lava that was blowing from below, threatening to bury us under it. We flew out of the crater of the volcano almost at the same time as the lava.

Sverr lost his balance and crashed down, and at the last moment cushioned my fall. We rolled down the slope, and rocks and pieces of burning embers flew after us. Bellowing ferociously, Sverr seized me again and surged

The Charmed Fjords

toward the twin peaks. Gorlohum was now spitting black clumps of smoke. At the bottom, the Confederation army was turning around their vehicles, trying to flee the wrath of the awakened volcano. There was almost something comical about the sight. Dragons thundered after them.

Sverr dropped me on the mountain plateau and slapped my loin with a leg so hard I wailed in surprise. But the black dragon turned and roared in my face so crossly that I decided to save my indignation for later. The hjegg's golden eyes, wild with rage, shone almost as brightly as the heat of Gorlohum. I wagged my tail apologetically and opened my mouth but didn't roar. I just shook my head toward the exploding Gorlohum. While the imminent eruption stopped the enemy's attack and precipitated their flight, we now had to calm Gorlohum if we didn't want to destroy the fjords.

Sverr understood what I was trying to stay and began to grumble in dissatisfaction. He circled the ground and let out a puff of black smoke. Finally, he nodded. I spread my wings uncertainly, trying to catch an air current. I soared up clumsily and circled the peak. The black beast remained beside me, watching carefully in case I dropped down again. But I strenuously beat my wings until I got to Gorlohum, which was now spewing embers and hot, crimson lava. I flew as close as I could and began to roar. I didn't know what I was supposed to do, but when the heat touched my nostrils, I suddenly felt a kinship with the volcano. It wasn't an enemy. It was the cradle of the fjords, the ancient source that gave birth to the dragons. I was no longer roaring. I was talking to Gorlohum, asking it to forgive me for waking it up. I told it about the fjords that it protected, about the wonderful people who populated these lands, and about the dragons that watched over it. I roared, and perhaps hissed, but the volcano heard me. The black smoke turned white. It flowed along the hardening lava of the crater, and on the ground it thickened

Book One: Beyond the Fog

and stretched like a piece of cloth between the twin peaks, along the mountain ridge, farther and farther, mending the holes in the shroud between the world of the fjords and the Confederation. And when I dropped down in exhaustion, the black dragon was right there to pull me up with his legs. But back on the ground, it was a man who embraced me — furiously, spitefully, and almost painfully, just like a dragon guards his most valuable treasure. I smiled as I looked into his golden eyes.

"It's over now," I whispered. "Does that mean you can tell me what you needed to now?"

"I love you," Sverr sighed. "I love you so much, Liv."

"I love you too," I began, but he was already kissing me just like he did everything in this life: furiously, passionately, like it was the last time.

Epilogue

I WAS STANDING between two stone columns around twenty-five yards tall. Each one was topped with an enormous stone dragon spreading its wings. The hjeggs' long, arched necks were lowered so that their narrow, amber-eyed, sneering faces nearly touched the ground. It was as though the beasts wanted to get a good look at everyone passing through the columns that joined the two worlds.

I protested until the very last moment, begging the council not to build these intimidating monsters, but the men only smirked. Well, what do you expect from men, and riars no less.

I looked at the creatures again and took a deep breath. No doubt about it, the guests would see right away what was in store for them on the fjords.

After a year of negotiations with the Confederation we managed to reach an agreement. The negotiations were by no means easy — quite the opposite, in fact. But the fjords had a strong argument on their side: the restored shroud of Fog. After Gorlohum was awakened it became more compact and it even shifted slightly toward the empty territory on the Confederation side. The people of progress did not yet know how to contend with this phenomenon, and we played that up in our arguments. Of course, public opinion also played an important role. I convinced the riars to return the

Book One: Beyond the Fog

prisoners, and first and foremost the scientists. In the scientific world, Anders's and Maximilian's authority still carried weight, and people listened to what they had to say. Our civilizations were different, but that didn't mean we had to be enemies. At least, many of us were trying to preserve what was still a fragile, yet cherished, world.

The outcome of the talks was the plan to resettle people from the Confederation on the fjords. This first group of volunteers consisted of thirty-five women and three men. I shook my head in awe at the thought. For some reason there were more women who wanted to find their happiness in a new world and live according to the local customs. They knew they would never be able to return to the Confederation. The council of hjeggs imposed that condition — the dragons weren't willing to share their secrets. To sweeten the pot, the dragons paid gold, diamonds, or other treasures for each volunteer. Perhaps there would have been more people willing to move, but another condition was that they had to be immune to the dragon's call. The fjords needed new blood.

I straightened the skirt of my simple, light dress. Unable to restrain myself, I turned around. Sverr was right behind me, as usual. I stood still for a moment, unable to believe what was happening. But then reality jolted me, and with a sharp, stinging clarity it hit me just how much my life had changed. Before, I lived only for science. But now?

Sverr smiled, came closer, and put his arm around me. "Don't worry. If we don't like them, we'll give them to that tribe. Let them dance at the shatiya."

"Very funny," I snorted. I quickly grew serious. "Maybe I shouldn't be the one to meet them. What if I scare them?"

Sverr planted a kiss on the tip of my nose. "Stop it, Liv. You have the most beautiful eyes and hair on all the fjords."

"They're red," I reminded him.

"Really?" Sverr asked in mock surprise. "You don't say?

The Charmed Fjords

I never noticed."

I elbowed him and sighed. Yes, my hair and irises had turned dark crimson, the color of my hjegg.

"You're the most beautiful woman in both worlds," Sverr whispered. "It doesn't matter what color your eyes are. I like all colors." Then he added peevishly, "I'm not the only one. They've already put up a monument to you in Varisfold."

I rolled my eyes. I'd seen the statue. It had rubies for eyes, red stone hair, and skimpy clothing. My hands held a blazing sword aloft, and a crimson dragon perched on my shoulder. The sculpture was attractive, but it made me uncomfortable.

"What if nothing comes of this? What if we miscalculated? What if — "

"Everything will work out," Sverr interrupted me, looking at me in amusement. He slowly licked my temple. "I hope the meeting of the Confederation people doesn't go on too long. I missed you. I want to go back to Neroaldaf, go to our caves, and pick up where we left off."

My cheeks blazed at the thought of our activities. Our study of human customs in bed was going full speed ahead and we'd stopped at a very interesting point — we seemed to think up things people didn't even know about. My barbarian's appetite for passion was off the charts. The caves were our place of hot nights and equally hot days. Not only that, another pile appeared alongside the gold in there: smoldering embers from Gorlohum's depths. That was now my place of strength.

"Liv," Sverr whispered ardently, pulling me closer to him.

"Not now!" I squawked.

"I'll hold my wife wherever and whenever I want," the barbarian interrupted me, and as proof fastened his lips over mine — greedily, wildly, without an ounce of bashfulness. I

Book One: Beyond the Fog

glowed inside. His wife. Could I really dream of anything more?

I was still recovering from my fright, remembering the vote to decide Neroaldaf's fate. Would Sverr continue to be the protector of his fjord, or would the council choose a new riar?

"If you reject Olivia and marry the woman you were promised to, we'll withdraw the accusation that you violated your oath," Magnus had said. I saw Sverr's lips blanch. Neroaldaf or me?

In that horrible moment I also bit my lips and prayed to the firstborn hjeggs for mercy, but I didn't interfere. On the fjords, the concept of honor is inviolable, and new customs shouldn't violate the laws that have been developed over centuries. A man's word is sacrosanct. A man's promise is eternal. Man himself is the cliffs. That's what the fjords are like. That's what Sverr is like.

I understood how much the choice cost him.

"Olivia," he had said calmly. "I choose her."

Silence hung in the huge hall for a few minutes. The riars frowned. Then they voted.

Of the twenty-two riars, eighteen decided to leave Neroaldaf in Sverr's hands.

He had to pay his former betrothed a huge ransom — a large portion of the gold from his caves — and issue a public apology. We arrived at the home of the woman who had been promised to Sverr, and when I saw her I was afraid all over again. The daughter of the riar of Rovengard turned out to be young and so beautiful that I felt even more like a monster between my scars and my red eyes and hair. I panicked that I'd read regret in Sverr's golden eyes and that he'd show interest in this young maiden. But Sverr just looked at her sullenly, without a trace of interest in his face. Then he squeezed my hand and looked amused, as though he

The Charmed Fjords

understood my inner torment.

The jilted bride looked at Sverr fearfully as she stood on the patio of her home, and then in a shaky voice she said she didn't fault the riar of Neroaldaf, accepted the handouts, and released him from his oath. Then she smiled at me.

"The love that Gorlohum is waking up for should not be impeded," she added.

Then we were on our way home, and I told Sverr about Irvin, whom I'd seen in the hall of the hundred hjeggs. He told me about the little boy whom the a-tem had sent to the south to start a new life. Now all of us would have a new life because the fjords remained standing.

Ten days later in his own hall of Neroaldaf, Sverr placed the marriage crown on my head and pronounced me his betrothed. And then he kissed me. He kissed me like he did every time — voraciously and tenderly.

Just like he was kissing me now. I lost control again until I heard Maximilian's snarky cough.

"I don't want to disturb you — I realize it's not a good idea to disturb two dragons no matter what they're doing, but the group of settlers has arrived."

I gasped and Sverr burst out laughing. Together we turned toward a new future.

End of Book One

Want to be the first to know about our latest LitRPG, sci fi and fantasy titles from your favorite authors?

Subscribe to our *New Releases* newsletter:
http://eepurl.com/b7niIL

Thank you for reading *The Charmed Fjords!*
If you like what you've read, check out other sci-fi, fantasy and LitRPG novels published by Magic Dome Books:

Reality Benders LitRPG series by Michael Atamanov:
Countdown
External Threat
Game Changer
Web of Worlds
A Jump into the Unknown
Aces High
Cause for War
Devourer

The Dark Herbalist LitRPG series by Michael Atamanov:
Video Game Plotline Tester
Stay on the Wing
A Trap for the Potentate
Finding a Body

Perimeter Defense LitRPG series by Michael Atamanov:
Sector Eight
Beyond Death
New Contract
A Game with No Rules

League of Losers LitRPG Series by Michael Atamanov:
A Cat and his Human
In Service of the Pharaoh

The Way of the Shaman LitRPG series by Vasily Mahanenko:
Survival Quest
The Kartoss Gambit
The Secret of the Dark Forest
The Phantom Castle
The Karmadont Chess Set
The Hour of Pain (a bonus short story)
Shaman's Revenge
Clans War

***The Alchemist* LitRPG series by Vasily Mahanenko:**
City of the Dead
Forest of Desire
Tears of Alron
Isr Kale's Journal
Tartila Mine

***Dark Paladin* LitRPG series by Vasily Mahanenko:**
The Beginning
The Quest
Restart

***Galactogon* LitRPG series by Vasily Mahanenko:**
Start the Game!
In Search of the Uldans
A Check for a Billion

***Invasion* LitRPG Series by Vasily Mahanenko:**
A Second Chance
An Equation with one Unknown

***World of the Changed* LitRPG Series by Vasily Mahanenko:**
No Mistakes
Pearl of the South
Noa in the Flesh

***The Bard from Barliona* LitRPG series by Eugenia Dmitrieva and Vasily Mahanenko:**
The Renegades
A Song of Shadow

***Level Up* LitRPG series by Dan Sugralinov:**
Re-Start
Hero
The Final Trial
Level Up: The Knockout (with Max Lagno)
Level Up. The Knockout: Update (with Max Lagno)

***Disgardium* LitRPG series by Dan Sugralinov:**
Class-A Threat
Apostle of the Sleeping Gods
The Destroying Plague
Resistance
Holy War
Path of Spirit
The Demonic Games

***World 99* LitRPG Series by Dan Sugralinov:**
Blood of Fate

***Fantasia* LitRPG Series by Simon Vale:**
Second Shot

***Adam Online* LitRPG Leries by Max Lagno:**
Absolute Zero
City of Freedom

***Interworld Network* LitRPG Series by Dmitry Bilik:**
The Time Master
Avatar of Light
The Dark Champion

***Rogue Merchant* LitRPG Series by Roman Prokofiev:**
The Starlight Sword
The Gene of the Ancients
Shadow Seer
Battle for the North
The Devil Archetype

Project Stellar LitRPG Series by Roman Prokofiev:
The Incarnator
The Enchanter
The Tribute
The Rebel
The Archon

***Clan Dominance* LitRPG Series by Dem Mikhailov:**
The Sleepless Ones Book One
The Sleepless Ones Book Two
The Sleepless Ones Book Three
The Sleepless Ones Book Four
The Sleepless Ones Book Five
The Sleepless Ones Book Six

***Nullform* RealRPG Series by Dem Mikhailov:**
Nullform Book One
Nullform Book Two

***The Crow Cycle* LitRPG Series by Dem Mikhailov:**
The Crow Cycle Book One

***Unfrozen* LitRPG Series by Anton Tekshin:**
Cooldown
Old-School

***The Neuro* LitRPG series by Andrei Livadny:**
The Crystal Sphere
The Curse of Rion Castle
The Reapers

***Phantom Server* LitRPG series by Andrei Livadny:**
Edge of Reality
The Outlaw
Black Sun

***Respawn Trials* LitRPG Series by Andrei Livadny:**
Edge of the Abyss

***The Expansion (The History of the Galaxy)* series by A. Livadny:**
Blind Punch
The Shadow of Earth
Servobattalion

***The Range* LitRPG Series by Yuri Ulengov:**
The Keepers of Limbo
Lords of the Ruins
The Guardian of the Verge

Point Apocalypse (a near-future action thriller) **by Alex Bobl**

***Moskau* by G. Zotov**
(a dystopian thriller)

***El Diablo* by G.Zotov**
(a supernatural thriller)

***Mirror World* LitRPG series by Alexey Osadchuk:**
Project Daily Grind
The Citadel
The Way of the Outcast
The Twilight Obelisk

Underdog LitRPG series by Alexey Osadchuk:
Dungeons of the Crooked Mountains
The Wastes
The Dark Continent
The Otherworld
Labyrinth of Fright
Showdown
Arbiter

Alpha Rome LitRPG Series by Ros Per:
Volper
Skurfaifer

An NPC's Path LitRPG series by Pavel Kornev:
The Dead Rogue
Kingdom of the Dead
Deadman's Retinue
The Guardian of the Dead
The Nemesis of the Living

The Sublime Electricity series by Pavel Kornev:
The Illustrious
The Heartless
The Fallen
The Dormant

Small Unit Tactics LitRPG series by Alexander Romanov:
Volume 1
Volume 2

In the System LitRPG series by Petr Zhgulyov:
City of Goblins
City of the Undead
Defending Earth

Citadel World series by Kir Lukovkin:
The URANUS Code
The Secret of Atlantis

You're in Game!
(LitRPG Stories from Bestselling Authors)

You're in Game-2!
(More LitRPG stories set in your favorite worlds)

***The Fairy Code* by Kaitlyn Weiss:**
Captive of the Shadows
Chosen of the Shadows

More books and series are coming out soon!

In order to have new books of the series translated faster, we need your help and support! Please consider leaving a review or spread the word by recommending *The Charmed Fjords* to your friends and posting the link on social media. The more people buy the book, the sooner we'll be able to make new translations available.

Thank you!

Till next time!

Made in the USA
Las Vegas, NV
01 December 2022